Glorious
Incorporated

Glorious Incorporated

THE JOSHUA CHRONICLES

STEVEN NEIL MOORE

Library of Congress Control Number: 2013909727
ISBN: Hardcover   978-1-4836-4754-8
                 Softcover   978-1-4836-4753-1
                 Ebook   978-1-4836-4755-5

This book was printed in the United States of America.

Rev. date: 05/28/2013

To order additional copies of this book, contact:
Xlibris Corporation
1-888-795-4274
www.Xlibris.com
Orders@Xlibris.com
116270

Contents

PART THREE

THE TRUTH

For my Lord and Savior, Jesus Christ, for without whom none of this would be possible.

To my grandmother Opal, the greatest woman on the planet.

For my family, Jessica, Jackson, Liam, and Declan.

Now is the dramatic moment of fate, Watson, when you hear a step upon the stair which is walking into your life, and you know not whether for good or ill.

—Arthur Conan Doyle

PART ONE

FIRST CONTACT

Chapter 1

Objects and Introductions

"I can't believe that I'm going to be late for this interview!" Josh was supposed to be looking at the early-morning New York skyline flash by him as he sped across the Queensboro Bridge in a taxi. Instead, he was stuck in traffic just inside the city as he listened to car horns blare out a panicked anthem, much like steers in a herd on their way to a cattle train. There were so many yellow taxis that it seemed impossible to count them all. He looked all around him. There was nothing but a sea of cars and people hustling to an unknown direction. They paid absolutely no attention to anything else around them. In front of him was a car that tried to merge from the left, in a vain attempt to get to the next lane to turn right on Second Avenue. That is where he needed to go as well and was not sure why this guy needed to get there quicker. Cars switched lanes behind him in the hopes that might provide a few more inches to get them to their destinations one second faster. His taxi driver contributed his part to the song of horns as he pushed his way forward. Josh leaned back in the rear seat of the cab, resigned that he was, in fact, late. *This is not going to be a favorable impression,* he thought. *This company is going to fire me before I even begin!* He became nervous over the thought. He felt lucky to even be considered for employment with the world economy in unrest.

Jonah International was one of two companies that seemed genuinely interested to speak with him at the campus recruiting event at Carnegie Mellon. He talked with a number of different companies throughout the day, but Jonah, and one other, seemed to pick him out of a crowd and warmly invite him back to their tables. Both recruiters discussed his academic achievements, extracurricular activities, his long-term plans for his future—standard topics that most spewed forth in their quest for new blood. Both were very forthcoming in their companies' mission statements and corporate agendas to "make the world a better place." The differences with these two were that they approached him. It was almost like they both expected him to be at this event. The Jonah representative made him feel like it was going to his grandmother's home for a holiday and being greeted by all the relatives whom he had not seen in a long time. He listened to each company talk about their prospectus. Then he heard a question that he did not expect.

"What do you think about the fate of the world?" asked the representative from Jonah.

A quizzical looked crossed Josh's face. "Excuse me?"

"Given the climate of the economy, the global unemployment rate, poverty, and famine across the world, how do you think the future of our world will survive?"

Josh was stunned for a moment. He did not understand the question and its relevance to his abilities to offer his business and financial management knowledge in the corporate world. After a few moments, the recruiter smiled. "Do you believe you can help us make it a better place for all humankind?"

Josh looked into the recruiter's eyes for a few seconds. "I would certainly like the opportunity to try."

"Joshua, that's all we can ask of you." The recruiter gave Josh a corporate packet along with a business card. "We believe that you have something special to offer our Firm. We also believe that we have something exceptional to share with you."

Josh was so immersed in his recollection of that day's events that he all but forgot where he was and the objective of the meeting.

"Hey, pal!" said the cabbie.

"Huh, what?" said Josh as he was jolted back to the present.

"We're here, Upper East Side, York, and Seventy-second. That'll be $34.75."

Josh quickly fumbled for the cash and handed it to the driver. He collected his satchel and coat and got out of the cab. He stood there in front of the corporate headquarters of Jonah International and soaked in the sight. The building was a modern structure of steel and glass. Above the revolving doors was the corporation's name with an image of a dove between the two. People walked into the building, some talked on mobile phones, others chatted and greeted fellow workers, all of them, though, seemed happy. He wondered if that was because they had a job, or if they were truly pleased to work at Jonah. He smiled at the thought of being part of a company with employees who really seemed to like their work. He had heard horrible stories of how miserable corporate work could be. He did not see any evidence of that here.

His smile faded when he realized that everyone that walked into the building was dressed a bit better than him. He had one suit that he bought over two years ago for the funeral of his best friend Harry's uncle. It was cheap because he did not have extra money after tuition and books. It looked okay for a funeral, but he felt out of place here in a corporate setting. Josh closed his eyes for a moment, said a silent prayer, and then walked through the revolving doors.

The long walk down the corridor was not a pleasant one. Kelan was on edge. The dossier on the Object was updated by the intelligence division at 10:09 pm yesterday. The DRONE traced the Object to it's localized residence where the Object remained for the rest of the night. At 8:05 pm, a take-out was placed: one order of spring rolls, one wonton soup, and one order of kung pao chicken. That order was delivered at 8:34 pm by a short, rotund gentleman in his midthirties. The Object paid $25 and told the delivery guy to keep the change. All systems tracked as tasked until this morning. Then everything went black at 7:03 am.

"Good morning, Mr. Tindal," said the admin.

"What frame of mind is he in?"

She looked tensely toward the double doors and quietly said, "You should be prepared for the worse. He received some Intel this morning as he came in the building and has been on a rampage since."

"Do you happen to know what the information contained?"

"He referred to losing something or other," she said.

Kelan rolled his eyes slightly. "Great . . . just great." *He already knows.* "Do you have a copy of his itinerary for today?"

She handed him a prepared handout of all his scheduled calls and meetings. He quickly searched and looked for anything that might indicate contact with a recovery team. *The last thing we want to do is overreact and pull the Object without more intelligence on the whereabouts.* Sometimes, the boss did not seem to think strategically. He had this primal rage when operations did not go according to plan. His agenda seemed standard. No evidence of contact with the RCT.

"Tell him I'm here."

She pressed a button on the telephone. "Mr. Blalock, Mr. Tindal is here to see you."

A strongly stated "Send him in!" blared back out. She looked sharply at Kelan. He turned and approached the door.

The boss was not happy, and this would not be a good conversation.

Joshua Arden was in awe by what he saw in the main lobby. Marble floor inlaid with brass grout, polished to the point of where he could see himself clearly as he looked down. It seemed to shimmer across the wide expanse of the whole area. There was very impressive artwork on the two massive sides of the enormous foyer. It was not too gaudy, which is what someone might expect from a corporation as big as Jonah, but modest in design. It was as if the intention was to impress without trying. The lobby looked like it was mostly brass and marble. Nondescript surroundings throughout, yet very modern and not out of style. The whole atmosphere seemed inviting.

It was strange, but he felt anxious when he got out of the taxi. Pensive, worried about the unknown of what to expect during this interview, and freaked out because he was late. He knew it was not his fault, but he also knew the interviewer would not care at all why, just that he *was* late. All that changed when he entered the building. Calmness swept over him. As if he was given a sedative as he passed through the revolving doors. He felt absolutely at ease, relaxed, without a care in the world. He questioned this change for about a millisecond and wondered what could have come over him when he saw her.

She was across the immense foyer just in front of the security desk, her eyes fixed upon him. On the other hand, maybe it was something, or someone, behind him. He was not sure. He held her gaze for about five seconds; and then with a natural reflex that most boys, and some men, had where they did not pick up hints that they could be the object of desire or attention, he turned around with a slight spin to see the true target of her glare. There was not anyone else behind him that gave any indication or returned her signals. The only object that was in the direct path of her piercing stare was the continual spin of the revolving doors. People casually moved through it without a look in her direction.

She's looking at me! thought Josh. *Yep. Me. Why is she looking at me? Oh man . . . It's because of my suit! That's got to be it. I'm the only person in here that doesn't look like a million dollars.* Josh began to look and pull at his suit in a manner that appeared to be a cross between someone who looked for his wallet and someone who swatted away a flying bug. He drew more attention from the passing people. She walked toward him.

The woman was in her mid to late twenties with chestnut brown hair, all one length, down to the middle of her back. She was dressed in a navy blue suit with a skirt, moderate three-inch heels to match, and white blouse with a visible silver crucifix. Simple, stylish, and professional. She had waited ten minutes. Her instructions were very simple. There was someone scheduled for interviews with the top brass in Finance today. She was to personally escort him to all the scheduled discussions. He was to be fast-tracked through all security measures. The candidate arrived five minutes behind schedule. He looked nervous, but seemed fine after he entered the building. *Nice to know the effect is helping him calm down*, she thought. That effect did not last long.

As she walked toward him, it similarly occurred to him that his composure and calmness did not last as well. He was not sure why he freaked out again. *It's just a girl. A very pretty girl. A very pretty girl who walked toward him with a purpose.*

"Joshua?" she asked as she reached him.

He stopped with his suit as he realized that it made no difference. She already saw the *before* picture. "Yes, hello."

She extended her hand. "Hi, Joshua. My name is Melina Vargas."

He returned the handshake. "I'm Joshua Arden." *Stupid! She already knows that. She said your name.*

She smiled at his discomfort. "I'm here to escort you to your interview sessions today."

Outstanding! he thought. "I'm sorry that I'm running late. Not used to the changing New York traffic yet."

"Completely understandable. Traffic can be a bit tricky here in the city." She turned toward the security desk near the elevators and gestured. "Are you ready to go up?"

He tugged at his suit one last time. "Ready as I'll ever be."

She started toward the gates. "Great! Please come with me."

The security desk was more like a podium. There were four in total. There was one guard behind each that constantly viewed what appeared to be a monitor built into the stand. They watched the people that passed through each gate. The gate was a bit of an understatement. It was the standard type of one found in an airport, but looked more high-tech. Instead of the large drab-beige-colored devices that had a multicolored display with lights that indicated you were worthy to pass or carried a concealed weapon, it seemed to be thinner, about two to three inches in depth and width. It was a perfect square from all dimensions. It was not freestanding like those airport machines. All four gates were built into the entrance hallway of all the elevator banks. When a person reached the podium, they placed their hand on a lighted pad. There was one on either side of each gate. It glowed green, and then the person stepped through the gate. The gate responded with a glow of blue, then the person made their way to the elevators.

Melina saw that Josh watched this sequence with great curiosity. "The security at Jonah International is state-of-the-art. I know that a lot of companies boast of the same, but Jonah's is the best. The bio-pads are biometric scanners that read specific genetic markers in each of Jonah's employees. These markers are encoded to each employee's security level and clearance. It tracks all movements in and out of the main building. The bio-gates"—she gestured toward the blue security gates—"ensure that each person has access to their respective levels only."

Josh watched more people pass through. "I notice that some people are using certain bio-gates more than others. Why is that?"

"Two of the elevator banks are specific to a lower clearance level. Talent Management"—she smiled and gestured to herself—"Human Resources, Financial Management, Consulting, Auditing Services, and other business divisions. The other two elevator banks are for higher-level personnel that handle more sensitive areas of the corporation."

Josh studied the distance from the gates to the elevators then looked around to see if there were any additional security personnel. "It doesn't seem like there would be any time for security to react before a threat could make it to the elevators."

"The security stationed at the gates is only for determining employee or visitor clearance and access privileges. Everyone has already been screened by Sentinel upon entering the building. If someone was a threat, they would be identified long before reaching the gates," she said.

"Sentinel?" asked Josh, puzzled.

With that, she approached one of the gates for the higher security levels and spoke, "Melina Vargas, Talent Management, security authorization alpha, 6, X-ray, 297. I am escorting VIP Joshua William Arden to the upper-level executive suites for scheduled interviews."

The security guard typed something into his podium then glanced up. "Please place your hand on the bio-pad, Ms. Vargas." Melina complied. The pad glowed red for about two seconds then transitioned to green.

"Approved and confirmed. Ms. Vargas, your clearance level has been temporarily raised for access to the executive suites for the remainder of today," said the guard.

He then turned toward Josh. "Mr. Arden, please place your hand on the bio-pad."

Josh did as instructed, but this time it did not glow. A bluish pulse-like scan started from the top of the pad to the bottom and continued for about five seconds. Then the pad glowed to a solid blue that transitioned to green.

"Identity and marking complete. Mr. Arden, you are cleared to the executive suites with Ms. Vargas. Please enter the bio-gates and board the elevators for access. Welcome to Jonah International."

Kelan knocked once and opened the door at the same time. The room was spacious, what you would expect for a CEO of a long-standing firm such as Alastar-McGlocklin? Overly extravagant large leather chairs with ornate details like it was handcrafted by a little Bavarian man hundreds of years ago. A long leather couch in one corner of the office that matched all the overstuffed chairs, a conference table surrounded by twelve leather chairs in another. The details of the conference table and chairs match all the other furniture in its decadence. The desk of the head man of Alastar-McGlocklin did not seem like a desk at all, but more like a judicial bench that you would see of a federal level judge. It was large, imposing, and seemed to sit higher than a normal desk. When Blalock sat at it and looked over, whomever was on the other side had no choice but to look up at him. This was by design.

All the furnishings in this office was carefully laid out and arranged by a decorator who specialized in projecting power, confidence, and it seemed like absolute domination for their clients. They charged a lot of money for this portrayal of appearance and stature. Blalock was quite pleased.

One wall of the office was a solid window from ceiling to floor. It was tinted so the sunlight would not glare the occupant. No matter what position the sun was in, it would not be intrusive into the spacious room. There were no curtains that covered any of the windows. The office was situated on the top floor. From the vantage point of where the window was, there were no other buildings that high within a visible range. There was a clear view of the Manhattan skyline from the Long Island office. It was at this wall of window where Kelan found Morgan Blalock as he stood and stared out.

Kelan shut the door, took a few steps into the office, and stopped. He waited to be recognized before he spoke. Normally, that was not his standard approach with the boss, but today had not started off well. Not well at all.

Blalock turned after a few seconds. "And what news do you have for me today?"

Kelan walked forward to the chairs directly in front of the judge's bench. "We received some Intel regarding the satellite tracking of Object 216."

Blalock looked at him knowingly then walked behind his desk. "Would this be the same Intel that I have here?" He picked up a file and tossed it toward Kelan.

Kelan glanced down at it. Some of the pages spilled out and verified that it was, indeed, the same information. Before he could say anything, Blalock barked at him in a raised voice. "What happened to the DRONE? Why did it stop functioning at the precise moment that 216 was on the move? Why didn't you task more than one DRONE to ensure redundancy measures? Do you have any idea how important Object 216 is to the future of our ongoing campaign?"

Kelan had no idea which questions to answer first, but he had better decide fast. "Mr. Blalock, Object 216 has been and always will be our first priority. The DRONE tasked to track was specially outfitted with all available intelligence on 216 and served no other mission parameters. Its sole purpose is to recon and deliver visual and audio—"

"I am quite aware of what the DRONE's functions are! I sanctioned the program! Can you tell me anything that I don't know about why a mission that I put you in charge of failed?" His tone was slightly louder than before.

"Mr. Blalock, sir . . . We are still in the process of retrieving the 216 DRONE. Once we have it back in house, we can run a diagnostic to better understand why it malfunctioned. It has a homing—"

"Yes, a homing directive in case of damage or mission failure . . . I know all of this. Again, I designed and sanctioned the program! Can you at least verify that the directive is operating properly? Is the DRONE following the return protocols and operating under a stealth umbrella? The last thing that we need is to have it tracked back to the RCT base."

"Yes, sir. I have reviewed the tracking coordinates and its location mapping and confirmed with the 216 commander. It is following the homing directive as designed. There is one thing though that doesn't make sense . . ."

Blalock just looked at Kelan and waited.

Kelan calmly opened his file to review what he was about to say before he was interrupted. "The DRONE lost visual feed at 7:08 am, for reasons unknown, and regained all system functions precisely twelve minutes later." He looked at Blalock to see if he understood and knew something that he did not.

He continued. "It was during this time that 216 obviously disappeared from our surveillance. What is interesting to me is that in all the months that we have utilized the DRONE, this is the very first time it has malfunctioned. Simultaneously, the RCT agents tasked to 216 lost audio feed and recon visual from the ground. By the time the team reached 216's last known position, the Object was already gone."

"What was the total downtime for the RCT's audio and visual on the ground?"

Kelan looked at him with a little admiration. "Two minutes."

It was like an orchestrated series of events meant to block out a specific amount of time for the Object to escape. Who could have had these types of resources to pull off something that precise? It could have been coincidental, but highly unlikely. They had tracked Object 216 for five and a half months without any hiccups in surveillance, visual recon, audio pickups, or system malfunctions. Wherever Object 216 went, Team 216 was there. They knew what 216's schedule was, from when the mail was picked up to what 216 had for breakfast. They knew who 216 associated with and all visitors who made contact. There were dedicated resources from agents and state-of-the-art digital surveillance on the ground to the DRONE in the air that tracked and watched every move. They had wire taps in the Object's home and on the cellular. Some agents shopped at the same grocery store as 216. The dry cleaner that Object 216 used was an RCT agent. All personnel involved were handpicked by Kelan for this initiative. They all had a specialty or skill set that was essential for the operation. All personnel were professionally trained and could operate in complete invisibility. They had all the angles covered with absolutely no room for error. Yet they lost the Object.

Blalock turned and stared out of his massive window. He tried to figure out the next move. He had to reacquire 216 as quickly as possible. The key to shape the course of future events, and of course his survival, resided in 216. In order to preserve his standing with the senior partners and show his commitment to the cause, he had to see this through to the end.

He turned back to Kelan. "What contingency plans have you designed to regain tracking of Object 216?"

Kelan's response was immediate. "Any plan for reacquiring, should 216 drop from our radar, was unforeseen as all avenues of coverage were accounted for."

"Really? Doesn't seem like that was the case, does it?"

"Our plan forward is to enact a search-and-retrieval pattern. We will increase the search perimeter and RCT agents on the 216 initiative, plus retask two additional DRONEs to canvas the entire New York City network. Their job will be to process all known digital signals from every electronic device wired into the global network. This includes traffic cameras, ATMs, personal cell phones, Internet connectivity . . . any and all communications both audible and visual. If 216 is anywhere near anything that can transmit a signal, we will pick it up immediately, triangulate, and converge."

Blalock studied Kelan for a second. "So what you're saying is that we wait for Object 216 to come home, and then we will resume surveillance, correct?"

An oversimplification, but in essence, the truth. Object 216 was completely off the grid, and Kelan did not even begin to know where to look. "Yes, sir, but we will also attempt to track the trail. We have a cleaner team in the Object's home now looking for signs of direction and intent."

For the first time, Kelan started to sweat. "Mr. Blalock, I understand the importance of what Object 216 means to this corporation and the balance of world power. We are doing everything that we can to maintain around-the-clock contact on the Object's activities. We *will* reacquire."

"You do realize where the Object might have gone, don't you? Have you considered placing a watch team there to verify?"

Kelan was tired of rehashing the same argument each time this subject came up. Unfortunately, he had to keep his frustration to himself. "Sir, every time that we have attempted to stake out that location, we continually get conflicting reports and error signals from electronic measures. The RCT agents in place have never had any successful operations when using our state-of-the-art equipment. The audio is garbled, the videos show nothing but static, and the DRONEs cannot seem to ever pinpoint the coordinates even though the longitude and latitude are preprogrammed prior to launch. They seem to keep delivering Intel from everything else but that location."

Blalock walked back toward the window as Kelan continued.

"We have tried old-school tactics with agents strategically placed in nearby buildings, on the streets, and at corner newspaper stands. All with binoculars or just casually eye-balling the place. Each agent comes back with similar stories. Sunlight interfering with their camera shots, binoculars with condensation on the lens, glares of illumination preventing them from seeing specific things, and my personal favorite . . . dense fog from steam tunnels that don't even exist near the location. There is some type of jamming grid surrounding that place at all times. We would have better luck trying to get into the White House."

"What is the closest range that we can receive uninterrupted signals?"

"From past attempts in surveillance and reports, the unexplainable jamming stops at a diameter of six city blocks in all directions," said Kelan.

Blalock looked through his large window at nothing in particular. "Continue with your plan to reacquire 216. I want all resources reassigned to this until the Object is back under our radar. Furthermore, put additional agents just outside the jamming perimeter on all major traffic and pedestrian throughways. I want constant eyes on subways, sidewalks, taxis . . . anything that can be used for transportation in and out of the perimeter."

He turned toward Kelan. "I want to know if Object 216 has made contact with them. You will do whatever it takes to find out. Do you understand?"

"Yes, sir."

"When do you expect the 216 DRONE back at the base?"

Kelan checked his file then looked at his watch. "The DRONE should be docked within the next thirty to forty minutes. I have all technical personnel standing by to figure out what went wrong. We will have an answer for you by the end of business today."

"Good," Blalock said. "Once you have made all the arrangements to reacquire Object 216, you will go there and personally oversee the analysis yourself."

With that, Kelan turned to leave the office. As he approached the door, he put his hand on the knob to turn it and heard, "And, Tindal." He stopped cold.

"Do not disappoint me again. There will not be a third chance."

Kelan stood there unmoved as the words hit him like a wave of nausea. He completely understood the meaning of the statement and the consequences thereof. He had seen what Morgan Blalock's temper and power could do to someone firsthand. He never thought he would be on the receiving end of it. He pulled to open the door and left.

Chapter 2

Security and Elevators

Josh and Melina walked through the gate toward the elevators. He noticed that Melina did not push the button to summon the lift. In fact, no one who advanced through the gate made a move to any of the buttons. He looked around curiously and wondered what this was all about. Then he saw why, there were no buttons to push.

Melina, again, saw the puzzled look on his face and explained. "Once someone has cleared security at the appropriate gate, the elevators are automatically signaled to return to the main level. It works much like a motion sensor when passing through the gate. It's like this on each floor, no buttons, just sensors."

"Hmmm . . . That seems pretty efficient. It saves time on moving between floors and prioritizes the queuing process more quickly without manual intervention," he said.

Josh looked at her and smiled. "Technology is great." He made it sound like it was a normal action and could not understand why the rest of the world used buttons.

She smiled. It did not occur to her that someone might be interested in such things. Most candidates were focused on the pending meeting and their potential for employment. She had never noticed anyone that seemed to be aware of the little things around them. Little things. She had taken them for granted in the time she had been with Jonah. Melina tried to remember the first time that she passed through the lobby on her way for interviews. What did she feel like when she walked through the doors for the first time? Did she have an escort? Was it a man or a woman? What did she wear? A thousand little first-day flashback moments in a split second. As she pondered these thoughts, all of those memories were fuzzy, except for one. She remembered that she did not interview on the executive levels. Not just the levels, but in the suites no less. Melina had never been up to the upper levels before. For a brief second, she considered the significance of the task for the day.

A few weeks ago, Melina was seated at her desk on the fourteenth floor. She worked through the paperwork of a technical screen for a candidate. Nothing at all remarkable about the form or, for that fact, the candidate. She had processed hundreds of these screens before, and they all seemed to blend into one another after a while. It was just another step in the recruitment process. As she assembled the recruits' interview package, her desk phone rang. Amy Langstrom, an executive assistant from the upper levels, was on the other end.

"Ms. Vargas, hi, this is Amy, Mr. Wessler's assistant. How are you today?"

"I'm doing great, how are you?" said Melina.

"I'm good, thank you for asking. Mr. Wessler is expecting a VIP for an in person two weeks from Monday and would like for you to escort the candidate through security and to the interviews. Are you free to help out?"

Melina responded without looking at her calendar. "I will be happy to assist in any way I can."

It did not matter what her schedule looked like. When a C-level executive asked you to do something, you say yes.

"Wonderful! I will tell him that you are confirmed as the liaison. You will be receiving the candidate's briefing package and profile via secured server access."

Secured server? Why not through e-mail like all other candidates? It's encrypted and the easiest form of communication. There had never been any type of information breach before. This was odd.

"Your security clearance will be temporarily bumped for access to the executive suites on the upper levels. This will only be in effect for the day of the interview. Do you have any questions?" asked Amy.

"Are all the details for the escort included in the package?"

"Yes. Furthermore, you need to be aware that you will be expected to remain with the candidate at all times throughout the schedule, except for the interviews themselves. The agenda has already been defined and will be included in the briefing package."

"When will the briefing package be available for review?"

"We will have it posted to the server some time mid next week. We'll send you an e-mail with the password access to the directory."

Melina was excited at this request. "Great! Thank you for the opportunity and consideration. I appreciate it!"

"You're very welcome. Mr. Wessler said that you would be the right one for this assignment. I didn't realize that you and he were on such close terms. He speaks very highly of you."

Melina was taken aback when she heard that. She had never met Jacob Wessler before. All she knew about him was that he was the CFO for Jonah International and subsidiary corporations, super nice and intelligent by reputation, and very well respected by everyone in the Firm, especially in the financial department.

"That's very kind to say. It is nice to be considered one of the choices for such an important interview."

"Ms. Vargas, you were the only choice. Mr. Wessler asked for you specifically."

After a few additional remarks and instructions, Melina finished her conversation and hung up the phone. *He asked for me personally?* She thought for a few seconds on why her. She was a lower-level resource in Talent Management. Her main role was to start the initial contact process for prospective candidates who came across her desk by referrals. Set up the phone screens and process the candidates through, if they measured up and had the qualifications. Being a liaison for a VIP recruit for the CFO was not in her job description. Then she figured that possibly she was recommended by her supervisor for the assignment. Maybe she was given a chance to show more responsibility outside of her current job role. She had been with the Firm for over two years, had various roles, always completed her appointed activities, and received good performance reviews. This was just another way to help her move up in the Firm. *That's got to be it!* With that, she smiled and completed her task with the happy thought that maybe better things awaited.

She looked at Josh and smiled. She wondered what was so special about him. He had to be intelligent; otherwise, he wouldn't be here. Seemed like any other recent graduate that was half-starved and would happily take a job in the mailroom given the economy. Even so, here he was. On his way to talk with the CFO of Jonah International.

He glanced over in Melina's direction; she smiled at him. He returned the smile and held her eyes for a few seconds. It was strange that she continued to look at him. It was like he was a celebrity, and she tried to work up the nerve to ask for his autograph, or that he had some hideous deformation and treated it like a car crash, and just could not look away.

He broke eye contact when the elevator arrived. He waited for the other two people to enter first then, with the gesture of a Southern gentleman, motioned for Melina to enter before him. "Ma'am . . ."

She smiled and entered. "I'm too young to be called ma'am."

"Aahh, but you deserve the respect that the label carries," he said with a slight bow then entered behind her.

He swaggered in and stood beside her, looked at her again and smiled. This time when she smiled back, it was with the look of respect. Respect for someone who appeared a lot wiser than his age. He came off as charismatic, but not in an arrogant way. He seemed like he had a good sense of humor, not that she would know, but he would be someone with whom she could hang around. Like that of a coworker that went out with a group of friends after work. Not in a romantic way at all, of course. She had a strict policy of not dating anyone from the Firm. Kind of silly in this case, as Josh did not work there. Even so, she started to secretly hope he would. There was something about him she could not put her finger on it.

The elevator doors closed. Again, there were no buttons. Josh looked at her. "I suppose that the lift will read your thoughts and take us to the proper floor?"

Melina openly giggled. "Not quite . . . but close." Her voice changed a bit to be more authoritative. "Sentinel, twenty-third floor please."

"Yes, Ms. Vargas."

The voice came out of nowhere but everywhere at the same time. There did not seem to be any speakers or intercoms that were visible. The other two people spoke to the elevator too and told *it* what floor they wanted, and the box replied in kind.

Josh raised his eyebrows and moved his eyes around to look for the invisible voice. He did not say anything. In fact, he just went with the flow. If Jonah put this much effort into an elevator, then he had higher hopes that the position he was interviewing for would be something akin to working with flying cars, or matter transportation of some sort. Not really sure what someone with a degree in financial economics would do in that position, but he would like to give it a shot.

Melina looked up at the ascending floor numbers above the doorway. She wondered if he would comment about the technology, but he seemed to be content with the smooth ride. Most applicants are ferried to interview stations on the lower levels, where there are actually buttons for the elevators. Since this bank of lifts was dedicated to the executive floors, the security was controlled by Sentinel. Someone wouldn't have gotten far if not authorized. Normal candidates would never see anything like this. Not until hired, or possibly had worked here for some time in a position that would require a higher security level. Even then, the new people that were exposed to the amazing technology of Jonah International found it hard to comprehend how tech like that existed and could not be found anywhere else. She had heard of stories here and there of some people that referenced the Firm as the maker of the gadgets used in *Star Wars* or *Star Trek*. She remembered how it was for her first exposure. She felt like a little girl that walked through the Barbie section of a toy store. Her mouth hung open for the first few days, until she learned how to control her zombielike expression and came to terms with the advancements in the technology world. She worked here for a little more than two years, and the more she discovered about Jonah's capabilities, the more her amazement returned, and she was right back in the toy store with the Barbie and My Little Pony, aisles and aisles of them. She was introduced to Sentinel over ten months earlier. Josh was introduced ten seconds ago and did not even budge.

Chapter 3

Replacements and Analysis

Kelan stood outside of Blalock's office for a few minutes. He tried to compose himself before he walked away. He was not sure if he was outright scared of the innuendo of the threat or angry that he was threatened. *Who does he think set up the reconnaissance on 216 to begin with? I arranged all the team deployment and retrofitted a state-of-the-art satellite that was in perfect working order . . . until today. All he did was raise his manicured hand and sign the order. I did all the work! He wouldn't even listen to my complete briefing on what we have accomplished to date with the surveillance. Arrogant, pompous, megalomaniac—*

Kelan looked up at that moment and saw an empathetic look from Blalock's administrative assistant.

Mrs. Betty Kincaid was a nice and kind person who tried to find the positive and good in everything. She had the misfortune of being Blalock's executive assistant for the past seven years. When his last assistant fell ill due to exhaustion, caused by overwork plus the diagnosis of chronic fatigue syndrome, his patience for the drop-in service and lack of commitment, because of some silly medical problem, prompted him to fire her. He cited that her performance was below the expectations set forth in her job description. Alastar-McGlocklin had a massive and expensive law firm on retainer. Blalock instructed them to find a way to make the decision stick without any legal backlash. Fortunately for her, the federal law against wrongful termination, coupled with a family friend who practiced law in the New York City District Attorney's office, prevented Blalock from pursuing his quest. In fact, things backfired so badly that the former assistant sued Alastar-McGlocklin, and specifically called out Blalock, claiming and proving proof of cruelty within the workplace. The suit yielded a nice seven-figure settlement. The board members did not wish to see any bad press in the news, so they voted unanimously to settle the case. Blalock fought back on the vote. There was no way he would lose face on something so insignificant, that would have displayed weakness within the corporation and, worse, showed he was vulnerable. He would not be made a fool. In most corporate structures, the CEO ran the day-to-day activities, but the board members carried the direction of the corporation. It was their collective power that brought reason and balance to any decisions that would, or will, affect the livelihood of the company and the individual, at their level of course. Let's not forget the lining of their overprivileged pockets. They could have cared less about this woman's medical problems, or her survival of this ridiculous lawsuit. However, they did care about theirs. Blalock's power was absolute. Regardless of the board's decision, he would still carry the majority vote. He planned to push this through to the end. She should have been satisfied with the involuntary separation. Because she fought back, he now intended to crush her. He aimed to show her, the board, the corporation, the world that Morgan Blalock would not now, or ever would be, challenged or defeated.

He would have gotten his way, if the senior partners had not stepped in. That was the one thing that Blalock was afraid of, the senior partnership. Instructions came down through a certified letter and were delivered by a private courier directly to his office. He was the only one allowed to sign for it. The instructions were on one sheet of paper with the senior partner letterhead and simply stated that he was to make a settlement with this woman. No repercussions of any kind would come to her and that they would monitor the situation very closely. The senior partnership would handle all collateral damages. With that, Blalock reluctantly did as instructed and settled the suit. There was no discussion about the event afterward. There was nothing in the press about the aftermath or even any indication that the suit ever existed. There were no records of the suit in any state or federal court. The sickly but now wealthy administrative assistant believed that she received the money as winnings from a lottery. She stopped pursuing a new job and concentrated on her health and enjoyed her life. Strangely, she had fond memories of her time with Alastar-McGlocklin. Everything that surrounded the event just disappeared, only Blalock had memory of it. That was by design. The senior partnership wanted him to know who was in control, who really possessed the true power.

A few months into her new retirement, she took her entire family on a ski weekend in the Colorado Rockies. On the way to the chalet, they passed a semitruck that carried a full load of timber as it made its way down the side of a mountain. They collided as they rounded a sharp bend in the very dangerous single-lane road. This sent the entire family careening over the side of a two-hundred-foot drop. There were no survivors. They were found two weeks later, only because the chalet's management attempted to collect the remaining balance and traveled up to the residence to check the condition. He wanted to see if they had arrived. They found the family at the bottom of a ravine. There were no traces of any other vehicles involved. The state police ruled it as a single car accident based on the road conditions and human error.

The accident was not newsworthy in the slightest, not even mentioned in the local paper. It was as if she and her family had never existed. She never did anything with the lottery winnings after it was deposited, so it was very easy for the financial lawyers of Alastar-McGlocklin to wire it back into the corporation. They took a small loss of only what she had spent, but recovered most of it.

Within a few days of the former administrative assistant's departure, there was an opening posted for the executive assistant's position in the secretary pool. No one wanted the job. Betty had thought this would be a step up, which could provide more money for her family. She happily took the position. The rest was history.

Betty just stared at poor Kelan. She saw that he was deflated and angry. Not that she had a choice, but she heard some of the conversation through the thick double doors. She did not intentionally listen, but Mr. Blalock's voice tended to carry when he was upset. Lately, his voice carried quite a bit. She gave Kelan an encouraged, supportive look followed by a smile.

He walked over to her desk. "That was *not* a pleasant meeting."

"Just give him some time. Once he has a chance to calm down, he thinks a little more clearly. I'm sure that he will follow up with you on your report and be more receptive to your plans," she said.

He looked at her with astonishment. Apparently, she knew a different Blalock than he did. He would never admit he was wrong, that he missed something, or for that fact, admit someone else might have had an idea that he did not think of first. "Anything's possible I suppose."

He looked at her like he had just noticed something unique. "How do you do it, Betty?"

She returned his quizzical look. "I don't follow?"

"How do you find a positive light in everything? You always seem to take an absolutely hopeless situation and find a way to weave some good throughout it. I don't get it."

Kelan genuinely tried to understand. He wanted to know what she did to stay so full instead of half empty.

She looked toward the double doors and hoped that she could speak freely without Mr. Blalock overhearing. She never knew when he would pop out with something he wanted her do or arrange. Sometimes he would use the intercom system, but he seemed to prefer to walk out and give instructions. He was not much into the technology of today. He was definitely a proponent of the old ways when it came to running a business. That was probably one of the main reasons that Mr. Tindal was employed here and worked closely with him. He had an advanced degree in computer science and a lot of technical experience when it came to surveillance. She did not really understand why that last part was important to Alastar-McGlocklin. The corporation's main global market was aligned with mergers and acquisitions. There were, however, other areas of interest within the companies that had been previously acquired. It was not really for her to reason what the corporate practices were when it came to business. Her job was to ensure that Mr. Blalock's agenda ran smoothly. Sometimes that included explanations of actions, both the companies and his, and now apparently hers.

"Mr. Tindal, I don't pretend to have a lot of experience in matters of business. My professional life has been mostly spent helping people like Mr. Blalock." She pointed to the doors. "If they are successful in what they do, I like to think that I have a part in that. I can't begin to understand the type of pressure the boss has trying to run a corporation as large as this. One thing that I have learned in all my years of serving this company is that there are things that happen in business, both good and bad. The good parts are simple enough to understand and accept. The bad parts are a little tougher to wrap the mind around. We wonder why some things didn't work out and try to put a logical reason around it to explain it in a way that we humans can comprehend. How we handle things in either situation is the key. Everyone is happy when some good happens, how long that happiness last is up to each of us. Now, the bad that happens takes more effort, but again, it's all in how you handle it." She smiled and paused for a second to see if the message registered.

"No matter good or bad, I choose to be happy and positive," she said.

Kelan looked at her with admiration. He still did not understand how she always remained positive, but was happy to have the privilege to work with her. Her attitude could be infectious, and he needed some of that.

"Your way of thinking is envious. I wish I could be as positive in all aspects of my life."

She turned serious for a second and looked him directly in the eyes. "You can. You just need to believe and have faith."

For a brief second, he felt like he connected with something greater than himself. Like his eyes began to open to something that he had never experienced before. Then his mobile phone rang. He looked at the caller ID.

THOMPSON (SECURED)

He held up a finger to indicate he would be back in a moment then turned and walked away to put some distance between him, Betty, and the double doors. He picked up on the third ring. "Tindal."

"Mr. Tindal, this is Thompson at base ops. The DRONE is ten minutes out. Trajectory is still operating within mission parameters."

"Stealth mode still intact?"

"Yes, sir," said the voice.

"Once the DRONE has arrived, secure in docking station alpha and prep for a level 1 diagnostic of the command module. Prepare to pull the motherboard. I'm en route. ETA, twenty minutes."

He flipped the mobile phone shut, slid it back into his jacket pocket, and walked over to her desk. "Betty, I need to go to the Long Beach facility, will you please have my car ready at the south entrance?"

"Right away, Mr. Tindal." She lifted the phone and dialed.

He turned and headed down the hall toward the elevators. He stopped after ten feet and turned back to Betty. She had just hung up the phone. "Betty? Has he ever said thank-you?"

She smiled again. "Not once."

"Me neither. We have something in common."

"How do you choose to handle that?"

He half-smiled. "Maybe I should try something different and find the positive?"

"I think that is an excellent idea, Mr. Tindal."

He turned and continued down the hall. As he reached the end of the corridor, he called out, "Thank you."

Alastar-McGlocklin owned a number of buildings and properties across the globe. Some of these were related to acquisition assets from floundering companies and varied in sizes and locations depending on their purpose and usefulness. As a rule of thumb, generally when a company was bought out, merged, consumed, or in certain cases, obtained by a hostile take-over, part of the process is to evaluate, categorize, and ascertain its net worth as it relates to the global market and to the purchasing corporation. These were standard practices for a pending parent company when processing the assets to determine future liability and market share cost of operation. If the assets did not currently, or was determined not capable, of yielding a profitable return on investment, they would be mined for whatever worth available and liquidated. During such processes like this, the legitimate assets of the dying company were registered within the negotiations and legally tracked, priced, and added to the overall total dollar value. Alastar-McGlocklin had an enormous team of crafty resources that handle these processes, and they had added a small additional step to the otherwise legal aspects of a purchase. If a property was discovered to be of *special interest* to the more sensitive and secretive operations of the corporation, those properties were buried in the legitimate acquisition minutia, and placed into operation and service for teams and resources that, for all intended purposes, did not exist. Kelan was on his way to one such property.

The Long Beach facility was just outside of the small community of Stony Brook. The compound was nondescript and blended well. The entrance was just off Old Field Road and not near any major high-traffic areas. The surrounding area was predominantly residential, but there were a few coastal buildings off of Long Island Sound that were used for commercial purposes. Alastar-McGlocklin owned one of these buildings and placed it in the special interest category. This facility was the base operations for all Dark-star Reconnaissance over the Northern Equatorial hemisphere activity. DRONE for short.

Kelan reviewed the brief that he received from the RCT tracking Object 216 while en route. He looked at all data transmission chatter between command/control and the 216 DRONE. Instructions were relayed and acknowledged per mission protocols. Nothing seemed out of the ordinary. Satellite recon snapshots were transmitted at operation intervals. Those snapshots were the backup to the live video transmission from the modified geographical imaging system housed in the DRONE's ventral fuselage. The GIS also provided high-resolution infrared thermal imaging for nighttime tracking. Facial recognition was operational and status checks and signals were tracking correctly. There was nothing remarkable about any of the data. The 216 DRONE operated at 100 percent efficiency. Why did it just stop working? If it were a system malfunction, then it would have registered immediately. If it could not signal, then it would have been picked up on the next signal status check, that's why they were there. If there was a failure in the signal capture, there were backup systems. When Kelan outfitted this DRONE to track only 216, he placed three redundant backups with relays that would cascade from one to the next in case of total catastrophic failure. If everything on the blasted floating junk pile just stopped working, then why didn't the stupid thing just fall out of the sky! Kelan threw the brief into the seat and floorboard.

He stared out the window and watched the buildings and trees zoom by. He considered himself an intelligent person. He was top in his class at MIT. Graduated as a normal person, not one of those snotty, arrogant little children at twelve or fifteen years of age. He could handle the social and single aspects of college and was most definitely able to fit in. He studied hard and played hard. That was the definitive phrase as they say. He always knew that he wanted to make an impact on the world, to contribute something that would put his name in books. High dreams of someone with a lot of ambitions.

He had worked various jobs after college. All were in his field of study, computer science, and all for very high-profile corporations. The jobs were satisfactory, if he wanted to be a worker bee and did as he was told, never able to excel, reach a career cap that he could not surpass. Always having someone else take credit for his work. That one bothered him the most. This was completely unacceptable in his eyes. He would never be able to develop anything that would showcase his talents or promote him to a status of global recognition. He wanted to be a person that people in his field would write legends about. Fame would naturally be followed by fortune. That's how it worked.

Along came Morgan Blalock with an opportunity of a lifetime. Promises of access to unlimited resources, a department division of his own to command as he saw fit. A ridiculously high paycheck. Most importantly, his name would be globally recognized. He would get credit for everything that he did.

Blalock said everything that someone with ambition wanted to hear. All Kelan had to do was sign a few forms that promised absolute secrecy for everything. A noncompete contract and disclosure agreement for anything that he did, saw, and developed for Alastar-McGlocklin. He also signed a binding contract that explicitly stated all intellectual properties belonged to the corporation. He only answered to Blalock, no one else.

One handshake and a few forms later, he was the director of Global Clandestine Operations for the multibillion-dollar corporation of Alastar-McGlocklin. Of course, his official title for everyone else was VP of International Technology Development. All advancements made or developed by his division would be credited directly to him under that title. It was up to Kelan if he wanted to share any glory from the cutting-edge science with which he was in command. Motivation of his division was of no concern to Blalock; he just wanted the rewards and spoils of the success.

All of that happened six years ago. Kelan continued to stare out the window. *Things were so different back then. If I had only known* . . .

The intercom system within the car sounded. "Mr. Tindal, we are seven minutes out from base."

Kelan put his finger on the Call button. "Thank you."

Thank you . . . humph. He figured that he could at least acknowledge the work of a subordinate when they performed *their* job.

He looked down at the mess of papers in the floorboard, sighed a little, and picked them up. He put them back in the order that he wanted and flipped through them again. He thought for a moment about what continued to work rather than what had stopped. He did a mental checklist. The flight systems continued to work and receive commands. Stealth mode continued to function. Telemetry worked because the orbital radius was maintained during signal failure. The transponder receiver was functional, or the DRONE would not have slowed the descent to navigate through the channel once it reached the outer marker. He wouldn't know if video continued to record until after diagnostic. It could have just lost the ability to transmit and continued to capture.

He went over the components of the DRONE, the mission parameters, and the telemetry objective several times. The only thing that failed was tracking or the ability to receive an acquisition signature. It was perfect timing with the ground unit's cluster of surveillance goof-ups. If this was sabotage, then it was one of the most precise, calculated, well-thought-out operations that he had ever seen. If that were the case, it would have had to have been an inside job. A handful of his people knew what the mission objective was regarding 216. Only they would have detailed mission Intel to know exactly when and what to shut down on the DRONE. That still did not explain the ground units. All RCT assigned to Object 216 had to be part of the conspiracy or witless pawns manipulated by a master. The latter part was the most plausible, but also the most elaborate and far-fetched. His head started to hurt. He did not like it when he could not figure something out. Everything could be explained. Whether the solution or results were good or bad, it could still be explained. He had to come up with that explanation. He was beginning to realize that his life might depend on it.

Chapter 4

Conversations and Watchers

The elevator's first stop let a young woman off. When the doors opened, there was the customary wall in front and, what Josh assumed, entry doors at either side. The doors closed, and the box continued upward. The next stop was for a man. Large build, broad shoulders, brown wavy hair to his collar, and the bluest eyes anyone could possibly have had. As he exited, he turned and gave Josh a smile then walked away. Josh did not think much of it. Everyone who came through the revolving doors in the lobby seemed to be happy and cheerful. Why would this guy be any different?

The elevator reached the floor for the initial interview. As the doors opened, Josh waited for Melina to exit the box first.

As he walked out, he looked over his shoulder. "Have a nice day, Sentinel."

"May you have a nice day too, Mr. Arden."

Melina about tripped as she came to a stop outside the elevator. She was dumbfounded. What just happened! She did not know what to be more astonished over. The fact that Josh wished the invisible voice a good day or the more bizarre event of Sentinel's response. Josh was not an employee. To her knowledge, he had never been to the corporate offices of Jonah before. She had never heard Sentinel respond to employees like that, much less a perfect stranger.

"Did Sentinel just answer you?"

"Sounded like it." He continued to walk past her.

He stopped and turned. "Are you okay?"

She was back in the toy store again. This time all the Barbies sang and danced just like the commercials from Saturday morning television. "I'm fine. It's just . . . Why did you say that?"

He looked at her innocently. "Say what?"

"Tell Sentinel to have a nice day."

"Seemed like the appropriate thing to say."

Joshua turned around to have a look at his surroundings. "Which way shall we go?"

Melina came back from the imagined toy store and motioned for him to proceed down the corridor.

In all the time, she had been aware of Sentinel; she was under the impression that it was an enhancement of a very sophisticated computer system that was networked throughout the building. Her understanding was that it only covered basic operations and electronic security. There were no direct interfaces with Sentinel on the lower levels outside of access to the upper-level elevator banks. Joshua's briefing package had her security access data, which included instructions for what to say and do, to get her and Joshua through to the upper levels. It was a machine with state-of-the-art software that only took explicit directions based on predefined commands. That was how things were supposed to work, or so she thought. Had anything like this happened before to anyone? The more important question was, why did she make a big deal out of this? Because this guy made more headway with an inanimate system than she did? Why would she care about something like that? She composed herself as she and Josh were approaching what looked like a directory of office listings and a kiosk. Not that it should have been a surprise to her, but once again, Josh did not react any differently than the first time Sentinel spoke.

Once they reached the kiosk, she placed her hand on the bio-pad. First, the light was blue, then it turned green. Just below the pad was a slot. It was a bit thicker than where a debit card might fit into an ATM. When the scan finished, a slight chime sounded, and a plastic card was produced. She reached forward and pulled the card all the way out then handed it to Josh.

"This is a high-tech version of a PDA. We call it a Proximity Information Card, or PIC. It has all the information that you will need throughout the interviewing process. It will give you access to your résumé, the bios for each of the people that you will be talking with, and the history of Jonah International. Most importantly, it has your itinerary. It is a temporary card that will only work in this building and be active for today."

He turned the card all around in his hand and examined it. It was the same dimensions but thicker than a credit card. It actually looked like it was about three cards thick. There was no writing, images, or bar coding of any kind. It was a clear piece of plastic with rounded edges. It did not feel like plastic either. It had more of a metallic feel to the touch, but it was very light. He had never seen anything like it before. "How do I access the information?"

"There is a conference table with a flat screen on the wall for each suite in your interview rotation. On the table, you will find a flat pad. It will look like a mouse pad with a credit card holder at the top. Place the PIC in the slot and put your hand on the pad. This will bring up the information on the screen. Scroll through the menu by swiping your finger on the pad. To select an item, just double-tap. When you are finished reviewing your information, just remove the PIC from the holder. Because you are interviewing with executives, their schedules are very diverse and busy. You will have approximately twenty minutes between interviews where you will have time to review the data on your PIC."

Melina walked Josh through a couple of hallways to the first suite. "Do you have any questions?"

"Can you tell me anything about the people that I will be talking to? Anything that may give me an edge?"

"I actually don't know who the interviewers will be. The PIC will have that data. It's not for me to see."

Melina's instructions in the briefing package were very specific in this area. She was to use her new temporary security clearance to retrieve the PIC for Joshua, after that, show him to the first suite. She was then instructed to wait in the common area near the elevators until she was summoned by Sentinel that Josh was ready for his next interviewer. Whom Joshua would be interviewing with was classified and not open to discussion with the candidate.

"Can I get anything for you? Some water perhaps?" she asked.

"No, thank you. I'm fine."

Melina opened the suite door for Josh. "Very well. Good luck." She smiled and motioned him in.

"Thanks." Josh entered the room, and Melina closed the door behind him.

The room was about what Josh expected. There was a sizable conference table with six chairs in front of a row of polished mahogany cabinets along the back wall. At one end of the table was the mouse pad that Melina mentioned. At the other end, on the far wall, was a fifty-two-inch flat screen monitor. Josh walked to the mouse pad and sat down in the chair closest. He looked at the PIC and shuffled it in his hand once more then placed it in the holder at the front part of the pad. He put his hand on the pad as instructed and looked at the monitor. It instantly came to life.

The main menu listed the categories just as Melina described. His name was at the top followed by subcategories: Jonah International, Itinerary, Résumé, and Exec Bios. Josh immediately double-clicked the Executive Bios. He was promptly given a message that stated this information was not accessible at the moment. He frowned. He did not understand. He paused for a second then selected his itinerary. He did not need to see his résumé; he knew he had no corporate experience and had no desire to see it on a big screen. Josh previously researched Jonah on the Net. He was pretty sure that area was covered. What he did not know was who the mystery interviewers were. His schedule for the day popped up. The odd thing was that only the first appointment was listed. Person, title, and time. The second and third slots were cryptic.

INTERVIEW 1: LANGSTON CAMPBELL, DIR/HR—9:35 AM
INTERVIEW 2: PENDING
INTERVIEW 3: PENDING

Very strange. Was the data upload not completed? No. Something else. It looked like it was a real-time update. He glanced at his watch. 9:15 am. What did Melina say? There was twenty minutes between interviews. Enough time for him to review the data on the PIC. It would stand to reason that he would have time before the first interview as well. It still did not explain why the other two slots were vacant.

Jonah International's headquarters was located in a subdued part of Manhattan. The building was comparable to any other structure that graced the New York skyline. It had thirty-nine floors and was intermingled with apartments and other businesses on the block. Most corporate entities shared space within commercial structures. It was, of course, New York City, and real estate was at a premium. Jonah owned their building, not a surprise as most buildings are owned by one company who occupies part and leases the rest. Jonah International, however, occupied every floor.

On one of these floors, a man sat behind and looked down at his desk. There was nothing on his desk. No paper, no family pictures, no computer. Not even a cup of coffee. Nothing. If someone came through his door and looked at him, it would appear as if he were just admiring himself in the shiny finish. If they came closer, they would notice an elaborate array of lights, video, and electronic files embedded within the surface of the desk. On one of those video feeds was Josh seated at a conference table in an executive suite. As Josh scrolled through the PIC, he was watched. The man looked as Josh picked the categories, studied him to see what he selected and why. Another man knocked at the door as he opened it. The man at the desk smiled and waved him in. The other man was tall with broad shoulders and brown wavy hair to the collar. He walked over and came around behind the desk to observe the feed with his blue eyes.

"What do you think?" said Blue Eyes.

The man behind the desk expanded the feed of Josh wider for better viewing. "He's looking through the data module right now. He went to the bios first," he said with a slight grin.

"He'll figure it out. He's a very smart and resourceful young man. I've seen him do remarkable things," said Blue Eyes.

He had a chuckle at the thought of the encounter at the elevator. "He didn't flinch with Sentinel. He even wished Sentinel a nice day. It was very amusing to watch Melina when Sentinel replied."

The man behind the desk slid back and faced Blue Eyes. "Is everything else in place?"

"We are ready for when the time comes."

"Will Joshua be ready?" the man said.

Blue Eyes looked at the man behind the desk with compassion and confidence. "Joshua Arden has lived a difficult life. He has endured much in his youth. Even so, he has come out of each trial a stronger person. He will overcome what lies ahead as well."

The man behind the desk looked relieved to hear that. He had high hopes for Joshua, but also knew what he would face. It was not so long ago that he himself had been where Joshua is now. He felt sadness at the thought of the near future and the events that would shape the young man on the screen.

As Josh studied the itinerary, it occurred to him that all the information *was* there. It was just that he could not see it, yet. He tapped once on the INTERVIEW 1 line. The color of the words changed from green to yellow. He backed out of the itinerary to the main menu then clicked on the bios subheading again. He was rewarded with a link: Langston Campbell. Joshua smiled. *Very ingenious!*

The men that watched Joshua smiled as well.

Josh read through the background on Campbell. As he scanned through it, nothing of interest popped out at him. *Whoa, hold up.* He did notice that Campbell's education listed him with a doctorate in Religious Anthropology. *What in the world is that?*

"Smart lad," said Blue Eyes.

"Yes," agreed the man behind the desk. "He's supposed to be the best one of us all. Past, present, and future. I would expect nothing less."

The man behind the desk entered a command. "Sentinel, please inform Dr. Campbell that Joshua is ready for his first interview."

"Yes, Mr. Holden."

Malcolm Holden, Global CEO of Jonah International, stood up, buttoned his suit jacket, and turned to Blue Eyes. "It's time to set events into motion, don't you think?"

Blue Eyes smiled and placed his hand on Holden's shoulder. "Events have been in motion for much longer than this, my friend."

Josh finished looking through the bio when a knock came at the door then opened. A gentleman in a very nice suit entered the room. He walked a few feet to the table and extended his hand.

"Hello, Joshua. Langston Campbell."

Josh stood and shook his hand. "Pleasure to meet you."

Langston gestured toward the chair. "Please."

As they both settled into their seats, interested parties throughout the building jacked into the video feed to watch this first interview. The people that watched all had a stake in how this played out. All had high hopes for the future and wanted to see firsthand the young man that would change everything.

Langston began the conversation. "I trust everything is going well so far?"

"So far, no complaints," Josh said.

"Good to hear that. Do you need anything? Can I get you some refreshments?"

"No, thank you."

"Okay, let's chat a bit about your background in finance and where you see yourself down the road."

For the first thirty minutes, Josh and Langston talked about his college studies and how he ended up majoring in financial economics. Langston listened intently but never took any notes. This was Josh's third big company interview, and in the previous two, each interviewer always took some notes. They might have scribbled or made out a shopping list for all Josh knew, but they made an appearance of writing the important stuff down. Langston responded with interested gestures, but nothing seemed worthy of a note here or there. Come to think of it, he did not bring anything into the room with him. Not even a copy of Josh's résumé. Oh well, maybe he had a photographic or eidetic memory.

When the dissertation of Josh's academic accomplishments was complete, Langston went a little off reservation with the remaining line of questions.

"So, Joshua, I'm curious . . . Why would you want to work for a company like Jonah International? We don't really start college recruits out in the best positions, and the pay is on the lower side of the competitive market. I'm sure that the other companies that you have spoken with have a more lucrative compensation package for new hires. The position you are interviewing for here is a market analyst on the lower levels. Not much in the way of upward mobility. We've got dozens of analysts all trying to get their foot in the door. You will more likely get lost in the herd."

He stared at Josh and waited for a response.

Josh had a game face. He used it when he and Harry would play cards on campus with the guys. Josh almost always bluffed when the stakes were really high, like when it involved food and rent money. He could not afford not to win regardless of what he held in his hand. He and Harry shared an apartment that neither could afford. Sometimes his paycheck plus the tips wouldn't cover the electricity, much less the rent. More often than he cared to remember, food was a luxury, not a basic necessity. He pulled out all the stops when things got tight. That game face proved quite resourceful when he needed it. He used it so many times; it was as automatic as a smile. Right now, the face was present, and it smiled at Langston.

"I'm not sure that I follow you, Dr. Campbell. It sounds like you are trying to talk me out of considering Jonah."

Langston shifted in his seat. "Not at all. I'm just wondering what would be the motivation for you to take a position with Jonah when there are other companies that would obviously offer you quicker advancement and pay, right out of college. Someone like Alastar-McGlocklin would be a perfect fit for anyone with ambition."

Langston watched Josh with anticipation, and so did the others that monitored the interview.

Josh maintained his game face, crossed his legs, and folded his hands in his lap. "Dr. Campbell, it has been in my limited interviewing experience that when a company asks a potential candidate to an in person, that candidate possesses a certain quality or skill set that will benefit the hiring company. If that candidate had not had the right stuff to begin with, then that candidate wouldn't have made it past the campus recruiting people, and the two separate phone screens. Now, we both know that I have absolutely no skills that would benefit your company. As you so aptly put it, you have dozens of market analysts. Nameless, faceless many that would love to move up the ladder as fast as they can scurry. I would think that they too could have chosen a better company if they wanted to move up quickly. Even so, they chose to work for Jonah International. What sets me apart from them?"

Josh uncrossed his legs and leaned forward. "I'll tell you what the difference is. On recruiting day at Carnegie, Jonah's reps came over to me. I didn't walk to them. I didn't see them do that with anyone else. That tells me two things. One: Jonah's reputation for being aggressive in the talent market is spot-on, and two: I've got something you want. I may not know what that is at the moment, but you can bet I'll find out. I do know this though . . . you don't want Alastar-McGlocklin to have it."

The other people who watched the interview were as silent as Langston. They all waited, almost holding their breath to see what would happen next.

"I saw how both companies were working the hype. About how they were the best choice, and that they would impact the world to make it a better place. Both were hitting all the right buttons and saying all the right words. What made Jonah stand out was not mentioning the possibilities of large amounts of money. That was basically all that Alastar-McGlocklin talked about. It seemed to have gotten the attention of my best friend," said Josh.

Langston started to get worried that he pushed Joshua too far with this line of questioning.

Josh leaned back in his seat again. "I'm not motivated by money. I have lived without a lot of it most of my life and survived. I've seen what the attraction of it can do to people. No, thank you. If it comes with the job, then of course, I'll take it. I would be a fool not to. However, that's not what gets me out of bed in the mornings."

Langston was genuinely curious now. "May I ask what does get you out of bed then?"

"I've seen a lot of injustice. Where good people are hurt by the decisions of others. Mostly big corporations, all in the name of the almighty dollar," said Josh.

He shook his head in disgust. "That's not right. Everyone in my life has been harmed or affected by corporate decisions made by someone, somewhere, who are not touched by the damage that it causes down the line."

Josh paused and leaned back for a moment as if he were in deep thought. He looked Langston in the eyes, his face sincere. "I just want to make a difference. I want to be able to speak for the people who can't speak for themselves. Big corporations need to see what they do to people. They need to understand that other things are more important than their market presence and money."

Josh immediately wished he had not said anything about big corporations. Jonah International was one, if not the biggest. It was like he wanted to use Jonah to get back at all the others because they were different. He thought for a moment. They actually *are* different, which is why he was here. But he did not want to use them per se. Well, that was not necessarily true. How would he explain his way out of this?

Langston was quiet, as were the silent observers. This was the first time that all had witnessed the resolve of what was to come. They saw the passion and commitment to truth, and it was marvelous.

Langston snapped out of it first. He sat back and slowly nodded as if in agreement with Josh. "Thank you, Joshua."

He was a little stunned by the statement. "For what?"

"For your candid response."

Langston was already committed with this path of questioning, so he decided to hit it head-on. "What makes you think that we don't want you to work for Alastar-McGlocklin?"

Josh simply replied, "Because you've already made up your mind about hiring me. These interviews are a formality."

He waited for this to sink in. Josh took a big gamble with that declaration. He had no idea if this were true or not. All the evidence pointed to this conclusion, but this was a bold play. This was not a card game, it was real life.

Langston had a game face too and did not want to tip his hand. There were two more interviews still to come, and now was not the time to be direct and let him know that he was absolutely correct. "What makes you think that we already have an offer pending?"

"I've already told you about the recruiting event. The phone screens were very basic. No hard-hitting standard questions that most college grads get, such as 'where do you see yourself in five years?' and 'what do you think you have to offer our company?' My other two big company interviews asked both of those plus others out of the standardized-textbook 101 questions to ask rookies. Jonah had not touched any of those.

"I had a hunch after the last phone screen. What really cinched it was today. I did some reading up on Jonah's interviewing protocols. All interviewing is done on the bottom levels with lower to middle management types. No one has interviews with department heads such as you, not in a corporation this size. You have people that do that for you. I am interested to see who the next two individuals will be. Certainly, no one interviews on the executive levels. Unless, of course, the candidate has something of value to offer or is an experienced hire gunning for something more than, say, a low-level market analyst," he finished.

He saw Langston blush. Josh was now pretty sure that he was right. The senior-level people that watched via the video feed were very impressed. He picked up a lot of details. Holden smiled to himself.

Langston composed himself. "I don't make the determination of who gets hired or not. I only make my recommendation based on the interview. The final decision will come from leadership. In your case, the Financial Director for Market Analysis."

Good answer. Safe, but good, thought Josh.

Langston looked at his watch. "We really only have a few more minutes before the next break and then your second interview. I would like to offer the opportunity to open it up for any questions that you may have."

Josh leaned forward and placed the PIC in the mouse pad, activated it, and navigated to the bio of Langston Campbell. "Yes, I do have some questions. I was wondering what someone with a doctorate in Religious Anthropology is doing as a Director of Human Resources. It seems like you are way overqualified for your current position. I don't mean to pry, but it looks fascinating, and I was hoping you could tell me a little about it."

Josh was not being malicious in any way. He was truly interested in Langston's education.

Langston smiled. "You know, you are the very first person to ever catch that. As with everything else, it's a very long story. I have a huge fascination with the human characteristics when it comes to their religious beliefs and practices. It was something of great interest in college, and I took a lot of courses around it. Next thing you know, I have an undergraduate degree in psychology and sociology. My master's program consisted of ancient religions predating Christ. I wasn't finished learning, so my doctoral thesis was the study of human beliefs. Hence, Religious Anthropology. If you get the position here, maybe we can catch up sometime over lunch and discuss in more detail."

Josh smiled. "If I do get the position here, I will most definitely take you up on it."

"I would very much that enjoy. Any other questions?"

"Yes, actually . . . I noticed that the other two interviewers on the PIC are blank. I'm curious as to why?"

Langston smiled again. "The others are picked based on the initial assessment from the previous interviewer. Once my evaluation is completed, the slot for the next person is selected based on recommendations. We try to tailor the people to each individual recruit."

Josh thought for a moment, considered Langston's response, and decided that it was not worth pursuing. He was satisfied with the answer. It was a little bizarre how this interviewing session was coordinated, but a company this large probably had its reasons.

"Anything else that I can answer for you?" said Langston.

"I'm good for now."

"Very well." Langston stood, and Josh followed.

They both extended hands and shook. Langston directed Josh toward the door. Josh pulled the PIC out of the mouse pad as he turned around.

Chapter 5

Surveillance and Actions

The car that carried Kelan turned onto the little gravel road that led to the Long Beach facility. There was a small fence that surrounded the building with a radius of a mile or so. This fence was not in any way meant as a security barrier that would prevent an intruder from entering. It was more of a perimeter line that would signal the security division that someone, or something, had crossed onto the property. The entrance was surprisingly open, no gate or guard. The corporation wanted this building to appear that it belonged in the little neighborhood and look almost abandoned to anyone who may pass by, which rarely happened. That did not mean that security for the installation did not exist. That was what made it the perfect place to run the surveillance and tactical operations. As soon as the car made the turn, all manner of security systems started to track it.

Kelan's car pulled around to the side of the building to the main entrance. This entry faced away from the drive and population of Stony Brook. With the building a mile from the main road, the only way that it could be seen was upon entering the property where security would automatically pick up the movement. The tree coverage made the entrance and most of the building impossible to see from the air. It also prevented satellite surveillance from unwanted attention.

As he approached, the loading dock doors slid open. Kelan's car drove through and found a spot within the building to park. There were a number of vehicles inside. In fact, it looked like that's all there was: various types of transportation. There was no rooms, people, or equipment, anything that would have indicated that this was a working facility, much less the base operations for the DRONE, just one small office in the corner.

Kelan exited the car and headed for the floor manager's office. He walked in and closed the door behind him then headed toward the lone locker against the far wall. He entered the code to the combination lock, and it opened. He reached inside and found a hook for a jacket and slightly twisted it. Inside the locker, a panel slid up; a numerical keypad glided out and moved into place. A voice quickly followed.

"Confirm identity."

Kelan entered his security code. "DCO. Bravo 26 Epsilon."

"Confirmed," replied the voice.

The keypad immediately glided back into the locker wall; the panel closed as Kelan shut the locker door. He turned toward the water cooler on the adjacent wall as it started to hum, and then an elaborate array of wall and floor moved out of the way to reveal an elevator. He stepped in, and the doors instantly closed.

The Long Beach facility was actually five massive subterranean levels of the most sophisticated complex that money could buy. NASA would have been envious of the technology. Nothing was spared in the outfitting of this facility. It is, in most ways, self-sufficient for long-term isolation. It had living quarters, a gym, an entertainment room, and commissary. It had been rumored that some of the engineers actually stayed there for weeks at a time without ever going to the surface.

Kelan went straight to his office and found the facility station chief waiting for him at the door. Margaret Havilland was a petite woman in her midthirties, her hair neatly pulled back into a ponytail, and she carried a technical printout of what Kelan presumed was the initial assessment from the 216 DRONE.

She skipped all the usual pleasantries and got right to business. "The 216 DRONE docked four minutes ago. The housing is being pulled. We expect to have internals completely available in the next ten minutes. Here is the flight data that we downloaded during initial descent."

She handed him the document as he sat behind his desk. "Mission protocols were followed to the letter. There doesn't appear to be any evidence of deviation. Flight path and trajectory were nominal," she said.

Kelan listened while he viewed the data. Upon initial assessment, there did not seem to be anything wrong with flight systems. "Video feed?"

"Capture is up and running. It appears that it never stopped."

Kelan looked up at her. "Aerial photography?"

"All operational and online the entire time. We're going to pull the digital recorder to verify once we have access."

The data looked normal, and that puzzled him. "It has been recording the entire time?"

"Yes, sir. The video and snapshots are being time-tracked and prepped for relay to your monitor. It shouldn't be any longer than a few more minutes."

Well, this day is just getting better by the minute, Kelan thought. So one of the theories that he hoped had been wrong, became very real. He needed to see for himself.

Margaret received a text message. "Video feed and snapshots are ready."

Kelan reached for the remote and pointed it to the flat screen on the wall. The video showed a very clear picture of the location of the apartment of Object 216. The DRONE made the mission orbital pattern and continued to capture from a circular angle around the structure. That allowed for all possible exits to be covered. The time stamp was 6:30 am. He fast-forwarded to 7:00 am and allowed it to continue from that point.

He needed to see it. Kelan had to make sure that the reports he received was not a fantastic story concocted from imagination. He would be the last authority to confirm that this was actually happening. Not *happened*, like in the past tense, but in the middle of and still unfolding.

Standard visual surveillance continued until the clock's time stamp in the corner of the screen indicated that it was 7:02:52 am. Then the feed looked like static as the clock still ran. He stared at the unchanged screen for thirty seconds then looked at Margaret. She looked at him with a blank expression. "This is what recorded until 7:15 am. We edited the video feed for your review. It should pick up at the 7:14:45 am time mark in about fifteen seconds," she said.

They both looked at the screen and waited. At the appointed time, the video came back with the same orbital angle, but this time, there was a flurry of activity around the building. Kelan could tell that the RCT attempted to locate Object 216 after the fact. It looked like something out of a breaking news flash from a 'we interrupt this program to bring you a special news bulletin' that could be seen from a television helicopter. All that was missed was the annoying commentary from a brainless, unaware reporter.

Twelve minutes. That was all it took to make the last eight months of the mission seem unimportant and a waste of millions of dollars. Twelve minutes was going to ruin everything that Kelan had worked for his entire professional life.

He looked intently at the screen. "Do you have the audio feeds from the tactical team on the ground during this timeframe?"

"Yes, sir."

"I want the video feed and the audio matched so I can hear what I'm looking at right now."

Margaret sent the command from her phone in an instant. Kelan viewed the debacle on the screen for a few more seconds then turned off the monitor.

"Do you want to view the snapshots?" she asked.

"Will I see anything different than the video?"

Margaret hesitated for a second. "No, sir."

"Then no, I don't want to see it. Who was on shift command for ground support during this mess?"

"Marseilles."

"Pull him in for a debrief. Call in the next shift commander to replace him. Tell him it's overtime."

"Right away, sir."

Kelan stared down at both his Intel package and the newly added flight data. It was everything that he had and knew about the breakdown in surveillance and the loss of Object 216.

It was nothing.

He had nothing to explain why they lost the Object. He had nothing tangible to trace back to a technical failure. He had nothing logical outside of human error, or stupidity, to explain why the 216 RCT lost the Object on the ground. He had absolutely nothing that would save him from the wrath of Blalock, yet. He looked at his watch. Object 216 had been off the grid for two hours and thirty-seven minutes. They were still in the black on the ground, there was nothing in the air. He needed a plan fast. Kelan hit his intercom button.

"Get all 216 department heads in the conference room in the next five minutes."

Margaret had seen that look before. Kelan came up with a plan off the cuff. He looked desperate, yet maintained his commander-in-chief cool, but he needed answers. He was going to find them, one way or another.

After surveillance on Object 216 was lost, all department heads were called into Long Beach. They knew it was the biggest and most important mission to date. It was the first time tracking was sanctioned for a human target. All previous missions were Artifacts. The cat and mouse game with Jonah International was tedious at best, but they could maintain a trace or location when it came to Artifacts. Sometimes they won and reached the targets first. Other times, Jonah beat them. They were evenly matched in those races. This mission was very different. They had no indication that Jonah was even involved this time. They needed more information. Kelan hatched a plan to get it.

Langston walked Josh back to the commons area where Melina waited patiently. As soon as she saw Josh, she smiled. She recognized the DHR that walked beside him. Joshua's first interview was with the Director of Human Resources. In her limited time here at Jonah, she had never seen an entry-level candidate, much less an inexperienced college recruit, get this kind of attention. She wanted to ask a dozen questions, but was prohibited by the instructions in the briefing package. The instructions had the digital signature of the Global CFO, Jacob Wessler. There's no way a sane person would disobey that directive. As they walked toward Melina, Langston stopped and thanked Josh for his time. They shook hands again, and then Langston turned down the corridor and disappeared.

Melina moved to intercept Josh. "I'll take you to the next room for your second interview."

As he rounded the corner, Langston took the stairwell up two floors. He entered the room where the watchers had observed the interview. Langston took a seat near Holden.

"Well?" Holden said.

"I like him. He's a very sharp and intuitive young man. It was impressive how he handled some of the questions. Do you think that I overstepped the line with the Alastar-McGlocklin reference?" said Langston.

"I think it was necessary to see where the boy's heart and mind are, but it could have been phrased a little more gently. Not to worry, both he and you came out of it just fine," said Jacob Wessler.

"He seemed to be relaxed, but cautious with his answers. He knew something was going on, but could not put his finger on it. He will make a good operative with the proper training and mentoring," said Ulysses Quaden, the Operations Technical Director.

"Agreed. Does he have any more outside interviews lined up?" said Holden.

"No. Jonah is the last corporation on his list," said Ulysses.

"How long before we make him the formal offer?" said Langston.

"We wait the customary forty-eight hours before contact. The offer letter has already been drafted and signed by the appropriate resources," said Wessler.

"Remember, this has to be Joshua's decision. He has to come to Jonah of his own choice. We cannot influence him in any way," said a voice.

All heads turned to the voice of the final member of the room. "He will need to be protected once he leaves the building until the offer is accepted. They may try to get to him," said Holden.

Blue Eyes looked at each of the people at the round table. "Joshua Arden is most important to our cause. This will be a significant turning point, and the Council of Twelve has committed to seeing it through. He will be secure. Of this, you have my word."

Melina and Josh moved toward the elevator, which happened to open right as they approached. As they entered and the doors closed, Josh turned to her. "Aren't you the least bit curious how things went?"

"Yes, I'm very curious, but it is not for me to know. The contents of the discussion are between you and the interviewers. I'm only the acting liaison for the day."

Josh inwardly shrugged then turned back to face the front of the elevator. He thought about how he could have responded differently to some of the questions. Especially the ones that were completely outside of what he expected. That was the way things regularly played out when confronted with the unforeseen and trying to come up with something on the fly. He always figured out the right thing to say after the fact. He could not turn back the clock though. He had to live with what was said. It was in the past now. The past was something that he had learned to adapt to and overcome. Dwelling on the things that could have been had caused more pain than he wanted to remember.

Melina could see that Joshua was distracted, deep in thought. She could not help but wonder what happened in the first interview. She wondered what was next and with whom. She desperately wanted to ask him everything. "What did the DHR say to you? Did he share any corporate secrets? Are you a secret spy here on an impossible mission of some sort? What in the world did they want with Joshua William Arden?" She used every bit of her will and mental strength not to ask these or any other questions. Whatever she had left after that was used to stare at the doors, and not at him.

They came to the next floor; the doors opened, and they emerged. As the doors closed, it dawned on him that Melina did not ask Sentinel to take them to their subsequent destination. The box just moved to wherever it was supposed to go as if it had already known. He really wanted to know how all of that worked.

The drill was much the same as before. They came to another suite; he entered, and Melina departed. As soon as he sat down, he placed the PIC in and performed the same sequence as before, only to find out his next interviewer was with a Financial Analyst Manager.

The process was more like he remembered from his previous two big company interviews. He was asked some innocuous questions, nothing obscure as with Langston. It was kind of boring in comparison. They talked about various subjects, asking each other questions that pertained to the actual position itself. After some probing information, Josh really hoped that he would get the job offer so he could put his education to some good use. It looked as though he would like the position from all indications of the description. When finished, he shook hands with number 2 and was escorted back to a waiting Melina.

Kelan and Margaret were the last to arrive in the conference room. There was a flurry of activity and chatter of the others that were already there. All had their paperwork, diagnostics, reports, technical specifications at the ready should they be called upon. Everyone quieted down when the DCO entered. Kelan took his seat at the head of the table; Margaret started prepping the videos, files, and snapshots on the principal computer for a push to each of the individual monitors and the main screen. He had his briefing package laid out in front of him. Margaret entered the last command then had everything ready. The monitors came to life with data.

"Object 216 has been off the grid for two hours and forty-four minutes," Kelan began. "I don't care how far-fetched the ideas are, I'm not interested in vague descriptions of known Intel. I certainly do not want any showboating or sucking up. I want options for reacquisition. We can discuss the failure for losing the signal after we have a plan forward. I want some answers. Who wants to begin?"

Kelan tried to be as sincere as he could under the circumstances. He did not believe in leading by intimidation or fear as Blalock did. He wanted to genuinely earn his entire team's respect. It was his belief that they would do anything for him if he had their respect.

"What little Intel that we have indicated that during the blackout, the Object left the apartment of their own volition or was moved by other interested parties to an alternate location," said one person.

"Ground teams confirmed this, and we sent in a cleaner crew to search the premises. There was no indication that Object 216 had prepared for a move or was forced to leave. All personal contents were accounted for," said another nameless person.

"What about asset tracking? Do we know what Object 216 was wearing at the time of the disappearance?" said Kelan.

It was widely known the importance of this mission, so no one left anything to chance. At the onset of surveillance, all personal assets that belonged to Object 216 at the time were cataloged and tagged. This included all new assets acquired during the mission.

"A chestnut suit, white shirt, pinstriped tie, brown dress socks, and a pair of Kenneth Cole dress shoes, brown, size 11, were missing. All other clothing assets were confirmed on-site or at the dry cleaner," said someone.

"Did those clothes have a tracking device embedded?" said Kelan.

All were silent for about two seconds. "The shoes had tags in each heel, sir. There was also a flat unit in the collar of the shirt." The speaker paused. "None of the devices were tracking enabled."

"Excuse me?" said Kelan.

The speaker was feeling uncomfortable. All eyes in the room were on him, each person thankful that they were not sitting in his chair. "All tags are passive until our surveillance units confirm movement, then they are activated. Once active, our satellites respond to signal and track all mobile activity for the Object. This includes the

216 DRONE. All electronic eyes were on target. The tags did not respond to commands. They did not activate," he said.

"You're telling me that Object 216 is wearing three tracking devices and none of them work, is that correct?" said Kelan flatly.

"Yes, sir."

Kelan rubbed his forehead and then his face. He was understandably upset. Here was yet another failure of technology with no viable explanation. So someone, or something, deactivated the tags as well as the DRONE. Again, more than one person would have to be involved if it were an inside job. These were two separate teams that were responsible for electronic deployment and tracking. They would have had to work together within some bigger plan. There had to be an endgame to all of this. If it was something and not someone, then what type of force, signal, or tech could have done this? Who could have controlled this? He had a thousand and one questions, and it became very apparent that his department heads could not provide the answers.

"Could the same signal that prevented the DRONE from capturing video and audio have disrupted the asset tags?" said Kelan.

"We're not sure. We cannot find a correlation between the two. We are continuing to research," said someone.

Kelan was already tired, and it was not even lunchtime. "All right, people, we need to find a plausible explanation for why we have lost Object 216 for the first time in over eight months. This has visibility all the way up to the CEO and the senior partners."

He paused for effect to see if that would spark some better answers or reasoning. Everyone in the room was genuinely stumped. There were PhDs, engineer techs, mathematicians that looked around and down at their notes and tried desperately to find something positive to add to the Greek tragedy that had unfolded. Kelan looked around at the people that had been handpicked to be his go-to leadership team on this mission. The best of the best, the smartest people that he knew. No one made any move to step up or even show that they had a glimmer of a plan brewing in their beautiful minds. He sighed and decided to engage them with a look straight in the eyes, to call them out one at a time until he started to hear some answers that he could literally live with.

He looked to the person at his left. "Options?"

"The 216 DRONE seems to be operating normally. The only issue pending complete analysis is the video feed transmission. We send it back up ASAP with the same mission parameters and widen the acquisition radius," said the flight command director.

"We won't be able to complete assembly within the next two hours as the diagnostics have already been initiated. Best-case scenario, we can have it back in the air by 2:00 pm," added Margaret.

"Unacceptable," said Kelan.

It was a full ten seconds before the next person in line said anything. Kelan played an eye contact version of chicken until the woman broke off and spoke.

"We hack into traffic camera surveillance on all known routes taken by Object 216 in the last ninety days. Run facial recognition patterns and cross-check with time index over the last four hours. See if we can get a match and path," she said.

Excellent. They had started to earn the money that he was paying them. "Good. What else?"

"We send single agents to each of the known locations patronized by Object 216 to watch known associates and try to pick up the trail," said the next person.

Flickers of hope at something salvageable surfaced. "Okay," said Kelan. He looked over at the mission coordinator. "What is the next operation booked for the Artifacts?"

"The Medallion of Souls. Object designation 582. Briefing for mission development is slated for the end of the month."

"582 is now on hold until further notice. Upload 216 mission parameters to a new DRONE and get it airborne within the next thirty minutes," said Kelan.

The mission coordinator looked disappointed, but picked up his cell and called his team to relay the new directive.

Kelan turned to the RCT director. "Get a tactical team on deck to widen the radius around Object 216's apartment. I want the entire area canvassed. Have a unit replace all passive trackers with fresh ones. Make sure all of them work before installation. What is the status on the current scrub? Any indication or trail as to the direction of departure?"

"An RCT tracker team has been on-site from point of lost signal fanning out in a ten-mile radius. They are still scrubbing for an energy sequence match with an orbital spectroscope. The scope itself has been outfitted and aligned to the Object's unique signature."

"And?" said Kelan.

"They still haven't produced a match or anything close within a 5 percent error of confirmation."

"How many foot soldiers are assigned?"

"We have ten in the dwelling and twenty-eight spread out over a ten-mile grid."

"I want a detailed report from Marseilles on my desk within the hour."

"Yes, sir."

Kelan turned to look at Margaret. "Exact status of the old DRONE?"

"Housing is completely removed. Digital surveillance and backups have been extracted and are currently in the process of a level 4 diagnostic," she said.

Kelan looked back at the rest of the smart people. "Whatever you and your teams have on your plates is now on hold until we have reestablished contact with Object 216. All other priorities are canceled until further notice. I want fresh tech in the air and on the ground ASAP. Widen the search radius. Use any means possible to reacquire. I want departmental reports every fifteen minutes. Dismissed."

Everyone gathered their paperwork, charts, and notes and left as quickly as they could. Margaret stayed behind. "Mr. Tindal, I realize that there are some aspects of the 216 mission that I'm not cleared to know, but . . ."

Kelan looked up at her.

"We are literally running out of options, and I'm assuming time as well?" she said.

The room was now empty. "Time is definitely the worse enemy right now. We need to reacquire the target ASAP." He leaned back in his chair. "Yes, Margaret, there are some sensitive areas that you have not been cleared for. Believe it or not, that has been in your favor. The less you know, the better."

Target? He's never said that before. It's always been an Object. Just like any other Artifact, she thought.

He looked at her intently for a few seconds. "Please close the door."

She walked over and closed the door and was back at his side within seconds. "Margaret, we are in a difficult position from a management level. We both are in charge of people that perform their duties as required without so much as questioning their directives. Up to this mission, their jobs have been understood at a very basic constant. Everything is black-and-white. Research an Artifact, locate, and acquire. Now we have a human Object. An Artifact that can think, interacts, and is mobile at any given time. Those are variables that some of these eggheads can't process, simply because they don't understand something that can have reason or logic within their current mission parameters. The color could not be grayer than this."

Kelan paused for a moment as if in deep contemplation. He tried to quickly decide if this was a path of discussion that he wanted to pursue with her. While he relished the thought of having a person on the inside, to know what he did about this mission, the stakes involved, the endgame, and the world-changing events that would shape all things to come, he did not know if this was something that Margaret could or would be able to handle. He desperately needed someone who had a calmer demeanor than Blalock. He wanted someone to talk to. Someone whom he could depend on to partner with in the completion of this maddening quest with which he was charged. How much could she handle? Could he trust her? This was a very slippery slope. Once he brought her in, he could not undo the revelation. He could not put her back into that world of simplistic understanding. She would not be able to just walk away. She would be part of the inner sanctum with no possibility of a return to what she probably considered a normal life.

His thoughts were to test the waters a bit to see if she could and would be capable of a commitment to see this through.

"We didn't hire these people from Camp Peary or Quantico. They don't have the necessary training that is required to run proper surveillance on a human being. That's why we created the Recovery and Containment Team. We knew that this particular mission was going to happen at some point, and we needed to have trained agents ready. Old-school surveillance techniques coupled with state-of-the-art technology. We used the RCT for each mission prior to incorporate them into the Artifact acquisition procedure. That way, when the time arrived, it would go unnoticed as to the true nature of their purpose," he said.

She looked a little shocked. "I had no idea."

He smiled slightly. "How would you? That's why we have clearance levels established. You and countless others are operating under the pretense that we are only tracking because those were the orders given." He paused for a second. "Object 216 is very smart. Graduated in the top twenty-five of the class from an accredited university. As far as we know, the Object is unaware of the surveillance and tracking measures. This is good, because that means we are doing our jobs correctly. There are some unknown variables as well. Information that is 'need to know' only, and has not been divulged."

She looked puzzled. "What type of information?"

"The kind that could help the team better understand what we're up against and provide more insight to our competitors and their culpability in the endgame."

She jolted for a second. "Mr. Tindal, I'm afraid I'm not following you. Is there additional information available that will either help us succeed or cause us to fail in completing the mission?"

"Yes."

She was mildly irritated with the implications. "Why hasn't this information been disclosed to the rest of the 216 team?"

"Because it is 'need to know' as I said before. Too many people know, and the operation runs a bigger risk of failure."

He had to be very careful. He could not tell her too much at once. He was not sure that she would believe him, even if he told her everything.

She looked a bit cautious. "Why are you telling me this now?"

"The game is changing and our clock is running out. I need to have someone closer in the shop that understands the true objective of this mission. You have constant real-time knowledge about the operation status and can provide sharper Intel when I need it."

There were other reasons to bring her in, but that was not important, for the moment. "I need to know your commitment to this division and the mission. Make no mistake though, once you are completely read in, the knowledge that you will come to possess will change how you view all operations going forward and the outcomes. This will affect every divisional decision you make from this day forward."

Conflicts of loyalty and apprehension swirled in her mind. "Mr. Tindal, will this additional intelligence that you provide make it easier for me to assist in completing our mission?"

"It will provide more insight for you to better direct the teams in their objectives. It will not make things easier for you as the station chief, in fact, it will be harder for you because you will have classified knowledge that cannot be shared with anyone else but me. You will have to learn to support all divisions with information that you maintain without divulging direct knowledge."

She lowered her head as if that decision for full disclosure would be a life-altering experience. Funny that she should view it that way because that was indeed the case. She looked at him and nodded the acceptance of the responsibility.

"Are you absolutely sure that you can commit and see this through to the end?"

She straightened up. "Yes, sir."

Kelan looked a little more relaxed and exhaled. He turned and faced her directly. "This goes much higher than the team, me, or even Alastar-McGlocklin's global CEO, Morgan Blalock."

He motioned for her to take a seat. "Margaret, there are aspects of this particular mission that have monumental ramifications should we win or lose."

She became annoyed with all the vague speaking and began to regret accepting the new responsibility. "Again, Mr. Tindal, I'm not following. You are talking like this is some sort of contest between teams. This doesn't make any sense at all. I cannot begin to help you through this if I first don't understand myself."

"Margaret, I cannot undo what I'm about to tell you."

She started to get scared. A very valid feeling, and that, if she had already known what he did, would have been completely justified. Kelan waited for just a moment before he continued. He did not try to be dramatic in any way; he just did not know how to approach the next part of the secret.

He remembered when Blalock first told him. As a man of science, none of it made any sense. He did not believe, so it was hard to accept. After some of the things that he had seen over the years, his views on life and the afterlife were very different now. Part of the acceptance was the blind belief. Now he was on the other side about to impart this knowledge to another person of science. He was not sure how this would to play out. "Do you have a religious belief?"

"Excuse me?" she said.

"A belief system that incorporates the supernatural or occult? Do you believe in a god?"

"No, not really. I mean, I've heard that some people need to have something bigger than themselves to rely on in times of stress or want. It's something that I never really gave any thought. As a scientist, it's not a rational or logical line of thinking."

"Were you brought up in a faith system?"

"My parents were not really into the church. They believed that you make your own way in the world and shouldn't rely on anyone, a god or not, to provide for you. What does this have to do with our mission or my role at hand?"

"Everything." Then he started to explain the unthinkable. As he walked her through the fantasy that fast became her new reality, he watched her expression change from dismissive to thoughtful interest and, finally, a panicked disbelief. He remembered the last expression very clearly himself when he found out.

When he stopped, he sat back in his chair and waited for her to say something. She looked almost catatonic, pale and sweating. Her heart rate seemed like it was out of control and became faster the more she processed. She tried to comprehend what she was just told. Margaret rapidly thought over all variations and outcomes of the mission itself, but now with a slight nudge of something impractical in the mix of her logical comprehension. She tried as hard as she could to work through the problem like she always did, but could not help to now apply this newfound information. In fact, no matter what she thought about, this illumination was part of the equation. Worse yet, as fast as her mind worked, she started to rethink everything in her life. How was something like this possible? The more she thought, the sicker she became.

Kelan leaned forward. "Margaret, are you okay?"

"Honestly, I'm not sure. I'm having a really hard time with this," she said in almost a whisper.

"I know that this is shaking the foundation of everything you understand. Some people say that this knowledge has a completely opposite effect on those who believe. They find a sense of calming and peacefulness indicative of serenity, of knowing that everything is somehow right in their world just by awakening to this truth and believing they will have their heart's desire. Honestly, I don't see it, and I've known for the last seven years. I guess I'm missing something in the translation."

Their eyes met as hers searched for confirmation. "Are you absolutely sure that this is the honest-to-goodness truth? That you're not just testing me to see if my loyalty or commitment to our mission is changing?"

He saw the hope in her eyes that she wanted this to be some sort of joke or a fanciful story. If she had really known him, she would have dismissed the thought of a joke. He was not like that normally, and today was anything but normal. He felt bad for her. He could not have told her at a worse time, but he needed an ally and needed her head in the game. He had to snap her out of this quickly. There would be time later to sit back and ponder the magnitude of this information.

"Margaret, I'm not testing you. I've told you the truth about our reality. I need you right now. We are going to lose the war if we don't reacquire 216 ASAP. Are you with me?"

Margaret straightened up and tried to compose herself as much as she could as the shock was still very fresh. "Yes, I'm with you. What is the next move?"

With that, Kelan got up and headed for the door; Margaret followed. They walked toward his office as he spoke in hushed tones. "It doesn't seem that we can trust anything electronic anymore. All surveillance measures appear to be in working order, but we are not receiving the intelligence that we need to make effective decisions. Continue with your diagnostics on the 216 DRONE. My guess is that you will not find anything conclusive. Once you have the report, bring it to me, and no one else. Do not post the findings on the central server. We're going to have to fabricate a false reading to explain the failure."

"Mr. Tindal, I don't feel comfortable with that."

He stopped and looked at her. "Margaret, this is how we play this out. As scientists, we have to have tangible, quantifiable evidence to explain causality and reason. There is no room for conjecture or hypothesis with this mission. As I said before, this goes a lot higher than this company. You know the truth now, think about the outcome. I have to provide a credible explanation for the failure of multiple measures in the tracking of one of the most important missions to date to some very unpleasant people."

He looked at her with some sympathy. "We have to provide answers that will buy us more time to get Object 216 back on the grid. You will not be admonished for a directive that I gave you. Besides, the outcome is my responsibility, not yours. Your involvement is transparent, and it will continue to stay that way. This is part of the job description now. We work together to supplement the facts as needed. Do you understand?"

She looked thoughtful as she considered what he said and weighed the recent shock of information with the request. "Okay, Mr. Tindal, I'll bring the findings to you.

We can't post the report until reviewed by department leads and signed off. Once that is completed, I'll make a note in the time stamp that will buy us more time before uploading."

"Good. I will alter the report as needed and get it back to you. Once the post is completed, I will inform the powers that be of the progress."

They continued their walk down the hall. "You seem pretty certain that electronic surveillance measures are no longer trustworthy. Do you have something else in mind?" she said.

"It's not that I think they're completely untrustworthy, it's the fact that the explanations for failure are not working in the mission's favor. The RCT unit is having the same sort of luck from the ground. I have another play in motion to help balance the odds."

They reached his office. "What do you mean?" she said.

They walked inside and closed the door. He looked at her with a slight smile. "We have someone on the inside."

Chapter 6

Boundaries and Tracking

Josh made it through the last interview with flying colors. At least, that was what the watchers thought. He had a different opinion. His final interviewer was a woman named Lilandra McDowell, the Director of Talent Management for the North American division. She also happened to be the boss, fourth removed, over Melina's department. As Josh talked with her, it appeared as if she did not seem to be interested in his qualifications as a financial analyst at all. She did not ask about 'why Jonah?' or any of the other standard new-hire questions. It looked like this interview was headed down the same path as the first. She seemed to be more interested in Josh's family life. She was very slick about weaving the questions together into an appropriate context. She never asked anything that would be considered crossing the line of too personal, but received just enough to piece together Josh's sad little background. This went on for about fifteen minutes. Josh was unaware at first what had happened. He answered the questions out of habit because he thought they were indirectly related to his ability to perform his possible responsibilities. During her series of a seemingly unending superfluous quest for nonessential information, she intermingled little ditties about her family and relationships. She spouted things like how important it was to maintain a bond with those closest to you. Then Josh got a question that stopped him cold.

She asked him about his mother.

More specifically, how she felt about his involvement and subsequent employment with a global corporation. "Coming from a blue-collar background, would your mother be proud of your achievements here at Jonah?"

As if on cue, she mentally picked up a bat and hit him right in the stomach. For the first time today, Josh did not know what to say. He hid the pain very well, or at least he thought he did. The watchers all shared a compassionate look with each other as this moment arrived. Lilandra asked this as instructed and waited. She also hid the heartache of having to ask such a personal question given the fact that both she and the watchers knew that Joshua Arden's mother was dead.

Josh sort of stared at her, but not directly. He looked through her and reached back into the past when his mother was still alive. First, one memory then another and yet another. They started slowly, but began to get faster as though a floodgate lifted and more and more water poured out. He inwardly smiled at the memories of his mom and the happy parts of his life. He knew that if he continued to run the movie in his head, that eventually it would become darker the closer he got to the end. He tried with all of his strength to slow the ride down and get off before he crashed into the final moments of his mother's life.

He remembered how long it took him to get over her passing. She was his entire world. He truly believed the word *mother* was the word for *God* as a child. He could not think of anyone else that would have loved him for who he was more than her. He remembered how angry he was at God for taking her away. Where was the justice? So many others probably deserved to die more than her. It was a senseless, meaningless death. He started to sink.

He had to come back, had to recover and push on. Coming back became easier now. On the other hand, maybe it seemed that way because he practiced it so much as a child.

"Mrs. McDowell, my mother was always at every Little League game when I was a child. She participated in the PTA and made cookies for the church bake sale. She loved

God and me. As far as I knew, he and I were her only objects of adoration. No matter what I did, whether foolish or sensible, she loved me just the same. It was completely unconditional. I never had to question how she felt. She always knew how I felt about her in return."

He focused on Lilandra; his blank, passive face looked her in the eyes. "My mother would be proud of any accomplishments that I made. She has always trusted my judgment since I was very young. There would not be any difference now."

He almost added "if she were still alive," but decided that this was a topic that he did not want to discuss any further. He waited for the interviewer to make the next move. She started this; he was determined to make her end it.

The more he stared at her, the more uncomfortable she became. Not sure if that was his plan, but it seemed an appropriate response to a subject that should never have been talked about, much less in an interview setting. There was a fine line between professional courtesy and a blatant disregard for personal boundaries. He began to question whether Jonah International was a place that he wanted to work.

Josh continued the game of chicken until she diverted her eyes and looked at her notes as if there were additional questions that she could fish out. As far as Josh was concerned, the interview was over.

Lilandra became uneasy. She tried not to show it, but tipped her card by looking away. She could feel his persistent stare. Lilandra knew the watchers had viewed the entire meeting and wanted them to do something to push this back on track or bail her out. She did not know where to go from there. She fumbled through the stack of papers like she had a purpose, but in actuality, had nothing else to discuss.

Right on cue, her PDA chimed with a message. "Excuse me for a second."

She looked at the screen.

WRAP IT UP. YOU HAVE ANOTHER APPOINTMENT THAT HAS JUST COME UP, AND YOU ARE SORRY, BUT HAVE TO CUT THIS INTERVIEW SHORT. HEAD IMMEDIATELY TO DEBRIEF.

She was grateful that the watchers had been perceptive and knew she needed an out. She tucked her PDA in her pocket and began to gather her papers into a neat stack. "Joshua, I'm so sorry, but I just received a reminder of another meeting that I must attend. Please forgive me, but I will have to cut our discussion short."

How convenient. "Of course. I understand," he said.

They both rose at the same time and shook hands. As they headed for the door, she offered the customary pleasantries of a typical interviewer along the lines of "If you have any questions, please don't hesitate to reach out" and "We appreciate your time" and so on.

Yeah, whatever.

He became passive about the prospect of working here. The personal stuff was now fresh in his mind and probably would be for some time.

He and Lilandra walked toward the floor's common area where Melina waited patiently. She shouldn't have been surprised to see Lilandra McDowell walk with Josh solely based on the VIP treatment that he had received so far. Still, she was impressed and a little stunned at the attention that this man had garnered.

Josh and Lilandra shook hands once more, and then she disappeared around a corner just as Langston did.

Melina smiled as Josh approached, but noticed that he did not smile back. "Is everything all right?"

Josh did not want to relive the experience or the memories, so he pushed through his feelings. "Sure. Just not feeling that well. I didn't get much of a breakfast this morning. As soon as I eat something, I should be fine."

She looked at her watch. "We have a full cafeteria on the fourth floor. It will open for lunch at eleven thirty. Would you like to get something to eat before you go?"

He raised an eyebrow. "Would you be able to join me?"

Melina smiled. "It would be my pleasure."

Lilandra walked into the conference room that held the watchers and took a seat next to Langston. She looked visibly shaken and rightfully so. This was an impossible situation for both her and Josh to have undergone. She was uncomfortable with this strategy from the beginning. The line of personal and situational questions that were to be asked had been discussed at length by the inner circle of "those who knew." She and Langston had both wanted to use a more subdued tactic to get an evaluation of Josh and his capabilities. It was ultimately decided that the only way to accurately measure his potential and place in future events was to put him in stressful positions and review the outcome. After all, his future would be getting a lot worse, and his ability to handle events and make decisions would drive the balance of global power.

The people that were going to ask the questions were carefully selected by a number of different factors. The one that carried the most weight was the fact that the selection pool could only be comprised of the people that knew the truth. The picks were based on some type of human neuro-response algorithm, originally developed in the mid-'80s by some Austrian sociologist and later refined by a plethora of psychologists, mathematicians, and scientists. It was then altered for studies of human behavior and reaction limits. The algorithm measured both the interviewer and the respondent on a number of different levels.

The idea behind all of that was to basically see how Josh handled specific scenarios and adapted to situations. With each given answer from Josh, the algorithm would calculate the proper sequence of questions against the types of personalities doing the questioning. The modified algorithm was far too advanced and sophisticated for a human to process as quickly as needed to stage the questions in the correct order. That was all handled by Sentinel.

It was decided weeks ago that Langston Campbell would be the first interviewer. He had more experience in these types of situations based on his background and could alter his questioning as needed to generate the desired scenario to gage Josh's responses. After the first few questions, a baseline was established, and Langston was then prompted through a tiny earbud with the follow-on questions. All the interviewers had these and followed the script to the letter.

Each of the watchers told Lilandra that she performed marvelously throughout the process. That did not seem to be much of a consolation to her. "Why would you want to ask him a question surrounding his mother? What on earth would possess anyone to bring up that pain from his past?"

"Lilandra—" said Holden.

"No, Mr. Holden, I agreed to participate in the screening of this young man with the sole understanding that we would gauge his moral compass and potential for honesty and goodness. Measuring these characteristics does not have anything to do with the boy's poor deceased mother. Everyone in this room knows what he has been through, what he has had to overcome to get to where he is now."

"We all had this discussion long before Joshua was even approached at Carnegie Mellon," said Wessler.

"Yes, and as you recall, I never agreed to this obtrusive and abrasive approach. He is very young, and the tragedy that he has faced is still fresh in his mind. Reliving this trauma is not healthy and, in my opinion, very poor taste on our part," she said.

"If he is the key to our balance of world power, he must face situations like this going forward. The enemy will not cut him a break once he emerges," said Wessler.

"So that means that we treat him in the same manner?" she said.

"Lilandra. Joshua Arden is one of the strongest candidates for the position that we have ever had. His name has been in the Book since his birth. His destiny has been foretold, and now we are seeing glimmers of his potential valor. We all know what he has been through. Look at how he has handled everything so far. Even with his mother's passing, he has kept his head up and continued forward. He knew that his mother would never have wanted him to dwell on what has happened, but would encourage him to focus on what could. He is a strong human being with a gift that he knows nothing about," said Holden.

He paused and looked at Blue Eyes. "We are only human. We have to be absolutely certain that Joshua can be ready when the time comes."

"I have been with Joshua since the very beginning," said Blue Eyes. "With great sadness, I have watched him endure cruelty and loss and suffer immeasurably. Nevertheless, through all of his choices, he has risen up and never accepted defeat or despair. He is the strongest human that I have ever had the privilege of guarding." He looked passionately at Holden. "Joshua is the hope that your world needs to keep the flow of power on the side of good."

All occupants in conference room 1A looked at Blue Eyes and prayed fervently that he was right.

They both sat in a corner of the cafeteria and ate their sandwiches. They discussed various topics from education to current world market events.

Josh was very interested in Melina's background in linguistic arts. She could speak seven different languages. Quite a feat for someone of her very young age. "How did you end up in the Talent Management Department at Jonah?"

"I was completing my undergraduate at Columbia here in New York when the university hosted a job fair one day. Jonah had a booth, I sat down and talked with them . . . Next thing you know, here I am."

She swallowed a drink. "Jonah made a very attractive offer. They paid for my master's with the option of moving into a field of my choosing when the timing was right if, at some point, I agreed to help them out in Talent Management. At the time, I thought it was curious that Jonah was requesting me to be placed specifically in this department," she mused.

"Why is that?"

"Because leadership also encouraged me to continue my language arts studies to expand my skill set. I don't really see the connection between my languages and TM. I have had to use some of them with a few of the candidates, but nothing more specific than that. I don't translate any documents, nor do I deal with any dignitaries at my level."

"Maybe Jonah has something more long-term in mind for you. You know, where your expertise in multiple languages will become your biggest asset."

Melina looked at him for a moment and wondered why she had not thought of that. A very simple statement but seemed to make the most sense. Maybe she indirectly worked her way up to something better, a higher position with her background. She thought the same thing when asked to escort Josh today.

Again, she sort of marveled at the intuitive nature that Josh seemed to possess. Melina observed that he appeared very composed and professional, but was carefree and accepted just about anything that crossed his path. She could still see remnants of something in his eyes that she could not put her finger on. There was a different story somewhere in there. When he came out of his last interview, he looked more upset than hungry. He was good at covering, but not great. She wanted to ask how everything went, but was bound by the directive to refrain from inquiring. She did not push the matter. Instead, she thought, it would be better to let this go with the hope that maybe someday she could actually talk with him about his experience. That is, if an offer is extended and he accepts.

Melina still felt embarrassed about her reaction to the Sentinel encounter earlier. She wanted to explain and apologize, but he did not even seem to notice or was very gracious and let the whole episode slide. A horrible first impression, she thought. However, now she had a whole new question that floated around in her head.

Why was she so concerned about what this man thought of her?

She had just met him only a few hours earlier. It could be all the attention that Jonah gave him. Not that she would be privy to all the pomp and circumstance VIPs are prone to receive, but never had she witnessed something like that for a college recruit. If Jonah thought he was important, then they also thought his opinion mattered. Maybe by association, so did she. She was obviously still having a hard time processing the whole situation. That made her natural curiosity all the more intense. She is not one to give into gossip or put her nose into anyone else's business, but this one really got the best of her. It was like a cub reporter who was the first to find out about the Watergate scandal, Melina wanted to know more. She tried not to obsess, but lost that battle the more she talked with him. What was the matter with her? She felt like a stupid little schoolgirl with a crush.

Oh no! Was that her problem? She turned her attention back to Josh. "You know, I haven't thought about it like that."

He took a sip of his drink and wiped his mouth with his napkin. "Jonah seems to have a purpose for everything that they do. I may not agree with their approach, but I understand their motive."

Melina noticed that Josh was saddened by that statement. Something happened today that hurt him badly. She did not know what to do or say, so she just listened.

Josh pushed his tray away slowly. "Jonah is a very large corporation with a lot of influence in many areas. In order to maintain their presence as market leaders, they need to be selective about the resources that work *with* them and *for* them. Each person that works here has a purpose in the overall mission, I'm not yet sure what that is though. It is through those people that Jonah connects to the rest of the global community. This place will most likely not function without key people in specific places, of that I'm pretty certain. I'm still trying to understand the techniques they use for finding the right people to serve this mission."

He looked out the window into the traffic below. "You seem like a very kind and caring person, Melina. I can tell that other people and their feelings matter to you. You display compassion when you see someone in pain, your empathy is genuine. Something like that speaks volumes of a person's character." He cut his eyes toward her. "Your skills have a purpose. You are meant for bigger things here. I'm sure all will be revealed in time. If I can see that, I'm confident that Jonah can too." He smiled.

Melina was absolutely sure now that Joshua was a special person with gifted qualities that Jonah International wanted on their side.

After they finished their lunch, Melina escorted Josh back to the main lobby. As the elevator doors opened, Josh said, "Nice to meet you, Sentinel."

"It was nice to meet you as well, Mr. Arden."

Melina smiled as they walked.

Just past the gate, Josh turned to her and held out his hand. "It was a pleasure to make your acquaintance, Melina Vargas."

She blushed slightly and hoped that he could not tell she was a little flustered by today's events. She took his hand and shook it politely. "It was a pleasure for me as well. I hope we have an opportunity to meet again. We have a car waiting to take you wherever you need to go." She gestured toward the doors. Just on the other side stood a driver next to a black sedan with the back door open.

"You never know what the future will hold," he said. With that, Josh walked through the revolving doors. He entered the car and said thank-you without a look to the driver.

"My pleasure," said Blue Eyes and closed the door.

"Object 216 is back online!" shouted a DRONE tech. He furiously typed in protocol commands to ensure that satellite capture was fixed and began recording.

Margaret walked with quickness to the tech's side. "Coordinates?"

"Still in the city, heading east on Fifty-seventh Street. Moderate rate of speed, not walking, most likely in a vehicle."

"Keep tracking." Margaret then yelled over her shoulder. "Get the RCT in a position for reacquisition!" She pulled out her mobile and dialed Kelan. "216 is active. Signal has been captured. DRONE has position fixed and is tracking. RCT en route."

Kelan hung up the phone. He spun around and continued his modifications to the diagnostic report from the DRONE analysis as quickly as he could. He wanted the report posted before he informed Blalock of the latest news. He was certain that the added information would prove authentic when reviewed, mainly because it would be validated as such by Kelan himself. As the main resource and acting head of the covert surveillance division, his word would be the final authority. As soon as he finished, he signaled Margaret with a text message so she would approve the record then post it to the central server.

He headed down to the tracking station with quickness and tried to look like he was not running. As he entered the room, Margaret approached him with the printout of the location and acquisition specs. "Object 216 came back online at 12:43 pm EST. The DRONE is in a standard orbital radius."

He caught her eyes as he took the specs. She nodded an acknowledgment that the altered report had been posted. "Has the RCT acquired a visual confirmation yet?" he said.

"They are still en route." She looked at her watch. "ETA, eleven minutes based on 216's current direction and rate of speed."

Kelan scanned the instruments and monitor with the DRONE visual. He could see the vehicle in which Object 216 rode. He wished he could get a clear picture or a positive ID with facial recognition captured from the DRONE. He needed to confirm this for himself before he reported back to Blalock. Kelan wanted absolute proof that they had, indeed, reacquired Object 216.

The black sedan that carried Josh arrived at his residence. The driver exited and walked around to open the passenger door. As Josh stepped out, he noticed Harry getting out of a cab on the other side of the street. He paid the cabbie then headed across to where Josh waited.

"Hey, man. Nice ride! What did you do to earn something like this?"

"A simple gift from an adoring company," quipped Josh. He turned to the driver with the Blue Eyes and held out his hand. "Thank you for the ride."

"My pleasure, Mr. Arden," he said as he shook Josh's hand. He got into the car and left.

Josh turned back to Harry. "Thought you were going to be on Long Island all day."

Annoyance crossed his face. "So did I. The F train got stuck under the East River right before I could reach East Broadway/Rutgers."

"You're kidding!" said Josh with some sympathy as he remembered his ride this morning. "What happened?"

"You know, I'm not really sure." They walked up the steps of the house they shared. "I got to the platform to catch the 8:05, and everything seemed fine. The train arrived on time, and remarkably, it was not as crowded as it should have been. Ten minutes into the ride—*bam!*—the train jerks to a stop, the lights flutter, and we stop moving. I was stuck for two and a half hours!"

Josh looked at his watch and did the math. "You never made it to *your* interview . . . Oh man . . . I'm sorry." He tried to think of something supportive to say. "Hopefully they understood the situation when you explained it to them."

Harry did not immediately respond. "You did contact them to let them know, right?" said Josh.

"For some unknown reason, there was no cell signal under the river. I still can't get one now, and I'm in the open." He pulled out his cell and looked at the screen. A big X was where the bars should have been.

Josh looked down. "Maybe there is something wrong with your phone." He took the cell from Harry and powered it down by entering a sequence of commands to reboot then handed it back to Harry.

"It's just been a horrible day. I didn't even have the right clothes for today when I went over to Katie's last night. I hope you don't mind, man . . . I borrowed some of yours," he said as he looked down at the shoes.

Josh shook his head dismissively. "Don't even think twice about it. You know whatever I have is yours."

Harry looked thoroughly whipped. "You think I still have a chance at this job?"

Josh pulled the cell from Harry's hand to check the status then handed it back. It had five bars across the top. "Call them. I'm sure they will understand."

Harry shook his head. "How do you do that? You seem to get everything to work for you. Straight As throughout all of school, graduating college at the top of your class. Big fat interview at Jonah International—" Harry stopped in midsentence. His expression change from aggravation to shock and remorse. "Dude! I am sorry, I forgot to ask how that went! I was so wrapped up in my *stellar* day that it completely slipped my mind."

Josh put his arm around Harry's shoulder, and they continued to walk up the stoop to the front door and entered the house. "It was very . . . different. Not even sure that's the right word."

Just down the street, on the other side, there was a tall figure dressed in black. He stood at the corner and looked in their direction. Neither Josh nor Harry was aware of his presence, and that was by design. It was his specialty to make sure that they did not notice him. He did not hide in a conventional way, but merely stood out in the open and faced them head-on. People passed him like he was not there; they never gave him the slightest glance or inclination that he was out of place or seemed different than the normal people that lived on the street or grew up in this neighborhood. His gaze was cold and would have been piercing if anyone were to look. All around him—from the sky, surrounding buildings, even some people on the streets who walked their dogs and removed groceries and children from parked cars—concealed the fact that they, too, watched the two friends as covertly as possible. The "eye in the sky" was in an orbital pattern and too high for a normal person to see, but the man in black glanced up and looked in its exact direction. All the trackers and agents were in place, and it was his job to provide a little extra assurance that they remained that way.

What the man in black did not observe was that he, too, was being watched. At the opposite end of the block, out of view of both Harry and Josh, was Blue Eyes. The sedan in which he drove Josh was nowhere to be seen. His service uniform gone, replaced by clothing that helped him blend into this neighborhood crowd, not that it was needed because the people that passed by did not seem to notice him either. Whatever this *power* that the man in black possessed to blend in and become unnoticed was apparently shared by Blue Eyes. Both men were unmoving with their gazes fixed on their targets. Just as the man in black had noticed the "eye in the sky," Blue Eyes was astutely aware of the people that were out of place in this neighborhood. He knew the agents were there, who they pretended to be: the young mother who retrieved her child from a car seat in a vehicle across the street, the city engineer who worked on a gas main around the corner. Even the little elderly lady who made her way down the street with her little chihuahua in tow. All appeared to be normal in their everyday activities, but were far from it. Each of them was a highly trained RCT agent sent there for one purpose: to track the target that was completely unaware of everything that went on around him. If they had really been flawless in their job, they would have noticed that at this time of day, the streets were usually deserted. The type of activity that happened now was indicative of late afternoon or evening, when children left school or adults came home from work. In turn, if Joshua and Harry had been more in tune with their surroundings, they would have also noticed this was an unusual amount of activity and people. However, the young men were each absorbed in their own actions of the day. Neither seemed eager to share their day's events, but was merely content just to shake them off. They casually walked up the steps into their row house without a second thought.

Blue Eye's orders were very clear; he followed them to the letter. He had never faltered in his charge to guard Joshua. The rules were made very clear upfront to both sides. He was there to make sure that the man in black followed his as well.

Chapter 7

Threats and Offers

Kelan remained in the tactical operations center and viewed the mission video and audio for fifteen minutes. Agents were on the ground and locked on the target. He finally received the confirmation that he had hoped. They had reacquired Object 216.

The *altered* tactical missions report from the DRONE analysis and all RCT agents debriefing sessions had been properly reviewed and approved by him and Margaret then uploaded to the central server. He had visual and audio confirmation that 216 was back in play. Kelan now believed that he had all the supported information needed to provide a briefing to Blalock. He checked his watch then looked at Margaret. She caught his eye and walked over. He spoke in a hushed tone. "I'm going to go to my office to call the chief. He has been itching for an update for the last two and a half hours. I don't want to keep him waiting for any the longer than necessary."

"I will continue to monitor all activity regarding 216. If anything deviates slightly from mission parameters, I will contact you immediately."

"Very good. I don't want any more surprises regarding this mission. We have unlimited resources at our disposal, and I will use them to my full advantage to ensure that we retain our target."

He walked toward the operations center's door with Margaret close on his heels. "Given the new information that you have received, you have full authorization on my behalf to enact any directive to ensure the success of this mission, do you understand?" he said.

"Yes, sir."

With that, he turned and walked out the door. Margaret headed back to the observation monitors for the 216 mission.

When Kelan reached his office, he closed the door and sat down behind his desk. He was still and silent for a moment as he pondered the exact words to use in the conversation. He did not want to provide too much detail, as that would open up the floor for more questions that he might not be able to answer. He wanted to be brief and concise. Kelan needed this to be a quick conversation. Unknown to his conscious mind, he took deep breaths at a rapid pace. He appeared to be hyperventilating. When he was finally aware, Kelan tried to calm himself and slowed the pace. In through the nose, out through the mouth. At first thought, he did not understand why he reacted this way. He gave many briefs to Blalock in the past. This one should not be any different than the others. But it was. This was one of the most important missions that he had ever commanded in his current position. Or at least that was the impression that he was given.

Kelan was very disappointed in his feeling of—what is this that he felt? He did a rapid search to the reservoir of his emotional data banks, never one to be prone to the many different irrational aspects throughout his life. He was always self-assured in everything that he did. Kelan knew what he wanted since, it seemed, before he could actually remember. When he achieved a goal, he was happy. When he did not, he was disappointed or angry with himself for not doing better. What he felt now was neither of those. His breath slowed a bit, and then it came to him. Kelan was afraid.

Fear.

That was how he felt at that moment, right then. But why was he afraid? Was he fearful that if the mission was not successful, he would be fired? Or was it? Was he afraid that something would happen to *him* if the mission were not successful? The memory of Blalock's last statement this morning was still fresh in his mind. "Do not disappoint me again."

The smoke-and-mirrors job that he did on the report would get him through this little hiccup. What if there is another problem during this mission? What if he did not live up to the *standards* that Blalock had? What if this, what if that?

Now, he was just angry. Furious that he would let someone like this get to him. He was good at what he did. That's why Blalock hired him. He had never been intimidated by anyone or let anything get to him, ever. This brief should be a slam dunk. Kelan picked up the phone and dialed. It rang three times before Blalock picked up.

"What?" he said.

He was obviously still disgruntled about the loss of signal regarding Object 216. There may have been more that bothered him, but that was not really Kelan's problem now, was it? "We have reacquired Object 216."

There was no response. Kelan could hear Blalock breathe on the other end. It was like he waited for something more than just that simple statement. Kelan was sure that he wanted more details, but another word would not be said until he got a response. This ridiculous stalemate went on for a full thirty seconds before Blalock finally broke.

"Has the report been filed and uploaded?"

He maintained his professional composure. "Yes, sir. The specific details—"

"Hold on." He pushed another button on his phone console. "Betty, there's a file located on the central server marked 216. Print it out."

"Yes, sir," said the intercom.

Blalock then proceeded to get back on the line with Kelan. "You were saying?"

Kelan attempted to keep his annoyance at being dismissed to a minimum. If Blalock had been perceptive to that, he might have made a statement toward the insubordination and the tone. At this particular point, Kelan did not really care. "I would appreciate it if you let me finish my report before putting me on hold to attend to other business."

Before Blalock could say anything, he continued. "Object 216 is now back on the grid. We have both visual and audio confirmation of identity and coordinates. The specific details along with the confirmation have been included in the report along with the DRONE analysis of why signal capture was lost. All passive tracking and tracing devices have been replaced, and we have tightened surveillance with agents on the ground. Everything that I have stated is inside the technical brief on the server."

"I'm pulling the report now. I will review it to see if it is satisfactory." This last statement was obviously a sign to Kelan to let him know who was in command.

Kelan was sick of this power play. He was assured that when he took the position of DCO for Alastar-McGlocklin, he would have complete authority to run his division as he saw fit. Things had deteriorated over time, but this particular mission changed everything. Blalock was determined to run point and used Kelan as a puppet. If that was not the truth, that is what Kelan felt. His regret for assuming this assignment notwithstanding had grown to the point of wishing he had never accepted the position with this company at all.

He swallowed his indignation and continued to maintain his position of professionalism. "I assure you, Mr. Blalock, that everything has been documented using standard agency protocols. All RCT agents involved have been debriefed on the loss of capture, audio and visual have been edited, time-stamped, and marked as per the mandated procedures. All information has been assembled by our department leads and reviewed and signed off on by myself and the station chief, Margaret Havilland."

There was a knock at Blalock's door. Betty opened it, walked across the room, and placed the 216 file on his desk. She left, closing the door behind her.

Blalock waited for two seconds and then responded, "We shall see . . ."

Fine, thought Kelan. He would say whatever necessary to get off the phone. "If there's nothing else, sir, I would like to get back to the operations center to supervise and monitor the mission procedures."

"There is one more thing . . . Do you have any secondary protocols to prevent something foolish like this from happening again?"

Kelan was a bit confused, but not really surprised. "As I said before, sir, we have integrated additional RCT agents—"

"That's not really what I had in mind."

Kelan attempted to ignore the interruption again. "What did you have in mind?"

"Based on the incompetence that I saw over the last twenty-four hours, I have taken it upon myself to add a secondary measure to ensure the success of this mission."

What was he talking about? This could be an impossibility, but Blalock seemed like he made even less sense. "Does this have anything to do with my division?"

Blalock thumbed through the file. "Indirectly, yes."

Kelan was now openly upset. "This is my division! You told me I could run it my way with absolutely no interference! This is a blatant disregard for my authority!"

"Do not take that tone with me! This is my company! I will run it however I want!"

There was a brief pause while Blalock composed his tone as the consummate commander. "Had you done your job correctly, my intervening would not be necessary."

"I *did* my job. If you take time to read the report, you will see that everything failed due to inadequate technology. Technology that *you* sanctioned."

"Do not blame your poor management of this mission on the technology that I provided."

"My management had nothing to do with this morning's failure," Kelan said, a bit calmer. He now realized that he treaded on very thin ice. The threat of physical danger was greater than he had originally thought. Kelan had witnessed firsthand the power that Blalock wielded; he had always pitied the people on the other side of it. His current attitude put him in that very position. He needed to smooth things over.

This would kill Kelan mentally, but he saw no other options. "My apologies for my tone and outburst. I realize the importance of this mission and do not wish to compromise the corporate agenda or success. I would like to know what your secondary measures are, if you don't mind."

"You would do well to remember your position in this corporation."

After a short pause, for dramatic effect, Blalock continued. "Your actions to date, notwithstanding, have been a little less to be desired in delivering results. The senior partnership has been monitoring this mission very carefully. They are not pleased at the progress."

Kelan was surprised to hear this. "Excuse me for saying this, sir, but I have been following the directive to the letter. The mission specifications outlined surveillance only. We were not to engage the Artifact at any time and were to maintain anonymity should something go wrong, or we were discovered. I'm a little puzzled as to why you and the senior partnership would not think that we are still on track."

"Today's example should be all the proof that you need."

Kelan rode a fine line, and he knew it, but it was very hard for him to remain calm and composed during a string of what he perceived as accusations. In the back of his mind, he started to think that the senior partnership came down hard on Blalock, and he, in turn, looked for another scapegoat. If this mission were a total failure, Blalock was the primary target, not necessarily him. Blalock would not have anywhere else to go and probably needed a plausible excuse as to why he failed. If he could pin the failure of this mission on Kelan, he might think that was a way out. If he made Kelan the fall guy, it would buy him another opportunity or chance. All of that made sense to Kelan, but why would Blalock pursue a worst-case scenario when they had reacquired Object 216 and tighten up measures to ensure that loss of capture would not happen again. Unless, the expectations of the senior partners were higher than Kelan originally thought. What if Object 216's fall from the grid was all that it took for Blalock to lose favor? What if a *second chance* was not an option given to him by the senior partners? Again, the original question popped into Kelan's mind: What would happen to Blalock if the mission failed? Kelan's blood ran cold as a second thought surfaced. If Blalock went down, what would happen to *him*?

Kelan was always pretty fast at thinking on his feet. He has had to use that skill a lot over the last twenty-four hours. At this moment, he needed it more than ever. He had to figure out a way to make himself indispensable to the mission and become the only asset that would make this operation a success. Over the span of two seconds, what seemed like a thousand possible scenarios played out in Kelan's mind. At first, he thought that a simple approach, recommending tighter controls with more agents dedicated exclusively to the 216 mission, would be the initial start, which he had already enacted. While Blalock was a megalomaniac, he was far from stupid. He would not see that as a value-added activity or any type of grand gesture that would secure his position. It would just be something that would have been expected given the situation.

No, he had to be more creative than that. He could not promote the use of additional technology as that was the primary reason stated in the report for the loss.

He did have one more approach, but he wanted to keep that one close to home. Not even Margaret knew about this, even though it was briefly eluded to earlier. He needed a hook, and that might be something that he could use as bait.

"Yes, today's incident was unfortunate, but I would like to point out that in the last seven months, this is the first time that technology has failed us. Granted, it seemed coincidental that we also had issues with the ground units simultaneously. You would have to agree that there's always going to be a certain margin of error when it comes to human intervention," said Kelan.

"I don't have to agree to anything. But . . . I will give you this, that is the very problem in which I am referring."

Kelan started to get a little suspicious on where this was headed. Did Blalock imply that the human aspect of this mission was a problem? If so, that would throw a wrinkle in his ability to become the primary asset. He was not sure if Blalock referred to him personally or the RCT agents in general or maybe both.

"I'm assuming this is where the secondary measures come into play?"

He was surprised by Kelan's intuitive ability and quick deduction. "A very perceptive observation."

Kelan waited for a bit to see if Blalock would offer any more information on his new *direction*. Blalock did not say a word. He waited for Kelan to make the next move. It was clear that Blalock wanted to be in command of this conversation, and he knew it.

Kelan operated under the original motive and tried to end this discussion quickly. "Are these new measures going to fall under my purview?"

There was a muffled laugh at the other end of the phone. "Hardly . . . The senior partners and I have discussed this in great detail within the last hour," he lied. "We have a special asset that will be engaged on certain 216 activities." He paused again to let this information sink a little deeper. "This asset will report directly to me and will not be associated with any activities that you oversee, is that understood?" Another lie.

The senior partners indeed informed Blalock that an asset would be assigned to the 216 mission. The asset would not report to him at all, but rather directly to the senior partners. They cut Blalock out of operation altogether.

"Yes, sir. If there is any assistance that I can offer at all—"

"No assistance will be required from you for this segment. There may be points where the asset will provide direction to you. You will follow those directions completely, is that clear?"

Blalock had been informed that this special asset would have, for the lack of a better phrase, diplomatic privileges that would provide complete autonomy throughout Alastar-McGlocklin. He had absolutely no say or power over this asset.

Kelan was now completely composed in his answers. A voice over the phone that was totally compliant and respectful in every way. It was a good thing this was a phone conversation and not in person. Kelan had a rage building and did not think that he would be able to contain it much longer. "Yes, sir."

He had to end this call now, but he needed one more piece of information. He needed a strategy in order to get it. In his best interest of self-preservation, he immediately decided that the way to remain on the better side of Blalock and the senior partners was to be a puppet . . . a "yes" man. Their unconditional servant in every way. If he could prove his value in ways that catered to their egos, especially Blalock's, there was a stronger-than-average chance that he would be included in the inner circle of executives. For the lack of a better phrase, he would be "in the know."

He could even find out the true nature of this mission. Of course, he was not disillusioned or naive to think that he had the complete picture of why Object 216 was that important. Kelan knew that he was treated just the same as he treated his subordinates. He only gave his people enough information to get the job done. As in every clandestine operation, there were always levels of need-to-know classifications. As far as he knew, he was at the top, since he ran point on this mission. Nevertheless, he knew there was more information *above* the top, and he wanted it. The only way to get it was to give the fat cats whatever they wanted, gain their complete trust.

Even if that meant he had to cross some lines into territories in which he had never been.

He prepared himself to take the position of Alfred, the butler to their Bruce Wayne. As with that character, he too knew there was a darker side, a side that was secret and haunting, a side that, when unleashed, could prove to be deadly when cornered. He had to play this one smart, cover all possible scenarios. While he facilitated their agenda, he would craft his own in complete secrecy. To begin his quest, he needed a name.

"Mr. Blalock, in order to ensure that all available resources are prepared to assist the asset, would it be possible to get one more piece of information?"

Blalock began to get annoyed. "What is it that you think you need to know?"

"The asset's name. If I'm to be of any help at all, I must be able to identify him or her to ensure that I provide the proper clearance packages and credentials needed to navigate all classified areas of Alastar-McGlocklin."

Blalock studied this question for a moment. He could not decide if Kelan fished for something or was genuinely interested in finally providing a useful service. Kelan had made so many mistakes over the last twenty-four hours that Blalock did not know if the boy's career would recover at the corporation. Truth be told, it was Blalock's career that hung in the balance, and he knew it. Not just his career he feared, but more like his life. If the mission went down the wrong way, he would make sure that it was not his fault. He needed someone to hang it on if everything turned south. Maybe he could use this asset to help him hook Kelan.

The question was very simple in nature; he just wanted to know a name. The reasons behind it were suspect though. Blalock knew the asset had no need for things such as clearance. This asset could, and would, go wherever it desired without so much as a second thought regarding boundaries placed upon ordinary material objects or property. Many times in the past, Blalock would find this very *being* seated in his office as he entered. At no time had Betty, building security, or anyone else between the front door and his door see this asset enter, let alone, pass through the corridors. There was never any record of the entry on any surveillance footage or badging at the security stations. This *thing* appeared corporeal, but moved like a ghost.

The very sight of *it* frightened Blalock, though he would never admit it. He was a very proud man. Fear was a weakness that he exploited in others. It was completely beneath him to stoop to that lowly emotional level. Even so, this *thing* made him feel hopelessly impotent and afraid; and now, it was here to do the bidding of the senior partners. *It* was here and used Blalock's property, his people, his contacts—anything that it wanted—to complete its own personal agenda. Blalock was its puppet. A humiliating departure from the top dog position that he was accustomed to since his inception at Alastar-McGlocklin.

Kelan was a fool, and Blalock knew it. If he wanted to get closer to this *person*, then who was he to stand in the way? Kelan could prove very useful as an informant on the asset too. If Blalock was going to be used, then he decided that he also would use anyone and anything to get what he wanted. Who knows, maybe Kelan would surprise him with Intel that even he did not know. Hard to imagine, but there was always that chance.

Blalock looked forward to playing any angle he could to secure his survival and success. He might even get the rewards that were promised to him when this mission was over. "You make a good point, Tindal."

Kelan swallowed a bit of vomit back. "Thank you, sir."

"The asset's name is Pymm."

"First or last?"

"Only."

As soon as they entered their home, both Harry and Josh headed their separate ways. Each moved with a purpose toward the first thing on their list: a change of clothes. As he dropped his backpack on the floor next to the banister, Harry bound upstairs toward his bedroom, while Josh moved to the right, through a makeshift dining room at the back of the house toward his. The house only had one bedroom at the top of the stairs. Josh insisted that Harry take it. The room that Josh had taken for himself was more like a small family room. The structure itself was old; it dated sometime around the 1960s. Much like some of the more compact designs of houses built then, the layout was pretty unconventional. There was no symmetry in any of the rooms. Each one had its own dimensions and doorways, and most did not match. The door to Josh's room was not actually a door at all, but more like an arched entryway. To give himself a bit of privacy, he had a folding partition that slid between the dining room and his space. Along with the main entrance from the dining room, it also had a side entrance that joined a much smaller room, which looked like it could have been for laundry back in its day. The laundry room had its own outside door that went into a very small and cramped excuse for a backyard. Josh used this room for a closet as well as storage. There were a bunch of boxes piled up in front of this exterior door. It was full of old textbooks and other things that he had accumulated over his teenage and college years, which he apparently could not bear to part with when he left Wisconsin.

After he slipped pass the partition, he took off his jacket and tossed it on his bed. He started to loosen his tie from the Windsor knot and then slowed to a stop. With a quizzical look on his face, Josh started to look around his room. Everything looked like it was where it should have been, but he had this strange feeling that something had been changed or moved. It was an odd sensation, although his eyes did not confirm his thoughts. He had a lot of stuff, probably too much, and it was all over the place. To the best of his visual observation, everything was the same as it was that morning. It was a lot like the feeling of being watched, kind of like somebody was looking, but they probably weren't.

Weird.

He shrugged and blew the sensation off then continued to take off his business attire. As he put on jeans and a rugby shirt, Harry's cell phone rang. Josh heard the muffled sounds of Harry as he walked downstairs. They both reached the point at the bottom of the steps where they had parted ways just a few minutes prior.

"Okay, babe. Talk to you later. Bye," said Harry.

Josh breezed by him on his way into the small living room, a smirk on his face. "Was that Kate or your job interview?"

"Har-har. Katie is coming by tonight and wanted to know if she could bring anything."

Josh flopped down on the couch and picked up the TV remote. "Why would she be bringing something over?"

"She's coming over to watch a movie. She didn't know if we needed anything else. We're probably going to order Chinese, are you in?"

Josh flipped through channels. "Sounds great, but I can't. I have to run periodicals and index seventeenth-century literature."

Harry headed toward the kitchen. "What time does your shift start tonight?"

"I'm on at 8:00 pm. Got the graveyard."

"Are you working all by yourself?"

Harry tossed him a can of soda. "Just me and the security guards."

He sat on the couch next to Josh. "Man, I don't know how you can stand that."

"Stand what?"

Harry feigned an overexaggerated shudder. "Working in that big creepy library, especially at night . . . and all by yourself."

"I don't really mind. It gives me a chance to do some thinking and read. Besides, not all of us can have cushy jobs at the Copy Caddy."

"Hey now, don't knock the Caddy. That pays my share of the rent for this magnificent and spacious dwelling."

Josh became animated. "This is just a temporary situation. You and I are both going to be extremely well-off at some point in our life. Just not right now."

He turned the TV off, picked up the home phone, and handed it to Harry. "Time to reschedule your interview."

Harry took the phone. "You're bringing me down, man."

Josh became a little more serious. "Harry, this is a good opportunity for you. I don't want to see you blow this by not letting them know the circumstances of your absence."

By default, Harry got serious too. "I'm almost afraid to call. Why would they want to give me a second chance when I didn't even show up for the first?"

Josh could see what was coming. He and Harry were friends, best friends most of their lives. Outside of Harry's mother, Josh knew him better than anyone else. Where Josh had been self-assured and raised to be an independent thinker, Harry had a self-confidence problem. His father was not around that much and, when he was, not a very positive influence. Harry did not get a lot of reinforcement until after his father was out of the picture for good. His mom worked as a nurse at a hospital in Kenosha. Her shifts varied, so Harry spent a lot of time with Josh or home alone.

It wasn't that Harry did not have the capability to do his best or try until he succeeded, he just did not have the internal motivation to keep going. Seven times out of ten, he would give up after the first roadblock. Each of those times that Josh was there, he would do his best to help Harry move forward. It looked like this was going to be another one of those times.

"Harry . . . have you had the opportunity to talk to them since the initial setup of this interview?"

"Well, no."

"Okay, how do you know that they're not going to understand what happened and give you a second chance?"

Harry became a bit annoyed at Josh for his logical thought process. "Well, I don't, Josh."

"Then what's the problem?"

He knew full well what came next. Josh waited for a second to give Harry a chance to respond. He really did not want Harry to have to say it or admit it, but he knew it was cathartic, and he needed it. Harry's self-esteem had to improve at some point. Josh would not always be around to help him through these situations.

Harry looked down at his hands folded in his lap. He sort of shuffled his feet back and forth on the carpet. He did not look up when the words finally came. "It's embarrassing."

Josh just waited; he knew Harry had more to say.

"I'm embarrassed to have to call them and ask them, no, beg them for another chance."

After all of these years, it saddened Josh to know that Harry still felt this way, that his thinking over what other people thought would prevent him from moving ahead. He and Harry had been closer than brothers ever could be. Deep down, he knew that Harry was not upset at the fact he shared his feelings with him. Josh would never make fun of him for something like that, and Harry knew it. He was there for Josh during some of the darkest periods in his life. Josh would not have survived if it had not been for his friendship. Harry was madder at himself than anything for allowing something this stupid to get in his way. Just as Josh knew, Harry knew what was coming next.

He leaned forward and faced Harry just a little and put his elbows on his knees. "Harry, you have to at least try. Opportunities like this don't really happen to guys like you and me. We both have a chance to make a difference, to be something that our parents never could. We can change our fates."

Harry smiled. That was the line he expected. Whenever Harry started going down this dark path, Josh always gave him the standard spiel about how both could do better than their parents and change the world. Sometimes he used the word *destinies* instead of *fates*, but it always ended with the same result. Harry picked up the phone and started dialing.

Josh playfully punched him in the shoulder and smiled as he moved to his bedroom. He tried to do his best Ward Cleaver impersonation. "You go get 'em, tiger."

Harry smiled. "Shut up! Where you going, man?"

"Pulling an all-nighter. I've got to get some sleep." He waved his hand and rounded the corner.

Josh awoke a few hours later. He was able to shake off most of the effects of the strange questions from that morning. His mind still tried to process why that lady would ask him about his mother. He wanted to talk with Harry to see what he thought, but was sidetracked with Harry's dilemma of the day. If it still bothered him tomorrow when he came home, he would chat then.

Josh quickly showered and dressed then walked to the living room. He could hear that Harry had some company.

"Hey, Josh!" said Kate.

"Hey, Kate. How's it going?"

"Can't complain. I was offered a promotion at work!" With exuberance, she turned to Harry and smiled.

He returned the smile and proceeded to wrap his arm around her. "That's my Katie Bell. The overachiever!" He looked proud of her on the outside, but inwardly he felt like he was not good enough for her. She had a great job as a regional representative for a large East Coast pharmaceutical company; he worked at a local copy shop.

Her territory was two of the five boroughs of New York. She was slated to get a third because the current rep had moved to another position and her numbers seemed to be above average. Neither Harry nor Josh had specifics of her job, but they both knew she had money, more money than they did. She bought a lot of the takeout.

"Hey, congratulations, Kate!" said Josh. He made an effort to be nice to her, for Harry's sake. There was something about Kate that he could not put his finger on. She always seemed sweet and affectionate when it came to Harry, but was not very supportive in his own quest to better himself. It was almost like she wanted him to depend on her. He could see a lot of the same patterns from Harry's childhood. Josh often wondered if the adage was true about surrounding oneself with elements of their early environment, because the individual did not know, or think, they could do better. Josh could see a volatile mixture of that, and Harry's self-esteem issues set him back even further. She was his choice though, and Josh would not dare to do anything to hurt his best friend. He would continue to support his friend until the damage of the relationship hurt Harry. Josh would not stand by for any of that.

Harry motioned to the coffee table. There were takeout boxes scattered about. "We've got some Chinese."

Josh walked over and grabbed a pair of chopsticks then looked over the spread. He grabbed a box of moo goo gai pan and flopped into the stuffed chair on the other side of the couch. He stabbed a big piece of chicken and part of a mushroom and shoved it into his mouth. "How did your phone call go? What did they say?"

Very excited, Harry snapped forward from his slouched position and jostled Kate and the food in the process.

"Easy!" shouted Kate.

He turned back to her, his excitement waned. His demeanor changed in an instant. "I'm sorry, babe."

This bothered Josh. He did not want anyone to steal Harry's thunder, so he pushed. A grin started to form on his face. "They're going to reschedule, aren't they?"

"Yes, they are! You were exactly right. They were completely understandable about the whole thing. They set me up again for next week!"

He stopped and pointed to Josh with both hands, a huge smile spread across his face. "You're the man!"

Josh tried to wave off the acknowledgment. "Harry, this was all you, pal. I just reminded you of what you can do with the proper motivation."

The statement was both an encouragement for Harry and a small jab at Kate. He wanted to glance over at her to see if she got it, but did not dare. She was obviously annoyed that the attention had been shifted from her good news. Josh did not really care. He may not openly acknowledge that he did not approve of their relationship, but he would do whatever he could to make sure that Harry was protected, even from someone he thinks is good for him.

Josh looked at his watch then choked down a few more bites. "Got to head out. Bus will be at the stop in about fifteen minutes."

As he finished up, he started for his room then stopped and turned back. "Harry, I'm very proud of you. You have earned the right for this chance to change your stars."

Harry smiled. "Thank you, Josh. Maybe we can both celebrate our newfound employment in a few weeks."

Kate turned to Josh. "That's right . . . you had an interview today too. How do you think you did?" Josh thought she sounded a little smug, but again, he really did not care what she thought.

"I did just fine. Not so sure about the interviewers."

She sneered. "What does that even mean?"

"It means, Katherine, that my answers were appropriate to the questions they asked. If they did not get all the information they wanted, then they should have asked better questions." He turned and walked to his room without even a look in her direction.

Josh stood up from the bench at the corner when bus 41 reached the sign and the door opened. He let all the other patrons exit and enter before he moved in. He walked up the stairs and slid his pass through the reader in one swift motion then turned to find a spot. Josh took an open place near the center on the driver's side. The bus driver waited until everyone was seated before he accelerated. To pass the time, Josh pulled out a book, opened it to the last page he had previously finished, and began to read. The driver drove down the street and watched Josh intently in the oversized mirror with steel blue eyes.

The central branch of the Brooklyn Public Library was on the corner of Flatbush Avenue and Eastern Parkway on Grand Army Plaza and was immense to say the least. It contained over a million cataloged books, magazines, and multimedia materials. Its local history division, the Brooklyn Collection, held over a million individual items, including photographs, maps, and manuscripts. Outside of the standard Brooklynites, the central branch hosted over one million people a year that passed through the main doors. The bus stopped on the opposite corner of those doors, and Josh was about to walk through them.

Upon entry, he was greeted by a night shift security guard. "Hey, Josh! How are you?"

He placed his backpack on the table next to the metal detector. "Hi, Sam. I'm doing just fine. How's Max feeling today? Better I hope."

Sam put the bag on the belt. It went through on the conveyor as Josh passed through the human component of the apparatus.

Sam grabbed the backpack off the belt on the other side and handed it back to Josh. "He's doing much better. The doctor said the cough was probably hanging on from the flu bug that he caught a couple of weeks ago. Nothing to worry about now though. If he's not getting any better in the next day or so, Janet or I will have to take him back in."

"Sam, that's great news. I hope that the cough is the last of it for him. I know it's been tough on all of you."

"Yeah, Max has had a hard go of it. The worse part for him was missing school." Sam shook his head in amazement. "Never knew a boy that loved to learn as much as him."

Josh could see Sam's love for his son. "Max is a great kid. I know that he will grow up and do amazing things. You just make sure he stays in school and keeps his grades up."

"Oh, you can be sure of that, Josh. That boy will be the pride of this family. I'll make sure that he does something really good with his life. See you later."

"See you on the next round." Josh smiled and walked toward central literature storage.

Josh worked on indexing specific books related to literature that had been recently acquired from other libraries. Most either went under due to lack of financial backing and donations or from property foreclosures or state sales to reduce the cost of expenditures. He was sickened by the thought that some of the people responsible believed that the best way to save money was to cut the arts out of the budget. Music was almost always the first to go. Now, it looked like reading ran a close second. The think-tank-in-command felt that books were becoming an archaic form of learning and technology, much like LPs and eight-track tapes. Anything that people wanted to know could be found on the Internet. That, of course, was stupidity at its highest level. It was very sad that such a low value on something so critical to development and culture, especially for the youth, would be arbitrarily tossed aside because a few people tried to watch some bottom line on some piece of paper, somewhere. One day, Josh hoped to be in a position where he could stop something like this.

He rummaged through the current stack related to the seventeenth century. He picked up one volume (*Cross-Currents in 17th Century English Literature: The World, the Flesh, and the Spirit, Their Actions and Reactions*, Herbert J. C. Grierson).

Josh punched up the index for the listing on the main library database. He was immediately rewarded with the indexing location of 820.9 G848 C. He printed out the index label, affixed it to the binder, and placed the book on the appropriate cart for filing by the next shift.

He stood up and stretched then checked his watch: 3:48 am. He yawned and decided that he needed a little caffeine to get him through the rest of the night. He walked toward the double doors that led out of central storage and turned left down the hall.

As Josh made his way through the massive library, he passed by one of the windows to the outside. He walked by these very windows dozens of times in the past. It went unnoticed, as did most of the elements in this building.

He had been with the library for eighteen months doing various jobs as needed. He sometimes worked odd shifts here and there, like this one, to accommodate schedules for possible interviews just like yesterday. His supervisor asked him weeks ago if he minded indexing the newly acquired books. He could have requested anyone to do that, but he wanted Josh. He trusted him to do the job correctly. Josh was a very dependable employee since the beginning. The supervisor gave him the option of working any shift he chose, as long as he could get the new books finished by the month end. Because of that, Josh could set his own schedule. He liked that.

He chose to work tonight because of the interview at Jonah yesterday morning. He originally picked it because it did not interfere or overlap with his responsibilities. Josh was glad he did now base on how the conversations went; he needed the distraction. He was still a little disturbed by the question about his mother and did not understand why. He never let anything like this bother him before, well, not since her death. Letting something or someone get to him took his leverage away; it caused him to let his guard down. That was the driving principle for him not caring what anyone else thought. It's not that it showed weakness like most people would think; it was that his mother had always told him he could do anything if he put his mind to it. "Don't let anyone tell you that you can't succeed," she always said. "Never let your fate pick you, *you* choose your own destiny." She was the wisest person he had known. He had tried to uphold that wish ever since she had passed. This was the one thing that he could keep alive, a piece of his mom that he could hold on to besides the memories.

Josh was deep in this thought as he walked to the vending machines. As he passed the window, he did not look out. From across the street, halfway down the block, the man with the Blue Eyes watched at the very instant Josh had gone by. He did not wait there very long. It was as if he anticipated Josh's movements and timed the observation perfectly.

It was his responsibility to ensure the safety of his charge. Joshua must remain free of any obstacles while he evaluated the initial contact with Jonah. Blue Eyes never moved from the fixed point on the window. He did not look around to see if anyone else watched or waited. He knew that he was the only one there at the moment. When he was satisfied that Joshua was safe, he vanished almost as quickly as he appeared and left no trace that he was ever there.

Josh completed two consecutive night shifts to get most of the seventeenth-century literature catalogued.

His weekend consisted of a Tuesday-Wednesday schedule that week. He planned to travel up with some friends to Montreal to see the Maple Leafs take on the Washington Capitals. As he walked out the door, his cell phone rang. He looked down and did not recognize the number. Normally, he would let an unknown call go through to voice mail, but on a whim, he decided to take this one.

"Hello."

A very pleasant female voice was on the other end. "Hi. Is this Joshua?"

"Yes, it is. How can I help you?"

"Joshua, my name is Gretchen Chambers. I'm a Talent Management Liaison for Jonah International. I'm very pleased to inform you that we wish to offer you a position within our corporation."

He listened to the rest of her speech with a smile that got a little bigger with each sentence. She ended the conversation with "And you should expect the offer package, to include the letter, by certified mail within twenty-four hours. Do you have any questions?"

"No, ma'am. I believe that you have told me everything I need to know."

"Great. My contact information should be included in the offer package. If you have any questions, please don't hesitate to reach out. We look forward to hearing back from you, Joshua. Have a great day!"

"You too, Ms. Chambers." He hung up.

Wow, his day began to look up, two offers within twenty-four hours. His friends pulled up to the front of his place and honked the horn. He waved and put his phone in his pocket. He grabbed his backpack, skipped down the steps to the car, and piled in the back. As the car took off around the corner, it passed a man who walked the opposite way. The man turned after the car was almost out of sight and watched it disappear. He smiled as he turned back around and continued down the street. He said hello as he passed a woman on the sidewalk. She returned the acknowledgment and thought to herself that he had the prettiest blue eyes that she had ever seen. She turned back around to get another look, but he was gone.

PART TWO

THE DISCOVERY

Chapter 8

Disaster and Details

Josh headed through the corridor on his way back to his desk. He just came from the cafeteria on the fourth floor, like he did almost every morning. He got in early today because Tina, the best lunch lady in the world, reminded him the Danishes were baked fresh that morning, and he did not want to miss them. He likened it to the sign at Krispy Kreme donuts: "Hot . . . Now . . . Off the line." The cafeteria always baked their fresh breakfast goods on Mondays and Wednesdays. Sometimes he did not get in early, but Tina would always save him one of her biggest and best when he came down to get his coffee. She was a great lady. He remembered how they had met.

She worked at the coffee shop three blocks down from Jonah. Josh stopped in almost every morning so he could to pick up coffee; he was Tina's regular. They worked their ritualistic routine into a blossoming friendship over a few months. One day after a couple of weeks, he noticed that she was no longer there. The staff behind the counter moved with a quickness to meet the demanding needs of patrons dying to get their daily caffeine fix; however, he never seemed to spot Tina. He always searched as he stood in the vast lines and waited for his morning brew. It turned out that the shop had cut her hours back and she no longer worked the weekday morning shift. They put her on for a few hours over the weekend, but nothing steady enough to make ends meet. Tina had a hard time with weekend work because of her family. She explained to Josh during one of their many exchanges that one of her children had special needs. Cystic fibrosis was a serious problem in her family. Two out of every five people on her mother's side developed some level of the affliction. In an unfortunate convergence of circumstances, one of her teenage daughters also had Down's syndrome. This caused a myriad of issues for Tina and her family. Since she was dropped down to part-time, she was forced to find other work that supplemented the family's income.

She was always nothing but nice to Josh. He could not describe the bond he had with her. On some level, it was a connection that he needed to keep and continue. He felt an overwhelming need, so he tried to help. He pulled some strings with the catering service at Jonah International and got her a full-time job with perks. The medical benefits at Jonah were second to none. Not only was Tina and her immediate family 100 percent covered with no co-pay, there was no clause, hidden or otherwise, that excluded them because of preexisting conditions. Tina could tap into the unlimited pool of health professionals and resources to assist her family. All medical services were completely paid. She gave him the freshest pastries ever since.

He had his coffee in one hand and, with his other, put the pastry in his mouth to hold it and then checked his watch. There was thirty minutes to review the financial report on the expenditures for the Hong Kong deal. Josh was the division head on all international activities related to foreign aid. It was his job to manage all the economic information related to the subject area in question. When this position opened up Josh jumped at the chance to take it. He liked the idea of being a part of a service that provided economic aid in the form of charity distributions and supplies. He felt like he made a difference, helped those who could not help themselves.

He loved his job.

His mom would have been proud.

Josh started in the resource pool doing data mining activities such as trend analysis for market options and developing executive briefs with supported budget estimates. The job was good and what he had expected for an entry-level position. His break came when an analyst for international affairs was out sick with the flu on a day that a big-budget finance meeting was set to take place. There were still some closing estimates that needed to be calculated and incorporated into the final brief. Joshua was asked by Jacob Wessler's staff if he could assemble the information quickly. For someone with Josh's educational background, it was completed with ease. Wessler was so impressed with his abilities that he pulled him into the International Affairs Financial Division and ultimately made him a co-lead. Between him and his partner, they were responsible for multiple areas aligned with financial analytics. Eventually, Josh outperformed his partner and was asked to lead the whole division. The timing was good for his counterpart as he was slated to move into another position more suited to his interest. Josh was the division head for the last eighteen months.

As he rounded the corner, headed for his office, one of his staff ran up and fell into step beside him. "Mr. Arden, do you have a second?"

He swallowed a mouthful of Danish. "Sure, Sally. What's up?"

She pulled out a file folder that contained some spreadsheets. "We have the preliminary analysis for the tsunami relief effort. We need your authorization on the initial assessment before we can begin the baseline estimates."

He handed her his cup while he took the spreadsheets. He scanned the file quickly as he walked; he never once looked up to see where he was going. Just as he turned down the hall to his office, he slowed a bit. "Everything looks fine except for the leadership compensation. Why are we estimating a percentage of the allocated budget directed toward that category?"

She stopped and set his coffee down on the nearest desk, pulled out another file, and began reading. "According to the original proposal, there is a clause that states the relief effort will be spearheaded by the Japanese Relief Council. Pursuant to their State laws, all disaster relief efforts are presided over by the council. Part of the contractual obligations in this area is compensation up to and including 25 percent of the total relief funds."

"What!? Twenty-five percent!" Josh just stared at her with disbelief. "So what you're saying is that the Japanese government is expecting compensation for their 'leadership' efforts"—Josh did the hand quotes with his free hand—"from a company that is giving them money and resources to clean up a disaster on their homeland *and* to support the victims of this massive tsunami that has wiped out hundreds of miles of their shoreline, correct?"

Sally took the spreadsheet back, put it in the folder, closed it and crossed her arms, then looked at him with a knowing smile at the corner of her mouth. "Yes, sir, that's exactly what I'm saying."

Josh just shook his head. "You've got to be kidding me! We are trying to help these people, and the government is trying to make a buck?" He looked down at his watch.

"I have a brief for the Hong Kong deal in twenty minutes, so I don't have time to deal with this now. Put a hold on the Japanese tsunami baseline." As it happened, he was standing next to his administrative assistant, Alice, who listened intently to the conversation between him and Sally. He turned to address her.

"Alice, please set up a meeting with Contracts, Legal, and the Foreign Relief Chairman for this afternoon. Tell them to be prepared to discuss the Japanese tsunami contract."

"Yes, sir," said Alice as she handed him back his coffee.

He turned and walked into his office. He spun around with a hand on the door preparing to close it. He addressed both Sally and Alice and said, "Please send the brief specific to the contract to my personal server. I will also need the disaster assessment and framework for the original estimations Jonah uses for disasters such as this." Then he looked directly at Alice. "Clear my schedule for the rest of the day."

As he shut the door, both Sally and Alice heard him mutter, "They have got to be insane . . ."

They both smiled at each other. Sally turned to walk back to her workspace. "I love working for him."

"So do I," said Alice. She picked up the phone and started putting the meeting together.

Everyone involved cleared their schedules for Josh's meeting. The right representatives were present as they started to pore over the specifics of the assessment. The slide presentation outlined the number of those impacted by the tsunami and depicted the devastation inflicted. Josh spoke passionately about the aid that was needed to give the Japanese people a chance of starting over.

His demeanor changed when he talked about the leadership compensation clause. He called it an unjustifiable expenditure that had absolutely no bearing on the relief campaign, outside of lining the Japanese Relief Council's pockets. After making his case, he addressed each of the affected departments in an attempt to find a way around this clause.

A representative from Contracts outlined the work breakdown structure for each one of the expenditures so everyone would understand how payment of relief aid was dispersed. Someone from Public Relations explained the significance within the Japanese culture and its role in governmental politics. This led to a somewhat reasonable explanation of why a leadership compensation clause would have been added. After everyone had a chance to digest the information, Josh turned to the legal department to understand their point of view.

He leaned forward a bit. "Caroline, are we legally obligated to pay this additional expense at this moment in time?"

As she shuffled through her papers, she took a few moments to ensure that she answered correctly. "At this moment in time, no. The baseline assessment must be approved and signed off by all departments prior to a formal contract of support."

Josh turned to the Foreign Relief Chairman. "Jonathan, what is your position on this?"

Jonathan Sinclair was the current Foreign Relief Chairman for Jonah International Global. He oversaw all relief efforts on a worldwide scale. Josh's current position technically was three levels below Sinclair's. Although most decisions on international relief are determined by

Josh, Sinclair would have the final word. Josh needed his buy-in.

"What exactly are you proposing for the statement of work surrounding this tsunami relief effort?" asked Jonathan.

Josh straightened up a little and faced him head-on. "My intent is to strip this leadership compensation clause completely out. The purpose of this meeting is to find out if there are legal precedents that permit or prevent us from doing this."

Jonathan looked thoughtful for a few seconds. He formulated a number of questions in order to see if something like this would be doable. He knew from past dealings that he would not have been called to such a meeting if Josh did not already have the bases covered. He was there to poke holes in the idea.

"If we pulled the leadership compensation, what would happen to the additional funds?"

"We would, of course, roll that into the overall total relief expenditure distributed from Jonah." Josh already had a separate presentation ready that outline where the additional funding would be best utilized. He picked up the controller and switch to it on the main screen. Jonathan sort of smiled. Joshua seemed to have done his homework. Jonathan wanted to find out how much, so he continued.

"Will there be any additional overhead as a result of this?"

"None at all. In fact, the supplies to help rebuild the smaller villages would be procured in country." Josh punched in commands on his flat screen computer within the conference table. "With the additional allocated money, a majority of those supplies will be discounted at a higher rate under the Japanese Disaster Relief Team Law of 1987."

Jonathan looked down at the figures and the governance law within his own personal screen.

Josh leaned back. "In essence, we would be buying in bulk. Not only would we be providing them professional services and aid in this relief effort, we would also be stimulating Japan's economy." He looked over at the PR guys. "That should go a long way in our favor toward the relations between United States and Japan, wouldn't you think?"

Sally walked into the conference room with a stack of blue clear-cover folders.

"The new outline for the proposal has been drafted in the statement of work that Sally is handing out now," said Josh.

As everyone received their copy, they started thumbing through various sections of interest. Jonathan looked through the parts that pertained to cost and legality. For a document that was thrown together in less than three hours, Jonathan was very impressed with Joshua's team.

Everyone took a few minutes to look through the document and their own files. A few people compared notes and chatted about certain sections. After Jonathan was finished studying the prospectus, he spoke. "Legal, where do we stand on the obligations under current Japanese law?"

Caroline was the one to respond. "After we sent the letter of intent to support, we have only received the governance laws from the State of Japan. Mr. Arden's team is currently in the process of assembling the baseline estimates. We are not under any obligation to the Japanese government in accordance with their laws until we complete the baseline package, formalize the contract, and receive the appropriate signatures from representatives on both sides." She paused for a moment and looked at both Josh and Jonathan. "As of right now, there is no legally binding contract between Jonah International and the Japanese government."

Jonathan turned to Contracts. "How long would it take to create a standardized contract that omits this leadership compensation clause?"

Contracts spoke at once. "Once a decision on the path forward has been made, we can have a draft contract completed within forty-eight hours."

"There is a strong possibility that this will not be well received by the Japanese Relief Council. What happens if they do not like this change?" said Jonathan.

"Well . . . that answer is really simple. We withdraw our intent to fund and support the relief effort," said Josh.

Everyone immediately got quiet and looked at him. Some eyes were wide at that statement; a couple of people had their mouths hang open. Josh looked around the room and knew that he just made a bold decree. He stared sheepishly at the table for two seconds and pondered whether or not he had made the right move. In some of his most heated negotiations in this position, he had always maintained his self-confidence and assurance. Never once had he faltered on decisions made. There was no second-guessing. All of his ideas came to fruition when discussed and worked through with his team. His ideas would lead to a plan. That plan would become actionable. Those actions would bring about change. And inevitably, that change would impact lives. That was why he thrived at his job. He had an insatiable need to make a difference in people's lives. That was what this deal was, a difference to people who desperately needed their lives changed. This time was no different than any of the others. There was a catchphrase in a TV commercial that he saw as a child that always stuck with him. "Never let them see you sweat." That phrase flashed into his mind after he looked down. He looked back up with his game face.

Jonathan raised an eyebrow and nodded. "So what you're saying is that the Japanese Relief Council should accept our terms to omit the leadership compensation clause or we'll pull out of the entire relief effort altogether, correct?"

Josh nodded. "Pretty much, yes."

"I'm not much on the legalese of this, but most people would consider this blackmail."

"I prefer the term *leverage*. It sounds more politically correct."

Caroline from Legal jumped in with both feet. "Mr. Arden, we have signed a letter of intent to support. Regardless of the outcome concerning this clause, we have all but given a written confirmation that we will aid this relief effort. The political ramifications for backing out of a deal of this magnitude, whether verbal or written, would have massive consequences on Jonah. This would be a public relations nightmare of which we may not recover." The two PR guys in the room nodded in unison.

"Not if the contract were structured under the laws of International Trade Agreements. Specifically, under the U.S.-Japan Regulatory Import and Trade Policy Initiative." Josh typed in a command on his flat screen again. After a few seconds, the pertinent part of the policy appeared on each of the personal monitors and the main screen for those that were not seated. As Josh spoke, he zeroed in at each level of the policy until he got to the paragraph and section that were binding.

"Paragraph 12, section D, subsection 8C specifically states, and I quote, 'Goods or services rendered between countries must meet both Japanese and American trade agreement laws as stated in Paragraph 3, section H, subsection 4N.'" He split the screen to show laws of the agreement side by side. "If discrepancies or disputes ensue and agreements cannot be reached by parties involved, then any and all contractual obligations for trade goods and/or services can be mediated by third-party arbitration. If arbitration fails to yield acceptable terms that will benefit all parties, then the original agreement is nullified and/or voided from further obligation, and the contract is dissolved."

Caroline looked intently at the screen for a few seconds then over to Contracts. He looked back and nodded. She then looked at Jonathan, who still examined the screen in front of him. He looked up at Josh then at Caroline.

"Will this work?"

"Yes, I believe it will," she said.

"Contracts?" asked Jonathan.

"Yes, we can structure the contract to fall under trade agreements if there are no exclusions specific to humanitarian services."

Josh moved forward and spoke. "There is nothing specific to the conditions of goods and services provided under these laws. It doesn't matter whether it is commercial goods under GATT or related to humanitarian services. The law should apply."

Everyone either thought about or looked at Josh with admiration. He found a way to help more people. He did it without compromising his own values or Jonah's in the process. "What do you think, Jonathan? Do we have your authorization to move forward with the restructure?"

Jonathan looked thoughtful for a moment and asked one more question. "If we move ahead with this, we will have to prepare the Japanese Foreign Relief Chairman. This can't hit him without some forewarning. Jonah and the Japanese government have a good relationship, and I don't want this deal to sour it. Do you have an approach?"

Josh motioned for Alice, who walked over and handed Jonathan a similarly bounded brief. This one had a red clear-cover folder. The title of the document was in large print and read, FOREIGN COUNCIL BRIEF ON TRADE AGREEMENT.

"This brief outlines the new direction of the contract to support the tsunami relief effort under the international laws of trade agreements. All relevant articles as it applies to the humanitarian support are highlighted, along with the platform for why this is a good idea for both Japanese and American relations. It also has all the same cost incorporated that was reviewed today. This is your copy. Another copy is ready for the Japanese Foreign Relief Chairman in his own language."

Josh continued to speak directly to Jonathan. "We are going to extend an invitation to Japan's FRC to come to the United States and discuss this change in person with you. Alice will coordinate the proposed dates with your admin. The objective is to have a signed contract before departing. Once we have the contract in play, we can begin support coordination within forty-eight hours."

Jonathan stacked his two copies of today's reports together and looked up. "You have my authorization to continue with the contract restructure. Well done, Joshua."

Some people in the meeting started to applaud. Josh felt a little embarrassed and rather silly. He just did his job. He saw an injustice perpetrated by paying this bogus fee when there was so much better that it could serve. He truly did not believe that he had done anything differently than anyone else would have in his position.

As people filed out of the conference room, some complimented him and patted him on the back. He was gracious and returned his thanks, but truth be told, he really did not like the attention. He liked being the man behind the scene that prepares the real stars for the camera. He did not feel that he could ever take a leading role where he was a key player in closing the deal. That was what people like Jonathan Sinclair did. He was the real master at crafting relationships and establishing long-term partnerships with other countries. Josh was just a supporting character in a much larger motion picture.

Alice walked back into the conference room. "You still have time to make your 3:30 pm with the American Red Cross."

He looked at her with a raised eyebrow. "I thought I told you to clear my schedule for the rest of the day?"

"You did." She handed him his PDA and grinned. "Since when does it take you all day to tie something like this up?"

He took his PDA, and in mock shock, he looked at her with wide eyes. "Ms. Williams, your assumptions of my abilities are greatly exaggerated."

She smiled. He smiled back. "Thank you, Alice. For everything."

"As you have said many times before, it was a team effort." She turned and moved toward the doors.

Josh had a really good relationship with his team. He relied on them heavily in all areas. He was certain that he would not have been successful in any of his tasks if it were not for the hard work and dedication of his staff.

Jonathan and a mystery guest walked closer to Josh as Alice moved away. He extended his hand. "Josh, very nice job on the presentation."

Josh felt a little warm in the face at the compliment. He did not visibly show his discomfort, but it was present. He was not sure at what point in his life that he started to really not like being in the spotlight or recognized for his achievements. He remembered something that his mother had told him growing up. "Flattery is all right, so long as you don't inhale." She got that from some famous author somewhere, off a napkin, or from a fortune cookie for all he knew. It did not matter, not to him. If it came from his mother, then it must have been something important. He never really understood what the phrase meant until people started complimenting him.

She always had little sayings like that, and they stuck with him. For a brief moment, just a flicker of a second, he remembered her smile when she first said this particular tidbit, the special one for when she was proud of him. She had many smiles for different situations and used them as the circumstances necessitated. He could not ever really remember a time when she did not smile. He loved them all. When she smiled, Josh knew she was happy; at least, that is what he thought right up to the end. When she got sick, she still tried, but he could see the light fading . . . He snapped out of it.

He shook his hand. "Thank you, Jonathan. The team worked very hard over the last few hours to prepare the business case for this proposal. I'm very proud of them."

"I can see that, but that's not what I meant."

Josh looked puzzled. Jonathan went on to explain. "Josh, your performance today has been one of many lately that calls out, for the lack of a better word, the *injustice* that you see in the fine details of these contracts and requests. You seem to have a gift, a remarkable gift, for spotting the negative in these situations and turning them into a positive.

"You command a presence with people that compel them to listen, to value what you have to say, take stock, and reevaluate their initial thoughts and understanding."

He guided Josh to the back of the room. "Of course, I'm not downplaying the contributions of your team, please don't infer that from my statement. I'm simply saying, Josh, this is a rare blessing in the corporate world. The power of persuasion is what most successful businessmen strive to gain. It's the main element that gives them the edge to control and manage outcomes to some of the most lucrative contracts and deals. What makes you different is that you never use this gift for a selfish advantage."

Josh listened in rapt silence as one of the most respected men at Jonah International gave him a huge compliment for a skill that he was completely unaware even existed. His mind thought back to the last few contracts and projects that he was involved with, to dissect the words that Jonathan had just said. He could not readily find anything out of the ordinary that would put him in the path of this compliment. Was he that obtuse in his thinking that even he could not justify the admiration? He never understood things like that. Everything that he had ever accomplished at Jonah was, in his opinion, part of the expectations of his job. It was his role to ensure that all expenditures and mission relief packages delivered the appropriate aid in whatever capacity that was needed. All monies and resources went directly to the relief effort. No exceptions. There would be no supplemental expenses to cover any costs that directly impacted the approved amount. Additional cost was always a separate WBS. This had been and will always be the policy, as long as he ran the international division that supported all Jonah's charitable operations.

Josh went through all the procedures, policies, and protocols when his train of thought collided with another train at super-high velocity. That was not what Jonathan meant at all. It was not about the policies or the relief effort, or even about the amount of money that he managed. He looked at Jonathan before he could build on his new line of thought.

"You genuinely care. You have a big heart and use that as part of the decisions that you make. Josh, part of being a leader is being able to understand those elements, knowing the objective, and affecting the desired outcome. The part that makes someone a great leader is the pure intention behind their influence toward that objective." He lightly pointed his finger to the center of Josh's chest. "With a good heart and a sharp mind, you have an amazing ability to balance and command both in harmony. That's the type of leadership that sets Jonah International apart from everyone else."

Josh did not know what to say. He never knew that was how people had felt about his work performance. Jonathan turned to catch the eye of the mystery guest who then walked over to join them.

"Joshua Arden . . . I would like to introduce you to Lucas Aldridge."

The man was immense. Josh was a fairly average-sized guy, around 5'10", 175 pounds. This man looked to be every bit of 6'5" with shoulders about the size of a single doorway. Josh tried not to look surprised, but his eyes were a little wide. He had seen him in the meeting, but never really took a good look. Josh vaguely remembered him as he stood in the background. That accounted for why he did not notice the enormity of this man's stature. Although Josh did not remember having met the man, there was something familiar about him. He had a feeling that this man was part of some snapshots from his past, of a silhouette that he had encountered over his lifetime.

Josh extended his hand. "Mr. Aldridge, it's a pleasure to meet you."

Lucas took it and gave him a strong, firm handshake. To Josh's surprise, it did not break his hand like he thought it would. This man had very good control with the amount of pressure and strength.

Lucas smiled. "Please believe me, Joshua, the pleasure is all mine. I would like to echo Jonathan's sentiments and say that your presentation was very impressive."

Josh looked sheepishly toward the floor. "Thank you, Mr. Aldridge. That's very nice of you to say, but again, I have to give credit to my entire team. They are the backbone of all my department's successful packages."

Lucas and Jonathan shared a slight glance. Jonathan smiled and placed a hand on Lucas's shoulder. "Josh, Lucas here has been monitoring your progress over the last few months. His division has a great interest in your abilities for aptitude around leadership. There may be an opportunity for you to advance within Jonah."

Lucas continued to smile as the direction of the conversation surprised Josh. For the first time, his inward embarrassment of the compliments took on a new meaning. What could everyone have possibly noticed that he did not? This question was the one that had him puzzled the most. He took pride in knowing all the signs when planning or facilitating a deal or a project contract for relief aid. He allowed a lot of latitude within his team when they tried to resolve or mitigate issues against deadlines. He wanted them to be able to recognize the specifics around all the aspects, to ensure that they could cope with different situations should they arise when he was not around. To his surprise again, he had an epiphany at the thought that this could be what Mr. Aldridge spoke about, his particular style of management.

"Mr. Aldridge, I—"

"Please, Joshua, call me Lucas. Aldridge is much too formal for me, and I'm not really suited to *mister* either."

Josh acquiesced to the suggestion. "Lucas, I don't know what to say. I'm very grateful to be considered for any advancement within Jonah International, but . . ." he trailed off.

Lucas looked at Joshua sympathetically. "You are concerned over your team and what you have built within them?"

"To a point, yes. But my hesitation is in the confidence that everyone seems to have an ability that I don't seem to recognize." He said that with open embarrassment. The cool assurance that always came with his game face was washed away. The doubt in his demeanor was very apparent, and he was positive that it showed to both Jonathan and Lucas.

"Joshua, some of the greatest leaders throughout history have never known their worth or their potential until thrust into situations where needed.

"Take Winston Churchill as an example. He was a very unhappy child with seemingly insurmountable odds against him. He came from an aristocratic background, of noble blood, yet he performed horribly in most everything that he did. His academic records were atrocious, his father's attempts to get him the best education were thwarted by Winston himself due to the rebellious nature of who he was inside. His relationship with his father was, at best, strained and tortured as Winston was constantly in opposition with everything that his father approved. When his father died at the early age of forty-five, it was only then when Churchill himself finally understood that it was his own limitations holding him back from greatness. He felt that he too would die young and only had a short time left to leave his mark on the world. And what a mark that would be. You have none of this riding against you. You just have a confidence problem."

Josh managed to get his game face back while Lucas educated him, but silently freaked out when being compared to Winston Churchill. Lucas talked as if he knew Churchill himself.

Sensing that Josh's comfort level faded even further, Lucas continued to encourage his latest charge. "Joshua, we have not yet discussed what the new role is or how you will be able to fulfill it. I'm only asking that you consider throwing your hat in the candidacy for the position. There are very few that have been identified as having the unique qualifications required to properly perform the duties. We believe that you have the potential to succeed and excel. You just need to have a little faith."

"I'm sorry, Mr. Aldridge—Lucas, but I need to ask . . . What is your role in this?"

"My apologies, Joshua, I introduced you, but didn't tell you what he does here at Jonah," said Jonathan.

Lucas smiled. "I am the corporate liaison between the executives at Jonah International and the Board of Directors, specifically the Chairman. In fact, it was the Board that asked me to review your performance history. You have been receiving a lot of praise at the C-level that has garnered this attention, and their reports have not gone unnoticed.

"When Jonathan"—Lucas gestured—"received an invitation to this meeting, he reached out to me so I could get a firsthand glance for myself, to see if everything that I have heard is true. Again, I would like to point out that the business case for change was well done and ably thought-out."

Josh stood there and listened. He was very quiet and did not move as he received all this information. He tried to come to terms internally with the compliments and the praise for his activities. He had never singled out his actions as an individual contributor to the accomplishments of his division. That was not how he was wired or raised. He started to wonder why all that success was being piled upon him when it was actually a team effort as he stated before. If he received recognition for the success of his division, the entire team should be rewarded and recognized too. It seemed that was not the case. He was targeted for something bigger that he still did not fully understand.

"I tell you what, Josh, why don't you let Lucas set up a meeting to discuss this new role a little further in detail. Absolutely nothing is written in stone. You have not been selected for any type of position, only considered as a very promising candidate."

Lucas chimed in. "That is correct. The choice has been and will always be yours to make. That being said, you are still the most viable candidate who we have seen thus far."

Josh rolled his eyes. "No pressure there."

Jonathan openly laughed and lightly slapped him on the shoulder. "Josh . . . This is not the Spanish Inquisition or the Crusades. It's only a meeting with a few key people to talk about a new job. Nothing more, nothing less."

For a brief moment, Josh considered the last statement fervently. It was just a simple meeting request. They probably only wanted to talk to him about his ideas and his methods for running the international affairs division. Meetings like that happened at corporate levels across the globe all the time. It was part of the moving-up-the-corporate-ladder process. He worked extremely hard once he had accepted employment with Jonah two and a half years ago. Just as he was considered for this new role, he worked his way up from financial analyst to division head for international relief. He thought hard for a second and tried to remember if he had been that reluctant when he switched from those positions.

In the brief instance all of that ran through his head, he squared off against Lucas and held out his hand. "Lucas, it would be a pleasure to discuss the opportunity of this new role with you and your division. My apologies for being so resistant."

Jonathan and Lucas smiled and shared a glance as Lucas took Joshua's hand. "Excellent! I'm glad to hear that you are considering this. Your reluctance is completely understandable. I have not given you a lot of specifics about what this position entails. You were merely probing for additional information. It is a sign of your leadership measure, to gain more information prior to making a decision. No one could fault you for your approach. Absolutely no apologies are necessary."

Joshua gathered his materials from the meeting. He headed toward the conference room doors as Jonathan and Lucas flanked him. "I will have my administrative assistant contact Alice with the details for a meeting. I am sure that between both, your schedule should not be altered or impacted in the slightest."

Josh hesitated for a second. "My schedule can be as flexible as needed to accommodate."

"Nonsense. We are requesting you to come see us. We can work around you."

They stopped just outside of the conference room doors for one final huddle. "Jonathan, again thank you for all of your support during this Japanese tsunami contractual glitch. I am very grateful that you saw the errors that I did and understand the need for a restructure. I will follow up with Sally as soon as I return to my office, but I would expect the new contract changes to be completed no later than 5:00 pm today. I will ensure that a soft copy is uploaded to your personal directory for review."

He turned and extended his hand one final time. "Lucas. I appreciate your attendance today. Any exposure that we can receive at the highest executive levels in support of our relief operations is always greatly appreciated. Again, my apologies, whether accepted or not, still exist for being so resistant to your offer for a meeting. I'm looking forward to opening a dialogue for the possibilities of a better future for all."

Both Jonathan and Lucas thought simultaneously that they could not have put that last statement better themselves.

"It was a pleasure to meet you, Joshua," said Lucas. With that, Jonathan and Lucas turned and headed down the east corridor while Joshua walked toward the north. As soon as he was out of sight, Jonathan and Lucas began to talk under their breath.

"Josh's performance today was exceptional. The way that his business case for change was laid out with the facts that called out the injustice of the leadership compensation clause . . . incredible," said Jonathan.

"Indeed. Not too many of the other candidates could have caught that small detail like Joshua did."

"From what I understand, none of the other candidates ever did."

"The details of the test differ for each one, but true enough . . . Joshua's abilities are exceptional."

"The passion that he expressed for what he truly believes in. He does have a good heart, and he knows how to use it when needed."

"That is what we are counting on, my friend," said Lucas.

"Is Ulysses and his team ready for an additional agent?"

"All preparations have been completed and are ready. We do not expect Joshua for a few weeks though."

"Why is that?"

"He has some personal business that he must work through."

"I didn't realize that he was going through anything of a personal nature."

Lucas glanced at him. "He is not . . . yet."

"Oh," said Jonathan softly. "I hope that he will overcome the challenge."

"If we have learned anything about this young man, it's that he will emerge stronger than before. I have every confidence in that."

They continued to walk until they reached a hallway that split into different directions; they slowed and faced each other. Lucas held out his hand. "Jonathan, my friend . . . Thank you for all of your help in getting events set in motion."

"It is my pleasure to be associated, let alone asked to be involved in such an important selection process."

"The next stages of discussions are pivotal in his choices. There will be much for young Joshua to contemplate as he decides on his course." Lucas bid Jonathan farewell and walked toward the bank of elevators.

Chapter 9

Explosions and Code

The little Ford Festiva roared to life after the third try, as much as it could roar for being a four cylinder. It sputtered and knocked a bit as it usually did, vibrated with a shutter that finally diminished, and then relented to the fact that it was going to be driven whether it was ready or not. For being over ten years old and having close to 163,000 miles on it, it still ran pretty well. By definition, with its advanced age and mileage, the term *pretty well* was very relative. It got her to and from work, and that was the important part. Her uncle always took care of the maintenance for her when needed. She tried to follow the standard schedule for keeping up the car with changing the oil every three thousand miles or so and getting what little wear she had left on her tires, balanced and rotated as necessary. Her uncle had told her the last time around that the left front tire was getting bald and needed to be replaced. He was in the process of trying to find a suitable replacement from a local junkyard that could get her through the winter months, until she could actually afford a newer tire. Again, by definition, newer meant one with a little more tread and less mileage than the one it was to replace.

When she had first purchased the car, there was a lingering debate between family and friends on the exact color. The final verdict was that it was an off-color, rust-type brown. Some thought that back in its day, it used to be a pretty candy-apple red. That would be hard to tell now by looking at it, as the paint was so oxidized. She had to have a car. That was a requirement to keep the job that she currently held. On the application form, it had asked her if she had "reliable transportation." She checked that box and filled out the rest of the information. She decided after she turned in the form, she needed to find an affordable version of "reliable." The car was not in mint condition obviously, and she had very little money to spare, so to coin a phrase "beggars cannot be choosers," she took what she could afford.

For a while, she worked the third shift at Moncrief Furniture Alliance, doing general janitorial services and cleaning up after second shift activities. She usually worked the section that dealt with fabrics and patterns for sofas, love seats, and dining room chairs. The work was only for four hours a night and prepped all the workstations and manufacturing lines for the 6:00 am shift the next day.

The first shift was the dream job. The pay was better, but not by much. The hours and the work were still long, but it had more stability. as much as a factory job could provide. The next shift up was second, which ran from 3:00 pm to 11:00 pm. That one was okay, but workers were always assigned to different areas each night depending on where people were needed to complete the production quota for the day. There was not much training involved, as it was mostly OJT provided by the first shift resources. It was only basic instructions for each one of the workstations on what needed to be finished before the next business day.

Moncrief did not make their furniture and products to stock to be placed in an inventory warehouse. Each item had a work order and was custom-made. One would think that handcrafted furniture would be better quality, as a customer would request something like a dining room table and chairs from a catalog, which would have a lead time of around three to four months for manufacturing. Who would want to wait for that long when someone could just go to a simple furniture store and buy something off a display and take it home that day? "You get what you pay for if its same-day furniture" is what the sales people always said. "Quality work takes time."

The people who actually built the furniture knew better. It was not about the quality, it was about meeting production numbers for each shift. If the workstation or a manufacturing line was behind on its hourly production, things were "overlooked" during assembly and the numbers were "cooked" to make up for the fallback. Most of the overlooking and the cooking took place between the first and second shift. That was one of the main reasons why resources on seconds never worked the same line or workstation each day. The fallback in production quotas happened in different places most of the time. Whichever line or workstation had the most immediate need was where the resources were assigned. It was always about the numbers.

Julie finally got her shot at firsts seven months ago. When a position opened in the finishing department for tables, she applied and got it. The training that she received was less than stellar, but it was provided by a twenty-five-year veteran on the line. He knew all the inner workings and all the tips and tricks on successful craftsmanship regarding the finished product. As with everything else, *craftsmanship* was a very broad term and used quite frequently. She paid close attention for the first three to four weeks, and then she was turned loose on her own. As much as she was allowed to, she provided exceptional quality to the pieces of furniture that came through her line. The final product was packaged directly after her station and then prepared for transportation.

She was one of five other finishing lines that produced different pieces each shift. She got along well with her other fellow workers in this area. They all chatted and laughed throughout the day. They took their breaks and lunches together; in a few cases, some of them were even on the same bowling leagues. If someone could have a second family, the people in her area within the Moncrief Furniture Alliance plant in Kenosha, Wisconsin, were them.

It was pretty cold that morning. She remembered seeing the temperature on the outside thermometer when leaving the house. It registered at 23°. No wonder the car gave her such a fuss when trying to start. It probably wanted to sleep in a little longer, just like her. She left the house at around 4:38 am that day, like she always did. The plant was just over thirty-seven miles away. On a good day, she could get through the gates of the plant between 5:30 am and 5:40 am, which would give her just enough time to go to the break room, get a cup of coffee, and chat a bit before going to her line. The third shift would always tidy up and restock supplies for the day's production quota. She knew this because that used to be her job. Julie still liked to inspect her workstation and line prior to the 6:00 am bell, much like a pilot wanted to examine his plane before takeoff. That morning, she ran later than normal and decided that the much-needed cup of coffee came first. Upon the initial observation, she could see her workstation area, and it looked like all the supplies for the day were in order as she approached her spot. She decided to forgo the usual line inspection.

As the first break at 8:30 am approached, Julie completed the final touch-ups on a curio cabinet that was part of a rush order placed by the wife of a well-to-do physician in upstate Wisconsin. According to the sales rep, it was a very prominent account, as there were a number of associated offices throughout the state of Wisconsin that needed furnishings, and she had established an exclusive contract with Moncrief to outfit each. As with most sales, priority was established with the accounts that spend the most money. Moncrief tended to go outside of their normal *quality* inspections to ensure that these exclusive accounts had the finest *craftsmanship*. When it came to finishing wood-based products, Julie was considered one of the best. In the short seven months that she had worked the line, Julie made it a point to become good at what she produced. The quota for her line today had been cut down due to the special order, so she took her time to ensure her best work. The buzzer sounded for a break-time.

"Julie!" shouted Dave from across the workstation. "Time for a break. Let's go."

Julie concentrated on one of the legs of the curio cabinet. "I need about five more minutes to get this one piece finished so it can sit and dry."

"All right. Don't take too long though. You know how short these breaks can get."

He started down the midway between manufacturing lines with the other workers. The break room was centrally located within the plant in a midsize room with surrounding windows. If a person stood in the middle, most aspects of the plant could be seen from each side. A number of people from his section were already there with their vending machine coffee, sodas, and snacks. He slid up to one of the machines, popped in a few coins, and out came a Snickers candy bar.

Tom from Fabric Coverings was seated at a nearby table. "What's up, Dave? Did you catch that Packers game this weekend?"

"Yeah, sure did," said Dave.

"It looks like they could've used Favre," snickered Tom.

"Ain't that the truth? I'm not really sure—"

A thunderous boom shook the room. Fluorescent lights that hung from the drop ceiling started to sway and move; a few broke their chains and crashed to the floor. The windows on the east side of the break room shattered along with the concussive sound. Most of the people that stood had hit the floor in an automatic protective posture. Dave and Tom reacted much the same way and dove to the floor as quickly as they could and covered their heads with their hands. Everybody remained in their positions as they waited for another explosion. Some screamed, while others told those who were screaming to calm down.

After a few seconds, when Dave realized that the explosion was isolated, he looked up from where he was lying on the floor. He quickly surveyed the damage. All of it seemed to be localized from one side of the room. The east side. The side of his department, the side where . . .

He scrambled to his feet as quickly as he could and started toward the east side door.

Tom shouted. "Where are you going?"

Dave exited the break room as fast as he could. "Julie!"

Tom got to his feet to follow. "Oh lord!"

Within fifteen to twenty minutes, there were all types of emergency vehicles that surrounded the plant. The fire consumed most of the finished furniture stored in the staging area, about thirty feet from the finishing department where Julie worked. The plant was mostly evacuated except for emergency personnel. Firefighters attempted to contain the fire within the specific area affected by where they thought the explosion had occurred, but it appeared that they were losing the battle. Something fueled the fire. The chief tried to get information from plant personnel on any chemicals that were in the area so he could better understand what he was up against.

The sheriff and local law enforcement officers worked with plant personnel to determine who was on shift that day, who might have switched shifts, and who might be missing based on a preliminary roster. EMTs and paramedics treated those that had already been evacuated. Workers who had minor bruises, cuts, and scrapes were attended to on the spot. There were a few that had broken bones here and there, and they were sent onto Fremont Medical Center. A small number of people did not look like they would survive.

The emergency personnel did the best they could to contain and handle the situation, but this was big stuff for the small town of Somers. After an additional ten minutes, the fire chief decided to call in a second and third alarm. He thought it was better to err on the side of caution and have more resources available, just in case. His fear was that since he did not know exactly what caused the fire, he should pull back secondary emergency personnel, except for the firefighters.

That decision saved an additional twenty-five people.

A second explosion lit up the sky like the noonday sun and shook the ground like an earthquake. Anybody within 150 feet of the plant had been blown backward.

Dazed and confused. A clicking sound. Fluttering eyes that once opened showed only splotches of orange and yellow blurs.

A clicking sound.

An inability to move hands and arms. Four of the five senses deadened or dulled.

A clicking sound.

A taste and smell of sulfur or metal. That did not make sense.

A clicking sound now replaced by a low and dull hum.

Vision slowly started to restore. Sound was still unavailable. Fingers and hands slowly made claw marks on the pavement. The fire chief felt movement and a poking along his back. A dull throb and something that sounded like a thumping began to fill his ears. Just one ear though, he could not make out anything in the other.

The chief thought he heard some people shout or scream; he could not really tell. Everything felt like a dream state; he did not know if it was real. Slowly, everything in his body came back online. His head ached from the pain. He was not sure if it was a headache or if he was wounded in the explosion or a combination of both.

The explosion. A second explosion happened. His people. He pushed himself up onto one side of his body; he did not have much choice as to which. He picked the side that responded to his mental commands. The clicking was replaced by the humming, and then the hearing process started to function again. It became clearer. The noise that he heard was shouting. It came from the other first responders that he ordered back right before the second boom. He looked around and saw that two of them ran toward him. They kneeled down next to him and did a quick assessment.

"Chief! Are you okay? Can you move?" screamed one.

The chief looked around for a moment. It was like he did not understand the language the person spoke.

The other one did a very quick once-over. "We've got to move him back. We don't know if it's going to blow again!"

Without a response from the chief, they both lifted him to his feet as gently as the situation allowed, pulled an arm over each of their shoulders, and ran back to the other side of the parking lot.

The area looked like a war zone. From where they stood, it appeared that what was left of the main manufacturing building was now ablaze.

When the structure was initially evacuated, all the employees were corralled in a nearby field on the other side that was not affected and were interviewed by law enforcement officers. Most of the employee parking was on the north side of the building, about two hundred yards from the east where the finishing department was located. There was an expanse between employee parking and the manufacturing plant which was where most of the emergency vehicles were positioned. After the second explosion, some of those vehicles were barely recognizable. The firefighters' vehicles took a majority of the force. One of the ladder trucks was flipped onto its side.

The chief had been patched up enough to where he could resume his duties. He attempted to get a head count of his firefighters that were inside the building prior to the second explosion. He had to make sure his people were okay. While he waited on all fighters to report in, he got one of his guys and a vehicle and drove around the building to survey the damage. When they made the complete circle, his assessment was that it was a total loss. The fire seemed to be spreading quickly. Too quickly.

Someone ran up as he got out. "Chief! We've been able to locate all fighters with a visual or by radio except Perkins and Caruthers."

The chief looked at him coldly as a shiver rolled down his spine. "What was the last contact you had with them?"

"They had just finished sweeping the west side of the building and were working their way toward the north."

The chief thought about this for a second. The first explosion looked like it came from the east side near the finishing department. Upon the initial assessment that his guys did after the second explosion and the loop he just made around the building, the entire east side was completely engulfed in flames. The northeast bridge between storage and transportation was blown away. Based on the building schematics, it looked like where storage had been was where the second explosion originated. That was on the north side.

"Heaven help us," whispered the chief under his breath. "Continue to try to raise them by radio. Do not, I repeat, do not send anyone else into the building."

"Chief. Those are our guys!"

His expression was solemn and compassionate. "Charlie, I know that. I would go in there and search for them myself, but you know that we cannot risk the lives of anyone else. We didn't know there was going to be a second explosion. We have no idea if there will be a third."

He turned back to watch the burning building. "We need to pray that the Lord will be watching out for them."

The first of the injured arrived at Fremont Medical Center in Somers. The facility was about the size of a health clinic, but served the small community well. It was not a full-blown trauma center who could handle any type of major accidents though. Anything that was bigger than a sprained ankle or a broken bone was usually sent on to Kenosha Memorial. There were two doctors and four nurses on staff when people started rolling in.

Most of the injured was able to hobble or walk in on their own, but one person was brought in on a stretcher, unconscious, and in terrible shape. One of the doctors rushed over immediately to run a preliminary assessment and get a report of the situation. "What have we got?"

"Twenty-seven-year-old female. Blunt force trauma to the head, back, and right shoulder. Dislocated left hip. Second—and third-degree burns to the face and torso."

The doctor evaluated the head injury first. It looked like she had a severe laceration to the right side just behind her ear. The skull appeared to be misshapen, and then he realized that it was her hair matted with blood and other debris. He turned his attention to her face. The burns were horrible. The hair to her scalp was nearly seared completely. Her face took a lot of the damage. He could not make out her eyes or any semblance that they still existed. It was almost as if they had been burned closed.

The doctor quickly examined the rest of the injuries. Her vital signs were very weak and became weaker by the minute.

"It looks like the blast hit her from the left. The force of the explosion pushed her into something very hard, causing the other injuries on the right side of her body."

A nurse quickly approached. "Andy, most of the other victims are stabilized. Crystal and I have completed the initial triage and prioritized what we can treat here versus what we need to send to Kenosha."

He did not take his eyes off the girl. "Has Kenosha been notified?"

"Yes. They have already dispatched ambulances."

"Get back on the radio and tell them to send a life flight medevac. Tell them to hurry. She doesn't have much time left."

He had imagined that before this accident, she was a very pretty girl. He was right. Trauma cases like this saddened him. He moved to a smaller community to get away from such injuries as this; he had his fill when he was an ER doctor in Madison.

He looked at the paramedic. "Do you have any information on her identity?"

"According to her fellow workers, her name is Julie Hanover."

"Has her family been notified?"

"I'm not really sure."

The doctor turned. "Crystal!"

She ran over. "Yes, Andy?"

"See if you can get in touch with the sheriff and find out if her family has been contacted. Tell him that she is being sent to Kenosha Memorial." He looked at her somberly. "Tell him that they need to hurry."

Julie had been stabilized as best as she could then prepped for transport. The medevac arrived within twenty minutes. From the time that the call was placed for transfer to delivery took fifty-five minutes. The hospital in Kenosha was ready for her arrival.

Kenosha Memorial was the largest hospital in the tricounty area. It was not the biggest in Wisconsin, but had all the amenities required to handle many types of emergencies. After the medevac arrived, the triage team quickly transported Julie into the hospital. She was still unconscious, which was to be expected, but the concern was the shock that her body received from the explosion. Fremont did not have the equipment to adequately assess the extent of the trauma damage to her head. That was the first priority.

As she was hovered over by doctors and nurses, they moved her as fast as possible to the trauma unit. The path did not run near the general public, which was by design and a good thing. There was no disguising that this patient had been through something terrible. Once they arrived, the doctors began shouting out orders. All the nurses executed each one of the commands in an automatic motion. Had the situation not been so tragic, it would have been beautiful to watch. One nurse handled all the vitals, another added specific medication to an already established IV drip, and yet another prepped the trauma room with things such as a burn kit in anticipation of what the doctors would need. If one were to observe the fluid movements of the nurses and doctors, it would be very evident that the team had worked together for quite some time. The day shift trauma/ER unit at Kenosha Memorial was definitely the A-team. The varsity players, so to speak, who worked their way up from all the horrible twelve-hour night shifts, holidays, and weekends to get to the cream of the crop schedule most medical personnel desired. In comparison, it was much like Julie as she clawed her way to the first shift at the plant. One of the best finishing people at Moncrief was now in the hands of some of the best medical professionals at Kenosha Memorial.

For all the residents and doctors in the emergency room, the chief of emergency medicine was in charge. For the ER nursing staff, it was the nurse manager. A registered nurse with the responsibilities for day-to-day activities, budgeting, and scheduling, who also performed the functions of a nurse day in and day out. The people who held this dual role were very skilled practitioners with a lot of experience. The nurse manager at Kenosha Memorial was Amanda Gibson. She happened to be on shift when Julie arrived.

The doctors worked frantically to get Julie stabilized. Fremont Medical Center did the best they could with what they had, but it did not prevent her from going into shock during transit. Amanda barked out orders to her nurses just like the doctors. Everyone tried to prevent any further blood loss.

"The burns are severe on her face," said one of the doctors.

"There are a number of small lacerations across her body. The biggest one is on the right side of her head," said another doctor. "Most likely hit by shrapnel from the explosion."

Amanda removed a stethoscope from Julie's chest. "Breathing is labored."

"Hypoxia," said a doctor. "Acute respiratory distress."

"Thermal inhalation?" said Amanda.

"The timing is about right. The explosion happened an hour and half ago."

"The skin has to be excised," said another doctor. He turned to Amanda. "Get Billingsley down here quickly." He was Kenosha Memorial's primary burn surgeon. Amanda nodded, turned, and ran to the phone in the trauma bay.

Before she could pick up the phone and dial, Michael Smithers, the hospital administrator, entered the room. "Is she stable enough to travel?"

Nobody turned to acknowledge him. They continued to work on Julie.

He raised his voice. "Is she stable enough to be transported?"

The ER chief of staff still did not turn away from Julie. "She might have a chance if we can alleviate the swelling in her head and get the burn area back to a porous state. She has absolutely no chance if we discontinue treatment."

"You need to find a way to stabilize her so we can move her back to Fremont."

The two doctors who worked on Julie stopped for a second and looked at each other then at Smithers.

"I'm sorry. Perhaps I misunderstood you or maybe you misunderstood me, I'm honestly not sure and I don't really care. She cannot be moved. She has no chance of survival, unless we continue treatment." He went back to work on her.

As the exchange went on between the hospital administrator and the chief of staff, Amanda had found Billingsley's number and was about to page him to the ER.

She had entered the first few digits when Smithers's hand reached over and hung up the receiver. "You need to find a way to stabilize her so we can move her back to Fremont. Her insurance has lapsed and will not cover the expense here."

"Have you lost your mind?" said the chief of staff. He said that more so as a factual statement rather than a phrased question. "Financial payments are not my first priority. Saving this young woman's life is."

"I understand that. Nevertheless, we also have a duty to control the expenses that this hospital incurs."

He turned to face Smithers directly. "I don't have any such responsibility. That particular clause was not part of the Hippocratic Oath. We will continue treating this young woman. This is my call as the medical chief in charge, not yours!"

Smithers looked ambivalent for about two seconds. "Dr. Ellison, we have specific rules that govern the medical treatment of patients and the procedures outlined to execute said treatment. Your job is to provide the expertise to cure, treat, or administer to those who require medical attention. My job is to ensure that we are properly paid for that attention. Ms. Hanover's insurance policy has been denied. For that fact, all the employees that worked at Moncrief Furniture Alliance has as well. Not one of them will be able to pay their bill. We cannot afford to provide extensive care pro bono."

Amanda removed Smithers's hand from the receiver. "So your answer is to just do enough to keep her alive for transport to another facility and then she becomes their burden?"

"I would not say burden, but more so their obligation to provide medical services more suited to her type of situation."

The doctor was clearly annoyed. "And what type of situation are you referring?"

Smithers was visibly upset. He was not accustomed to being challenged. "The type where payment of services are not mandatory or required. We are not going to treat every person that walks in here who presents a risk for nonpayment. Anytime someone comes into Kenosha Memorial, they sign a waiver of services and agree to payment if their insurance does not cover their expenses. Ms. Hanover never signed one, and there is a huge risk of nonpayment now that she has no insurance."

"She was blown up and doesn't even know what has happened to her! She couldn't sign your stupid paper if she wanted to," said Amanda.

Smithers directed his anger toward her now. "Nurse Gibson, this is not a debate, and you are not in command of this hospital! If you wish to remain on its payroll, you will keep your opinion to yourself and do what you are told."

Her blood boiled. She walked a fine line with this talking head now. She turned to look at the doctors with pleading eyes.

The chief attempted to get the situation back to a manageable level. "Mr. Smithers. If this young woman dies because we refused to treat her due to a policy being enforced, then why bother to treat anyone? We should just turn everyone away regardless of whether they can pay or not. We all took an oath to help those who could not help themselves. My job is to save lives, not just those who can pay for it."

Smithers stared at him. The plea did not get through, so the doctor tried a different approach. "If the word gets out that we turned this woman away and the reason why, this hospital will not recover from the fallout. The press alone will eat this up. Is that something you are prepared to handle?"

That statement made Smithers pause. Amanda and the chief of staff could see the gears click as Smithers ran a number of scenarios through his narrow little mind. His main objective was to ensure and control the financial impact of all expenses to the hospital. The Hospital Board of Review did not take kindly to a negative trend of the revenue each time the cost of running the facility exceeded the intake of money. Obviously, the medical emergency at the furniture plant would be exceedingly expensive now that the employees' insurance was invalid. If Smithers had any type of soul or heart, he might have wondered why the insurance had lapsed in the first place. The complication with the Hanover woman posed a new problem. She would be the most expensive case that Kenosha Memorial has had in a long time. All of a sudden, the expenses took a backseat to this new suggestive comment. Negative public press. Smithers was a weasel, but he understood what this meant for the hospital and his job.

He feigned concern for the poor woman's predicament. "All right. Here's what we will do . . . Continue with your course of treatment, and get her to the point of where she is out of immediate danger. Do not go above and beyond the care required to prevent her death. We will ensure that she has medical attention here at Kenosha Memorial for a minimum of fifteen days. Beyond that, we will need to transfer her to a facility more suited to ongoing treatment and recovery."

"So he has a heart," Amanda said under her breath.

"What was that?"

"You have a big heart. Thank you, Mr. Smithers," she said this loud enough for everyone in the trauma bay to hear.

He was somewhat embarrassed at the compliment. "Well then, please continue to aid Ms. Hanover." He nodded and left the unit.

Amanda rolled her eyes then punched in the page for Billingsley. Smithers was not that sharp and did not recognize the sarcasm. She was not really surprised by that though. Once she was finished, she went back to aid the rest of the staff.

After ten minutes or so, Julie was stabilized and prepared for surgery. The burn surgeon was scrubbing up, and the OR was prepped and ready. Amanda supervised the trauma protocol and procedures, posttreatment. After she signed off on the chart to account for all medical supplies used, she left the bay to head back to the ER main triage station. She noticed through the open bay window at the front of the desk, the chief talking with an elderly man. She slowed a bit to assess the demeanor. The doctor was very sympathetic with his gestures; the man was obviously distraught. She assumed that the gentleman was related to Julie. A feeling of complete sympathy washed over her. She looked very sadly at the man. She hated this part of her job. Delivering good news was one thing. When something this bad happened, there was always the unavoidable conversation with the family.

She was a nurse and, therefore, not the one that had to deliver the catastrophic news. Nonetheless, it was still hard to watch as the family reacted. She continued to walk toward the desk bringing her closer to the conversation. She did not intentionally try to eavesdrop, but she did hear bits and pieces. He was her uncle. He was the only family she had and did not have the means to care for her and did not know how he was going to pay the expenses.

Her heart was breaking all over again. Why couldn't good people ever catch a break?

This was just like the ordeal with Madeline. She did not deserve anything that happened to her. There was nothing Amanda could do for her, except care for Josh. That was one of the last things that she promised Madeline. Amanda was saddened by the thought of her best friend; she missed her dearly. Living life had not been the same without her. She had not heard from the boys for a couple of weeks. She realized that both were busy with their lives in New York and would call when they could. She never wanted to call them for fear that she would be interrupting their schedules. Funny how parents will think that way. Amanda finished her depressing train of thought a few seconds later then went back to performing updates in other patients' charts.

The smell of coffee filled the room as Kelan walked down the hallway toward the kitchen. He took in the aroma with a deep breath through his nostrils, closed his eyes, and spent a few seconds in total euphoria. He poured himself a cup and glanced to the right. Just outside the kitchen archway on the credenza, he saw a copy of today's *New York Times*. He smiled slightly then walked toward it. He took a drink upon picking it up as he skimmed through the headlines. Kelan took a seat at the dining room table across from the floor-to-ceiling glass on the other side, which held a magnificent view of the Manhattan skyline. It was impressive during the day, but it was breathtaking at night. He enjoyed this view on many different occasions and settings over the last two years. He loved this apartment. It was impeccably decorated with all the latest Greco-modern pieces of works and furniture that he could find. It was a style unlike any other he had ever seen.

He had been impressed by a number of different places before he settled on this one. He paid top dollar for the best interior design company in Manhattan. Kelan gave them some ideas of what he was looking for, and the company put this ostentatiously decadent style together. He was absolutely thrilled and loved showing off his apartment whenever he had the chance. He was certain that anybody who came into his home would be completely and totally envious.

He drank a few more sips then placed the mug on the table. He wanted to flip through the financial section and check out today's stock market quotes. As he scanned markets, a very slender female arm wrapped around him from the back. She softly kissed the nape of his neck. He smiled. She smiled as her head came around to kiss his cheek and ultimately found his mouth.

After a passionate kiss, she pulled back and smiled again. "Good morning."

"Good morning to you. Thanks for starting the coffee and getting the paper."

She pulled herself away and sat in the chair next to him. "It was my pleasure. I had to get up and check some of the system specs anyway."

He picked up his coffee to take another sip. "Anything that I should be concerned about?"

"No, not at all. Just standard system specifications to ensure that we are still tracking on missions and that all mains are nominal."

Kelan smiled playfully. "Good. I hate to start off my mornings with bad news."

She got up from the table and moved toward the kitchen. "What's on your plate today?"

He took another sip. "Not much. I've got a breakfast-brunch with the boss."

She poured herself a cup. "Oh? Anything that I should be concerned about?" she asked with a smirk.

Kelan chuckled. "No, not at all. Just the standard briefings on current and pending operations. I don't have to ask you about your day because I know."

She openly laughed. "Yeah . . . I guess you would."

"What time is the station briefing this morning?"

She turned, leaned against the counter, and took a sip. "Ten am."

Kelan looked down at his wristwatch. "You're probably going to have to cover for me since I will be with the boss."

With one last swig on her cup, she placed it in the sink then looked at her own watch. "No problem. Oh, I've got to run if I'm going to beat rush hour traffic."

She moved toward him and leaned down and gave him another passionate kiss. "Last night was great."

He smiled. "Absolutely."

She leaned back. "Tonight?"

"Let's see how the day goes."

She smiled then walked toward the door and picked up her accessories, cell phone, and keys. "I'll see you at the facility around lunchtime?"

He nodded. "Depending on how things go with Morgan this morning, yes. That is the plan."

"Okay," she said softly with another smile then Margaret left.

He smiled back at her until the door clicked shut. Once she had left, he moved quickly behind her and listened. He had to ensure that she was indeed gone. When he was absolutely certain, he locked the deadbolt and went into the kitchen. Kelan opened up the trash compactor to the left of the sink, reached under the open part and felt for, and found, a switch. He flipped it, which triggered a secret panel just above the stove on the back side of the kitchen. It popped into the wall slightly then slid upward. To the naked eye, no one would have ever noticed that section of the back wall and splash guard. Once locked into place, an electronic flat screen board moved to its position. The screen itself was simply powered on by touch. Once activated, Kelan punched in a few simple commands. The statistical display to the left side of the panel moved back and forth as if it scanned for something. That lasted for three to four seconds, and then a green light came on. His apartment was now secured. It jammed all frequencies that came in or went out. If there were any bugs or wiretaps on his phones or any miniature cameras within the confines of his apartment, they were now rendered useless. It was crafted by Israeli intelligence, and Kelan paid quite handsomely for it.

Blalock did not know that he had this; neither did Margaret. If any camera saw the flurry of activity, it simply looked like he put something in the trash and then turned on the stove. Kelan needed insurance against any activity that he wanted to keep under the radar. All electronic media and equipment that were used within his apartment while the jammer was active continued to function as normal. However, it could not be hacked, even by his specially trained experts.

In order for him to continue the plan, he must maintain absolute secrecy. He was not sure why he felt the need for stealth, but paranoia had manifested after the perceived threat from Blalock years ago. Kelan's ongoing mission since was self-preservation. He looked for anything that would guarantee his safety and corporate standing at Alastar-McGlocklin. He was not sure what he would find, but when it was found, he would need a strategy that would protect his interests. Blalock was a very clever man and should not be underestimated.

After the signal suppression was active, Kelan walked into the spare bedroom. The room had what would be expected: a bed, a dresser, and a nightstand. The closet had double-doors that stored standard items such as hanging clothes, a rack with shoes, and some miscellaneous items scattered about on the top shelf and on the floor. Nothing would be remarkable if anyone should open and poke through the articles. He bent down to the floor and moved the items that were just to the inside and the right. The exposed area looked completely inconspicuous. Kelan pressed the floor with the flat of his palm once then twice. Upon the second press, a floor panel popped open. There was a small nondescript keypad at the bottom of the opening about four inches below the base of the floor. He entered a series of numbers, closed the panel, and then stood up. There was a slight hiss of air pressure and a faint whirling sound as the entire inside of the closet moved to the left, revealing a thick metal door. Once the closet had finished moving, the metal door opened to give him enough room to walk through.

When he moved into the apartment, it was remodeled to suit his needs. The contractors removed a wall here and there and carefully picked the ones that were not considered load-bearing. Once he had the construction of the model framed, he brought in some service providers that specialized in panic rooms. This particular room was designed to be self-sustaining in the event of a home invasion. If someone were to compare the apartment against the blueprint, they might notice a slight error in the mathematical dimensions.

This was not an ordinary panic room. Israeli intelligence also outfitted this 12 x 12 space with state-of-the-art technology, which enabled Kelan to do covert information gathering and analysis. He had everything from satellite surveillance to spider bots programmed to comb through both secured and unsecured Internet sites, hitting on key phrases and words of Kelan's choosing. If it plugged into a network, he could hack it.

Thus far, he could gather standard Intel such as financial activity like market and stock options, offshore accounts, and legal mergers and acquisitions. That last part was actually the true nature of Alastar-McGlocklin, or at least that is what the world was meant to see as the corporate front for their business affairs. The clandestine operations in which he was responsible was, of course, off book. The company also practiced illegal seizures of assets that usually benefited Blalock's personal agenda.

Blalock had shadow accounts that were undocumented within the corporate structure. Kelan was sure that Blalock was unaware that these had been discovered. By normal means, Blalock would have been correct, but Kelan was smarter than that. Once he discovered these undocumented accounts, Kelan set up a tracer on financial transfers to and from. He tracked all sorts of activity across the globe between various organizations in which Alastar-McGlocklin had either purchased or did business with on the side. Blalock was a very busy man, and Kelan wanted to know why. Over the course of the last eighteen months or so, he had seen a pattern between financial transactions and acquisition accounts that did not necessarily match up.

Kelan knew that some of the underground funding went specifically to his department. If that money were on book, then that would defeat the purpose of the term *clandestine*. Neither Blalock nor Kelan wanted any spotlight on these types of activities. That was probably the only thing that either of them agreed on. From both a professional and personal aspect, they did not want any government agencies or financial investigations targeting the company. Kelan, not so much because of his loyalty to Alastar-McGlocklin, but more so that he did not want to get caught doing anything illicit. He did not really mind doing the illegal mission here or there; he just did not want to be fingered. A stain on his record such as that would be a career-limiting maneuver; he would lose everything, and that was unacceptable.

As he stripped out the balance of money that his department incurred, there were still some anomalies across the financial landscape. Nothing so much on the legitimate side of Alastar-McGlocklin's monetary holdings, this was more on the *undocumented* funding accounts that Kelan had discovered. In certain cases, there were large sums of money transferred to an unknown account and, then sometime later, transferred back in. He noted at least three transactions like this. The only thing all three had in common were that they originated from legitimate holdings of purchased companies traded on the market. All of them were split off and sold for whatever they were worth. For monetary amounts that large, the transactions had to be monitored and filed with the Federal Trade Commission to ensure that all competitive practices with the liquidation were completed legally. The Securities and Exchange Commission was involved as well to ensure that the stockholders were rightfully compensated at the time of the dispersible. The cash liquidation distribution seemed to follow the letter of the law regarding regulations for trade and sale, but the money disappeared once the transactions were completed. Kelan tried to figure out how Blalock was able to basically reverse the money-laundering process and not get caught. He wondered if the senior partners were wise to what was going on. However Blalock was doing it was of principal interest to Kelan. He thought if he could tie all of this together, his leverage against Blalock would strengthen his position with the senior partners and possibly get him a seat at the top. That was, after all, the ultimate objective.

Kelan keyed in a few commands at the computer console, which pulled up an elaborate array of data across the monitors stationed in various positions around the far wall. He wanted to see if any new activity developed in the last twenty-four hours before his little meeting with Blalock in, he glanced at his watch, eighty-four minutes.

He roamed through the data and looked for outstanding anomalies. Kelan was always one to be prepared for meetings. He wanted to have all the information at hand, always know more than his colleague, in this case, his enemy, Morgan Blalock.

Data results were static; nothing new was pending. Kelan was somewhat disappointed, but then again, that was not the first time that no changes had occurred within a small period of time. He still tried to analyze the pattern of timing of the account fluctuations and correlate those with market events and such. There was a connection here somewhere, and Kelan wanted to find it. The big question was, once he did, what would he actually do with it? Developing the strategy and executing it were two different things. In his business, information was only worth something if it was used.

Part of the perks of Kelan's job was to have his own driver and company car at his disposal. He was allowed to pick a new car every twelve months. This year's model was in the latest Mercedes series. It was coal black, with the darkest tinted windows allowable by New York State law. The car was definitely an eye-turner whenever people saw him get in or out. Kelan arrived on time at Venue Delacruz, a swanky five-star restaurant on the Upper East Side of Manhattan. Blalock loved this place. It was prestigious, overly expensive, and most importantly, it was the place to be seen.

The car pulled up to the valet, and he opened the door. Kelan thanked the man as he exited. Kelan learned the value of showing appreciation. A little politeness goes a long way to gaining respect and admiration. A life lesson that he got from Betty years ago. She probably would not approve of his motives for extending the courtesy, but nonetheless, he was trying to be a better person.

Upon entering the restaurant, the maitre d' greeted him openly. This was not his first time here as Blalock usually liked patronizing this place. He and Kelan almost always met here to discuss high-level company activities. Blalock was already seated at his table, sipping a morning cocktail. *His* table. Apparently, he was such a good customer that he had a reserved table every time that he came in. Kelan wondered what Blalock would do if he walked in and someone was already seated there. He knew this though, and he felt very sorry for whoever it was.

He walked through the crowd passing tables toward his prey. As he got closer, the performance mode kicked in. By the time he reached the table, he was all smiles and full throttle.

"Morgan! Good to see you!" he said with enthusiasm.

Blalock rose and shook his hand. "Kelan. Thank you for meeting me this morning. I hope that I didn't drag you away from anything too important?"

"Absolutely nothing that I can't address later," Kelan lied.

Blalock motioned to an empty chair right next to him. "Please, sit."

Kelan continued to smile and unbuttoned his Armani suit coat as the maitre d' pulled his seat out for him. As soon as he was seated, the maitre d' motioned for the servers right away. The way they moved, one would have thought that the president of the United States was at the table. The servers immediately began the ritualistic process. They placed the napkin on Kelan's lap, poured him sparkling water, and brought him his morning drink of choice. They seemed to know his likes and dislikes; Kelan really enjoyed that. He did not have to say a word, and the servers bent over backward to make him happy. He wondered why the rest of the world could not operate that efficiently. He saw the appeal of why Blalock enjoyed coming here. Of course though, everything came at a price. To get quality service such as that, Blalock would drop about $500. In Kelan's mind, it was worth it to be pampered. Moreover, he did not pick up the tab, so as far as he was concerned, the sky was the limit.

They both knew the routine. They never talked except in generalizations while there were prying ears about. In the business world, one could not be too careful with information, that was, and always will be, the hottest commodity in the world. In the beginning, Blalock was a bit timid to talk about anything specific to Alastar-McGlocklin outside of the security of the building; however, over time, Kelan had managed to coach him in the fine art of speaking in code. Sometimes that was necessary if there was important information that

Blalock felt needed to be shared and did not want to be conspicuous about it. It also came in handy if there were ever any conversations that were recorded; nothing could be substantiated in a court of law should it come to that.

He noticed that Blalock had the *Wall Street Journal*. "Anything happening in the market today?"

"Not much on the international front. There is a start-up that looks promising though." Another Artifact has been identified.

"Really? What industry?"

"High tech, out in Silicon Valley." Continental United States, West Coast.

"What are they manufacturing?" Identify the Artifact.

He made eye contact with Kelan as he took a drink. "You know, I'm not really sure, but I hear that it will change the industry."

Kelan almost choked on his beverage. Blalock did not know what the Artifact was. This was a new development. In his entire time as DCO in pursuit of these objects, he had always known what the target was. How was he supposed to track and retrieve something without knowing what it was? He needed more information.

He wiped his mouth with his napkin and apologized, feigning that the drink went down the wrong way. "What do the market analysts say?" Need to establish the source of information.

"Top senior analysts are feeling pretty good about it." The senior partners at Alastar-McGlocklin.

Kelan thought through that for a moment. The last acquisition was 877, the Lorne Stone. A private buyer paid a substantial price for its possession. It did not even have the chance to enter the sanctuary for cataloging. There had been a few other Artifacts over the last couple of years, but nothing as significant as 216. That was the longest-running mission to date. Kelan wondered what this new discovery could be.

"What are the initial growth projections?" Establish a location for grid search.

The server had just returned and waited patiently to be acknowledged.

"Excellent," said Blalock as he turned the paper to the alphabetical market listing. Once he found what he wanted, he handed it to Kelan. He then waved to the server to take his order. Kelan looked at the section in which Blalock had folded the journal. There was a listing circled for this nameless company, and specific projection values were highlighted. Each number meant something in their little code communication.

Coordinates. Longitude and latitude.

Kelan made a mental note and quickly memorized the numbers. The server finished with Blalock's order and turned to Kelan. He rattled off something, and then the server walked away.

Kelan wanted to get conformation that this should be pursued. "Are you thinking of investing?"

"I believe it would be foolish not to. The *Street* has a very good feeling about this one." Mission profile and execution have been sanctioned.

As soon as he got to the Long Beach facility, he would begin to work up a plan with Margaret. "Maybe I should look into it as well. I'm always willing to invest in a company with a viable future." Confirmation of directive received and understood.

"That's a good choice, my boy. Investing in a company's future can have stimulating monetary possibilities for the shareholders in the not-so-distant future." This is a high-priority mission. This Artifact was very valuable and important to the senior partners.

Kelan handed the paper back to Blalock. This appeared to be the main purpose of the meeting. He wanted to make sure that Kelan was aware of a new Artifact. The thing that puzzled him was, why do it here and not through the normal channels at work? They established a protocol for mission formation surrounding Artifacts, which had always been sufficient and secure in the past. Blalock specifically chose to give him the data here and now. He needed more information to confirm his suspicions.

"Before I do any additional research on the start-up, have you heard whether they are more poised as a venture capital investment, or will they consider factoring?"

Blalock looked at him and smiled. He finally asked the right question. He leaned forward a bit. "This new start-up will be solely owned by a private corporation. It was just recently announced that it would be seeking financing in the form of a cash advance in exchange for receivables at a nominally discounted rate."

This time, Kelan tried to keep his surprise at bay. Blalock just referenced a factor; he wants this mission classified black. Minimal support staff for location and extraction. No one below Kelan was cleared for the operation. That had not happened before. Not even 216 rated a black status on the clearance level. Kelan understood now and was very curious. "It must have amazing potential. I will definitely look into this company as soon as I can."

Orders and instructions understood. No one lower than Kelan would be made aware of this operation. The largest obstacle was how to manage this without a support team. Kelan had his next assignment, and he had to figure out how to execute it all by himself.

Chapter 10

Sadness and Relationships

Josh poured over some contract stipulations in his office when Alice knocked on his opened door. "Can I do anything for you before I leave?"

Josh intently studied a clause then slowly looked up with a puzzled look. Alice had seen this before and half-smiled. She pointed to her watch. "It's 6:00 pm."

He looked at his own watch, not necessarily questioning her ability to tell time, but more like a double-take as if he did not believe it. "Wow! Last thing I remember was getting this review contract from the server. I could have sworn that was about an hour ago."

"Nope. I've been in twice to bring you a juice and drop off your messages. You didn't move, but you thanked me each time."

Suddenly, he felt the fatigue in his shoulders and dryness in his eyes. He stared at the computer for quite a long time. He leaned back in his chair and rubbed his eyes. "Thanks for checking on me, Alice. I'm fine. Have a great evening."

She turned to leave. "Don't work too late."

Josh looked around his desk and then noticed the messages that Alice mentioned sitting on the edge. He reached over to pick them up and thumbed through each casually. Most of them were work related: contract questions and approval requests. He got to one message and perked up a little. It was from Harry. Josh smiled until he read it completely. Harry canceled, again.

His posture and spirit slumped at the words. "Can't make it for Chinese. Duty calls." Wednesday night was their take-out night. Josh really looked forward to these each week. With his schedule at Jonah and Harry's at Alastar-McGlocklin, they barely got to see one another anymore. Chinese take-out night was the only time they had together. They both agreed early on that no matter how busy each was, they would always make time for this. It was a chance to shake off all the minutia of the business world and get back to some semblance of a personal life, for them to unwind and lose themselves in caveman-type activities. Just Harry and him, like it used to be when they were kids. Sometimes Kate was there, but Josh had learned to live with the fact that she was becoming a permanent part of Harry's life. He still tried to respect Harry's choice, but he did not like it. All these years, and he still did not think that she was a positive influence for Harry.

This was the fifth week in a row that Harry canceled their Wednesday night routine. It had been work related each time, or at least that was what Harry claimed. Josh threw the note on top of his desk and leaned back in his chair. He swiveled the seat to look out his window. Each time that Harry canceled, Josh usually worked late too. He did not really have anything to go home to on take-out night. Doing Chinese by himself defeated the whole purpose of a Chinese take-out night. The last three weeks that he missed take-out, Harry spent the rest of the night at Kate's afterward. He guessed that Harry did have some type of personal life after all. He was just spending it with Kate now.

The last two weeks, Josh had even suggested that they could hit some late-night dinner after Harry was finished working. He would say that it was not fair to make Josh sit around and wait or that he did not have any idea when he would be finished. It sounded like he purposely blew him off, but Josh knew that could not be the case. Harry would never do something like that, not even if Kate were involved.

Josh made a conscious decision that he was not going to work late this time. He needed to get out and do something, but was not sure what. He decided he would figure it out on the way home. He closed the open files on his PC, packed up his bag, and walked out of his office.

Josh arrived home about an hour later and did not feel any better about the situation.

He missed his friend.

It never used to be like this between them. In fact, he and Harry were in some arguments in recent months regarding, of all things, Josh's advancements through Jonah. He did not want to think that Harry was jealous, but that was how the confrontations came across. He never came out and accused Harry of it, but that was in the back of his mind when Harry would spout off things that seemed irrational and over the top. Josh did not even understand how the arguments started, but tried to be considerate of Harry's situation. He was really stressed out at work. Apparently, Alastar-McGlocklin had been pushing Harry and his team to complete some financial accounting records that were backdated ten years in preparation for an audit that was coming at the first of the year. The company loaded down Harry's entire department with all this extra work on top of their normal workload, with no additional incentives. He had often warned Harry not to work too hard, that it would burn him out and the stress was not worth it.

In the small moments that Josh actually got to see Harry, he would complain about how his schedule was grueling and that he did not know how much more he could take. On more than one occasion, Josh offered to help get Harry in the door at Jonah International. That was usually when the arguments started. Harry would almost always take the offer as offensive and that Josh tried to get Harry to work for him because he felt sorry for his situation. He claimed that Josh was flaunting his position and Harry needed his help. Of course, those thoughts never entered Josh's mind when he made the suggestion. If Harry were to accept his help, Josh would just get him connected with the right people and let Harry take it from there. Josh helped a lot of people out with various positions at Jonah, but he did not have the same emotional connection with them that he had with Harry. Although he had a big heart and compassion for the well-being of others, Josh thought of Harry as his brother. He was not going to abuse his standing at Jonah International to fast-track someone in his family above anyone else, especially for a skilled position. In fact, with all the people that Josh helped, or got jobs for, none of them were in an influential or professional position. They were all service oriented, people that were just trying to make ends meet. They were not trying to make a career choice. Their jobs had always picked them, not the other way around. They just wanted to earn a decent wage for a hard day's work.

They were just like his mom.

Josh entered their apartment and tossed his keys into a bowl on the credenza. He and Harry moved from their fifty-year-old starter home about sixteen months earlier. Since both had corporate jobs and earned more money, they decided to upgrade their living quarters to something a little nicer and newer. The old neighborhood they had originally moved to upon their arrival in the big city had a nice appeal for anyone who was on a streamline budget. It was not run-down or under the protection of the local mafia, and it offered the look and feel of where Josh and Harry were brought up in Wisconsin. They could afford it coming right out of college, and it did the job. A little familiarity was something they both needed in this brave new world. With a little more experience and cash, they both decided to elevate their standard of living. There was a slight difference of opinion on where to locate and how much they could afford though. Josh wanted to move to a more practical area that offered security and more convenient access to both work locations. Harry, on the other hand, wanted a little more. Now that he had a taste of having something left over after bills and taxes, he wanted to fast-track to the good life and thought that downtown Manhattan would be the better way to get there.

Josh had always been the practical one in their friendship. He was the one that took a step back to assess a situation, weigh the options, and then pick the more pragmatic course. Harry flew by the seat of his pants. His decisions were almost always based on a gut feeling rather than a solid foundation of common sense and research, which was fine, if he were Richard Branson and right. Josh was the one to talk him down from lofty thoughts and actions, which would most certainly have cost him more in the long run. Harry's mother loved him dearly, but knew that he was not the type to take his time and think things through. When he and Josh had left for New York, she pulled Josh aside and asked him to watch out for Harry and keep him safe.

Josh had eventually won out in the end, and they settled on a place that was not too far from either of their jobs. It afforded them the ability to save money and live comfortably for two new corporate minions. Although Josh did get Harry to agree, this particular win was hard fought, and Josh knew why. Kate was leading Harry like a dog on a leash. Her influence was like a drug with him. At every turn, Kate was always trying to get Harry embedded into her in crowd of friends and hangouts. Kate lived on the edge of the New York fabulous scene and wanted Harry right there with her. She also wanted him to pay for it.

Until recently, she was accepting of his relationship with Josh. In fact, she encouraged them to remain roommates after they started their careers, stating that he and Josh would miss each other too much and separating now after coming all this way together would have a "negative impact on his career aspirations and friendship." The thought of them not maintaining their bond with each other was something that she just could not let Harry go through. Josh was too important to him, and she did not want him to suffer.

Harry ate this up, like the addiction that it had become.

Of course, Josh could see through the ruse that Kate was painting. Her taste was very expensive in everything that she did. Her love language was materialistic in nature. The only way that Harry could convince her that he cared was to buy her things, ridiculously expensive things. To keep up the continual stream of affection, he had to share the living expenses with Josh, whether it was by choice or not. Kate did not understand that there was more to Josh and Harry's friendship than just expenses. She would spout all the right words to him in order to get what she wanted, but that was all they were to her—words.

In the last six months, Harry grew more distant. Josh was almost certain that the wedge coming between them was driven in by Kate and could not understand her change of heart around their friendship. Where they once spent quite a bit of their time together, which in most cases included her, now they were spirits that just passed each other in their apartment. Harry spent more time over at Kate's to the point of where he took more of his clothes every week.

Now, Chinese take-out night was gone.

That was the last bit of their time that Josh had left, and it had all but vanished. The schizophrenic way that she wanted Harry to still see Josh, but did not want them to spend any more time together, had puzzled him. Quite frankly, he was not very surprised. It basically confirmed that she was a bad influence and, in Josh's opinion, certifiable.

Josh understood the first couple of times that Harry canceled, but now that understanding had turned into anger. He would completely support Harry if he knew what had changed and why. Kate was involved, and Josh knew it. Of course, there was no proof that he could produce without sounding like a jealous little brother who was not allowed to play with Harry's toy truck. Harry knew that Josh had always had an issue with Kate. For the sake of Harry, both Josh and Kate got along. They were both an important part of Harry's life and did not want to cause him any of the pain that a situation like this almost always generated. Now, the tables have turned, and Josh was being cut out.

Why?

Josh stood there in the empty apartment and just listened to the silence. It was deafening. He had to do something to get his mind off the situation, fast. He quickly changed from his business attire to more casual clothes and left the apartment.

He walked down the street for a bit, trying to figure out why things had changed, then heard his stomach growl. He did not want to eat, on the off chance that Harry would call to tell him that he was blowing off work and on his way home for the Chinese feast, but that was not going to happen, and Josh finally accepted it.

He hailed a cab and decided to check out that new Thai place he and Harry talked about last month. The cab rolled up just short of the entrance. Josh got out, paid the driver, and walked in. It was decorated a lot like an upper-end Chinese establishment and packed with a ton of people. That was to be expected as it was close to 8:00 pm.

Josh approached the hostess stand. "Excuse me, where do I go to order take-out?"

The hostess was semipleasant in her response. "The far end of the bar." She pointed then looked around him to the next guest.

"Thanks . . . and you have a great evening too."

He was not sure if she appreciated the remark or not because he had already begun weaving his way through the packed crowd. He arrived at the bar and told the server that he wanted take-out. He handed Josh a menu and stepped away to serve another patron. Upon his return, he took Josh's order, asked if he could get him anything while he waited, then gave him the requested drink. Josh sipped the soda and looked around and through some people, as he was deep in thought about his disappointment of a night. Then he noticed something. He was not sure what he saw was correct, so he maneuvered his gaze a bit to get a better look.

At the far end of the room, at one of the cocktail tables, was Kate. She laughed and tossed her hair about like some girls do when they tried to pick up guys while she stirred her drink. Seated directly across from her, with his back to Josh, was a man. Josh continued to look without making it look like a stare. He was angry, more now than before. How could she do something like this to Harry? What was Josh going to say to him? Should he even tell him? All of these thoughts raced through his mind in a microsecond. Then they all stopped, as if a comet had just hit the restaurant. The guy shifted slightly in his seat, and Josh got a good look at his face.

It was Harry.

Josh was frozen for a moment as he processed the realization of what he saw. All the pieces to the Kate-and-Harry puzzle started to fall into place. This was just another signal to Josh that confirmed he was outside the trusted friendship that had taken decades to build. A girl managed to break up Butch and Sundance. Josh's train of thought crashed when the server behind the bar told him that his food was ready. Josh paid and thanked the man, finished his soda, and looked at Kate and Harry again.

A young lady serving drinks happened to walk by, and he got her attention. "Excuse me. Can you do something for me?"

The young lady then walked over to Harry and Kate with two fresh drinks and placed them on the table. "Compliments from an admirer."

Harry looked a bit puzzled and giddy at the same time. "What admirer?" He looked at Kate, who shrugged, then back at the young lady.

She merely tapped the coaster underneath Harry's drink, smiled, and walked away. He lifted his drink and saw the note. The blood drained from his face.

"Don't work too hard, Harry. You'll burn out from all the stress."

Harry jerked his head around to look for the person that sent it. He saw nothing. Kate asked what had happened, but he ignored her. She took the coaster from his hand and read the note. Harry sat there like a child in timeout. Kate looked around and could not find anyone that she thought would have written this either.

In the opposite corner of the room with his back to the wall was a man dressed in black, observing the entire exchange. He took a swig of his drink and smiled.

Alice walked into his office and handed Josh another message. Without even breaking his concentration, he kindly accepted the piece of paper and, with one fluid motion, deposited it in the trash. "I thought I told you to stop bringing me these."

She stood there with her arms crossed. "He's your best friend, and he's reaching out. You need to give him another chance."

He looked up from his computer. "I will talk to him when I'm ready. I am not ready and, therefore, will not talk to him."

"It's been a week. How long are you going to make him suffer?"

Josh looked incredulous. "You can't possibly be serious? Make him suffer? Not that it's any of your business, but he's the one who has blown me off for the last month and a half. He knew that Chinese take-out night was important, and that didn't seem to matter to him. We had an agreement that we would always save Wednesday nights for bro stuff. He broke the deal."

He swiveled in his chair to face her. His demeanor changed from anger to hurt. "He lied to me, Alice. I don't know how to handle that."

"He might have had a reason to do so. You won't know until you talk to him."

Alice was very sad for her boss. She cared because she knew how much character and honesty meant to him. If it had been anyone else, he might have dealt with the situation differently. She saw how much this hurt him and did not know what she could say to ease his torment. She decided that she was going to let him be until he could get past the anger.

"Listen, Josh, I can't imagine the kind of pain that you are going through, but I know that ignoring him is not going to help. I'm not going to push you on this anymore, but I am going to still bring you his messages. It is a sign that he cares and wants to keep trying. You should consider the effort and factor that into your feelings."

Josh started to protest and make his case, but instead just slumped in his chair and made a grumbling sound.

"I hired you because you are smart, but I don't want your intelligence used against me." He looked at her and smiled slightly. "I'll be fine at some point. I just need to wallow in my self-pity and anger for a while longer."

"It's not good for you to spend too much time inside your head right now. You should throw yourself into work! That might help," she said sarcastically.

"Get out," he said playfully.

She left and closed the door behind her.

He looked back down at the brief in front of him. What should have been an easy review became harder as he read. He seemed to continually read the same sentence over again. After the fourth time, he decided that he should focus on something a little more distracting and a little less important. He did not want to make any rookie mistakes because his head was not in the game. He got up to head to the cafeteria for a juice and noticed that Alice had already brought one in and set it on the edge of his desk. He was impressed and frustrated at the same time. *It's like that woman is a witch*, he thought. He flopped back down into his desk chair and looked around his office. Then he started to swivel in a circle. He kept turning just like a kid would if given the opportunity. He tried to think of anything that would allow him to cut the pain of Harry's betrayal out if his head. Alice was apparently too efficient at everything that she did. There was nothing left for him to do except his job. That bummed him out. If he got up to take a stroll through the halls, he would most likely attract unsolicited attention and be offered assistance that would be equally unwanted.

He thought about it for a few more seconds and figured that there were only two viable options to get him past this. The first was to decide to talk with Harry and clear the air. He was still angry and very hurt. The talking part was just not ready to emerge. The second was the only distraction that he could do, and that was to continue to reread the same sentence until his mind allowed him to move onto the next. There was a potential for a third way out, but his lame excuse would bother him. He would not feel right about taking the afternoon off because he was angry at his best friend. He was not about to act like a high school girl who was upset that she did not make the cheer squad and just could not cope with the humility in front of her friends.

Crap.

He took a deep breath, tried to find his center, and then started reading the brief again.

An hour had passed when the door opened. He did not look up, as he was now in a groove, and did not want to break his stride. A phone message was dropped on his desk. He looked over and felt the angst coming back; the groove was gone.

He turned then grabbed the message and crinkled it in one hand. "Alice. I thought I told you—" He looked up.

"Hi," she said.

His distraction now stood before him. A few seconds went by, and still nothing came out of his mouth. He finally inhaled then let out a breath. "Melina! Hello."

"Alice said you were in a mood. She really wasn't kidding."

"What?" he stammered. "Oh! No, there's just something going on with Harry at the moment. Totally unrelated to work . . . Well, it's obviously causing an issue for me, not that you're here mind you . . . that's not the issue . . ." He continued to babble.

She dropped her purse off her shoulder and sat down in one of the chairs in front of his desk.

"Same old Josh. Can talk a person off a ledge, but still has a difficult time articulating in front of a woman." She laughed.

He remembered how much he liked that laugh. He had not heard it in such a long time, but could never forget it though.

Melina Vargas.

The first person that he met when he walked through the doors of Jonah International almost three years ago. After he accepted the financial analyst position, they got together for lunch from time to time in the cafeteria. Eventually, they became good friends. During that time, he learned that she had a hard-and-fast rule regarding dating coworkers. He respected that and tried to keep his level of attraction in the friendship zone. As more time passed, they started doing activities outside of the company: ball games, movies, hiking, even things with Harry and Kate. The more time that he spent around her, the more his feelings changed. He was not a very perceptive person in that area by nature, but he thought that she began to feel the same way. Of course, he had no way of knowing. He was certain that her career was important and she did not want any distractions to deviate from her advancement. One evening, while they were at dinner, everything came to a head.

"You've hardly touched your chicken cacciatore. Is everything okay?" said Melina.

Josh looked pensive. He took his fork and ran it in slow circles through the rice. "Actually . . . There's something that I would like to discuss with you."

She continued to eat and looked at him then smiled. "Sure. What's up?"

Josh looked down at the table. He fiddled with his fork a bit and started folding and unfolding the napkin in his lap and still did not say anything. Melina noticed.

She put her fork down and leaned in with a look of concern. "Josh? What's wrong?"

He saw the concern on Melina's face. "Oh no! No, no . . . It's nothing bad."

He looked down at his lap again and continued in a hushed tone that was barely audible, "At least I don't think so."

"I'm sorry, I didn't hear what you said."

Josh looked up, fidgeted in his seat, and then leaned forward. "Nothing, I was just babbling to myself."

Melina giggled a little. She could see that Josh was uncomfortable. She did not want to make him any worse by laughing out loud, so she waited patiently for him to continue.

He found his courage after a few more seconds and a long drink. "Listen, I think that you and I have become pretty good friends over the last nine months. Do you agree?"

She nodded. "Sure."

This was where the hard part came in. "Since we've been spending more and more time together, things have become . . . a little different for me."

She cocked her head a little to the right. "In what way?"

"Well . . . I've started to have feelings for you. More than just a friendship."

He closed his eyes for a second and hoped that he could just die. He did not want to open them and her be gone at the thought of him being attracted to her. He opened one eye at a time; she was still there. That was a good thing he thought.

He looked at her expression, and that good-thing thought vanished.

She looked shocked and uncomfortable, very uncomfortable. Melina looked down at her plate with an apologetic expression. He thought that she was going to cry.

I've completely stepped in it now, he thought.

Josh backpedaled. "I'm sorry, Melina. I didn't mean to offend you-"

It was Melina's turn to quickly counter. "No, Josh. No . . . You didn't offend me at all. I'm honestly and truly flattered. It's a great compliment that you like me."

Now, she was the one to look down and fiddle with her napkin. "It's just that . . ."

He was now concerned that something terrible had happened instead of his revelation of feelings not being reciprocated. He could see that she was in pain from something. He wanted to help. She was his friend.

"Melina, you don't have to explain. You don't owe me anything. It was stupid for me to come out and say something like that. We are really good friends, and I don't want anything to come between us. Please, just forget what I said, okay?"

He reached over, grabbed her hand, and lightly squeezed it to show her that he was on her side and expected nothing in return for his declaration.

Melina squeezed his hand back and looked up. She had tears in the rims of her eyes. She smiled slightly, letting him know that she was grateful for his selflessness.

He was a good friend. Deep down, she knew that and wanted desperately to be able to tell him how she truly felt. She just couldn't. "Josh, there's something that I've been meaning to tell you too."

He smiled at her. "What?"

"You were right all those months ago about Jonah's plan for me."

"What are you talking about?"

"I was offered a position at Jonah Paris as a contracts' translator."

Josh did not move, not an inch. He held his breath and waited for the impact of the next bomb.

She took a breath and released the inevitable. "I accepted."

Josh slowly pulled his hand back from hers. He did not react outwardly as bad as he felt inwardly. He was thoughtful about his next words. He did not want to make the situation any worse for either one of them.

"Melina, that's great news. I'm very happy for you. I know this is the best move for your career."

This is absolutely the worse day of my life since . . .

She tried to smile. "They gave me some time to think it over before I needed to give them my decision. I finally made up my mind today. This was what I wanted to talk to you about tonight."

"How long have you known?"

She looked down again. "About two weeks."

Josh could not hide his surprise. "Why didn't you tell me?"

"I didn't want things to change between us. I didn't really consider taking it until yesterday. If I turned it down, then I wouldn't have had to sit here and watch the pain that I'm obviously causing you."

Josh pulled back a bit. He felt very stupid for pouring out his feelings to her two minutes ago. If he had kept his big mouth shut, she would have delivered her news first, and this completely awkward and extremely uncomfortable moment would never have happened. He was off in another world of his tumultuous thoughts and did not think that this night could get any worse.

He was completely mistaken.

"Friday will be my last day at Jonah International."

Now he was sure that she could see him shaking. "Friday?" he whispered.

His voice was louder where she could hear. "That's really soon."

"Yes. There is a big proposal in development between two of France's largest cargo transports, Alpiniste Air Transit and France Cargo-Unis, with the German trucking company, Albert Fracht International. Jonah Paris is mediating. They need a translator who can speak both languages next week."

Josh could not hide his disappointment. "Sounds exciting. I wish you would have told me sooner, Melina. It would have been nice to be a little more prepared to lose one of my best friends."

She reached for his hand. "This is not good-bye, Josh."

He pulled his just out of reach. She picked up on the signal then slowly pulled hers back. "Josh, we will not lose touch. I promise."

That was such a long time ago, but seemed like it was only yesterday. He sat down at his desk now and stared at her. It had been over eighteen months since that dinner. He remembered a few phone calls over the first few months after she left. The calls became more infrequent and then stopped altogether. They were both at fault for allowing the contact to die. Melina used work as an excuse; Josh used the time change difference. Sometimes, they swapped the reasons for evasion. Evidently, it was too painful for both to continue to pretend that nothing was wrong.

He stopped staring. He calmly reached over to his computer, tapped a few keys, and closed the brief that he used as a major excuse not to think about Harry.

Time for the game face. He coolly waited for her to start; she was obviously there to see him for a reason.

She began to look a bit uncomfortable, but nevertheless, started talking. "It looks like you've done really well for yourself over the last year. International Affairs Division Lead for Relief. Nice job, Josh." She really meant that.

"Thank you, Melina. How have you been doing over in Paris? Still performing contract translations?"

She nodded. "Yes, I'm in the same division, but now I run it."

"Melina, that's great!" He was very happy for her. So much for the game face. Who was he actually kidding though? He could never really hide his feelings under the pretense of a body language that he developed for something other than interacting with a woman, especially Melina. Only she and his mother could see right through his cool deportment. Maybe that was one of the things that attracted him to her.

What she said next could not have been any more direct than a slap in the face.

"I've missed you, Josh."

He was pretty sure that his mouth hung open while she continued.

"There hasn't been one day since I got on that plane that I haven't thought about you."

He was dumbfounded. This was moving too fast. He could not process the right words in response, and then she kept piling on more bombs. "Melina, I—"

She held up her hand. "No, please, let me finish before I lose my confidence. That night we had dinner and you told me that you had feelings for me was the most thrilling night of my life."

His eyes got wide at that. There was no possible way to come back to a semblance of a game face. "Excuse me?"

"I know you think I'm crazy, but I felt the same way. I got scared and ran as far as I could."

"Paris is pretty far," he agreed in a disbelieving tone.

I'm losing my mind, he thought.

She nodded in total agreement. "Yes. You have no idea how much it hurt me to see the pain that I caused you. I had been thinking outside the friendship box for quite some time and was trying to figure out what to do. I had this rule—"

"A stupid rule," he countered.

She nodded again in agreement. "Yes, now I know that it was a stupid rule, but at the time, it was the best protection that I could have."

"I'm not following . . ."

She looked down at her lap, much like she did during the horrible dinner debacle that set all of this craziness into motion. A few seconds passed. "Jonah International was not my first job," she said softly. "I was an intern at another company prior to finding an opportunity here."

She paused for a few more seconds. Josh could see that she was reliving some kind of nightmare. He saw the same look in her face when she dumped him before they became anything that was worth dumping. He got up, walked around his desk, and sat in the chair right next to her. He leaned in, but did not make any physical contact. He had a bad feeling that he knew what was coming next. He decided to let her off the hook.

"Melina, I can see that there is a demon haunting you. I don't want you to say anything that is going to make you relive a horrible time from your past. You do not owe me anything."

She looked at him immediately with a compassionate expression. Tears started to form. "You said that exact same thing to me at that dinner. You really don't want to hurt me, do you?" That was more of a statement than a question.

Josh had a look of love upon his face. "Of course not! You are and always will be my friend. I would never willingly do anything that would hurt you. What would that make me?"

She reached over and took his hand. "I dated someone from that company. He was very nice to me, said the right words, gave me some nice gifts. Did pretty much all the right things that a young impressionable and very stupid girl wanted. He was the first man that I ever really cared about."

Josh closed his eyes and prayed that the next words would not be what he dreaded.

"He abused me emotionally. Told me I was worth nothing, and that I would never succeed at anything, that it was a *man's world*, and a woman should know her place in it."

He opened his eyes right after and thanked God that his worst fear was not realized. He squeezed her hand to show his support and understanding.

"Melina . . . none of that has or ever will be true. You are so much more than anything this moron could ever be. He was most likely threatened by your amazing intelligence and was trying to bring you down to a level of where he could feel better about himself," Josh said that with conviction.

She smiled. "I know that now. But I wanted you to understand why I did what I did."

Josh *did* understand. Melina did not want to get hurt like that again. She found a better place to work, threw herself into her job, and vowed never to date anyone else from her company. Everything made sense now.

Now came the truth that he had been waiting to hear for the last eighteen-plus months. "You left here because you cared about me and didn't want to be hurt like that again, right?"

She nodded.

"You want to believe that there are good men out there, and that you deserve to be happy, right?"

She smiled and nodded again.

"Great. That's two for two. I'm on a roll. I have one more."

She laughed and held both his hands now.

He was way out on a limb with this one, but hoped beyond all hope that he was correct. "You came halfway around the world to sit here in my office, to see if there is a chance that we can still be friends, with a possibility of becoming more."

She was apprehensive. "Actually, I was wondering if we could skip the friend part and go straight to possibly more."

His dreams were finally coming true. "Long distance is not going to work, and I don't speak French."

She smiled and leaned in closer. "I've already tendered my resignation at Jonah Paris. I'm moving back to New York."

"Well . . . that's a very good start."

He stood and pulled her up with him. He looked at her like there was nothing else that existed, gently held her face with both hands, and kissed her for the very first time.

After Josh had seen Harry and Kate at the Thai restaurant that night, he took his take-out home then ate it as he sat in front of the TV. He was in no hurry because he knew that Harry would not be coming home anytime soon. That was not how Harry worked. When he got spooked about something or caught like in this case, he kicked into an avoidance mode. Harry was notoriously adept at disappearing until he could figure out his next move. Most of the time, Josh was there to push him along to quickly get him back on track, but this one was a conundrum. Since Josh was the focus of the disturbance in Harry's force, he would not know how to handle it. If he took advice from Kate in lieu of Josh, he would dig himself in even deeper, which meant that Harry would most likely be underground for quite some time.

That gave Josh a little extra time to figure out his next step. He tried not to make any irrational choices in the midst of his hurt feelings and anger of betrayal. The scene played over and over in his mind. He tried to rationalize why Harry would avoid Chinese take-out night for five consecutive weeks.

He looked at the angle of Kate's involvement in the matter. She obviously knew that Wednesdays were supposed to be him and Josh. Kate would weasel her way into the evening's activities on more than one occasion. Josh went back to the psychopathic tendencies that he observed. Her open display of how important the friendship was to maintain one moment, then at the next, led the sabotage that poisoned Harry's mind. Kate was not stupid by any means; she knew that Josh did not like her and might have used that as a catalyst to sway Harry's free time away from him.

Josh pondered all the possible reasons why Harry would lie, and could not come up with a hint of a plausible cause. He was not going to figure this out in one night. He sure did not want to be near Harry in his current frame of mind though.

He needed some space. He decided that he was going to find other accommodations until he could cope with this in a more rational way.

Jonah International had partnerships with many different organizations and businesses that provide various services across the world. In certain cases, these partners had exclusive club-like corporate programs that catered to the more elite clientele, to provide incentives and rewards for doing business. Jonah was a very elite client. Some of these incentives were available for the employees at a greatly reduced price and sometimes even free, depending upon the management level. Josh had decided he would reach out and see what he could find. He made the necessary calls and, within twenty minutes, had secured a suite at one of the affiliated hotel chains, for as long as he needed. He was very impressed with the quickness and service. He did think it was odd that as soon as he gave the representative his name, he received the open-ended booking very quickly. They also stated that a corporate charge account number would not be needed;

his stay would be comped by the general manager of the hotel. Normally, he would have pushed back and insisted that he be charged at least the reduced rate, but he did not want to argue the point, not tonight. He discarded his take-out containers, packed a bag, and took off for the hotel.

That was two weeks ago.

Harry was badgering him with phone messages almost every day, and Josh lost sleep practically every night.

Then Melina came back.

The day that she arrived and overwhelmed him with all the wonderful feelings, he slept like a baby. Just having her back in his life made a night and day difference. His mind started to gain clarity about a lot of things, but mainly opened up his eyes to the situation with Harry. Josh decided that tonight, he was going to go back home and talk to him.

Josh left work at his customary time and arrived back at the apartment shortly after 7:00 pm. As soon as he walked in, Harry jumped up from the couch. He just stood there while Josh dropped his backpack on the floor then tossed his keys into the bowl. He turned and looked at Harry. For the first time since they had been friends, neither of them spoke. They stood facing each other for what seemed like an eternity.

Josh was the alpha male in the friendship, so he started. "Hello, Harry."

Harry fidgeted. "Hey, Josh."

He noticed that Harry was nervous.

Good.

Josh turned and walked to the refrigerator. He pulled out a soda, popped the top, walked over, and sat down at the kitchen table. He took a drink and just stared at Harry. After two more drinks, he finally started. "Why?"

Harry looked puzzled for a second, and then it clicked. "I didn't mean to hurt your feelings, Josh."

"Really? If you didn't want to do our normal take-out-night routine anymore, you could have just said something. Instead, you chose to go behind my back and lie."

"It was just a few weeks, Josh, it was nothing-"

Josh slammed the soda down on the table and jumped up. "It was everything! You lied to me! Not by omission, but on purpose! In the twenty years that we have known each other, you have always been the one person that I could count on to be there, in any form. You were there when my mother died! You held me while I cried and didn't judge me. I trusted you, and you have always had my back. I have never kept anything from you."

Harry just looked sick with grief. "Josh, there are things going on that—"

"No!" Josh exclaimed. "I will not accept an excuse for this one."

He walked over to Harry with a purpose and pointed his finger directly at him. "I have always, *always* been there for you. If something were really 'going on,'" Josh said with finger quotes, "you would have come to me. I'm the one person that you could have counted on. You deliberately cut me out. So back to my first question . . . why?"

"I can answer that one," said a voice from the hall.

Josh turned to find Kate standing there with her arms folded.

"Well, I guess I shouldn't be surprised. She's been doing all the thinking for you lately, so I suppose that it's only fitting for her to speak for you too."

"Now wait a minute!" shouted Harry.

"What? Tell me I'm wrong. Tell me that she has not been instrumental in the demise of our friendship."

Josh turned to Kate and dug in, ready for the fight. "You got something to say?"

Kate was ready too. "You have been pushing Harry away, and he's tired of it. The petty jealousy because of me is causing a rift in our relationship. He needed some time to figure out what he wants to do and where our relationship is going."

His game face was full on now. Josh pulled out his big guns for this fight. He looked at Harry. "None of that makes any sense. Did she discuss this with you before flying in on her broom?"

"I don't know what you think you're doing—" started Kate.

He pointed his finger at her, but looked directly at Harry. "You, shut up. Why don't you just hand over your man card right now, Harry? She's obviously the male in this relationship."

Harry became angry. "You don't talk to her like that! She has been there for me a lot over the last few months. You were so wrapped up in your high-powered position at Jonah, you never even gave me the time I needed when things got tough at Alastar-McGlocklin."

"So that's the reason why? You feel that I've abandoned you and our lifelong friendship for my job? What a crock of—"

"It's not just that, Joshua," said Kate. "You have been working ridiculous hours to compensate for your inability to keep Melina—"

Josh was on fire now. "You pick the next words that come out of your mouth very carefully, Katherine."

There was a pause on all sides. Lines were crossed on a massive scale.

Josh spoke in a very low tone. "I'm only going to say this once, so both of you listen up. What has happened here is not a result of anything related to Melina. The issue is that you lied to me," he said, pointing at Harry, "and she is the reason." He pointed at her.

"I thought that you were my friend, Harry, that nothing would ever come between us. I guess I was mistaken. For whatever reason you think you had to do this, to lie to me, you were wrong. All I've ever wanted was to be there for you, like you've been there for me. You are my brother, Harry. I love you, and nothing could ever change that."

"You're not my brother, Josh! You never have been."

Josh recoiled like he had been shot. His eyes were wide with disbelief. This was it. The day that he never thought would come. Josh would never know the true reason for the deception now. It was too late. Harry just killed everything, every moment of the lifelong friendship with that line.

It was over.

Josh steadied himself against the wall as Harry showed remorse for his comment. Kate walked over and stood by Harry.

Josh could think again. "I'll be taking some things with me to the hotel. I will have the rest out by the weekend. You've won, Kate. He's all yours now."

Josh walked over, picked up his backpack, and headed for the door.

"Josh, wait!" said Harry. Kate held him back.

"I really hope you two will be happy together," said Josh as he closed the door behind him.

Harry fell to his knees and wept. This was not how it was supposed to go.

Kate knelt beside him and wrapped her arms around him. "I'm so sorry. honey. I'm so very sorry that this is happening to you." She held him for a bit, then got up, and pulled him to his feet. "Come on. Let's get you onto the couch. I'll go make us some drinks. That will help." She walked into the kitchen.

As soon as she rounded the corner, she pulled out her cell and hit a number in her speed dial.

"Yes?" came the voice on the other end.

"It's done," she said.

"Good," said the voice, and both hung up.

Chapter 11

Suspicions and Positions

Kelan reviewed some of the mission expenditures in his office. He tried to find the funding for the special off-book directive that Blalock had given him a few weeks prior. He already began the initial information retrieval on his own. That particular activity had cost nothing but time and had yielded enough data to satisfy Blalock regarding the status. He was a little concerned that Blalock did not push harder to complete due to the urgency of the Artifact retrieval. He made a big deal about how important it was to the senior partners and was very cryptic at the brunch that day. Fortunately, Kelan could utilize his panic room to gather the necessary Intel. Once the parameters had been entered, his computer algorithm did most of the work. This afforded him the ability to continue his normal job responsibilities during the day, while have around-the-clock data crunching and background processing. It was also very convenient that it was removed completely from the Long Beach facility. Since he had to operate on his own, it was nice to have the separation of the two, preventing any slippage in clearance and time.

Funding was going to be an issue though. Only he and Margaret had full knowledge of the shadow accounting ledger. He would have to be creative in cooking the books to siphon the money required to the retrieval expense.

Kelan did not yet devise a strategy for how to accomplish this mission without an officially sanctioned team such as the RCT. They were the best as far as he was concerned and could complete the job with less than a 2 percent error. Not very good odds when applied against a large sum of money, but acceptable when performing a service.

Kelan operated off a ghost server within the facility, which only he knew about and controlled. It was not on any type of maintenance schedule, so Margaret was not aware of its existence. He had a program with a specific hot key command that allowed him to mask the screen and file manager with another program of his choosing, should he be compromised by anyone monitoring keystrokes of his activities or even looking over his shoulder. To ensure that all information was integrated, he incorporated a stealth variable to keep this server and his panic room synchronized at all times. He felt very confident with his security measures.

Heavily immersed in his research, he noticed a flag on one of the Artifact accounts. It was 216. His eyes popped off the screen for a split second to ensure that his door was closed, and then he clicked on the account statistics.

The flag was specific to an activity deviation on the mark. He drilled in a bit further and discovered that an alert notification had been set for review, regarding an address change. Object 216 was no longer living within the designated range of coverage by the DRONE. It was set to be retasked to the new coordinates pending the approval. Normal operating procedures expected anything that was specific to the 216 operation to be immediately forwarded to Kelan. The alert status change was listed seventy-two hours ago. He had not been notified per protocol and was not happy about it.

Before he called Margaret for further information, he noticed another anomaly in the mission parameters. The 216 operation had need-to-know security levels. Kelan's clearance level allowed him complete visibility to all 216 data. That included specific mission objectives outside the facility's purview. It was in that very area that Kelan noticed that covert Agent 775 did not file their latest report brief. This seemed a bit coincidental, a location change and a missed report deadline within a week of each other, when no other flags on the 216 operation were tripped in the last three years. Kelan was glad he saw this before alerting Margaret. She knew that he had an operative on the inside, but nothing else. He did not trust her enough to bring her into everything.

He reached for a remote in his desk and pressed two separate buttons, one to secure his office door and grey the windows, the other to activate a jamming signal to prevent any external listening measures within the facility. He turned around to the credenza behind his desk and opened a drawer to reveal a secure communications terminal. He took his cell phone and clicked it into the open slot on top. After punching in a code, he waited for the digital monitor to change from red to green, which indicated his cell was now secured. He pulled out the phone and dialed.

"Yes, sir," said the voice on the other end.

"You missed your last report. Why?"

"My apologies, sir. At the time it was due, I was unavoidably detained and could not get away."

"Were you with 216?"

"Yes, sir. There has been a change in status—"

"I'm aware. I'm looking at it right now. Understanding that you could not compromise your cover doesn't mean that you couldn't file the notification as soon as you were available."

"Yes, sir, I understand, but unfortunately, the situation is still in progress, and I have not yet been able to get away. I'm requesting operational leeway to complete my current contact, with the expectation of a detail report to immediately follow."

Kelan thought for a moment. Something big must have gone down. Agent 775 had been in deep cover for a very long time and not missed a filing to date. No reason presented in the past ever indicated this agent's inabilities to deliver as expected, or that they would not have a justification for doing so. "Granted. I expect that detailed report ASAP."

"Yes, sir."

Kelan hung up.

After a late-evening dinner with Margaret, he made an excuse for not asking her back to his apartment for the rest of the night. Kelan had some work to do of a sensitive nature and did not want her snooping about, so he told her that the Château Brion was not agreeing with him and made his apologies. She bought it and did not put up a fight.

He went through the normal process to secure the apartment before he entered the panic room. The synchronization of the ghost server data broadened the research regarding the new Artifact. This was good. Maybe he could modify the algorithm to find some funding if he incorporated the shadow accounts into the parameters.

A status beacon flashed on his screen. It was specific to his ongoing search for dirt on Blalock. He switched the monitors over to review the latest Intel. Kelan's eyes widen.

The panic room computer system had been processing and correlating both the Blalock dirt-digging and the new Artifact acquisition research. The files were separate initiatives, but worked from the same basic processor on a shared drive, so there was a possibility that some of the research from either would be cross-checked. To date, nothing remarkable or outside of the normal yield of data retrieval was gathered by the merge of the two tasks. Today, however, when Kelan pulled the 216 mission data onto the same processor for review, it was also synchronized with the panic room information. The advanced computer algorithm assumed this was new Intel and started to cross-check all and found multiple hits across the board. All three projects were connected.

216 was the catalyst.

Kelan quickly flipped through the many linked points of data. The detailed analysis would take much more time, but the preliminary findings were unbelievable. The more he read, the more concerned and disturbed he became. The initial pattern matches were subtle, to a degree, with connections specific to financial transfers from the operations and shadow accounts. This was not news to Kelan. It was very likely that he would be able to determine where the money was going now with the additional data factored into the equations.

His thinking, for the moment, was from Blalock's perspective. Questions formed around how 216, the new Artifact, and the secret accounting was related.

What is Blalock's involvement? Why are these three things connected? What is he trying to hide?

Kelan started punching keys and navigating the data. The further he moved through the connections, the more information he assembled. Bits and pieces of certain things he could not put together, but knew they would be integral later. He began cataloging everything that had a hit. Insurance policies, trucking manifests, estate purchases . . .

Wait . . .

Kelan's skin got cold. He stopped.

There were mission logs that were not part of his department, records of activity that looked more military than anything he had ever sanctioned.

Mortality figures.

Dossiers of both operatives and targets, deceased.

Names of people that he knew.

He pulled back from the monitors. He sat there and stared at one name that practically jumped off the screen. Julianne Anderson. She was Blalock's assistant before Betty. As he read the final mission brief, he started to sweat. *Her entire family! He had her whole family eliminated . . .*

Kelan spun his chair around and quickly punched in a command at the station he used to link the panic room with the facility. He severed the connection and made certain to wipe any IP routing and satellite traces. It did not matter anymore whether the data exchange was in place. He had the baseline information needed to continue his research. Kelan did not want his little panic room remotely tied to anything that could subsequently be linked back to him. As he typed the separation command, his hands shook. He did not know if this meant he was scared for his life, of his indirect involvement, or for the simple fact that he had been correct all those years ago. Blalock *did* threaten him.

The screen flashed a message.

CONNECTION TERMINATED. SECURITY TRACE WIPE COMPLETE.

He backed away from the station slowly as he tried to piece together everything that he just discovered. His mind was a blur of activity, thinking along many different threads of reality, scenarios, and pulling out some rough hypotheses.

The key to everything that he just found was 216, that was the center of all activity. He had some unknown variables where the results were not specific, such as the massacre of the Anderson family, but those could possibly tie into an overall objective. An objective, which would be the question of the century. For everything he did not know, he understood this. He was in over his head and did not know to whom he could turn. He looked back at the monitor with the profiles and names. He was going to need some help to prevent his own from being added to that list.

Josh had struggled over the last couple of weeks. The loss of his friendship with his best friend hit him really hard. He had not felt this type of hurt since his mother had passed away. The pain itself was different with his mom, but Harry's initial betrayal and subsequent comment had the same type of intensity. It was a deep wound in his soul. He felt like an idiot for believing Harry would never cut him out of his life, for thinking that giving Harry his complete trust and loyalty was something he would cherish the same way Josh did. Harry was as much a part of Josh's essences as his own beliefs. He was the only remaining constant in Josh's life that still connected him with the piece of his past he held in the same regard as his mother. Now, that seemed all but gone. Something fragile that slipped out of existence. Something that was going to haunt him for the rest of his life.

Understandably, he moped about, but was in control enough to keep it from affecting his work. Josh thought he put up a good facade when interacting with others. Most did not even know that something was wrong. However, there were a few select people who monitored the mood from a distance.

"How do you think he's holding up?" asked Holden.

"This is a tough situation for him," said Lucas sadly. "All he had left was Harry, and now he feels as if there is not anyone else with whom he can be himself, confide in, or count on."

Holden and Lucas watched him through one of the monitors via a security camera positioned in the hallway just outside of Josh's office. Both felt compassion for the young man, for they had been in very similar circumstances with differing perspectives, so they empathized with his feelings of loss and sadness.

"How long has it been since you and Jonathan approached him?" asked Holden.

"Four weeks. We were expecting a delay in the meeting due to the emotional stress that he is currently undergoing. I do not expect that it will last much longer though."

Holden smiled. "How are things going on that front?"

Lucas returned with a grin. "It appears very well. The timing of her return worked to our advantage. She has filled an emptiness in Joshua's heart that has been there since his mother's passing."

Holden cocked an eyebrow. "It goes without asking, but I'm going to anyway . . . You did not influence her decision to come back to Jonah International, did you?"

"My friend, you know that is against the rules. We can only guide without directly affecting any predetermined outcome. All decisions must be made of her own free will. I can say this though. I have had Marko watching out for her over the last few months to make sure that she has been safely free of other forces that could prevent her from considering a future with Joshua."

Holden turned to Lucas. "Is something happening in which I should be involved?"

"No. This will not be your fight. There has been quite a bit of activity in the enemy camp. It seems that there is a plot hatching, which we are not privy as of yet. When the time comes, and we are instructed to do so, it will be addressed with a force, the likes of which have not been seen in a very long time."

Holden tried not to be conspicuous with his body language, but there were many times that Lucas had eluded to exploits from his past that Holden found fascinating, but was too intimidated to ask. He knew that Lucas had seen, and more than likely participated in, many historical events that have shaped the outcomes of civilizations, both old and new. He and his companions were a walking history class.

"Is this something that Josh will be ready to handle?"

"The timing of his leadership will precipitate the coming battle. He will witness those events. Only the Chairman will know of his readiness," said Lucas.

Josh sat in his office and gazed out the window. He wondered how things could have gotten so bad. He tried to determine if his approach was wrong when he confronted Harry. He contemplated whether he should have handled the discovery of Harry's ruse at the restaurant differently.

He ran through all the possibilities over and over, desperately hoping that he could have found some way around what had happened, in hopes that their friendship could be salvaged without Josh compromising his feelings on the matter. The more he thought about it, the more nauseous he became. He was lost and did not know where to go.

Alice stood in his open doorway. She had a lot of respect for Josh, and it saddened her greatly to see him in what seemed like a constant state of pain. She knocked on the door softly. "Hey, Josh, you had asked me to remind you of your lunch with Langston today. His assistant called to confirm."

Josh turned his chair away from the window and looked at her thoughtfully. "Okay, Alice, thank you. Yes, Langston and I are still on for lunch. Please let Jenny know that we can go wherever he would like. I'm not picky."

She nodded her head slightly. "Okay. I'll take care of it." She started to turn then stopped. She looked back at him with hope in her voice. "Is there anything that I can do for you? Anything at all?"

He halfheartedly smiled. "No, thank you, Alice. Time will eventually take care of this. I want you to know that I see what you are doing, what everyone has been doing, and I greatly appreciate it. I know that you are trying to help. I'm sure that this may not make sense to some people. It may not seem like it, but it makes me feel warm and loved to know that you are all my friends and want to be there for me."

He turned back to the window. "I just need some time."

She nodded slowly to nobody in particular and left the room. The two men watched through the camera and continued to feel bad for the young man.

Holden turned the monitor off.

Lunchtime with Langston Campbell was good for Josh. He could forget about his problems with Harry for a brief moment and discuss things about work and the special projects in which Langston was involved. Josh mentioned that he was invited to discuss an opportunity with a new division, but did not know much about the responsibilities. Langston encouraged him to seek this meeting and find out for himself whether he would be a good fit. Josh was indecisive, mostly, because of his current funk with Harry. He did not want to let leadership down if he could not perform at his very best. An admirable trait, but did not seem possible given Josh's track record within the company. Langston said this opportunity may be just what he needed, to help him cope with the stressful situation. Josh did not think of it in that respect.

When Josh returned to the office, he asked Alice to call Lucas Aldridge's assistant to set up the meeting. What they did not know was that Lucas did not have an admin. Unbeknown to them, her call was handled by Sentinel. The meeting was set up for a Thursday morning.

It was scheduled to be in the upper levels. Josh had not been on those floors since his first interview. Alice gave him a quick reminder that it was 9:45 am. Josh finished up his last task then headed toward the elevator. Because there was a separation between the lower—and upper-level lifts, he could not take the regular ones from the lobby. However, there was one singular elevator that allowed movement between all floors. It was used mostly by the fat cats upstairs and required a special clearance and code, much like when Melina escorted him on the first day. There was no mention of an authorization procedure or any type of code needed. Josh was so preoccupied with his current responsibilities, and the thing with Harry, that he did not think to ask.

When he arrived at the special elevator, the door opened automatically. Josh remembered the first lift ride to the upper levels and that the box had a voice.

"Hello, Sentinel."

"Hello, Mr. Arden."

"I'm going to assume that you know why I am here and where I'm going?"

"Yes, sir."

"Great. Let's be on our way then."

"Very good, sir."

The elevator, and Sentinel, conveyed him to the proper floor and opened the doors. Just on the other side was Langston Campbell. Josh was surprised. "Langston! I didn't expect to see you here. Are you going down?"

Langston smiled. "No . . . actually, I'm here to escort you to the meeting."

"Oh! Well, all right. Thank you, Sentinel. Have a nice day."

"Thank you, sir. May you have a nice day as well."

The lift doors closed as he and Langston began to walk. They went to a small conference room where inside waited Lucas and someone whom Josh had not yet met.

Lucas stood and extended his hand. "Joshua! Thank you for coming and speaking with us."

"My pleasure, Lucas. I'm very sorry that I have kept you waiting all these weeks. I have . . . been a bit preoccupied as of late."

"Nonsense. As I stated earlier, you are a busy man, and we would work around your schedule."

Lucas turned to his guest. "Joshua Arden, I would like to introduce Ulysses Quaden, the Operational Technical Director for Jonah International."

Josh shook his hand. "Pleasure to meet you, sir."

He shook Josh's hand vigorously. "Please, no formalities . . . call me Ulysses, and the pleasure is all mine!"

Ulysses looked like he was in awe of Josh's presence. Langston caught his eye with a warning look to pop it down a notch. Ulysses picked up the hint and stopped the handshake and the momentary gush of starstruck admiration as naturally as he could.

"Operational Technical Director of what?" asked Josh.

"All in due time, my friend. Of course, you already know Langston." Lucas motioned to him.

Josh now looked a little confused. "You're going to stay?"

Langston smiled. "We are going to be working together now. Lucas thought it would be a good idea for me to sit in on the discussion."

Working together? Josh thought.

"I'm not sure that I qualify for anything connected to Human Resources."

Langston laughed. "Josh, do you remember when we first met? You asked me a question about my degree and why I was in Human Resources."

Josh was thoughtful for a moment. "Yes! I remember asking why someone with a degree in . . . Religious Anthropology was working as a DHR."

Langston, Ulysses, and Lucas exchanged knowing looks with each other. "DHR is one of my more public talents."

Lucas motioned for all to have a seat. As they settled in, he glanced toward the corner of the ceiling. Malcolm Holden watched via closed-circuit camera from his office. This was the second phase of Josh's rise. He would not have missed this for the world.

The conference room door opened, and two attendants entered. They proceeded to serve beverages and light snacks of their choice. Josh was amazed at what took place. He had never been afforded a position that would warrant attention of this sort; he certainly did not think he was in that type of position now. Once they were finished, they exited as quickly and efficiently as they had entered.

Not wanting to be unappreciative, the question was just sitting there on the end of his tongue. "Excuse me, but what was that all about?"

Langston stirred his tea. "What do you mean?"

"I've been to some fancy dining establishments that have charged ridiculous amounts of money and received lesser quality service than what just happened here. If they are from the fourth-floor cafeteria, I don't recognize them, and I know most everyone."

Ulysses and Langston laughed. Lucas just smiled. "Don't be alarmed, Josh," said Langston. "The upper level has a few extra . . . amenities than the lower. This is mostly due to the executives and the clients that we do business with from all over the world. We have a catering group on the fifteenth floor that provides extraordinary service and cuisine. They are separate from the fourth-floor services, which is why you may not have known about them."

"Does something like this intimidate you, Joshua?" asked Lucas.

Josh had a look of someone with an opinion, but was going to be polite enough not to share it with everyone else.

"Go on. You can speak freely here," continued Lucas.

Josh cocked his head slightly to the side. "Well, I'm not the type of person to expect to be served like that. If I wanted some tea or scones, I would have had them brought in and set on the outer table prior to the meeting then gotten up to get it myself. I don't expect anyone to do anything for me that I wouldn't be willing to do."

Excellent! thought Holden as he watched. Lucas had a look of approval while Langston and Ulysses slightly grinned and continued to eat their snacks.

"You have just passed the first part of this job interview," said Lucas.

Josh was really confused now. "I'm afraid that I don't follow."

Lucas straightened up in his chair. "Joshua, there is an element of this position we seek for you to fill that is in need of traits that are, shall we say, characteristic of someone with no hidden agenda and pure of heart. Good judgment, self-sacrifice, a moral understanding between right and wrong, and nobility are indicative of such a person."

Josh tried hard to comprehend, but still did not have a clear picture of what Lucas was saying.

He leaned forward a bit. "Okay, let's pretend I know exactly what you are talking about . . . even if I possessed the traits that you have listed, I am, by far, not from a noble background. I'm a kid from the east side of Wisconsin. I don't have any family to speak of, and my mother was a blue-collar factory worker. If memory serves from my Western Civilization class, nobility is a birthright bestowed from generations down in a royal lineage." He leaned back in his seat. "I am 180° from that."

Lucas continued to make his point. "Do not discount yourself so quickly, Joshua. Nobility is not just by birthright. It can also be bestowed by decree. Kind of like a knighthood, if you will."

Josh was a little taken aback. A look of dread started to come across his face. "And who would make such a decree within Jonah International?"

Lucas looked at him and said very elegantly, "The Chairman of the Board."

Josh's eyes widen at the title. The top position at Jonah International. All the Jonah subsidiaries, acquisitions, affiliates, partners—everything rolled up to the Chairman. He had heard stories about the Chairman and the Board of Directors since he had been with Jonah, but never gave it much thought since he was a nobody. He knew a lot of the C-level executives, but did not know any that had actually met with, or personally knew, the Chairman or any of the Board Members. All that knew of them seem to hold each member in the highest regard, almost in reverence. Leaders that high up would never look down through the hundreds of thousand employees in Jonah International just to find someone like Josh, or would they?

Josh's tone lowered. "Does the Chairman know who I am?" He wanted to vanish or possibly become part of the wall before he heard the answer.

"Yes, Joshua," said Lucas. "He knows exactly who you are."

Josh felt dizzy for a second. Thoughts of how he ended up in this moment from birth to now flashed at the speed of light through his mind. Why would someone that important want, or even care, to know him?

"Joshua, do not despair. Being noticed by the Chairman is a very positive thing."

Ulysses and Langston nodded their heads in agreement; then Langston leaned forward. "Josh, let us tell you what we have in mind for this position and why we agree with the Chairman that you are the best person for this job."

"All we ask is that you give us the time to explain how you can help us, and then you can make your decision," said Lucas.

Lucas, Ulysses, and Langston gave him a minute to let everything absorb. He was hit with a wall of information, and they did not want to scare him away. Josh had to come to the new role all on his own, of his free will only. Those were the rules; they were not to be broken. When Langston thought the appropriate amount of time had passed, he leaned forward to start from the beginning.

"Josh, Lucas and I are going to tell you some things that may be hard for you to understand. We don't expect you to come to terms with this immediately, but we are going to ask that you accept what we have to say as the complete truth." He paused for a second. "Does that sound okay?"

Josh tried to pull it back together. Now was obviously not the time to act like a scared child lost in a strange place. If ever he needed his game face, it was at this moment. "Yes. I can listen to what you have to say."

"Can you do it with an open mind?"

Josh nodded. "Yes, I will do my best."

"Great! That's all we ask," said Langston.

As Josh paid close attention, Langston and Lucas began to give him the background of the position and job responsibilities. This new role would be as an analytical consultant within a division of Jonah International, which specializes in research and acquisition of Artifacts.

"What is an Artifact?"

"An Artifact is an object that was handmade by humans for a purpose of subsequent use. In our case, manipulation of a religious or spiritual nature. These Artifacts, although just a material item, hold meaning to certain cultures and have great influence over their beliefs and are fundamentally worshiped," said Langston.

Humans? Who else would make these? thought Josh.

"Artifacts have been created and scattered throughout the world for hundreds of centuries," said Ulysses.

"Why are these important to Jonah?" asked Josh.

Lucas answered this one. "Jonah International has a larger purpose than just international trade, relief support, and economic commerce." Lucas had to be careful going forward. He was not allowed to tell Josh everything yet. "Jonah has a pivotal role in the balance of the positive and negative influences on a global scale."

Josh showed a look of intrigue now. "What type of influences?"

Langston shared a glance with Ulysses. They both wondered how Lucas was going to approach the explanation.

Lucas leaned forward and spoke in a lower volume. It was not really necessary, but more as a dramatic effect to ensure the seriousness of the answer. "The type that can bring about world peace or plunge it into another world war."

Josh had a very difficult time maintaining his game face, so he just stopped. His brows furrowed as he wondered how he could possibly make a difference that would bring about something that huge. He decided to go for broke on the questions. "Please forgive me if I seem ungrateful for an opportunity that can change the face of the world, but what makes all of you, and the Chairman, think I have anything of value that could pull something like this off?"

"Josh, here is where the rules can be a hindrance to our discussion. At this point, we are not at liberty to divulge certain answers such as why you are important to this cause. The answer to that question and others will come in time, but only if you accept the offer of this position. I do not mean to mislead you in any way. As we said in the beginning, we offer only the truth and the position as evidence for your decision," said Lucas.

"I don't understand what you mean when you refer to rules," said Josh. He maintained his calmness, but it rode a very thin line. He was not sure how much more vague information he could handle.

Lucas grimaced and shook his head. "The rules have been placed for a specific reason, Joshua. They are meant for the protection of the decision process and must be obeyed at all times to ensure that the right person, with the purest intentions, is chosen correctly. At this moment,

I cannot give you any further information regarding them. As mentioned, in time, you will come to know the truth behind why."

"Okay . . . I'm going to give you the benefit of the doubt, for the moment, but I still need more to go on. May I continue to ask questions with the understanding that you may not be able to answer?"

"Absolutely," said Lucas.

"Right then . . ." He straightened up in his chair in preparation for the onslaught of thoughts churning through his head. "My questions will most likely be directed toward you," he stated, motioning to Lucas, "but there are some that I have for both of you too." He motioned to Langston and Ulysses.

All three gentlemen nodded their agreement. Holden continued to watch his monitor.

"What makes my experiences essential for this position? You obviously know my background and what I have done for Jonah. This position seems like it is way outside of my wheelhouse."

"It is not what you have done, it is how you have done it," said Lucas. "You are very passionate about the job that you do because it affects people's lives, you want to help them. Through your due diligence and effort, you go to extra lengths to ensure accuracy in all that you do, to ensure that all details have been presented to allow for a more methodical and authentic assessment of a situation. The Japanese tsunami campaign is one of many examples."

Lucas looked at Langston who nodded in agreement.

"Your experiences in leading and researching the details are key to this new role," added Langston.

Josh looked thoughtful for a moment, as he accepted the answer, and pondered his next question. He nodded his acquiescence and moved on. He turned to Ulysses. "Lucas mentioned that you were an Operational Technical Director . . . Can you tell me of what?"

Ulysses looked at Lucas who nodded approval. "I am the technical lead of all the Artifact missions. I assemble the data packages, technical armament for retrieval, and mission specifications. I usually lead the teams to retrieve the Artifacts themselves."

"Technical armament? Does the retrieval process have an element of danger?"

"There are some risks to the recovery of an Artifact from time to time. We take all the necessary precautions to ensure the safety of our team though."

"Will I be on your team?"

Lucas answered, "Yes. You will be working with both Langston and Ulysses to research and rescue Artifacts."

"Will I be working here in New York at Jonah International?"

"For the most part," said Langston. "There will be fieldwork depending on the findings of the research and the necessity of travel. Think of this position much like an archeology dig. You may need to travel to where the Artifact is located."

"As an analytical consultant?" probed Josh.

Langston shared a look with Lucas. Josh was getting into a gray area, and they needed to maneuver the conversation in a slightly different direction.

Lucas interjected. "Joshua, every member's role will allow a blending of expertise across the board. Ulysses has the technical knowledge to supply the equipment, specifications, and mission intelligence from a more tangible and practical point. Langston has the historical knowledge needed to know the origin and relevance of the Artifact, which will allow us to understand its direct relation to folklore, the occult, and cultural religions. That part is essential for Jonah to ensure that the Artifacts are handled appropriately."

Josh listened intently. All of this information could be very overwhelming if he allowed it, but he continued to try to keep an open mind as asked.

"You will bring a perspective born of analysis and leadership," Lucas continued. "You have a deep commanding aptitude for persuasion and leadership and are very perceptive. These abilities, coupled with the details that you are so good at uncovering and developing, will allow this team to pinpoint Artifacts more efficiently and bring a more structured and methodical approach to the table."

"And your role?" Josh asked to Lucas.

"My role is to serve the Chairman. I will remain as the primary liaison between Jonah's leadership and the Board of Directors." Lucas looked at each one of them then back at Josh. "I will also be available as necessary to provide you support during your transition within Jonah. Think of me as a personal assistant of sorts."

Langston and Ulysses shared a look of surprise. Although they were cognizant of the true nature of the Artifacts, neither had ever worked directly with Lucas. They both knew that he was a VIP with a lot of pull and the complete support of the Board, but had never known him to bother with someone of Josh's level before. When they did see him, Lucas was mainly with Malcolm Holden. Most people at their level thought they knew who Lucas was and what he did. Those people were very wrong.

Josh tried to find a weak point in the explanation, but was sidetracked by the same question that kept popping into his head. "Why are the Artifacts so important to Jonah?"

Holden had wondered how long it was going to take Josh to get back to this particular question. It was the same question he had asked all those years ago when he first joined the mission teams as an agent. Ulysses and Langston did not want to field this one, not because they did not know the answer, but simply because they did not want to give Josh too much information, or not enough. Lucas was always very good at giving the right amount.

"The Artifacts have a different significance to everyone. From Jonah's perspective, they represent an object that will shape the beliefs and faiths of countless people worldwide. Sometimes, but not always, objects or Artifacts are held in high reverence, and promote idolatry, whereby distracting one from their true nature of choice without duress.

"It is not Jonah's place to prevent the choices made by people, but instead remove any of the elements that sway them one way or the other. It is part of the overall service that Jonah International and their subsidiaries provide to ensure there is equal balance across the plain of spiritual existence," said Lucas.

He paused to see if this was making sense. He did not want to overload Joshua, not yet.

Josh slowly nodded his head as if he sort of understood, but was still crunching the data. "Okay, if I can ask the same question a different way, just so I can connect the dots . . ."

"Yes, go on," said Lucas.

"Why is the spiritual welfare of people important to Jonah?"

Holden smiled. Langston and Ulysses knew what Lucas was going to say.

Lucas leaned forward a bit. "I am sorry, Joshua, but I am not at liberty to answer that question now, but I assure you, at some point, you will find what you seek."

Josh kind of figured that he would hit a roadblock with that one. He picked up on something rather important though, in that Lucas did not say he would never know, he just would not know, at the moment. In fact, all the questions that he had, and some that were asked, had not directly been dismissed. All would be revealed in time. It was almost like a role-playing game where the player had to advance to unlock codes or gather more information to get to the next level. Josh decided that since he was not shot down completely, he could wait until the appointed time as determined by the powers that be.

"Not a problem," Josh said that casually, much to the surprise of Ulysses and Langston. Holden was not surprised in the least. He knew what was in store for young Joshua and that some of the answers he wanted would come directly from Holden himself.

Josh had another question, and probably the most significant one yet. "Is there anyone else interested in the Artifacts besides Jonah International?"

This question was anticipated by Lucas. "Yes."

Before he continued on, Lucas was thoughtful on how to respond. He knew Joshua well enough to know that once he gave him the answer, his mind would begin to run through the points of information and start, as Josh aptly put it, connecting the dots. Connections would not only come from this particular discussion, but points from his past that would eventually weave its way into a tapestry and become clearer to Joshua as he progressed through his learning and understanding.

"We are competing directly against Alastar-McGlocklin," said Lucas.

This response caught Joshua by surprise, and he did not hide it in his expression. His mind started moving into overdrive. Joshua reacted in an automatic mode of gathering Intel and piecing together scenarios. The three interviewers did not make a sound or move. They could see that Joshua was working through some things and did not want to interrupt. When he was ready, he would come back to the conversation.

Josh processed data at Mach 2 with his hair on fire. The questions poured in; he categorized, cataloged, and placed answers to the ones that he could figure out. The last one in line, him like a brick wall, and his mouth popped open. He quickly looked at Lucas and hoped that he would have the answer Josh needed to hear.

"Harry? Is he in any danger?" He assumed that all three knew that his best friend worked for Alastar-McGlocklin.

Langston quickly leaned forward. "No. Not that we know of. Harry works for a separate division outside of the Artifact operations. He should be completely removed from the situation."

As bad as Harry hurt Josh, he still cared about him and his well-being. He would never want him to be in any type of danger. Joshua's expression of dread and despair changed after he heard the answer. He composed himself and was back to business with one more follow-on question. "Are people's lives at risk as a result of who gets the Artifacts?"

"Well . . . yes," said Langston.

"I'm in," said Josh.

Ulysses and Langston were pleasantly surprised at the quickness of his decision. Separately, Lucas and Holden were not surprised but equally very pleased.

"I would not be able to live with myself knowing that if I did not take this position, people's lives would be in jeopardy. If there is anything that I can do to prevent loss of life or injury, then I am in. I'll figure everything else out as it comes," he said.

Looking down at his watch, Josh stood, and the others followed. "If you will forgive me, I have some other business that I need to attend to." He began to shake each person's hand. To all three, he said, "I'm assuming that the transition period will be worked out between my current position and this new one?"

"Of course," said Langston.

A small look of sorrow creased Josh's face. "My team?"

Lucas put his hand on Josh's shoulder. "They will, of course, be taken care of, but you should not despair. This new position has additional perks that you may find very attractive."

Josh was interested in that response. "Really? I'll have to get together with Langston, while he's using his public talent as a DHR, and go over the new package benefits." He said that playfully to mask the uneasiness and uncertainty he felt of the unknown and a future that seemed to be out of his control.

Holden was pleased to see Josh responding well to the information that he had been given thus far. Inwardly, he felt a pang of guilt knowing that Josh's trials were not yet over. Now that he was on his way to enlightenment, Holden and the rest could be more open about helping him to cope. He would need the whole support of Jonah International before everything was said and done.

Chapter 12

Friends and Origins

That night, Josh had plans to see Melina. They were going to have a light dinner and catch a movie, but something came up with Melina's new position as Director of Linguistics at Jonah. She had only been appointed to that position in the last few weeks, but was already exceeding expectations, much like Josh did in his role. The *something* happened to be an impromptu replacement for a translator at the United Nations for a video conference between Bosnia and South Africa. She had others in her department that could have handled the job, but she did not want any of them to work after hours on such short notice. If he were in that situation, Josh would have done the same thing.

With the help of Jonah Real Estate, Josh found a gated condo community after parting ways with Harry. The community also happened to be owned and operated by an affiliate. Jonah International did an excellent job of taking care of people that bought services and products from their partners, as well as their own employees, and it made him very proud to be associated with them. They were not the typical corporation that was out to make a buck off unsuspecting victims, like he and Harry used to talk about in college. Josh suspected that Alastar-McGlocklin fell into that category in the worst way. He was certainly going to find out with his new position just how much.

He was both anxious and sad to begin his new job. On one side, he was very determined to do his best when the transfer was complete. On the other, he hated leaving his team behind. Alice, Sally, and the others had been very loyal to him over the years. They all worked hard to do their best, put in overtime when needed, and never complained. They understood that the clock started once a request for relief support came in, so they did what they could to get the aid to the victims as quickly as possible. They knew Josh's dedication to the cause, and they were always there to back him. He had to find a way ensuring that they would, indeed, be taken care of as Lucas had said.

He hoped that he could discuss a lot of this with Melina tonight over dinner, but apparently that was not to happen. He was not upset about missing time with her, just a little disappointed. This was not a big deal in the whole scheme of things. He wanted to support her work and encouraged her as much as possible. That is what a good boyfriend should do. He was saddened by the thought that Harry gave more in their relationship than Kate did. Josh could see that, had always seen that. Harry never could though. Their relationship was a poster child for the saying that love was blind. In this case, very blind, deaf, and extremely dumb. Harry made his choice and was very clear about it. Still, Josh missed him.

As usual, Josh was one of the last people to leave the office. He arrived home in record time, mostly due to the company car service that provided after-hours transportation. This was another perk of working for Jonah. The best part about this one was that it was offered to any employee regardless of their level. Josh did not mind taking advantage in this case, because it was freely available and did not represent a privileged amenity that only the exclusive upper class thought they so richly deserved.

On the trip home, he reflected on how far he had come over the last few years. He smiled at the thought of his first job when he came to the city: the library. He did not make a lot of money, which was never his focus to begin with, but there were aspects about it that he missed. He liked working the graveyard shift in periodicals and new editions. Josh enjoyed the part-time solitude of nights, as it allowed his mind to wander in areas of how he could cause a change given the opportunity. While stocking and cataloging was a mundane task, it also allowed him to look for work in his field of degree during the day. He really liked the people that worked there. They were content in their positions and did not seem to want for more. Neither did Josh, for that matter; he just wanted to cause a change in people's lives, and that was what he did now.

The old job was not that challenging and did not hold the large responsibilities that he handled now, did handle. He was going to miss this job too. He did not know what type of new responsibilities he would have yet. All of these thoughts ran through his head as the city lights flashed past him. He gazed out over the Williamsburg Bridge and wondered how his former coworkers were doing, and then an idea came to him. He would drop by and see them. His old supervisor and others should be there tomorrow, so he would see if they were available for lunch.

Josh finished up what was probably his last full review of a relief package and looked at the time. He had Alice give the central branch a call earlier that morning to ask if his old colleagues would be free for lunch. He told her to sweeten the deal by letting them know it was on him.

Alice arranged a reservation at a restaurant that he thought they would enjoy, Angelo's Italiano Cuisine. One of the new *perks* that Lucas referred to in the interview was, ironically, a personal car and driver at his disposal twenty-four hours a day. He did not feel comfortable at first, which was why he used the corporate after-hours program the previous night. At the same time, he did not want to insult Lucas and the position by not showing his acceptance of this new responsibility and the associated benefits. This was something that he supposed he would get used to, but still thought it was a waste of resources.

Josh's car pulled up to the corner and dropped him off. He wanted to walk the block a bit without it being seen. He did not want them to think that he was showing off his corporate position by having a driver pull up directly in front of the restaurant. He was in business attire since it was a workday; he could not do anything about that. He took off his coat and tie and left them in the car so it would seem a little more casual and decrease the possibility of making his old working-class colleagues feel awkward around him. He did not have any idea whether any of them would, but he did not want to come off as any better than them or anyone else. He was still the same Josh they knew, and he wanted to keep it that way.

Upon entering the restaurant, he saw them all immediately. Same group of miscreants that he remembered. There were some cheers, hugs, and handshakes all around. His old supervisor, some other coworkers, and a couple of security guards that Josh knew really well were at the table. They exchanged a few comments around how long it had been, how good Josh looked, and that he was truly missed at the library. They all figured out what to eat. The server then took their order and left them to their conversations. When the food arrived, they all started in and continued to talk and reminisce about people, places, and current events.

"It sure is good to see you again, Josh," said Pete, one of the security guards. "You was always really nice to us lower-class citizens," he said, laughing.

Josh gave Pete a shot to the arm. "You know that I never thought of you guys like that. I want to thank you for being nice to a kid from Wisconsin who didn't know anything about New York."

"Oh, and you do now?" laughed Joe, the other security guard.

Josh laughed. "Better than I did when I got here." He swallowed his current mouthful of food and took a drink. "In all seriousness though, all of you were really kind to me when I worked there, and I truly appreciate it."

"It's really good of you to take us to lunch, Josh," said his old supervisor. "I don't pretend to know how much money you're making, but something like this can't be cheap. It's a very nice gesture. Thank you."

"Yes. Hear, hear," came a lot of voices in agreement.

These folks appreciated the simple things in life, and that was what Josh missed the most.

"You guys used to go to lunch a lot back in the day. I'm sure this isn't any different. I'm just happy I can do something in return for all the kindness that you've shown me."

Josh took another bite. "I'm really sorry that I missed Sam. I was hoping he would have been on days by now."

The two guards shared a solemn look. The others got quiet. The supervisor looked like he was a little uncomfortable. Josh picked up the change in the mood quickly.

"What?" he said seriously. "What's going on with Sam?"

The supervisor looked at a few individuals before answering. "Josh . . . Sam's family is not doing too well right now. He's been having trouble with Max."

No! thought Josh. "What happened?" said Josh as more of a statement than a question.

Still feeling uncomfortable, the supervisor continued. "I'm not sure how much you know about Max, but he's always been a little sickly as a baby."

"I remember that he had a lot of colds," said Josh. *Please tell me that he's okay, that he's not . . .*

"Turns out that Max was always getting sick due to an underlying cause." The supervisor paused. Josh could tell that this was a very difficult subject for him. He needed to know more.

"What is the cause?"

"Max was diagnosed with leukemia," said Pete.

"About eight months ago," said Joe.

Josh sat there stunned for a second. He did not know. How would he? He left the job over three years earlier. He thought quickly and had a lot of questions. He did not believe they would know all the answers, so he started to pair them down to the more basic ones. "Where is Sam now?"

The supervisor looked at his watch. "He is probably working his shift at the docks."

"The docks? Doesn't he still work for the central branch?"

"Yes. He still works the night shift, but he needs the extra money for all the medical bills."

Joe chimed in. "He had been offered the promotion of the day shift just after he and Janet found out how sick Max was, but turned it down because he needed more money to cover the doctor expenses. The bump to days would only give him an extra fifty in his pocket. It wouldn't even scratch the surface of the bills." Joe lowered his head. "Library offered the position to me. I couldn't turn it down."

Pete put his hand on Joe's shoulder. "Don't beat yourself up about this again. You know Sam was glad that you got it."

"Anyway," said the supervisor, "Sam couldn't make ends meet by taking the day shift, so he continued to work nights—"

"And took another job during the day to supplement," finished Josh. He hung his head for a second and thought why such a good man who just tried to take care of and provide for his family was going through all of that.

"What about insurance? The library is run by the state and federally funded. Employees should have good insurance, especially if the condition is not preexisting," said Josh.

They all grumbled and shook their heads in disgust.

"Insurance for all the central branch employees was privatized over a year ago," said the supervisor. "Benefits were basically cut in half, and the rates went up. We all got hit pretty hard with that."

"Sam was hit the hardest. With the new insurance plan, he maxed out his allowed coverage three months into the treatments for Max," said Pete.

Josh's eyes widened at this news. How could he have let so much time pass before getting in touch with his friends? The bigger question was, how could he have not stayed in touch? Sam was one of the nicest people that Josh had ever met. He was the very first person at the central branch who made him feel welcome to New York City and always had a smile for him when he showed up for work. Sam was so proud of his son and of his accomplishments and achievements in school. The longer Josh thought about it, the more he hated himself for letting his friend down.

"So Sam has been paying all the additional expenses out of pocket?" asked Josh.

Pete and Joe nodded their heads, and the supervisor said, "Yes . . . what he can."

Josh thought for a second. "Do you know what hospital Max is being treated at?"

"I believe it is the Brookdale Hospital Medical Center on Lindon."

"Do you know if Max is currently admitted?"

Pete answered this one. "Yes, I talked to Sam a couple of days ago, and he said that Max was going in for another round of treatment. They usually hit him pretty bad, so they want to keep him over for a few days."

Josh made a mental note of the hospital. They all finished up their meals and had light conversation, but the tone and the mood had changed since Sam entered the topics. When lunchtime was over, everyone stood, smiled, and thanked Josh for lunch. The central branch employees filed out and left Josh behind. He paid the bill then exited the restaurant. Josh immediately pulled out his cell and made two calls. The first one was to bring the car around; the second was to Alice.

"I'm going to be a bit late getting back to the office. I need you to do something for me."

Josh explained what he wanted; she would get back to him as soon as she could. Upon entering the car, Josh told the driver to head to the Brookdale Hospital Medical Center.

As he arrived at the hospital, Josh entered and approached the information desk. He asked for Max Schulman's room. After she briefly looked through the computer, the volunteer stated that he was located in the cancer ward, pediatric hematology-oncology division. The volunteer pulled out a hospital map and highlighted a route and drew him a path directly to the cancer ward. Josh thanked him politely and headed through the marked corridor.

Josh found Max's room and slowed. He peered through the slender window embedded in the door. If Max were sleeping, or if someone were visiting him, Josh did not want to disturb. Max's mother, Janet, sat by his side, doing a crossword puzzle. Max looked like he was asleep. There were a couple of fluid bags attached to Max's arm intravenously. Josh figured that one of them had to be the chemo drug.

His eyes drifted back toward Max. The last time that he had seen Max, Sam, and Janet was at the library picnic about three years ago. Max was about eight then; Josh did the math in his head. He should be around ten or eleven now.

Max looked horrible. He remembered a young boy with olive-colored skin, a little on the chubby side, and full of energy. The boy he saw now was a pale comparison. His thick black hair was now cropped short and looked to be a little curlier. It was also a lighter color, a darkish brown. There was a noticeable difference in his weight as well. Max looked years beyond his actual age.

Cancer was an ugly beast that would do things like that to a person. Josh knew the effects that chemotherapy could have on the human body. He remembered the drastic changes in her appearance when he watched his mom suffer through both chemo and radiation. Memories of that horrible time in his life started coming back in waves. As with all the other bad memories around his mom's illness, he pushed those into the back of his mind and focused on now.

Josh tapped lightly on the door then opened it. As he approached Janet, he reintroduced himself and told her his connection with Sam. He explained that he had heard about Max's situation through some of Sam's coworkers earlier that day.

After he talked with Janet a bit, to find out about Max's current condition and status, he asked how she and Sam were holding up. There were tears on the rims of her eyes as she explained everything that had happened over the last year. Josh just sat there and listened. He figured this was cathartic for her, as she might not have anyone else with whom she could talk.

Josh told Janet how sorry he was this was happening; if there was anything she, Sam, or Max needed, to please not hesitate to let him know. He handed her a business card and asked if it were okay if he came by their home later that evening to see both her and Sam. She did not see a problem with that and even said she would make dinner. He did not want to put her out, but graciously accepted. It was about that time that his cell phone rang. He pulled it from his pocket and looked down. It was Alice.

He explained that the call was business and apologized, but he had to take it. Before picking up and speaking with Alice, he confirmed a time for him to arrive that evening then said good-bye. As he departed from the room, he then picked up the call. "Alice. What did you find out?"

She began filling him in on the research he requested regarding Sam's position at the central branch, Max's medical records, and the hospital expenses to date.

"Please call Langston's office and tell him that I need to speak to him once I return." He looked down at his watch. "I should be back in about forty-five minutes." A few more instructions were exchanged, and then he hung up.

Josh arrived at Sam and Janet Schulman's home on time. He was greeted warmly at the door by Sam with a great big bear hug; he was very happy to see his friend. Janet put out a nice spread of hors d'oeuvres, and then they sat in the family room and chatted for a bit. Inwardly, Josh felt bad because he knew Sam and Janet did not have the money for an extra mouth to feed, but he did not want to make things worse by insulting them and refusing her unselfish offer.

Sam and Janet had told Josh that their son had to spend one more night in the hospital before he could come home. They both apologized that Max could not be there to share the dinner with him. That broke Josh's heart.

They had a very delicious meal of beef stroganoff and a dessert of banana cream pie. Josh complemented the chef with a smile and then politely asked them how they were both really doing.

Sam played it off. "We're doing just fine. It's been a struggle with money here and there, but we are making both ends meet."

"Sam . . . I know that you are working a second job," said Josh.

He looked a little embarrassed. "Well, the money could be a little better at the library, but the part-time job down at the pier is helping."

"Pete and Joe told me the insurance changed at work. They said that your benefits were cut in half and your rates went up."

Sam's expression deepened a bit. He did not want to discuss his hardships outside of family. He knew Josh was not prying into his business, that he was only asking out of concern. It still did not make the subject any less painful. "I could deal with the fact that the insurance was changing companies. I even understood the rates, that usually comes with the territory. Even so, it was really hard when they denied existing benefits under the current plan."

Josh's brow furrowed. "I don't understand."

Sam leaned forward a bit. "Leukemia is a really hard form of cancer. Certain treatments are effective for some people, but not on others. The doctors had to try some different types until they found one that worked for Max." Sam looked as if he were about to cry. "His little body just couldn't handle some of the side effects." He paused.

"Some of Max's treatments cost more than others. The new insurance denied all but one type. It's the cheapest, and one of the hardest on him."

"That's why he has to stay in the hospital each time. The doctors want to monitor him to help get him through the initial dose of chemo," said Janet.

"Wait . . . The only treatment that the new insurance company will pay for is the cheapest one on the market?" asked Josh.

Both Janet and Sam were silent, but their expressions spoke volumes.

"So Max has to stay in the hospital longer due to the type of chemo administered. Does the insurance company cover the cost of the hospital stay?" he asked.

Sam shook his head. "No. That was one of the cuts. They will only pay if it is necessary like an operation or something, they called it a nonessential liability. Max is viewed as an outpatient case." He looked a little disillusioned now. "The doctors said it would be better for Max to be on a newer type of treatment plan, one that doesn't have nearly the side effects, but insurance won't cover it and we don't have that kind of money. Staying in the hospital for a few extra days is the more affordable option," he said with some shame.

"We're doing the best we can. I started teaching part-time down at the community center. It doesn't pay much, but every little bit helps," said Janet.

Josh frowned at the thought of her having to work. She should be with her son. He looked at Sam. "Do you have any health benefits with your part-time job at the pier?"

"Nah, they don't give mooks like me insurance for part-time work," said Sam as he tried to lighten the mood. "I'm just grateful for the pay that I do get to help out with . . ." Sam lowered his head.

Janet put her arm around her husband and patted him on the shoulder.

Josh made a mental note to check into this new insurance company. He leaned forward. "Sam, I would like to help."

He straightened up. "No, Josh. I'm not going to take money from a friend. I may not have much, but I do have my pride."

Josh grinned and shook his head. "Sam, I'm not here to offer you money . . . I'm here to offer you a job."

"What?" said Sam. Janet gasped.

Josh reached around to the satchel he had brought in with him and pulled out a manila folder. "A position has opened up in my company. It's much like what you do now at the library, a security gate attendant at the corporate headquarters of Jonah International. It will be the day shift, Monday through Friday. No weekends." Josh smiled as he handed the folder to Sam. He opened it up. There was an official offer letter attached to a bunch of other documents. "I believe you will be happy with the starting pay?"

Sam's eyes widened. "This is twice as much as I make at the central branch!" Janet put her hands to her mouth.

"Let's talk about the important stuff," said Josh. "As an employee of Jonah International, the health benefits package is second to none." He pointed to the papers in Sam's hand; he flipped to the section highlighted two or three pages into the offer.

"One hundred percent coverage, no co-pay, no preexisting conditions are exempt," said Josh.

Janet started to cry. "What does this mean?" asked Sam.

"It means, Sam, that Max will get the best health care coverage going forward without any out-of-pocket expenses from you or Janet."

Josh pulled an envelope out of his satchel. "What is in your hand is the offer of a job. What I have here is something that I want to give you personally."

He handed the envelope to Sam. "Whether you choose to accept the job offer or not has nothing to do with this," said Josh as he pointed to the envelope. Sam opened it. As he read the information, tears pooled up in his eyes as well. Janet asked, "What is it?" Sam could not speak. Janet looked toward Josh.

"All of Max's current medical expenses are paid in full," said Josh.

Janet started to openly weep and put her head in her hands.

Sam dropped the envelope and hugged Janet tightly. "Oh my lord!"

Josh remained silent. He did not want to ruin this moment for either one of them. When they separated, he continued. "Also included in that envelope is a letter of reference to one of the best cancer treatment hospitals in the country. Johns Hopkins Hospital, in Baltimore Maryland, is less than five hours away. As an employee of Jonah International, a housing expense for you and Janet to stay in Baltimore will be established. Whenever Max needs to go, and for however long he needs to stay, you and Janet will be with him the entire time."

Janet stood up and walked over to Josh, pulled him up from his seat, and gave him a warm and long hug. "Thank you!" she whispered softly. "You are truly a gift from God."

Josh was stunned to hear these words. In his mind, he wanted to help out a good family who was in need of his connections. Max did not deserve this disease, and the Schulman family did not deserve to suffer when Josh could do something about it.

After a few moments, when all the emotions had subsided and they had a chance to recover, everyone sat down and continued to talk.

Josh took the information and pointed to a card. "Call this number when you decide to accept the job"—smiled Josh—"and they will begin the process for hire. They understand your medical situation and needs. You will, of course, have all the necessary time off needed when Max is being treated."

He looked down at his watch then stood; Sam and Janet followed. "It's getting late. I need to let you folks get some sleep. You have a lot to think about." Josh grinned.

First, Janet gave him another big hug then Sam. His bear hug lifted him off the ground. He put him down and shook his hand. "I don't even know what to say . . . I can't express enough how grateful I am to you."

Josh was still bashful and had a hard time accepting compliments, but tried anyway. "Max doesn't deserve this, you're a good family. I'm just glad that I was in a position to help out a friend."

They said their final good-byes, and then Josh departed from their home as both Sam and Janet watched. His car was waiting right where he had left it.

The driver got out and opened his door for him. "Home, sir?"

"Yes, please." Josh smiled at tonight's events. In the car, he pulled out his cell phone and dialed Melina.

"Hey, you!" she said softly. "How did it go?"

"Wonderfully!" Josh said happily. "I can't begin to tell you how great it was helping people who deserve it. How was your night?"

"Lonely . . . but I'll survive," she said playfully. "Heading home?"

"Yeah . . . It's been a very exciting night. I'm not sure how much more I can take."

"Are you up for coffee?"

"You know I don't drink coffee," he said with a grin.

"Well, it's a good thing that I have other things to drink here."

"I'll see you in a few."

"Don't take too long. You've been keeping me waiting all night." She laughed then hung up.

Josh told the driver the new destination, and he acknowledged. As they turned the corner, the driver looked through the rearview mirror and smiled at him with sparkling blue eyes.

Morgan Blalock reviewed the morning stock market numbers from the comforts of his massive English manor in Southampton, New York. As with his office, his house was just as ostentatious. The decor was something out of late-nineteenth-century England. There were over thirty rooms with lavish and ornate furnishings, impeccably decorated by some of the best English designers whom Blalock could find. He only actually used around ten of the rooms. The rest were basically showpieces for entertaining. The exterior lawn, and the gardens behind, rounded out the decadence. The citizens of Southampton were not jazzed about this monstrous structure, as it did not fit the village motif or the historic New England guidelines that made the Hamptons a top attraction for notable celebrities or dignitaries. Nonetheless, Blalock used his considerable influence to secure a large section in the Hamptons to erect his mansion and circumvent any local laws prohibiting him from building what he wanted.

It was a beautiful morning, so he was drinking his tea on the veranda. His footman had just finished serving crumpets when his butler approached. "Sir, Mr. Pemberton is waiting for you in the library."

Pemberton, thought Morgan. *Who is he trying to kid?*

"Tell him that I'm still eating my breakfast, and I will be there momentarily."

"Begging your pardon, sir, but he was quite insistent," said the butler without moving.

Outwardly, Morgan very calmly folded the paper neatly and placed it next to his plate. He picked up the tea and took one more sip then retrieved the napkin from his lap and blotted the corners of his mouth with dignity. Inwardly, however, he was seething. How dare that *person* come into his house and demand an audience, not that Morgan ever had a choice in the matter. *He* showed up whenever *he* pleased. It was not like Morgan would have heard the door chime either because of the vastness of his manor. He had servants who took care of those types of things. If he *had* heard the door chime, what would he have done? Assumed that it would have been *him* and then tried to duck out the back or hide? Morgan's pride would have prevented either of those options under normal circumstances, but this visitor was different. He would have absolutely run away if given the chance.

Morgan caught himself in midthought. He knew that his visitor was anything but conventional. Coming through the door was not his style. That is what bothered him the most. The *thing*'s ability to come and go as it suited. Sometimes Morgan would be in his office at work, turn around, and there he was, as if appearing out of nowhere. It was a nice little parlor trick, one that Morgan would not readily admit, but scared him greatly every single time it happened. He knew that *it* was not aware of this or any other thoughts that he had though. Morgan had figured out a long time ago that for all the power he held, *it* could not read his thoughts. Morgan tested that theory numerous times during their encounters. There was never any retaliation toward the line of thinking. Morgan took great satisfaction in this discovery. His mind was free to roam in the disgust for everything that this *thing* represented. Morgan also wondered if that applied to *its* boss as well as the senior partners. He did not believe so, because if that were the case, they would have killed him a long time ago based on just his thoughts and intentions alone.

As soon as he was finished, Morgan looked at his houseman and waited for him to pull his seat out. Once the butler had performed his duty, he escorted Morgan through the house to the library. Upon entering, the butler closed the doors behind him as he left. There, sitting in Morgan's favorite chair, with his legs crossed and his hands folded in his lap waiting expectantly, was Pymm. Sharply dressed in a black pinstripe suit, which looked to be ridiculously expensive, he smiled upon Morgan's entrance and motioned for him to have the seat next to his. As much as he could, Morgan attempted to return the smile, but it was very difficult. He had absolutely no joy of speaking, or meeting with, this agent from the senior partnership. His distaste became more apparent every single time. His fear was that Pymm could now see that.

Morgan took his seat as *recommended* and waited for Pymm to speak.

"Good morning, Morgan," slithered Pymm. "How are you on this fine day?"

"As well as to be expected. To what do I owe the honor of your visit this morning?"

Pymm laughed. "Straight to the point. I like that," he mused.

"I realize that you are a very busy . . . person," said Morgan. "I do not wish to keep you from your daily activities any longer than necessary," he said politely.

A devilish grin spread across Pymm's face. "Well said."

Maintaining his perfect posture, Pymm continued. "I'm sure that you know my only objective is to ensure the success of the 216 operation."

"Of course."

"Good," Pymm said with a nod.

Ten to fifteen seconds passed in silence. They both just stared at each other. Each waited for something, but Morgan was unsure of what. Pymm was the one who barged into Morgan's manor without any invitation whatsoever. This was obviously his meeting, so Morgan just waited patiently and hoped he would state his business then leave. Pymm continued to stare Morgan down. Finally, Morgan said, "Is there more to that, or are you just merely confirming the obvious?"

"The success of this operation depends on absolute secrecy between you and your trusted advisor, Mr. Tindal."

Morgan cleared his throat. "I wouldn't necessarily classify Kelan as a trusted advisor—"

"It doesn't matter what you want to call him; nonetheless, you have brought him into the fold. Therefore, the trust is implied, wouldn't you agree?"

"I suppose so, yes. Is there something that you wish to inform me about?"

"Not directly, no. I want you to be clear on the collateral damage, should anything go awry with the operation."

Morgan cleared his throat again. "Nothing has gone astray from the plan in over three years. Why, you yourself have been directly involved. I am certain that you would have brought any deviation to my immediate attention."

"What I share with you is of my own choosing," stated Pymm matter-of-factly.

Morgan started to perspire under his suit. He hoped beyond everything that it was confined to his undergarments and was not visible to Pymm. As he stared at Morgan, the irises of his eyes began to turn a bright crimson. Morgan had a hard time containing his fear.

"I am assuming that you have started gathering your information for the next Artifact acquisition," said Pymm.

"Absolutely. I have already started Kelan on the initial research."

"We are aware. We had Familiars on-site that monitored the entire meeting that morning at Venue Delacruz."

The blood drained from Morgan's face. That seemed to please Pymm. He took great satisfaction in letting Morgan know that he had always been watched.

"Tell me, Morgan, how much do you trust Kelan?"

He eyed Pymm carefully. He was afraid that he might say something that was not true and get caught in the lie. He thought as fast as his old mind would allow and tried to come up with the most truthful answer possible.

"There were some insubordination issues in the beginning. Once we cleared up who was in command, Kelan has been on board ever since."

He watched Morgan for a brief moment, cocking his head from one side then to the next. "You didn't answer my question."

There was a longer pause.

"Yes. I trust Kelan," said Morgan finally.

"Very well. Understand that any actions he commits will be in your name. You will be held accountable."

Morgan cleared his throat for a third time. "I understand."

"Good." The bright crimson of Pymm's eyes turned back to a coal black. "There are two more Artifacts that need to be acquired," he said, getting back to business. He reached inside his jacket pocket and pulled out a small business card with neatly typed information regarding the specifics of each new Artifact. As he handed the card to Morgan between his first and middle finger, he noticed how long and sharp Pymm's fingernails were, almost, if not, like claws. This was yet another indication of what he was.

Pymm settled back into his chair. "The 216 operation is nearing closure."

This surprised Morgan. "Oh?"

"Yes," said Pymm as he looked down and brushed imaginary lint from the sleeve of his jacket. "Not that it is any of your concern, but events are now being set into motion, whereby 216 will no longer be of use to us."

"What are your plans?"

Pymm looked at him directly in the eyes. "As I stated, it is not any of your concern. You have your directives."

He stood and walked toward the library doors. To Morgan's surprise, the doors opened by themselves as he walked through and then closed. Morgan began to shake and shutter. He looked down at the small business card then closed his eyes as he tried to calm himself. He slumped into the chair, resting his head on the back. Hundreds of thoughts ran through his mind in that moment. The most prominent was how he got himself into this deal. It all started with the foundation of the company: Alastar-McGlocklin.

Over three hundred years ago, a Hungarian carpet merchant by the name of Johan Alastranosif lived and worked in what is now the town of Dornbirn, nestled in the state of Vorarlberg, Austria. He was the seventh of ten children from a very poor family, who struggled daily just to stay clothed and sheltered. He vowed when he was older, he would not live in such conditions. As he endeavored to survive, fate had thrown him into the path of someone with similar aspirations for material attainment, Vladimir McGlocktonstein. They were both very poor, but dared to dream of fortune and prosperity. Johan and Vladimir spent many nights discussing what they would do if they were wealthy men. Vladimir's specialty was as a land broker for a local nobleman. His detests for the nobleman was apparent in their conversations. According to him, the noblemen knew nothing of land value or how to maximize an opportunity for a deal. Vladimir was paid a pittance for what he believed the value of his skills were worth. He was tired of being the brains behind all the riches of the nobleman.

Johan and Vladimir would discuss plans and schemes for a better life, night after night. On one such night, they had this very discussion in a local pub when a stranger two tables away had overheard their conversation. A devilish smile spread across his face. He approached Johan and Vladimir and joined their discussion. He appealed to their egos for materialistic gains and completely agreed with all of their ideas and plans. He told them that he could help them achieve their dreams, for a small price.

The stranger weaved a tale of "what could be" and "you could have it all" with a little "you would not at any time be poor again" on the side. He topped it off with the pièce de résistance, "You will never have to work for anyone else ever again."

Sold.

As with most humans that hear of the chance to grab something of tangible worth, both Johan and Vladimir did not really listen to the cost of the proposed prosperity that the stranger offered. Worst of all, they did not understand it.

The stranger made Johan and Vladimir an offer that they could not possibly refuse. Both men were not very well-educated, but understood the value of a barter or a trade. When the stranger was finished, and their eyes stopped dancing in their heads, they asked what he wanted in return. The smile that rebounded was condescending, not that either of them would understand that either. The syrupy syllables that followed were like sweet music to their ears.

"Why, simply a small portion of your earnings and an occasional favor now and then," he said. "There are some other things that will pop up from time to time, but that is nothing to be concerned about now."

They were enthralled at the potential of making more than just ends meet. They truly believed that if they partnered with this stranger, they could have more wealth than they ever imagined before.

Power. Fortune.

They looked at each other in stunned silence, as if in some sort of trance. The stranger waited expectantly for their answer. As if telepathically connected, Johan and Vladimir nodded very slightly at each other. The stranger knew at once; he had them—mind, body, and most importantly, soul. There was, of course, one major formality.

"Well? What say you?" said the stranger.

Vladimir held out his hand. "Sir, you have yourself an accord."

The stranger looked toward Johan. "And you, my friend?"

Johan extended his hand too. "Yes, sir, I am in agreement as well."

The stranger almost leapt with delight. "Excellent!" He shook both Johan's and Vladimir's hands with vigor and excitement. "Now . . . There is a formality of a contract that must be signed by you both."

Both Johan and Vladimir bristled with anxiety, for they knew a contract meant an ironclad deal. They had the stranger right where they wanted him. Once this deal was signed, there was no possible way the stranger could get out of providing his end of the bargain.

Of course. the stranger knew better.

"Not a problem, my good man, just tell us where and when we should be to sign your contract," said Vladimir proudly.

"I happen to have the contracts with me now," said the stranger. With that, he produced two scrolls that looked very ancient, along with two individual quills and ink. He laid out the contracts on the table so they could see them, dipped the quills into the ink, and presented them both at the same time.

There is nothing more dangerous than an individual who thinks he is smart, but in actuality is not. A smart individual would have questioned why contracts were already created for a deal that had only now been struck. A smarter individual would have asked why the stipulations in the contract matched the very items that they had precisely discussed that night.

Alas, Johan and Vladimir still danced among the stars with the thoughts of prosperity, wealth, and power.

Both reached for a quill simultaneously. Something pricked their fingers within seconds. Blood from their hands dripped onto the individual contracts at the precise area where the signatures should have been.

The stranger immediately yanked them up from the table. "That will do."

He quickly rolled the contracts into a tight spiral and slipped them into individual protective sleeves.

"Congratulations, gentlemen," he said through a smile. "You will now have everything that you so richly deserve." He bowed courteously to Johan and Vladimir. "When you awaken tomorrow, your lives will be forever changed."

With that last comment, the stranger swiftly departed from the tavern. Upon exiting, he quickly moved around to the back, out of sight. If anyone had watched, they would have sworn that the man *floated*. A devilish grin spread across his face again. His eyes morphed into blackness the color of coal. In the blink of an eye, he vanished.

The very next day was the beginning of Johan's and Vladimir's new life. True to the stranger's word, events began to unfold that, at first, were very subtle, such as Johan's carpet business increased and Vladimir's ability to barter and trade land deals improved. After a few additional days of local business prosperity, they both came to realize that every business transaction they engaged in went in their favor. Over the course of the next few months, they had made more money than in the last two years of their earnings combined.

Money can change a person if allowed. The differences are quite diminutive in the beginning, but as time progresses and wealth and possessions increase, thought patterns would begin to alter. Johan and Vladimir were not immune to this effect. Their status in the community was on the rise. They were both becoming known as business entrepreneurs, but only in their field of expertise: a merchant for exquisite carpets and a land broker for the rich and royalty all over Austria. They now had the wealth that they were promised, but they wanted more. They continued to plan and scheme, even after all of their successful ventures. Thoughts riddled their minds of how they could acquire and control more. They had decided that since they were both successful as individual businessmen, they should combine their efforts to create something bigger, something that would leave its mark and let the world know they were there. From the birth of that decision came a two-person company, a team that would appear to be unstoppable. As with any company formation, they needed to have a mission objective, a service that they could provide that was in desperate need. Since they were not very smart, they pondered what to do night after night. As with the fateful night that their lives changed, they were in the exact same pub, scheming and planning, with no hope of coming up with a way on their own, to further expand their wealth.

As if by divine intervention, but in reality, far from it, the very same stranger entered the pub. He saw Johan and Vladimir and greeted them as if they had been lifelong companions and friends. All three laughed, drank, and talked about recent events. The stranger could see that Johan and Vladimir liked their new lives. He could also see that greed had started to become their deadliest and the most powerful sin.

He smiled. He had them right where he wanted them.

As with the first meeting, he crafted an extraordinary tale of how to expand their business beyond the borders of their small country, how to have people working directly for them. How to capitalize on the misfortune of others to improve their control and dominance.

Brokering deals, selling and acquiring, seemed to be what both Johan and Vladimir excelled in doing. The stranger convinced them that they could do that with anything, not just carpets and land. The stranger produced a list of regional and continental merchants and businessmen who were in need of financial assistance in one form or another, which could also help them with their quest for more worldly gains. He guaranteed that if Johan and Vladimir contacted those people to see how their services could be mutually beneficial, their wealth and possessions would double within the next year. The only requirement was that when they talked with these people, they provided the exact services requested; and once the deal was struck, Johan and Vladimir must seal the bargain with a signed contract. The contracts themselves would be provided by the stranger. He volunteered to take care of all the legality dealings for their new company at no additional cost, outside of the small percentage of earnings stipulated at the beginning of their *partnership.*

Johan and Vladimir readily agreed, once again thinking they had the best of the stranger. Had they been more religious in their lives, or at the very least superstitious, they might have seen the stranger's true purpose.

Time passed for both Johan and Vladimir. Months turned into years, and years turned into decades. As they grew older, so did their greed. The ways of a noble businessman fell to the side in their pursuits and conquests for more. They no longer played by the standard rules or etiquette for barter and trade. They did what they had to in order to gain what they wanted. In their minds, the ends justified the means. They saw no harm when it came to the practical or legal matters of fulfilling a deal. If a loan was defaulted upon or goods were not delivered as promised, per the terms of the contract, their collection tactics were swift and very hard.

Their company was so vast that it stretched over the entire Eastern European region. Before corporations were even in existence, Alastar-McGlocklin dominated the business world, specializing in mergers and acquisitions, with a large emphasis on acquiring. Of the many areas within their company, the stranger had the most interest in Contracts. He requested that Johan and Vladimir allow him to select and place his own team to handle all the contracts for company, people who were completely loyal to the stranger and did whatever they were told.

He called them Familiars.

It was odd that every time through the decades that Johan and Vladimir had met him, the stranger did not seem to age. In fact, he looked exactly the same as the first day of their encounter.

Over the years, they had kept their end of the bargain and paid him a small percentage of their earnings. As sizable as the company had become over time, that *small percentage* eventually turned into a very large sum of money.

During that time, the *favors* were also honored. They varied in range between the hiring or placement of certain individuals to finding and acquiring objects. The stranger referred to these objects as Artifacts. Neither Johan nor Vladimir really understood their importance or why they were so special to their silent partner. The ones that they found did not provide substantial value of any sort that they could see. Some of them made no sense at all. One such item was an old stained cloth. If one looked closely and possessed a working knowledge of religious culture, it may have resembled some sort of deity or something. They really did not have a clue, as religion was not one of their primary concerns or pursuits. The cloth served absolutely no purpose in their eyes. It could not be used for anything practical. The material substance that made up the cloth could not even, technically, be classified as garment-worthy. It was very thick, much like a cross between burlap and wool. Not wearable or usable at all in their minds. Nonetheless, they did as they were requested and fulfilled each and every one of the favors.

As the years rolled by, Johan and Vladimir became older and wealthier. They continued to manage the company, which by now had stretched across to the brand-new world as it existed during that time. The Americas were fast becoming the modern land of prosperity. It was obviously a market that Johan and Vladimir wanted to tap, but were now too feeble to handle. The stranger had met with both, one last time, and made them one more offer to assist in the expansion of Alastar-McGlocklin to the new world. In exchange, he asked that he be the one to name the successor to their company, after they both depart from this life. His reasoning was that he was in a better position to recognize the proper qualifications to continue the successful evolution of the company. After all, they would not live forever.

They were correct; the stranger did not age one day. In all their years alive and together as partners, they never once really considered what that meant, never questioned the stranger about the irregularity of occurrences involving him. They trusted him throughout all the business opportunities and decisions. In hindsight, his lack of aging should have been in the front of all the questions never asked. It was too late for any of that.

Johan and Vladimir pondered the stranger's request for a few days and, when he returned, gave him their answer. They both agreed to his terms, but wanted to know how this transaction would benefit them so late in their lives. The stranger smoothly said that they would be forever known all over the world for their shrewd and unmatched business sense and also as the most famous and powerful duo that had ever lived. Thousands of people will someday work under the name of Alastar-McGlocklin. Their legend would live on forever.

Immortalized.

Forever.

They did everything that they set out to accomplish. Now it was time to enjoy the fruits of their labor and let their trusted friend continue forward. The stranger produced two contracts. With no issues from the quills, they signed them without even reading the fine print.

That single event sealed their fates forever.

Just like before, after they were signed, a very evil smile crossed the stranger's face. Instead of yanking the new contracts aside, he looked at both Johan and Vladimir and briefly reflected on their pitiful existence in this life. They gave up everything for material possessions and money. They never experienced love; neither the sensation of giving nor receiving. Neither of them knew what it was like to be generous nor appreciated. They would never know admiration from colleagues or, for that matter, anyone else. Not one person in all the years that they have been doing business respected them, for they were ruthless in all of their dealings. They had signed away their souls, and they were completely unaware.

Johan and Vladimir were utterly alone in this world.

The total value of their self-worth was wrapped up in one specific task, acquiring as much as they could. That mission had been accomplished. Their obligation to the contracts presented by the stranger was now fulfilled.

He picked up the soul-sealing contracts and looked at them. Satisfied that the signatures were now complete, he rolled them up and placed them in his satchel. "Gentlemen, I cannot say that it has been a pleasure over these last five decades doing business with you, but I would like to convey my appreciation for your services to our cause."

Both Johan and Vladimir had a puzzled look. "I'm not sure that I fully understand?" said Johan.

The stranger looked bored and began to brush imaginary lent from his jacket sleeve. "No . . . I don't imagine that you do. Your services are no longer required."

With that, the stranger turned and walked toward the door, leaving them both for the last time.

Johan Alastar became ill within the next week. He had displayed symptoms of smallpox soon after, dying within three weeks. Vladimir McGlocklin, fearing that the raging epidemic surrounding them would make him sick as well, journeyed to the Spanish countryside in hopes of finding safety in the seclusion from diseased-infested people. During his travel there, he came into contact with a baggage steward, who appeared to have a cold. Within four weeks of that contact, Vladimir died of the Spanish influenza.

The ageless stranger already began the proceedings for appointment of the next head for Alastar-McGlocklin in anticipation of Johan's and Vladimir's demise. There were some prime candidates who would gladly do the bidding of the stranger and his partnership, in exchange for the material wealth and control that Alastar-McGlocklin offered. As time rolled by, the proceedings for the changing of the helm stayed the same. When each CEO had fulfilled their contractual obligation, they were *retired*, making way for the next occupant. Each successor knew not what happened to their predecessor, only that they had moved on and were living a lavish lifestyle, or so they were told. The same held true for Morgan Blalock.

Morgan was approached some twenty years ago with the same deal as the other former leaders of Alastar-McGlocklin—money, power, and control in exchange for a percentage of the earnings and some *favors*. Over the course of three hundred years though, certain individuals such as the stranger began to dictate the direction of the company and its holdings. They were never seen and rarely heard from, but everyone at the executive level was very aware of the influence they possessed. They eventually became known as the senior partners.

The Chief Executive Officer role was merely perfunctory. The senior partners made most, if not all the decisions. Their CEO acted as their puppet.

Morgan sat there, slumped against the back of the chair. The conundrum of his situation became all-consuming. He had asked himself many times over the years whether the price was worth it. After careful deliberation, every single time, the conclusion was always the same. He would never go back to manage a general store in Utica, Illinois. That type of life was always beneath him. He was better than that, he knew it, and so did the senior partners at Alastar-McGlocklin. Besides, he knew that it was too late to go back. He made the deal when offered, and he signed the contract. Contracts were binding when it came to dealing with the senior partnership.

Or not, thought Morgan foolishly.

He had worked a lot different angles and activities to secure a more independent position within the company. The senior partnership and their little agents could not read his thoughts, and he believed that was one of his biggest advantages. Because he was not aware of which people were Familiars within, or for that matter, outside Alastar-McGlocklin, he had to be very careful of his movements so as not to draw any unwanted attention.

The day is coming soon when he will make his move and disappear. Everything must be in place.

Chapter 13

Selflessness and Surprises

Her shift at Kenosha Memorial ended thirty minutes ago, but Amanda had stayed on a little later to finish up paperwork and to finalize the shift roster. It was not uncommon for her to stay after to transition to the next shift, but she was visiting Julie today. She hoped that she could get this done quickly enough to get at the burn center in time to have dinner with her.

Twenty minutes later, she was on her way to the University of Wisconsin Hospital and Clinics Burn Center in Madison. Julie was in long-term patient care for the last couple of months.

After the run-in with Smithers, Kenosha Memorial's Hospital administrator, he permitted her to stay for fifteen days posttrauma, allowing time for Julie to be stabilized and to find a long-term care facility to treat her severe burns. Julie's situation was unique because of the extensive damage during the explosion. The issue of her care and treatment came down to money.

The primary insurance carrier at the plant defaulted on all claims. After further investigation, it was discovered that Moncrief Furniture Alliance had been bought out by an undisclosed corporation five months prior to the explosion. During the transition of ownership, Halifax Medco, the company that covered the insurance, was terminated and released from its contractual obligations.

Under standard federal law, secondary coverage should have been provided under the Acquisitions and Mergers Act by the new ownership within fifteen days of termination of the primary. This applied to companies that were qualified under the act's coverage laws. That never happened due to the type of acquisition.

The new ownership had plans to dissolve and liquidate the assets of Moncrief for redevelopment of the land, with no plans for future manufacturing. There was a legal challenge to the claim between the town and the company, pertaining to the livelihood of the current employees and what that would do to the township. An injunction was filed to stop the acquisition proceedings just ten days after the primary insurance contract was terminated. Due to the red tape of legal claims, filed petitions, judicial inquiries, and depositions, the secondary insurance to replace Halifax Medco was never activated. The attorneys for both sides missed that little detail during the back-and-forth barrage of legal suits. Nothing was in place to prevent any gap of coverage.

Moncrief's employees had no idea that their insurance was gone. For that fact, they had no idea that they were about to lose all of their jobs. The explosion accelerated the awareness of both. Moncrief was the main employer for most of the townsfolks, and this horrible accident was the worst thing that could have happened for the people and the town. The plant was all but destroyed. The remaining employees were forced to go on unemployment or find other work outside the town of Somers.

Of all the survivors, Julie was hurt the worst. After her vital signs had improved and became stable, some of the staff at Kenosha Memorial's Emergency Medical Trauma Unit had taken it upon themselves to give her a little extra attention throughout her stay. Amanda continued to keep up with Julie's progress since the accident. The UW Burn Center in Madison, Wisconsin, was one of the best in the state and had offered considerations for patients in Julie's situation. Funding for special needs' cases such as hers were provided to offset the cost of the treatment and rehabilitation within a reasonable period of time. Julie was moved there after her fifteen-day stint at Kenosha Memorial.

Amanda had developed a friendship with this young woman, and it appeared to be beneficial to both. Julie always looked forward to her visits.

She arrived just in time for dinner. As always, Julie was very happy to see her. After their meal, they sat and chatted a bit. As Julie's friend, Amanda was interested in how she felt, but the nurse inside of her always probed.

In the last couple of months, Amanda developed a pleasant relationship with the burn center's nursing staff. After leaving from a visit, she would stop by and talk with them. The scars started to heal, but Julie would require extensive surgery if she wanted any semblance of a normal life. As with everything, it was always about money. There was never enough to give her the full care needed, and the hospital could just do so much. There was no insurance to count on; her only living relative was her uncle, and he could not do anything to help. The UW funding allowances were depleted for Julie's case. Her bills were mounting, and she still had a long way to go.

Throughout the entire ordeal, Julie's spirits remained high. If she sank into some type of depression, she never showed it. The staff confirmed that Julie was always in a cheerful mood, no matter how she felt. She would volunteer as much as possible by working with other burn patients, showing them the ropes. Though there were times when Julie's pain kept her confined to her bed, she still managed to remain positive.

That broke Amanda's heart. Julie was such a decent and vibrant young woman. She had so much to offer the world, and yet this happened to her. As a nurse, Amanda regularly questioned why bad things happen to good people. It was always an age-old dilemma, and no one ever had a valid answer. Decent people did not deserve anything like what Julie was going through.

The next day, after Amanda's shift, she decided to give her boys a call. She tried Harry first, hoping that he would pick up this time. She was disappointed to go into voicemail yet again. She left a cheerful message telling him how much she missed and loved him and that she hoped to hear from him soon. She immediately dialed Josh after and was rewarded with a live voice after the third ring.

"Hi, Amanda!" said Josh.

She smiled into the phone. "Hi, sweetie! I hope that I'm not disturbing you."

"I don't believe that could be possible," he said playfully.

Harry, Josh, and Amanda had made a deal when they left Wisconsin. They were to try at the very least to communicate once a week. It did not have to be by voice; it could be by e-mail or a simple text message. Amanda did not care; she just wanted to stay in touch with her boys, but also give them the freedom to live their lives. She did not want to be overbearing, but the mother in her still needed to be connected in some way. The arrangement worked out very well in the beginning. Both Harry and Josh would find time here and there to drop a line, one way or another. Embracing the latest technology, sometimes it was an e-mail after work; others were a simple text message on a subway. Amanda's schedule varied as well, so she followed the same patterns.

Both were faithful to their promise; sometimes they even did it together. As time moved along, Harry's and Josh's careers started taking off, and Amanda tried to adjust her expectations as she realized both boys were getting older and beginning their new lives. Of late though, she had seen some distance between contacts, especially from Harry. She had been pushed to his voicemail more and more lately. He never returned any of her e-mails or text messages either. Josh was still pretty good about taking and returning her calls. She was not really surprised when he picked up.

They exchanged standard pleasantries, how great it was to hear from each other, Josh's new job, and Melina's return. Amanda was very pleased to see that Josh had found someone special. He had earned the right to be happy after everything that had happened in his life. Then the subject of Harry came up.

"I can't seem to contact Harry. I know that both of you have busy corporate schedules, but when you see him, can you please tell him to return his mother's calls?" she said half amusingly.

Josh cleared his throat. "I wish that I could, Amanda," he said with a hint of sadness in his voice. "But Harry and I aren't speaking right now."

Amanda's voice changed. "What's going on? What happened?"

Josh did not want to go through this again. It was not a shock to him that Amanda did not know about their disagreement, if it could be classified as that. Harry had always been bad about contacting his mom anyway. Josh would push and nag him each week to make time to call. The nagging obviously decreased the less time they spent together. He wondered if Kate had ever encouraged him to contact his mother.

Josh started out with the highlights of the events that led up to the split. He told her that he had not seen or talked to Harry in months. Amanda, concerned about both boys, pushed for more details.

Josh opened up the gates and let everything out. "He lied to me, Amanda. How am I supposed to handle that?"

She could feel his pain. "Honey . . . Did you give him a chance to explain why he lied?"

Josh was surprised. "What?"

"I'm not excusing what he did, please don't misunderstand, but did you stop to think that maybe he had a good reason?"

"How could there ever be a good reason to lie? We have never done that to each other. Harry and I are closer than two brothers could ever be. To be quite honest, that is what did it for me."

"What?"

She could not see it, but Josh looked down at the floor. Every time he thought about the comment that Harry made, the explosion of hurt washed over him in an instant. As with everything else that was a challenge in his life, he pushed the pain to the back.

"Harry told me in the heat of his anger that we were not brothers," said Josh softly.

"Oh, Josh, I am so sorry that he hurt you that way."

There was silence on the phone for a few seconds as Amanda tried to piece together a response out of all the information. A thought popped into her head.

"Do you think that this girl, Kate, had anything to do with the trouble between you and Harry?"

"I think she had everything to do with it," stated Josh emphatically.

He told her about the sequence of events and Kate's involvement in everything regarding his and Harry's relationship.

"She is a bad influence on him, Amanda. I could sense it from the beginning. How was I supposed to tell my best friend that?"

"Honey, I am sorry. I wish I had a good answer for you," she said sympathetically. "As much as it pains a mother to say this, he is a big boy and must make his own decisions. If this is the woman whom he chooses to be with, then who are we to say any differently? I do know this, you boys have been through a lot together. You have been best friends most of your lives. I'm sure that if you both sit down and talk this out, you will get through it."

"Well . . . I hope that you are right. Someday, I would like to get past this. For right now, the feelings are still too raw."

Putting closure on that topic, Josh asked her how everything was going at work. Amanda talked about the general misfortunes of the daily grind at the hospital and the good parts that were too few and far between. Her tone changed a bit when she brought up Julie. Josh asked for more specifics on what had happened. Amanda detailed the unfortunate circumstances that brought her and Julie together.

"How many fatalities were there?" asked Josh.

"Five, including two firefighters," she said.

"And Julie is still at the UW Burn Center?"

"Yes, but we're not sure for how much longer."

"Funding issues?" Josh said knowingly.

"Isn't it always?"

"Has anyone formally requested relief aid?"

"I don't understand," asked Amanda, interested.

Josh explained that under tragic circumstances such as, but not limited to, natural disasters, domestic relief can be provided to assist in the reconstruction of damaged property as well as the medical expenses of those injured through no fault of their own. He thought that Julie would have a good business case based on her circumstances of the plant explosion.

"Do you think something like that would work?" Amanda said hopefully and excited.

"I don't see why not. I used to do this very same thing on an international level. Tell you what . . . I'm going to send you an e-mail with all the information to request aid. There are going to be some forms that Julie will need to fill out. While she's doing that, I will start the relief packet for processing the aid on my end. I have a very good relationship with the Division Lead for Domestic Relief at Jonah. I think we can get this fast-tracked," said Josh confidently.

They both talked about a few more things before saying their good-byes. Amanda continued to thank Josh for his help. She was so proud of the work he was doing. His mother would be too, if she were there. Amanda was the closest thing to a mother he had now. It warmed his heart to know that she cared for him, just like his mom would have. After Josh had hung up, he was thoughtful about this new project. He needed yet another distraction from the problem with Harry. First thing in the morning, he would start to do some digging on this new company. It was yet again another example of how big corporations can hurt little people.

He wanted answers, and now he was in a position to get them.

Kelan was in his office at the Long Beach facility reviewing a few of the open mission's parameters that were currently in an active condition. It was a standard procedure as the DCO to ensure that status was current and all operational requests passed his approval. As he reviewed, he also multitasked on additional agenda items, both requested and personal.

The secret Artifact mission assigned by Blalock proceeded as planned. Kelan managed to find the funding needed to adequately back the additional research and assemble an extraction team. The problem was, he could not use anyone within the RCT. Kelan was pretty sure that Blalock understood the difficulty in classifying this particular extraction as a black op. Nonetheless, the instructions were implicitly clear. Kelan would have to find another way. Interestingly enough, he had never headed a mission where diplomacy was the first consideration for acquiring an Artifact. An outright legal acquisition, which by definition was what Alastar-McGlocklin was publicly known for, was not Morgan Blalock's style. He preferred taking what he wanted rather than negotiating.

Kelan explored different options in the *taking* category, such as mercenaries. They could be depended upon, if the price were right, but there were all sorts of other classified considerations when using them. They would complete the mission, provided enough information was given, but their loyalty would only go as far as the highest bidder. They could not be controlled after the mission was finished; therefore, secrecy and discretion would be a higher risk. He added this topic to the list of things that he was going to discuss with Blalock for the 2:30 pm meeting today. As he continued to review, he jotted notes down into his tablet for both the sanctioned and unsanctioned missions.

There was an application on his tablet that allowed him to keep other information of a more *personal* nature. He made sure that tablet was not on any of the network servers. He also ensured that there was no wireless connectivity that it could access. For all intent purposes, it was a stand-alone unit. The only way to see any information on it while he was at Long Beach was to access the tablet directly, and it was never out of Kelan's hands. Since the discovery of Blalock's secret agenda, Kelan severed all the direct network connections to Alastar-McGlocklin's central servers and data banks. Now, during working hours, he downloaded data needed directly to his tablet using a flash drive. Any additional Intel beyond that was fat-fingered in. Once he returned to his panic room, it was a simple task of jacking in his tablet and uploading the new information.

The supercomputer nestled into the panic room continued to seek and retrieve information based on Kelan's data inputs and modified algorithms. Each time that he discovered something new, he changed the search parameters to expand or narrow the focus. The objective was always the same: secure his position within Alastar-McGlocklin and bring down Morgan Blalock.

There was a knock at the door.

As per protocol, Kelan locked his computer with a password. He also saved and closed the most recent information entered on his tablet and then placed it in his top desk drawer.

"In," stated Kelan.

The door swung open; it was Stanley McManus, the missions' auditor. "Hey, Chief, got a minute?"

"Sure, Stanley, come on in."

He entered, closing the door behind him. He carried his portable notebook and sat down in the chair in front of Kelan's desk. "I was running numbers for our active missions and came across a few discrepancies. I was hoping to discuss with you before I filed a report."

Kelan tried not to outwardly panic. "What kind of discrepancies?"

"Well . . . ," said Stanley, scratching the back of his head. "Per my standard process, I run bimonthly audits on each of the active operations to account for total expenditures against the allotted budget for each. As you are aware, any expenses that goes above and beyond that have to be approved by you."

Kelan's brow furrowed for a moment. "I don't remember signing off on any extra expenses recently."

Stanley was quick to catch the direction of Kelan's thought. "Oh no, that's not what I'm saying at all. The books for each mission match the expenses to the penny."

He stared at Stanley expectantly, making him feel like he was wasting Kelan's time. "Then what seems to be the problem?"

Stanley started to feel uncomfortable. "It looks like the budgeted amounts for some of the missions have been changed."

"Changed, as in how?"

"They've been lowered."

Kelan tensed a bit. "I'm afraid that I'm not following you."

"Record logs indicate that no changes have been entered since the last operational meeting a week and a half ago. Whenever we have the monthly meeting, I run an ad-hoc audit to capture any incremental changes between the bimonthly audit cycles to ensure I have the most recent reconciliation available." He paused. "The numbers have changed."

Stanley leaned forward, opened his notebook, and faced the monitor toward Kelan. "Out of the nine active missions that we are currently operating, five of those missions have had their budget numbers altered."

Kelan looked at the screen with great concern. Stanley turned his notebook around and punched in a few keys to bring up another screen then turned it back toward Kelan.

"Upon noticing that the budgets were different than my previous report, I did some further digging and found that the expenses matched each of the five operations' budgets completely. I ran a comparative analysis between the last report and today's and found the overall discrepancy between the five altered missions' budgets to be around $2.3 million. Further research confirmed that the sanctioned budgets were approved and funded appropriately. That means that the money was already allocated and in each operation's respective accounts."

Kelan sat straight up in his chair. "Just to be clear, you are telling me that we are missing a total of $2.3 million from our overall operational budget for our current active missions, is this accurate?"

Stanley leaned back. "Bottom line . . . someone went to a lot of trouble to ensure that the accounting was correct and siphoned off the 2.3 million."

Concerned creased Stanley's face. "Boss, someone is skimming from this division's assets."

"Have you discussed this with anyone else?"

"No, sir. You are the first person that I have talked to."

"Good. Please send me all of your findings. I have a meeting with the CEO this afternoon and will bring this matter up."

Kelan stood up from his desk, indicating this discussion was now over. "Stanley, I need you to be very discreet about this. If someone is taking our assets, we need to determine why and to what end. I will definitely be looking into this one personally. Thank you for bringing this to my attention. I'll let you know what I find out."

With that, Stanley acknowledged his instructions and left.

Kelan waited until the door closed behind him, reached for the secure remote on his desk, and hit the lock. Once he heard the click, he sat down roughly in his chair, leaned back, and began rubbing his forehead. Fearing someone passing by might see he was unsettled, he grayed out his office windows as well then tossed the remote on his desk in frustration. Kelan began shaking his head back and forth in disappointment. He wondered how he could have gotten careless, so sloppy in his process to reallocate the funds. His mind started racing to understand another part of Stanley's discovery: how it totaled to 2.3 million. Kelan's original estimate only came to 1.7 and was not spread over five accounts. Something else was going on here, and he had a feeling it might be linked to Blalock's activities. He would begin checking his theory once he received Stanley's data.

He could not fault Stanley for finding this. That is, after all, why Kelan hired him. It was not so much he was worried the trail would lead back to him, but the fact he thought this was a foolproof exercise into account shifting. He would clearly be mistaken to believe he was the smartest person at Long Beach, but at the very least, thought he covered his tracks well enough to slide past any type of real analysis.

Kelan reached into his desk to retrieve his tablet and opened the programs back up on his computer. He would have to step up his game going forward to ensure that all possible contingencies for surveillance on him would be considered. One thing this job has taught him very well, was no one was above reproach, not even himself.

He arrived thirty minutes before his scheduled time with Blalock. He had some nonessential tasks to take care of under his official Alastar-McGlocklin moniker of Vice President of International Technology Development. Even though a majority, if not all, of the important work was done as the DCO, he still had to keep up appearances as far as the stockholders and the board of directors were concerned. He found it fascinating that the board had no idea of his real purpose. He attended the normal corporate functions, as a matter of social convention, but never once discussed any of the clandestine operations that he has performed over the years. The true nature of Kelan's role has obviously been kept secret from the board. To no one's surprise inside the circle, only Blalock, the senior partners, and he knew the truth, or so he thought.

He went through the normal office motions of reviewing messages and e-mails for his pseudo-role when he came across the annual invitation for the Global Innovations of Technology Conference. The information packet came with a three-day agenda and a listing of the major technological players of today. Among those who would be in attendance was Jonah International. They were involved with the GIT for many years in one capacity or another, but this year, they were listed as keynote presenters, and their topic was biometric imprinting. Kelan was very intrigued. He picked up his phone and called his assistant to register him for attendance and book the travel. Of course, it went without saying that he wanted the optimum tier package for the three-day event. In his mind, that would ensure the best possibility of having an all-access executive package, plus it would look good to anyone from the outside. Perception was, and always will be, an important part of his corporate position. Kelan looked at his watch at about the same time a calendar reminder went off on his PDA. *Time to go,* he thought.

He smiled at Betty as he approached Blalock's office. "Good afternoon, Betty." Their relationship had gotten closer over the years, mostly, due to the respect he had for her as a person with conviction and beliefs. She did not push her religion on him when they talk about things, but he could see that it had a very positive influence on her attitude and outlook on life. With all his power and wealth, that was still one area in which he struggled. Sometimes, when he needed an espresso shot of positive affirmations, he dropped by to chat with Betty.

A smile broke out across Betty's face. "Hello, Mr. Tindal! How are you today?"

"I'm doing very well. Thank you for asking." He nodded toward the double doors. "I've got a two thirty with the boss."

"He's expecting you."

"Thanks, Betty. We'll chat soon," he said with a smile as he continued to walk toward the doors.

There was no longer any intimidation, or what could be considered a strained relationship, between him and Blalock. Each had their own understanding of how the working relationship moved forward as employer and employee. Kelan said and did what he needed to maintain the freedom of his position. As long as he delivered results, he could write his own ticket. Blalock had a massive ego, and Kelan tried to validate it as much as possible. The old adage of attracting more flies with honey rather than vinegar was one of the main cornerstones of their *partnership*. Blalock like to be worshiped as a corporate god, so Kelan obliged, reaping his own benefits in return.

As a testament to the informality of their arrangement, Kelan knocked twice as he opened the door, that never would have happened in the old days. Blalock was engrossed in something at his desk when Kelan entered.

"Morgan, good afternoon!"

"Kelan, my boy . . . how are you on this fine day?"

"I'm doing very well, thank you for asking."

Morgan gestured to the conference table. "We can review the open missions' statuses in a few moments. I have some things that I must tie up here first."

He was completely agreeable with whatever Morgan said. "Of course. I have the files prepared for your review when you are ready."

Kelan had a number of folders for each one of the open missions. Contained inside were printed copies of operational milestones, mission timelines, and financial expenditure statements. Blalock was never much of a technical aficionado and preferred paper copies for reviewing over pie charts and bar graphs on an electronic monitor. In fact, numbers plainly entered into a spreadsheet format without all the flash and glam of color and graphics was exactly how Morgan liked his updates. For all of the years Kelan had known him, Blalock still did not have a computer in his office. As with his dependencies for everything else in his business world, Blalock had Betty. Anything that could not readily be pushed out by using paper was taken care of by her. She was the technical wizard behind the curtain to his Oz.

Blalock seemed pretty engrossed in what he worked on. Kelan looked in his direction a few times and wondered what held his attention. He checked his watch and noticed that five minutes had passed and started to get a little frustrated. Not only was this wasting his time, but now curiosity over the files that Blalock studied had slowly become an obsession. Kelan had to give props where they were due though by using paper for almost everything, some of Blalock's old-school habits prevented him from using electronic measures to spy on his activities directly. This, in turn, made gathering evidence and dirt a little slower, but not impossible. That did not matter in the long run, or affect Kelan's agenda. He would continue with his plan to bring Blalock down.

Motion in the boss's direction indicated that he was finishing whatever it was he was doing. Blalock made a notation in the current file, closed it, and stacked all the files neatly at the side of his desk. As he made his way over to the conference table, Kelan looked in the direction of those files and wondered if it would be worth the trouble to develop a plan to copy them. He was sure that the hard copies within those folders came from something that Betty had printed and, at the very least, would have knowledge from where they originated. To print them, she would have soft copies, easy enough to find and duplicate. The only problem with that idea was getting her involved. This battle for power was between him and Blalock. Betty would be collateral damage if she was found out, and that was something that Kelan would have a hard time dealing with, given the discovery of what happened to Blalock's last assistant, Julianne.

No. This was something that he had to do on his own. As self-absorbed and greedy as he was, Kelan had personal limits as to what he would do for money and power, and hurting or killing people crossed a line.

Morgan took a seat at the head of the table. Displayed in front of him was an array of active mission files with the updates highlighted. As per standard protocol, Kelan covered the financial expenditures and the statuses of each. When the overall operational briefing had completed, all new business items could be discussed. As Kelan assembled the loose briefing papers, he was the first to bring up said items.

"Morgan, there are a couple of things that have come up, and I would like to get your input."

Morgan sat back a little with a genuine curiosity. "Yes? Go on."

Morgan, of course, had his own topics, so allowing Kelan to go first was completely out of character for the CEO. Things had changed over time between them. Once, where Morgan would have insisted on interrupting and covering his agenda from the start, he was now more noncomplacent and appeared thoughtful and respectful of Kelan's ideas. The DCO practically fell out of his seat when Morgan allowed him to speak first on one such occasion, but had since grown bold enough to put his items on the table first, given the ever-changing nature of their working relationship. Morgan no longer appeared to be the hostile, dictatorial tyrant who had to have things his way no matter whether he was right or wrong. Appearance or not, Kelan knew better. The stripes on a predatory tiger cannot be changed.

"The Global Innovations of Technology Conference will be held in San Diego in a couple of months. I have booked an executive package to attend, but plan on being there for the entire week," said Kelan.

"How many days is the conference?" asked Blalock.

"The same as last year . . . three days, but I was hoping to get in a little R&R while I was there. I haven't taken a vacation in the last two years. I figured a couple of extra days wouldn't matter much."

"I don't see a problem with that. Is there a particular reason that you want to attend this year?"

"Actually yes, Jonah International will be a keynote," said Kelan, waiting to see his reaction.

Blalock had looked like he was half-listening up to that point, but when Kelan had mentioned Jonah, his eyebrows raised and his eyes shot up to meet Kelan's.

"They are presenting biometric imprinting. It couldn't hurt to gather a little additional intelligence on their technology," said Kelan with a smile.

Blalock returned his grin. "Not a bad idea, my boy. If they're going to be foolish enough to publicly share some of their security secrets, why not exploit the exposure to find a flaw or a weakness."

Still smiling, Kelan said, "My thoughts exactly!"

He was pleased to see that Blalock had drawn his own conclusions as to why Kelan wanted to attend, although, he could not have been further from the truth.

It was time to see if he could make Blalock sweat and tip his hand, so he approached his second item. He shuffled a bit in his seat and changed his expression to one of concern. "Morgan, it was brought to my attention by one of my auditors that we seem to have funds missing from some of the accounts."

He waited for Blalock to reply, while watching his body language. Morgan did not make a move, but to only look Kelan in the eyes. He seemed to be processing the statement in preparation for his next question.

After Stanley had brought up the missing money, Kelan had thought of how to approach Morgan, or if he should say anything at all. At least half of the funds from those accounts were siphoned by Kelan himself, so if Morgan questioned him on the amounts, he could simply say that he had reapportioned certain funding to cover the cost of the black op mission. Morgan might give himself away if he reacted to the difference.

His eyes finally diverted from Kelan's and looked down to the table. A split second later, their eyes met again. "Do you have an exact amount of the missing funds?"

Here we go.

As he opened one of his folders, Kelan pretended to search for the number as if he did not have it off the top of his head. His eyes moved through the sheets looking for nothing in particular. After a few seconds, he picked a random sheet that meant diddly to the topic and used his finger to trace a few lines.

"Yes, here it is . . . $2.3 million," he said.

Blalock's eyes widened a bit but not as much as Kelan hoped. "Are you sure that is the number, 2.3 million?"

"Yes," said Kelan, picking up the sheet to hand it to Blalock for confirmation. He hoped that he would not call his bluff. "I have Stanley's findings right here if you want to see them."

He folded his hands and brought them up to his chin as if in deep thought. "No. That won't be necessary."

"Morgan?" feigned Kelan. "Is everything all right?"

He could not have cared less whether Morgan was all right or not. He wanted so badly to catch Blalock red-handed that he attempted to befriend him in order to coax a confession of some sort. If it came to it, he also did not care if his testimony were admissible in any type of legal proceedings toward an embezzlement charge. Kelan was not interested in pursuing justice per say; he just wanted Blalock to know that it was him. That his downfall came by Kelan's hands.

Blalock cleared his throat. "Yes . . . I'm fine, it's just that this is a little disconcerting."

Oh, come on! You can do better than that, thought Kelan. He decided to push him a little further.

"It's never a good thing when funding is misappropriated. I can assure you, the budget numbers were approved by both you and me at the beginning of each of these missions, but in the best interest of full disclosure, I would like to point out that I reallocated 1.7 million to cover the expenses for the unsanctioned mission in which you've assigned to me," baited Kelan.

"Well, that seems to be the answer," Blalock stated confidently. "There is your missing money."

Kelan put his acting to the test by shaking his head in deep thought, as if trying to rationalize Blalock's statement himself. He needed Blalock to think that he was in agreement with him, to show him that he was on his side. "I'm not sure about that, Morgan. The money amounts don't match up. We are still missing $600,000."

He waited for Blalock to catch up. Now, it was time to show him Kelan's dedication to this cause. "I had my auditor do some more digging, and the affected accounts don't match up with the ones that I touched. This means that there was someone else besides me pulling money."

He could not exactly be sure, but it looked like he was cracking Blalock's composure. He noticed that there was a little sweat gathering on his forehead. "I want to assure you that this has my full attention. I can absolutely guarantee that I will find out where the residual money has gone."

With a wave of his hand, Blalock said, "Six hundred thousand dollars seems negligible compared to the hundreds of millions that we've already invested over the years in the Artifacts missions. I don't want you to waste your valuable time tracking this down. I have other objectives I want you to focus on."

"Morgan, $600,000 is a sizable amount regardless of the total expenditures. If not for the money itself, we need to find out who's been taking it and bring them to justice. We don't know if it's one person or many. As a whole, Alastar-McGlocklin should not abide by stealing within the corporation. On a personal note, this money came out of accounts under my purview. I want the head of whoever did this on a platter," said Kelan with conviction. He actually meant the last part. He knew that Blalock was the likely suspect, and now he had the crime evidence provided so conveniently by Stanley. All he had to do was tie the two together.

"Kelan, while I appreciate your tenacity to correct a financial wrong, I cannot spare your time to look into something like this when we have higher priorities."

He persisted; he would not let up. If he could get Blalock to lose his temper and shut him down on this pursuit, this would be one more piece of evidence toward his culpability. This would definitely mean that he was hiding something.

"Morgan, I—"

"Tindal! Enough! This matter is closed. You will adjust the budgeted amounts for the affected accounts accordingly less the 1.7 million you used for your personal assignment. The $600,000 will go away as if it never existed. Do you understand?"

Gotcha.

Kelan assumed a submissive look much like a dog after he had been beaten by his master. Blalock needed to think that he had him under his thumb.

"All-All right, Morgan. Whatever you want. I was just trying to prevent something like this from happening again. I hate to see the good name of Alastar-McGlocklin stained by internal espionage and embezzlement," he said respectfully.

Blalock's mood and expression softened. It looked as if he was almost ashamed of his outburst. "Tindal . . . Kelan, please forgive me for my manner. There are . . .

things going on at my level that you are not privy to, and the pressure is starting to get to me a bit."

I'll bet, thought Kelan. It was nice to see Blalock humbled, but that did not change anything. Kelan still did not care, but he continued to keep up the act. "Morgan, I understand . . . Is there anything that I can do to help?"

That offer sparked Blalock to get back to his professional demeanor. "Actually, yes. There are a couple of things that we need to discuss. One has to do with two new Artifact acquisitions."

Kelan picked up his pen to begin taking notes. Blalock got up and walked to his desk and opened a drawer. He pulled out one sheet of paper then grabbed one of the files from his desk and walked back over. He handed only the paper to Kelan. He began reading immediately as Blalock waited for him to finish.

Kelan's eyes widened a bit. "The Wallace sword?"

"Yes. Are you familiar with it?"

"Somewhat, it's the sword that William Wallace used to lead the Scottish revolution against England hundreds of years ago. What is the significance of this item?"

"I'm unsure. I was not involved in the selection of this particular Artifact."

Their eyes met.

"Pymm?" stated Kelan.

Blalock frowned a bit, then with a wave of his hand, looked away. "Of course. The senior partners sent their lapdog to my home to give me these targets." Then in a gruff manner of a dignified old codger, he said, "They didn't even have the common decency to wait until business hours. It interrupted my breakfast."

Kelan looked back to the sheet to study it a bit more. "Will both missions be on book?"

"Yes, you will have the full resources of your division available for these acquisitions."

Kelan started to crunch some numbers mentally, more specifically to resource availability.

"We currently have nine active missions. What are the priorities of these two new ones?"

"Standard. Why do you ask?"

"We have limited resources left for simultaneous operations. We are stretched pretty thin at the current nine. I will know more once I complete the mission specifications and allocate the appropriate resources for the plan."

"That brings us to our next topic of discussion."

Kelan was still deep in thought and half-listening as Morgan continued on. "You should have more resources available in a short time."

"How so?"

"The 216 mission is coming to a close."

Kelan almost fell out of his seat. He was usually pretty good about concealing any shock or surprise, but this one caught him way off guard. A hundred questions sprang into his mind instantly. Before he could even begin to bombard Blalock with them, he held up his hand in anticipation. "I know you have a lot of questions. I only have a few details that I can give you though."

"I absolutely have a lot of questions," started Kelan, "but please continue."

"The surveillance of Object 216 will no longer be necessary given the conditions set forth by the senior partners. I am not privy to the *conditions* in which they speak. When Pymm came on board a few years ago, it was made very clear to me that he had his own personal agenda as relayed to him by the senior partners themselves. I was not to interfere with any objectives that he had with regards to the disposition of Object 216."

Kelan's eyes narrowed a bit. "You told me that Pymm reported straight to you."

Blalock had been caught directly, so he confessed. "I lied. It was my belief, at the time, that a single line of leadership should remain intact to maintain a command structure, whereby leading to compliance by subordinates."

Blalock paused as Kelan continued to look at him. He could see that Kelan was rethinking all the events since Pymm's appearance, most likely wondering how he could have missed the disconnection of authority.

That was not what he was thinking at all though. It was not about the line of leadership, it was about the control.

Blalock could not control Pymm.

That must be eating away at him. Kelan could almost understand why Blalock was stressed. He ruled with an iron fist, most, if not all the time. He often thought that Blalock would have done exceedingly well back in the days of the Russian czars. Some were merciless in order to grow their empire. It appeared to Kelan that Blalock followed the same game plan. He was not used to anyone challenging his authority in any capacity. When Pymm came along, it basically neutered him, stripped away the very essence of who Blalock was. He did not know how to process something like that.

This was great.

The big man was vulnerable, and Kelan was going to seize the opportunity to capitalize on it. "Okay, I can accept that. I'm disappointed that you did not have enough faith in our relationship to tell me the truth, but I can live with that, for the moment. The thing that we both should be concerned about now is that neither one of us know the endgame for Object 216."

"Agreed."

Kelan would put aside his hatred for Blalock to actually do what their business arrangement had originally intended: work together. "Morgan, I've got to be honest with you . . . In the limited dealings that I've had with Pymm, I've never really liked him or his arrogant attitude when it comes to sticking his nose into our affairs. Underneath his suave charisma and his impeccable good taste in clothing, he strikes me as one of the slimiest things to walk on two feet."

Morgan broke out into a laughter that surprised Kelan. In all the years that he had known him, he had never heard Blalock laugh.

When his amusement finally died down, Morgan said, "My boy, I couldn't agree with you more. Nonetheless, the senior partners felt his participation was necessary to achieve the objectives of the operation."

Kelan was puzzled a bit. "What exactly is the objective? When you gave me this assignment five years ago, the mission statement was simply surveillance and pattern tracks of known contacts."

"When I assigned this to you that was exactly the purpose. We were to simply monitor him as a person of interest. His value to the senior partnership was unknown, even to me. To this day, I'm still in the dark as to the true intentions."

He seemed to relax a bit and slumped back into his chair with his arms folded. He continued with what Kelan assumed was honesty for the first time.

"The sole purpose of your division and your current position as DCO was to research and collect Artifacts. Your division was meant to be kept secret from the rest of Alastar-McGlocklin. No one besides the senior partners and me are aware of its existence. That included its board of directors."

Kelan smiled. "That much I knew. Whenever I chatted with them at formal functions, it was quite clear they had no clue as to what I truly do."

Blalock smiled too. "They really don't have a clue in general."

They both laughed.

"Their only concern was that the company was making money and their quarterly dividends got fatter as time passed," said Blalock.

He looked down and appeared solemn. Kelan sensed there was something going on emotionally for him. For a brief millisecond, Kelan almost had a little compassion for the old man.

"Their position is as much a joke as mine. The senior partners apparently control everything within this company. Every time that I make a decision of significance that does not fit within their agenda, I get shot down at every turn."

Kelan wondered if Morgan heard what he just said, for that was exactly how Morgan treated him. This would have been an excellent opportunity for Kelan to point that out, but common sense dictated that he should let this one go. In fact, he needed to throw the old man an ego bone.

"Morgan, I don't believe that they would've hired you just to be their yes man. You bring a lot of valuable insights to your position, and they recognize that. They couldn't run this company without you." He was only mildly nauseated at that statement.

"Well, thank you for the kind words," he said, genuinely grateful. "But that doesn't change the fact of where we are standing at the moment."

"How do you want to play this?" asked Kelan.

"Do you still have your person on the inside of the 216 mission?"

Kelan eyed him cautiously. "How do—"

"Please, Tindal, I'm not as uninformed and out of the loop as you might think. Just because I don't have a computer doesn't mean that I don't get information."

Inwardly, Kelan had to smile. *Bravo, Morgan*, he thought. He was almost impressed that Blalock had a pulse on his activities. The inward smile faded though as he started to think about how Blalock got this information. Betty could only do so much, and she was unaware of the secret division. Of course, Blalock knew of all his resources and staff as the approval for hire had to go through him. Any one of them could easily provide Blalock Intel that was sanctioned. The problem with that scenario was that his inside person was not part of any mission briefings and reported solely to him. The only person that might have possibly known . . . he paused.

Margaret.

She did not know everything, but knew just enough. He had confided top secret things with her over the years, which the rest of the staff did not know or need to know. He did mention to her, once upon a time, that he had someone on the inside, but never identified them. He was having a relationship with her, if one could call it that. She had been in his apartment on multiple occasions and had access to everything outside of his panic room. She came and went in his office at Long Beach. She was, for the lack of a better term, his *right-hand man*.

Margaret was the most plausible source, but he still did not know how she could get information that was only known to him. Would it be possible that there was another person, or could she be working with someone else on the inside?

So many questions and obviously not enough time to get the answers. The fact of the matter was, Blalock knew he had someone, so there was no skirting this topic. He would have to find his answers later. He would also need to escalate his failsafe.

Kelan cleared his throat and tried not to sound uncomfortable. "Very impressive, Morgan. Yes, I still have my person on the inside."

"How close are they to the subject?"

"Fairly close. It looks like the relationship is moving forward as planned."

"Very good, and the roommate?"

"Estranged for a little over five months now."

"Excellent. Not having experienced the loss of a best friend myself, I would imagine that he is under a lot of stress." He was thoughtful for a moment then started nodding his head. "Good," he reconfirmed as he reached for the file folder on the table and handed it to Kelan. "We need to keep him in a pressure cooker state until we find out what the senior partners plan on doing and how. I don't want him to get distracted or motivated to do anything outside of our designed scenarios."

He pointed at the folder. "I have taken the liberty to draw up a few contingencies due to Pymm's involvement. Very rudimentary, but should give you some ideas on how to circumvent any decisions that come down from them, in which you and I are not in agreement."

Kelan thumbed through some of the sheets as Blalock spoke. Morgan was very busy, very busy indeed. Some of these additional ideas were not that bad. Kelan might take those under advisement as he started strategizing the desired outcome.

He shuffled the sheets, placed them back in the folder, and closed it. "So the assumption is to maintain the status quo . . . continue with the 216 surveillance, but build in controlled measures to account for the unknown variables presented by the senior partnership at a time of their obvious choosing."

Blalock nodded. "Easier said than done I'm sure . . ."

Kelan shrugged a bit. "That's why you hired me."

"I will continue to try to gain as much information from Pymm and the senior partners with regards to 216. Anything that I come across, of course, will be shared with you."

"It goes without saying that I will extend the same courtesy to you."

He started to rise from the table as an indication that he believed the meeting was over. His assumption was correct as Morgan stood as well. As Kelan gathered his files for departure, Blalock said, "Since 216 is a high priority for the senior partners, I would like status updates from you every forty-eight hours. If anything new turns up that is not on our radar or is off mission, I want to know about it."

Kelan raised one eyebrow. "You think Pymm will do an end-run around us?"

"I wouldn't put it past him," stated Blalock emphatically.

With that, they both said their good-byes, and Kelan departed. As the doors closed behind him, Blalock made his way to the massive desk. After he heard the click of the door, Blalock's demeanor turned evil.

Fool.

The seed to Pymm and the senior partners' involvement was planted. If Kelan does as instructed, it should provide enough evidence to pin the 216 operation on him, should it fail. Blalock could feign lack of knowledge and claim that Kelan went rogue in his directives. The best part of this plan was that Blalock did not have to lift a finger to provide the evidence, Kelan would do that himself.

Blalock was very proud of his actions. He put a lot of time and effort into devising the strategy. Kelan was the puppet to his puppet-master. In the back of Blalock's mind, he remembered the last statement that Pymm said regarding accountability for Kelan's actions. Surely, he and the senior partnership would understand, if enough evidence were provided, that Blalock could prove his innocence in the matter. Contract or not, they would see that Kelan orchestrated the entire thing. Blalock could turn additional evidence of the incompetence throughout the mission once his own inside person was finished. On that thought, he picked up the phone.

It rang three times before the person on the other end picked up. "Yes, sir. How may I help you today?"

"Are you free to speak?"

"Please stand by . . ."

Blalock assumed that the other person was compromised and needed to find a more secure location.

Another ten seconds passed. "I'm sorry for the delay, sir. There were others around, I needed to change my proximity." She heard the call waiting beep on her phone, but ignored it.

"It's not a problem, my dear. I understand that you are in a precarious position, and I do not wish our arrangement to taint your current connections or ability to operate."

"Thank you, sir."

Blalock got straight to business. "Have you been able to extract anything unusual regarding Kelan's connection around the 216 operation?"

"Sir, to my knowledge and observation, Kelan has been operating within the standard mission protocols."

He was disappointed. "And you are absolutely sure?"

"Yes. sir. As requested, I have been trying to spend as much time in and out of the office and with him as possible. There has been nothing out of the ordinary, but he has been tied up with a lot of external work. He told me that it was something assigned to him by you, so I took it at face value and didn't push."

"Hmmm," said Blalock. "He's quite right on that front. I have him working on something that is for his eyes only, do not pursue the matter."

"I completely understand, sir."

Blalock was thoughtful for a second in silence. It seemed that his trust in Kelan was validated, for the moment. Kelan had done exactly what was asked of him. Blalock knew that he could be ruthless when he needed to though. He was surprised that Kelan could maintain a relatively squeaky-clean image throughout the 216 process. He almost felt ashamed that he had someone watching him, but Blalock had to be sure he was performing to expectations and not delving into areas he should not. This was going to make things harder for Blalock to plant the evidence needed to make Kelan his fall guy. He might have to solicit this young lady's services in that task. More of an internal question rather than a moral dilemma, but he needed to decide how involved he wanted her to be. Right now, her only objective outside of working directly for Kelan was to observe and report his activities straight back to Blalock. Thus far, the extra money that he had paid her had yielded nothing of substance. Either she had stunk at her job or Kelan was very good at covering his tracks.

"Continue your observations as per our agreement, and if possible, monitor his electronic transmissions as well."

The voice on the other end was inquisitive and asked, "Sir, are you expecting something unusual? If so, it may be of benefit for me to have more details so I know what to look for."

"The specifics of the new activities are not your concern. What I need you to do is follow my direction and orders and report back to me per our standard schedule. If anything appears to be out of the ordinary in general, you contact me immediately. I want you to focus on his communications, both incoming and outgoing."

"Sir?" she asked.

"I want to know whom he talks to at all times."

"Understood, sir, but it's going to take some time to set up the taps and will be particularly difficult without his knowledge," she said.

"I have the utmost confidence in your abilities. Get this done as quickly as you can."

"Yes, sir," she said dutifully.

"And, Margaret."

"Yes, sir?"

"My agreement is with you and you only. You will not under any circumstances divulged any of the activities that you and I have discussed with anyone, is that understood?"

"Yes, sir, I understand."

He hung up and frowned into the phone for a moment. He had hoped there would actually be something new that could be used as a starting point for the evidence he needed against Kelan. *All in good time*, he thought. There were other issues at hand in which he actually needed Kelan's help. Regardless of how well Kelan had been performing, Blalock did not want to be caught unprepared. He liked to have his cards stacked. Losing was not an option; he did not believe in the no-win scenario. Kelan's inside person was of special interest to Blalock. He loved the look on his face when he mentioned it. Blalock knew something like this would eat away at Kelan as he tried to discover how he knew about the informant, and most importantly, wondering *what* he knew. Ironically enough and much to Blalock's dismay, there was a third player in this game who supplied information as well. Blalock had no idea how Pymm found out about Kelan's inside person, but that was inconsequential. Once Blalock received the name, he set up a little side job of his own to ensure that the deck was again stacked in his favor. He pulled out his cell phone and dialed the second inside person.

As soon as Kelan had closed the door to Blalock's office, his demeanor changed as well. He walked with the quickness past Betty's desk; she was busy with other things and did not notice. With a quick look at his watch, he pulled out his cell and dialed Margaret. He was disappointed when he was sent to voice mail and hung up, not bothering to leave a message. It was probably better to discuss the specifics of 216 in person anyway. Once he entered the elevator, he looked down at the file and wondered what was actually in store for this young man. This entire mission had been odd from the start, but after a while, it had become commonplace for most of his teams assigned. He wondered if Blalock even knew the monumental amount of time, money, and effort it took to maintain the 216 initiative. Now, because of something the slimy henchman for the senior partners had said, it was coming to a close. No timeline, no details, and an unknown outcome. One simple statement, and now he would have to figure out how to continue to operate with no specifics. On top of that, Blalock wanted to toss in his little ideas for subterfuge against the senior partners and Pymm. Kelan was not a magician, but he was paid quite handsomely to act like one. Just another day, just another rabbit out of his hat.

All this time, he saw this young man as nothing more than a number and a mission. At first, it did not bother him that he was surveilling 216, but now Kelan became a little more than disturbed based on what he discovered Blalock was capable of and the lack of details of the mission closing. Kelan opened the file again and looked at the dossier. He read the header.

NAME: Harrison Jeffrey Gibson
DESIGNATION: 216

Chapter 14

Missions and Concerns

Josh loved his new job. Just as in his two previous positions, the thrill of something different and challenging made him excited and thankful to be part of the Jonah International team. Upon accepting his brand-new position, Josh threw himself into his new role. Financial economics and analysis was one thing, but learning to hone his skills as a leader seemed to be a bit of a personal roadblock to him, especially since, at the moment, he had no team to lead. Langston, Ulysses, and Lucas worked with him in different areas to help him adapt, according to the three of them, a naturally gifted skill into what Josh thought was a pseudo-role of an analytical consultant. All three were convinced that the problem was not that he lacked the wisdom, but rather the self-confidence. Given time, they knew that Josh would improve, but it needed to come at a pace in which he was comfortable. The issue with that was that time was not necessarily on their side.

The analysis part of his training was pretty easy. His eye for details was astonishing to begin with, so it was naturally easier for him to learn the specifics around these targets: the Artifacts. Josh learned the rudimentary skills at Carnegie Mellon, but that was purely in economics. The rest was basically by experience from his previous roles within Jonah and from Lucas, Langston, and Ulysses.

During the course of three months, Josh noticed that Ulysses's team seemed to be of one single mind, very fluid in their movements and always anticipating each other's thoughts and actions. Ulysses was the team lead and ran all the tech op on briefings, while Langston provided the historical relevance based on their missions to the rest of the acquisitions team. Josh spent most of his time with both. The three of them became very close.

The Artifact Acquisitions Retrieval Team consisted of twenty-five members in total, ranging from field operations to what they called Watchers. The Watchers were the information analysts and operators who covered everything from topography to reconnaissance. Each field agent had their own individual watcher. They monitored environmental settings, movement tracking, and telemetry, even the field operative's vital signs. They were the eyes and ears to the field operative and literally gave them eyes in the back of their heads and provided intelligence throughout their missions. They did most of their work from the AAR hub. Josh did rotational work in each one of the areas of the team in order to provide him a well-rounded view of their purpose and function. He had been working with that group as of late. Unlike the other Watchers though, Josh was privy to all the leadership briefings and decisions. He thought that was going to be an issue with his fellow teammates, but they seemed to be in acceptance of his position as part of the management team.

The AAR hub, also called rHub, was located in a sublevel of the Jonah International headquarters, below the electrical, facilities, and parking levels. It was one single level that ran the dimensions of the entire building. Growing up, Josh was a big fan of movies and TV shows that featured adventure, action, and suspense. He loved all the gadgets that he would see in James Bond flicks and some of the newer television shows that featured secret agents and technical wizardry using the latest special effects so glorified by Hollywood. Those could not hold a candle to the stuff that he had seen on Ulysses's team. The situation room was an amazing piece of technology. The monitoring stations that outlined the room had real-time high-resolution graphics powered by next-generation technology that was not released to the outside world. The conference table in the middle was a 12 x 12 octagonal platform with fusion-powered illumination from beneath. Above, hanging from the ceiling, was a lighted receptacle matching the exact dimensions of the table. When both were active, it projected hard-light three-dimensional images between the two and allowed manipulation of the illuminated elements, either by voice command or mere touch. The artificial intelligence behind all of this was Sentinel. Each cubicle and workstation throughout the rHub had identical technological capabilities. All were powered by the same self-supporting ColdFusion reactor that took care of the entire building. It was clean, green, and safe.

When Josh joined the team, he was offered an office right next to Ulysses, but refused stating that it did not make sense based on his title of analytical consultant and, of course, being the freshest meat on the team. His view of his role and title was founded on his college background. An analytical consultant was probably an entry-level position in the world of financial economics. An analyst does just that, analysis. It is their job to assess market and financial conditions and report those back to their managers. In Josh's world, those are considered peons and minions, and not necessarily worthy of said corner office. His last title as division head for International Relief probably warranted the office, the team, and the assistant. Nobody reported to him in this new position though. He was okay with that and understood it was going to basically be a step down when he accepted; but Lucas, Langston, and Ulysses insisted that this new position would be above and beyond anything that he had ever had experienced before. So far, he did not see any of that.

He completed six weeks of analysis with Richard Frampton, the Data Assimilation Lead, prior to his training on the Watchers detail. Before that, he was ramped up at an accelerated rate on all the amazing technology now at his disposal. However, everyone in rHub had treated him like a C-level executive, and that had him stumped. In the back of his mind, he wondered that if he was going to be in such a critical position, why was he doing only menial analysis activities? Not that they were no less important, and why did the title on his business cards basically say Acquisitions Consultant? He was an acquisition analytical consultant. He analyzed probable acquisitions at a consultant level; he was a consultant that provided analysis on potential acquisitions. It did not really matter how one said it; he was just basically an entry-level consultant, no more, no less.

Josh was not jealous by any means; he just did not understand the correlation between everybody's excitement of working with him and the big talk from Lucas and Langston versus the activities that he performed. He discussed certain aspects of that during his off hours with Melina. She explained that it was a brand-new position for him and he did not know anything about it. That everyone had to go through some type of training phase before being propelled to *greatness*. He often smiled at those types of lofty comments as a matter of courtesy, but inwardly, it still made him feel a little self-conscious. He had told her in past discussions he had with Lucas and Langston, they would both make references to what would happen in the future when Josh "would do this" or when he "would do that"; they always spoke in a future tense. It was almost like everyone was reading the same book, but Josh was in chapter 3 and they were in chapter 10. He understood that someday he would most likely have answers to all of these growing questions, but it still did not change the fact that all of these *unknowns* made him feel uneasy and out of the loop. There was some type of big secret in which he was the subject, but not part of it. He always maintained his professional countenance and tried very hard not to ask more questions he knew he would not get answers to, but he wanted to know. He felt like a kid on Christmas morning just about to burst in anticipation of the presents under the tree that he could not yet open. Josh would sometimes reflect on that, but tried not to let it interfere with his responsibilities. Today, he was busy working with his assigned field operative on a simulation test when Ulysses approached him.

The exercise was a field op extraction of an object, whereby Josh provided his operative intelligence and guided him through different facets and obstacles to reach the goal for retrieval. It was almost like a video game where Josh controlled his man in the field. Ulysses stood at a distance in order to let Josh finish the exercise.

"Alpha 6, closing distance to target: 600 meters north by northwest. Spectrum analysis indicates no electromagnetic signatures present. I've sent the data to your OpSat. You should have visual over the next ridge," said Josh.

"Copy that, base ops," said the voice on the other end.

Ulysses just smiled. From the reports that he received from his last two trainers, Josh had exceeded expectations at all levels. He was a very quick study, not that it was any surprise to Ulysses.

Josh's hands moved over the hard-light imagery as gracefully as a professional ballerina dancing at a recital.

"Geographical radius scan completed. No active movement within six kilometers of your position. Should be a cakewalk to target. Please confirm status," he asked.

"Systems nominal, 5 x 5," said Alpha 6.

Josh finished up his last comment when he noticed Ulysses out of the corner of his eyes and smiled. "Mr. Quaden, to what do I owe this auspicious visit? Spot inspection?"

Ulysses laughed. "You know that I don't check up on you." He laughed a little harder.

"Right . . . ," said Josh as he swiveled back to his station. "Distance to target: 150 meters."

"Roger that," said Alpha 6.

"Are you about finished with this exercise?" asked Ulysses.

Josh looked over his hard-light imagery. "At present speed, this will be completed in the next five minutes. Is everything okay?"

"I need all the senior leads in the situation room as soon as possible. We have a new development."

Josh completed his exercise and was the last to enter. He took his position at the conference table, and then the outer doors to the room closed and sealed.

"Sentinel online. Authorization, 3 lambda 64," said Ulysses.

The table came to life.

"Sentinel is online."

"Load Project Herald."

An array of hard-light data images immediately came to life. Within them were folders and files that outlined specific information regarding the current Artifact cache, to include both retrieval and holding locations, dates and time stamps, security status, and the historical relevance research and assessments provided by Langston's team. There was a secondary grouping of images for Artifacts that were pending retrieval, and a third classified as "orphans." This last category held bits and pieces of uncataloged Artifacts that were known to be in existence, but had not yet been identified with a hard lead to the whereabouts.

"As you all know, so far, we have been able to retrieve seven Artifacts that we believe play a significant role in religious doctrine as documented by Langston and his people," said Ulysses. "The impact of each Artifact has multiple levels of meaning across the board."

Langston manipulated some of the images to show the Artifacts being discussed. "Of these seven, as well as the known Artifacts that we currently do not possess, we have been studying the historical ideology of each cultural society in relation to the Artifact itself in an attempt to find a commonality. Each Artifact is a piece to a bigger puzzle that we are trying to decipher. The research into each has been long and arduous, but we've been able to shed some light on a few things. One of which," he said, focusing the imagery, "is the Cavaliere Lama . . . the Knight Blade."

A three-dimensional image of the blade swirled slowly in motion.

"Although Italian in origin, the Cavalier Lama first came to notable prominence in seventeenth-century France under King Louis XIV's reign. The blade belonged to the one king's personal guard in the Garde du Corps, a musketeer named LaMont Delacroix. The uniqueness of the blade was that it wasn't the typical fencing rapier made so famous by the books and movies. This blade had an ornate hilt with a crested symbolic design depicting spiritual forces in battle." Langston focused the image to magnify the hilt for closer observation. "This was a one-of-a-kind crafted piece. The legend of the blade states that it held immense power and that those who possessed it would never be defeated in battle. Legend or not, Lamont defeated all of those who opposed King Louis using this very blade. Mousquetaire Delacroix found himself in favor of the king and was eventually assigned as his personal bodyguard."

"Sentinel, display findings from a molecular structure," said Ulysses.

Chart analysis and elemental results came into view. "Carbon dating of the Artifact puts its origin right around the fifteenth-century. Metallurgy and geographical analysis indicate that the point of origin was somewhere near Ponte Linari," said Langston as a topographical map of Italy appeared. He manipulated the imagery again. "Around the same time frame appeared another Artifact. I think you will be particularly interested in this one, Josh."

The swirling image changed from the blade to a larger than life amulet.

"If you wouldn't mind, can you take the rest of the team through this one?" asked Langston.

"Médaillon des Âmes," said Josh with a near perfect French accent. It paid to date someone who could speak seven different languages. While on a two-week rotation within Langston's team, this particular Artifact was the subject of his training in his crash course introduction to historical and religious anthropology.

"The Medallion of Souls," he continued, "is also a seventeenth-century object rooted in the foundation of its strongest influence back then: religion. There were two factions competing for religious allegiance, Protestants and Roman Catholics. During that time, Spain was a dying power, but possessed immense amounts of European territory, of which France took a great interest. In one of their many pursuits for global domination, France offered their services and protection to unify Spain in exchange for ruling the kingdoms under one Bourbon monarchy. The European communities were not happy about this and so ensued the War of the Spanish Succession. The war was fought between 1701 and 1714 out of fear of the unification between France and Spain. After a decade or so of blood loss, the war was finally ended in the signing of the treaties of Utrecht (1713) and Rastatt (1714). This enabled Philip V to remain as King of Spain, but would remove him from the French line of succession, averting a union of the two kingdoms. What is not well known in the history books is that a symbol crafted from the spoils of war was given to Philip as a reminder of the countless souls that perished during this struggle . . . the Medallion of Souls." He nodded toward the three-dimensional amulet.

Josh paused for a minute as his fingers danced over the controls to bring up his research. A chronological timeline appeared. "As far as we can tell, the medallion remained in France's possession up until the revolution of 1789. I haven't been able to trace the object past that."

"Until now," said Langston.

"We've just received some Intel outlining the current location of the medallion," said Ulysses as he pulled up an outline of France.

The senior leads started to mumble a bit at this news. Josh leaned forward in excitement and waited for further information. As Ulysses continued to speak, the topographical outline narrowed to a location. "The medallion is currently located at 10/12 rue Andras Beck 92360 Meudon-la-Forêt, just outside of Paris, France, a plastics manufacturing plant."

"And the irony does not fall short that the location is about six clicks outside the Palace of Versailles," said Langston.

"Wait a second . . . that address . . . Sentinel, confirm address and cross-match with known points of interest," said Josh.

"Address confirmation completed. Location is directly above storage facility designation SV8."

Josh looked at both Langston and Ulysses. "This is one of the security vault locations for Alastar-McGlocklin. They're in possession of the medallion, aren't they?"

Both Langston and Ulysses shared a look.

"Yes, they are," said Ulysses.

"How reliable is this intelligence?" asked Josh.

"Very. We've reviewed the data provided so far, and it checks out. Sentinel has authenticated. The asset checks out as well and has agreed to continue providing us ongoing information. We now have someone on the inside of Alastar-McGlocklin, code name: Herald," said Ulysses.

Josh had a realization then smiled, nodding his head. "Messenger."

Ulysses and Langston smiled at Josh's quickness. Other senior leads in the room looked puzzled.

"Another name for *herald* is *messenger*, a bringer of news," said Langston.

Ulysses continued. "Our new asset has given us visibility to all the Artifacts currently in possession by Alastar-McGlocklin. This includes locations, security systems, and protective compliments. We also have their next two targets for retrieval. We will be working interception packages up for those."

Josh's thoughts processed at Mach 2 around all of this and its meaning for the cause. "What's our next play."

"Simple, we are going to take the medallion," said Langston flatly. "It's not stealing if it was stolen to begin with. I realized that's a bit of a moral stretch, but it must not remain in the hands of the enemy. This Artifact is one of the key pieces to the aforementioned larger puzzle. As with all the others that we have acquired, adequate compensation will be given to its original owner, if the possession was legitimately documented."

Ulysses manipulated the building's image to show the substructure. "According to the information from Herald, the medallion is stored in a secured vault on the fourth sublevel, three-quarters of a mile below the plastics' plant."

The senior leads studied the schematic. "I would imagine that the security would be quite difficult. Did Herald offer any details?" said one.

Ulysses raised his eyebrows at the obvious simplicity of the question, yet prepared himself to present the complexity. "The 36 x 12 room is surrounded by construction grade concrete at least a meter thick with reinforced rebar. The only way in or out is through a class 1 steel vault door. Entry is controlled by a four-point biometric security system, in which only seven people on the planet have access. There is a singular tunnel that runs from this surface entry point," he said, touching the hard-light image and tracing it, "to the vault door. Approximately 1,500 feet in length at an 8 percent grade slope, surrounded from all sides by the same construction grade concrete. Both the tunnel and the vault have security surveillance installed at every feasible vantage point."

"Traps?" asked Josh.

"Throughout the entire tunnel, according to Herald," said Ulysses.

"Sounds impossible to penetrate," said another senior lead.

"Getting to the vault door is the easy part," said Ulysses. He manipulated the image further to show a digital wire frame of the room itself.

"The medallion is encased in a solid, unbreakable transparent aluminum shell. The entire room has an interlocking, multiphase laser grid that sweeps every inch of the vault at variable speeds. When the chamber is locked down, a state-of-the-art compression system extracts all O_2 and replaces it with halon gas once the vault door has been sealed. If anything biological has the misfortune of being inside during consolidation, they have 4.3 seconds of life left," he said.

"That'll ruin your day," said another senior lead.

There was silence within the room for a few seconds. Finally, Josh came out and said what everyone else was thinking. "So . . . exactly how are we going to get the medallion?"

"At a predetermined time, Herald will shut down the protective grid and security surveillance," said Ulysses.

"That will get us into the vault, but we still need to figure out how to remove the medallion," said Langston.

Josh manipulated the hard light to zoom in on the medallion's case. "Herald provided the most current schematics to the vault to include the medallion's security pedestal, correct?"

"Yes," said Ulysses.

"And you're 100 percent sure that you can trust this source and the data provided?" asked Josh.

"Sentinel detects no deception in the intelligence. This is the closest we have ever come to capturing the Medallion of Souls. It's an opportunity that we cannot pass up. Both the medallion and the Knight Blade are at the top of the list for Artifact acquisitions. We need them both to continue our analysis of the endgame," said Langston.

Josh nodded his head slowly. "Okay . . . I've got an idea . . ."

Josh had never actually told Melina the specifics of his new role within the acquisitions division. She was a very smart woman though. At a high level, she knew that this position was a stepping-stone to greater things that Jonah had in mind for him. Later that evening, Josh had dinner at her place. The conversation evolved from exchanging pleasantries about each other's day to sporadic details of the upcoming mission to Paris. It was not until Josh had told her he was not going to work the intelligence this time when she started to feel uncomfortable.

"I just don't understand why you have to go on this mission," she said.

"Honey, this is my job. I was never meant to stay behind a computer at rHub. I've finished out my Watchers rotation, and this is the next logical step."

"I understand that you feel this move is necessary for progression, but it doesn't make sense to send you out so quickly without the proper training."

"Melina, I will be fine. Ulysses and the other agents are going to be there. They have enough training to protect me. There's nothing for you to worry about." Josh could see that she was getting more upset and wanted to bake in some reassurances. For a minute, he thought that she was buying it, but again, she was a very smart woman.

"Since you have been in this position, you have explained to me, in a roundabout way, what this division does. We have had many dinners with Ulysses and Sandra, and Langston and Debra, and while you men thought that the ladies were chatting about girl stuff, I listened to you boys talk shop.

"I listened to you talk about surveillance and satellite images, telemetry updates, and data packages for the Artifacts. I've also heard you discuss coordinating training schedules with the military specific to explosive ordnance disposal, testing results of antiflak Kevlar exposure to high-impact projectiles, target practice with nonlethal weapons such as an M234 Riot Control Launcher and a variable velocity weapon that uses a propulsion energy source. I thought Ulysses was going to wet his pants over that one," she said emphatically.

Josh did not say a word and tried not to look slack-jawed at everything he had just heard.

"Don't sit there and tell me there is no element of danger to any of the field agents on these missions. I have sat back and tried desperately not to remember any of the things that I heard the three of you discuss and, for the most part, have done very well since you were safely behind a desk. Now, that's all changing," she said.

She was visibly shaking now. Melina was truly scared for Josh's safety. He looked down at his plate. He had never given consideration to how something like this would make her feel. Josh knew there were risks involved when he accepted the position. Danger is a very broad umbrella that covers countless situations. Just walking across a street in Manhattan has an element of hazards, but that is something that most people take for granted in their day-to-day lives, much like he was doing now. Josh never really gave it a second thought as in his activities, at no time, had he ever seen any action from either the intelligence side or through the computer from an agent's vantage point. He had been involved in one Artifact extraction, and that went like clockwork. Textbook extraction as Ulysses put it, not even a hint of excitement, and it all happened from his workstation.

Josh was in the game now, moving from observation to participation.

He now realized that his decisions going forward would affect her too. He had never been in a position where he had to think about the well-being of someone with this type of an emotional attachment. His mom and Harry were the closest that he had ever come, but they were both different than Melina. His love for her was . . . distinct.

Love. He loved her.

He loved her and did not ever want her to leave again. Mark Twain had once said that if people told the truth, they wouldn't have to remember anything. If Melina was going to be a permanent part of his life, Josh had to include her in everything from this day forward and always tell her the truth.

He got up and walked around to her side of the table then knelt down so he could look her in the eyes. He gently picked up both of her hands and held them. "Melina, I am so sorry for not considering how my work makes you feel. I have been very selfish in the decisions that I have made, not only with this mission, but in accepting this position in the first place. I should have discussed my options with you prior to agreeing, but my thoughts were only of those people that could be affected if I didn't take this job. Langston, Ulysses, and even Lucas more or less said that people could get hurt, and I couldn't have that on my conscience. If there was anything that I could do to prevent harm in any way, then that's what I was committed to doing. You are right. This mission is going to be dangerous, but please believe me, that I will be safe."

"Josh, you don't owe me any explanations—"

"Yes, I do. You are the most important person in my life. What I do now, and forever, will affect both of us. It's not just about me anymore."

She smiled. "Now and forever?"

He smiled back. "Yes. I love you, Melina, and I don't want you to ever question that."

They embraced and kissed. Melina pulled back a little. "I love you too."

"Listen, why don't you come to Paris with us?"

"Are you serious?" she said, surprised.

"Absolutely. You can monitor with the intelligence team during operation and see for yourself firsthand that everything will be fine."

"Is something like that even possible? I mean, I'm not authorized for a lot of the stuff that you do. I wouldn't want to put you or any of the other teams in jeopardy just because I'm insecure about your safety."

"Don't be silly. I am in pretty good with the boss. We'll make this happen." He smiled. "Besides . . . we are going to Paris, and you know it better than any of us. We will need somebody to show us where the closest McDonald's is and interpret our order."

She laughed and shoved him over.

Chapter 15

Lessons and Destiny

Josh, Ulysses, and the team practiced retrieval simulations for the next four days. The tactical field agents went over various maneuvers based on what-if scenarios that ranged from textbook extractions with no resistance to full-scale assaults from both an offensive and defensive posture. Incorporated into each of the scenarios was Josh's idea for retrieving the medallion. It was simplistic in nature, but brilliant in its ingenuity. Ulysses wished he had thought of it first. The only drawback was that it required more equipment and a little more manpower. Ulysses wanted to keep this operation small as possible to minimize exposure and the time for extraction. Josh's plan would still fit within those parameters if everyone did their part with no mistakes. Precision had never been a problem for the Artifact Acquisitions Retrieval Team in the past. Josh and Ulysses ranked each of the possible outcomes based on probability and the accuracy of details provided by Herald. Neither of them saw any flaws during the simulations with the extra equipment or men. They felt good about the success of this mission.

Herald contacted them with the optimal timeline for extraction. All the equipment was packed and prepped for international travel; field agents and on-site intelligence operatives were en route to the airfield. Ulysses, Josh, and Melina were the last to leave. They boarded a Bell 525

Relentless from atop Jonah International headquarters and headed northeast.

They arrived at Hanscom Air Force Base, Massachusetts, in less than two hours, touching down right next to a C-130J Hercules Tactical Transport. Both Josh and Melina tried not to look enamored with the helicopter, or the plane, but could not help to be impressed. Both were state-of-the-art aircraft that far surpassed any mode of transportation either of them have ever ridden in. Ulysses let the kid-in-a-candy-store looks go when they got in the Relentless, but watching their eyes bug out when they saw the Hercules prompted him to explain what they both would most likely perceive as extravagance.

"Jonah has many affiliates whom they do business with across the globe. Some are even Associates," he said.

"Associates?" asked Josh.

"Associates are believers in what Jonah International stands for and provides to the world as a whole. They understand that the enemy poses a serious threat to the balance between good and evil and supports the ongoing cause to prevent them from . . . let's just say, 'increasing their market share' worldwide," said Ulysses.

"We are ready to disembark, sir," said a voice over the cabin speakers.

"Thank you," said Ulysses to no one in particular. He turned back to Melina and Josh. "All people that are affiliates and Associates have basically made their choice to serve on the side of good. They have pledged their loyalty, services, and"—pointing to the Hercules through the window—"resources for the cause."

The cabin door to the Relentless was opened from the outside by two air force personnel. As the three of them grabbed their carry-ons and began to exit, Ulysses said, "It all comes down to a choice, everyone has to make one. If you choose our side, Jonah takes care of you."

"What if you're on the other side?" asked Melina.

"Well . . . they're going to have a really bad day in the end," said Ulysses.

The three of them were met halfway to the Hercules by a group of what looked like air force officers. The man who appeared to be the leader snapped to attention and saluted with his entourage following suit.

"Col. Raymond McCready, Commander, Nineteenth Airlift Wing out of Little Rock." He dropped his hand and shook Ulysses's. "Welcome to Hanscom Air Force Base."

"Thank you, Colonel. Ulysses Quaden, Director of Technical Operations," he said.

"Your equipment has been packaged and stowed on the Hurc. Your team arrived forty-five minutes ago. They're currently aboard double-checking the manifest. Simmons here will stow your personal gear," said the colonel, motioning to his people. They took the bags and headed toward the Hercules.

"Col. McCready, I would like to introduce Melina Vargas, Director of Linguistics at Jonah International," said Ulysses.

"Ma'am," said the colonel as he shook her hand.

"And this is Joshua Arden," said Ulysses with a grin.

"Mr. Arden, it is an absolute pleasure to meet you, sir. When I found out that you were going to be joining this mission, I flew up with the crew from the Rock to meet you personally," said the colonel as he shook Josh's hand.

"Um . . . thank you," said Josh, a little confused.

"I look forward to working with you. You can always count on our support for anything. I mean that, sir," said the colonel.

Josh shared a glance with Melina. "Thank you, Colonel. I appreciate your assistance."

The colonel smiled then gestured toward the Hercules. "Let's get you folks squared away. Dust off is at 2300 hours."

One hour after takeoff, most of the mission's personnel found a rack to bed down for the night. A few milled about with diverse activities, from checking the tactical harnesses to a simple crossword puzzle. Josh was at a table station with his laptop open and various files scattered about. He did not really pay attention to anything; he just looked out the porthole window into the blackness.

Melina tried to get some sleep across the way when she turned and looked at him. "Josh?"

He did not respond. She got up and moved toward him then sat down. "Hey . . . you should try to get some sleep."

She lightly touched his arm. He looked around slowly, caught her eyes, and then smiled.

"You look troubled. What's on your mind?" she asked.

"Up until about fifteen minutes ago, it was this mess on the table," said Josh.

"And now?"

He glanced down to the table then turned to look back out the porthole.

"What is it?" she urged as she wrapped her arms around his then took his hand.

"This whole business about my future and the destiny of mankind. It's becoming overwhelming again. I have been asking Lucas, Ulysses, and Langston for months about the half-comments, innuendos, speculations, the looks I get from people I've never met, like Col. McCready, and they keep telling me a little here and there, and that I'll just have to be *patient* and all will be revealed in due time."

Melina did not know what to say. This was not the first time that Josh has been disturbed over this subject. She did not know what to say then either. "I'm sure that they are not keeping you in the dark on purpose. If they have told you that you'll find out everything at some point, then I believe that to be true. Especially coming from Lucas. He doesn't strike me as someone who would not keep his word."

She was right; he was frustrated. "I know . . . I know, it's just that I feel like everyone is looking at me like Harry Potter, the savior of everything magical. It took him years to figure out what apparently everyone else around him already knew. That lasted through seven very large books and eight ridiculously long movies. Look at everything he lost to vanquish the enemy, and he still couldn't prevent Hogwarts from being blown up."

"He did play a mean game of Quidditch though." Her failed attempt to lighten the mood did not go unnoticed by Josh, but it still did not help. "Honey, that was just fiction, things imagined by a very talented author."

"Real or not, the principles remain the same. I seem to be very important, not just to Jonah but to the world, and

I don't have clue one as to why." He looked down at the table again.

Melina followed his gaze then had an idea. She picked up some of the papers and looked at them. "Why do you have copies of insurance records and carrier's portfolios?"

She did not try to blow off Josh's frustration or feelings regarding this matter, but needed him to focus on something that he could control.

Josh was frustrated, but not stupid. He knew that she was trying to provide him a distraction, to keep him from spiraling down that path again. It was now something else that, if allowed, he would obsess on, which could cause him a great deal of anguish and, worse yet, loss of focus. It was almost like when he had dark thoughts about what happened to his mother. The two situations were completely different, but at the same time caused him a lot of inner turmoil. Just as with his mother, he had to come up with a way to push it backward and get himself, and his head, back in the game.

He assembled some of the folders. "There were a couple of situations that I encountered over the last year where some good people were struggling because of something awful that had happened to them, and both situations had to do with insurance payouts."

He leaned over and gave her a kiss. "Nice job on the distraction, by the way."

She smiled. "You're welcome."

Melina picked up one file and looked at the name. "Max Schulman?"

"Great kid, got dealt a bad hand . . . leukemia. His father and I worked together at the library before I joined Jonah."

She looked at another file. "And Julie Hanover?"

"She got caught in a plant explosion near where I grew up. I found out about her from Amanda."

"Harry's mother?"

Josh hesitated for a second. "Yeah, Harry's mom."

He shuffled through some of the files and pulled out specific information on each of the health care insurance carriers. "I asked for the case files because when I heard about each separate situation, something didn't quite sit right under the circumstances. In both instances, Max and

Julie had legitimate claims. All the appropriate paperwork, plus proof of individual insurability, was processed accordingly and, in Max's case, paid out, although under his father's new plan would only cover the bare essentials. Sam and Janet, his parents, could barely supplement the needed medical treatments, and Max was not getting any better."

"Oh my, that poor boy."

"Don't worry, Max has a happy ending. I helped his father get a job at Jonah. I put in a recommendation for transfer to a specialist at Johns Hopkins and paid off their existing medical debts." He looked at Melina and smiled. "Max is currently in remission and back in school."

Melina gave her boyfriend a hug. "Your heart is as big as this plane. What about Julie?"

"Her case is a bit different. Apparently, the plant that she worked at was being sold for disposal."

Melina looked puzzled, so Josh explained. "Some big-shot corporation wanted to buy the plant for its land value, sell off its assets, and develop it for a strip mall or something silly along those lines, leaving the local folks out of work, pretty much bankrupting and closing down the town. The plant is the main employer for three counties. The town filed an injunction to stop the sale of the plant, but proceedings for the purchase had already started. There were some inconsistencies between the present owners and the purchaser regarding paperwork. That resulted in the loss of the current insurance carrier, leaving the employees with no coverage at all. Somebody dropped the ball. That's when the plant exploded."

"Were there any fatalities?"

"A few, yes. Of the remaining survivors, Julie was hurt the worst. She had third-degree burns over most of her body. She was sent to a specialist in Madison, but none of her bills were getting paid. She had no family to speak of that could help, so Amanda has been doing her best to support."

"How did you step in?"

"I hooked Amanda and Julie up with Jonah's Domestic Relief Division, and they're doing what they do best. Julie is mending slowly, but surely. The legal department is also advocating on behalf of the townsfolk regarding the sale of the plant."

"What about Julie's bills?"

"They were taken care of."

"By whom?"

He looked her directly in the eyes. "By someone who cares about people more than corporations."

Melina smiled. She knew that Josh's heart really had no limits when it came to helping people. That was one of the many qualities that she loved. "So I take it that you found something else when you started your investigation?"

Josh looked down at the carrier files, straightened them, and placed them side by side. "Well, when I continued to look at the parent companies, I found that they shared one thing in common."

She looked closely at the two files and scanned for anything out of the ordinary. Her eyes caught the names of both companies, and she stopped. She looked at Josh with some concern. "Both insurance carriers were subsidiaries of Alastar-McGlocklin?"

"Yes . . . and that's not all." He pulled out the contract for purchase of the furniture plant in Wisconsin. "They are also the company that is trying to buy the plant."

"This is the same company that directly competes with Jonah International, isn't it?"

Josh nodded. "In a lot of key markets, yes. It's not unusual for a corporation that specializes in acquisitions to purchase diverse companies as part of its corporate strategy. For whatever reasons it may have, good business sense dictates a purchase that will be beneficial to the parent company's bottom line."

He reached into the file and pulled out the financial earnings for both insurance carriers over the last two years. "Neither one of these completely separate insurance carriers met their fiscal year budget nor market earnings. In fact, they have been steadily losing money for the last couple of years."

"Then why purchase them?"

"Exactly. I've been trying to find the logical business sense in their decision to buy, but can't. A tax write-off is the most practical reason, but they would have to pay taxes for that to be an advantage, that's a whole different discussion." He hesitated. "Then something else occurred to me."

"What?"

"What if these seemingly unrelated events have an underlying theme, something in common?"

"I'm not following."

"Sam's insurance changed at the library. Alastar-McGlocklin bought out the state's library contract and replaced the carrier with their newly acquired company. I used to work at one of the libraries affected. The insurance coverage for the people at the furniture plant was dropped. The plant exploded, which resulted in sending the severely injured to Kenosha Memorial. The explosion also happened while my legal guardian, Amanda, was on shift. Her job has been placed in jeopardy due to her determination not to give up on a young woman who has no one else and no means to pay until I stepped in. Alastar-McGlocklin dropped the ball on the insurance and is trying to buy the plant. The plant is close to the town that I grew up in."

He pushed the papers back into the folders and looked at Melina. "Alastar-McGlocklin's first year to participate in college recruiting was the year that I graduated. Their first and only job fair was the one that I attended at Carnegie Mellon." Josh reached into the last folder and pulled out a few more papers that backed up everything he stated and handed them over. She looked through them with growing concern.

"The day after my interview at Jonah, I was contacted by a representative from Alastar-McGlocklin, not for a job interview, but a job offer," he said.

"Wait a minute . . . You never interviewed with Alastar-McGlocklin?"

Josh shook his head. "No. The only time that I have ever talked with them was months before that day at the job fair. Their reps were actually following me from one station to another, kind of like they were waiting for an opportunity to sell me some knock off Rolex out of the back of a car. That discussion didn't last long. I found them very pushy and too full of themselves. They pretty much supported everything that I hated about corporations, throwing big phrases around like 'we are the leading company in . . . ' and 'we are the best at . . . ' It was a huge turnoff. I thought their approach was kind of odd. They were all about the kindness to lure me back to their booth, then they laid on the power play of how great they were. I didn't give any of this much thought until recently." He gestured to the files on the table.

"Anyway, I didn't hear a word from them at all after I moved to New York. Harry and I both struggled just to get by, he at the copy shop, me at the library. I wasn't in any hurry to get a high-paying Wall Street job. As silly as it sounds, I was happy with the little life that I had. I remember being at home one day and looking for something in a pile of books and papers in the corner of my room. I moved a stack and out fell a business card that I got from a Jonah rep at the college fair. I picked it up, held it in my hands, and remembered something they had said to me. They asked if I believed I could help them make the world a better place for all humankind. There was something special about that moment, and for a brief second, I wanted to make that difference. After a couple of days, I kept being drawn back to the thought of actually making an impact and helping people. I gave the rep a call, and the rest is history."

She squeezed his arm. "I'm really glad you made that call."

"So am I," he said with a smile. Then it faded.

"Right after, I mean the very next day, I received a call from Alastar-McGlocklin's HR department offering me a starter package. No phone interviews, no face-to-face . . . nothing. To this day, I have no idea how they knew I had talked to Jonah. It was almost like they were watching me, waiting for me.

"I'm not sure if you know this, but I grew up hating corporations. I came from a very poor background where money never meant anything except basic survival. There was no McDonald's every day or toys whenever I wanted them. My mom struggled just to keep the lights on, a roof over my head, and food in my stomach. Throughout my childhood, my life had been plagued with hardships that were basically caused by big companies."

He pointed to some of the papers on the table. "The automotive belt manufacturing plant that my mother worked at was bought by a big company that ultimately cut their benefits and laid off 40 percent of the workforce. She was not laid off, but had to work double shifts to make up for the lack of production, if she wanted to keep her job. She had a basic education and nowhere else to go, so she worked twice as hard for the same money. She worked herself to death to survive."

Melina looked through the papers then her jaw dropped. "You're kidding! Alastar-McGlocklin was the company?"

"An unlikely coincidence, right?" he said skeptically.

She kept looking through the papers on the table. She reached around him and pulled some other files, specifically, the ones that noted Alastar-McGlocklin's direct attachment to the events that Josh just described. She darted back and forth between different invoices, purchasing contracts, official letterheads of subsidiaries with acquisition announcements, etc. Her concerned look grew deeper.

"What if the commonality of all of these specific events wasn't about big business at all? What if these weren't random actions of buying and selling tangible assets that directly, or indirectly, affected people's lives?" he said.

She looked at him with a horrific expression that told him she finally understood.

"What if all of these events were orchestrated to get to me?"

Chapter 16

Briefings and Breach

Mission packets were distributed to each team member once they were airborne from Hanscom. They included detailed specifications of the operation timeline, activity management plans, team call signs, mission objectives by phases, geographical data pertaining to the target, facility blueprints, satellite and thermographic images, number of personnel at target and their shift schedules—everything needed to ensure that all Intel was current and accurate. There was even a weather forecast. Total flight time was a little over six hours. The expectation was for all team members to know their assignments and intelligence inside and out prior to arrival.

The captain of the Hercules announced their approach to Paris-Orley. With forty-five minutes left in total flight time, Ulysses assembled the team for the operation briefing.

He checked his watch. "We should be landing at 10:00 am local time. Associates have secured a hangar to hold the Hercules and provide cover until the mission has been completed."

He picked up a remote control and pointed it toward one of the monitoring stations. A holographic projection displayed the mission parameters, much in the same fashion as a standard business presentation. He cycled through the mission specifications as he spoke to each section.

"Based on the latest intelligence from Herald, the plastics' manufacturing plant has a shift change between 4:35 pm and 5:00 pm. This means there will be a lot of activity between employees entering and exiting the facility. During the same time, raw material delivery from external suppliers and cross-dock pallets will be moving in and out of the production staging area to inventory storage, just behind the east corner of the main building. This can be both good and bad. We want to be able to blend with the locals without drawing too much attention to our movements. The decoy and look-out team, code name Lancer, will be dressed as dockworkers moving inventory pallets and masking our ingress and egress to the vault tunnel.

"The entrance is on the southeast side of the main building, just behind the electrical substation, through a doorway marked Danger 10,000 Volts. External video security surveillance is managed by the plastics' plant and not included within the service that Herald is providing us within the tunnel and the vault. The intelligence team, code name Eyeball, will be stationed in an AGS moving van two kilometers away. Beginning at 4:25 pm, Eyeball will tap into external video feeds and, at random intervals, loop security surveillance. If the guards aren't paying close attention, they will never notice.

"At approximately 4:37 pm CEST, Herald will flip the switch, tunnel and vault security will go dark. The tactical team, codename Brushfire, will enter the tunnel door at 4:38 pm. The clock starts upon entry. We will have eight minutes to breach the vault, obtain the medallion, and exit before Herald reactivates internal security systems. At 4:47 pm CEST, the medallion will be placed inside a pallet and loaded onto one of the deployment trucks scheduled for shipment. That truck will be operated by Lancer and will rendezvous with Eyeball for the exchange. Once the exchange is completed, Eyeball will head back to the hangar. Brushfire will exit the facility via one of the raw material suppliers' transports at 4:50 pm. That particular transport is owned and operated by an Associate who will deliver our team back to the hangar. Watchdog will be monitoring the entire operation from rHub," he said.

Ulysses switched off the holographic projection and put the remote back in its slot. He turned back to his team. "Are there any questions?"

"Are we expecting to encounter any Familiars or resistance?" said someone from Eyeball.

"According to Herald, this is a passive installation, electronic surveillance and automated countermeasures only. No RCT within striking distance. However, the plastics' manufacturer is sympathetic toward their movement. It is quite possible, Familiars will be present during the operation. Watchdog will be monitoring all satellite communications specific to their known frequencies and alert Eyeball should anything surface. Any other questions?"

After a few seconds of silence, Ulysses said, "Okay . . . Estimated time until the Hercules is secure: seventy minutes. Once we are inside the hangar, we will stay there until the mission starts. No one is to leave the hangar."

The team disbursed to their various activities while Josh moved toward Ulysses. Melina was right behind him.

"Familiars?" asked Josh.

"Those are the people who assist and serve the other side. They are similar to Associates, but the difference is, Familiars have some sort of personal investment in their cause. They understand what they perceive to be the truth, as told to them by the enemy. They have been promised something in exchange for their loyalty and services, such as wealth, power, material gains, or status," he said.

"Enemy?" asked Melina with some concern. "I don't understand."

"This would be one of those things that is supposed to be explained to me later," said Josh.

Ulysses looked sympathetic toward both Josh and Melina. He knew it was difficult to come into this new world of understanding with so many questions and not given any answers.

"Listen . . . I know that this is hard for both of you to understand. I promise you, there will be a time and a place for each one of your questions to be answered.

All I can tell you is this, the enemy cannot be trusted under any circumstances. They will lie, steal, and cheat to get whatever they want or need in order to succeed in their endeavors. If Familiars know what they are getting into and that they are willing participants, it is too late for them. In the enemy's eyes, a contract is a contract, regardless of the means."

This was the most information that Josh had received from anyone in a long time. He was not even upset that it all sounded very cryptic and appeared disjointed to the point of a cross between science fiction and a cold war novel. Ulysses talked as if the entire world was involved in some elaborate conspiracy, that some participants were willing and others were not. Josh could not make any sense of it. He needed to understand what was going on. What were the sides in this war?

Was it a war? If so, was it fought with conventional weapons? Psychological, biological, or a combination of both? So many questions still floating around that Josh tried to put in order.

"Okay . . . so we've got them versus us, good versus evil, or however you want to classify it. For those who have not yet made a choice, there is still hope, correct?" said Josh.

"There's always hope, if there's a little light left in your heart," said Ulysses.

He pulled out his tactical harness for inspection one last time. "In the immortal words of Bob Marley, it's our job to 'light up the darkness.'"

All teams arrived at their designated spots at 4:20 pm local time. Ulysses ran a COM check and verified readiness. Both he and Herald had burner phones for communication. They were to be used for text messaging only. The sole purpose was for Herald to contact the retrieval team to inform them of the status to the surveillance and countermeasures system. The codes were simple: # meant the system was down, $ meant that the system would be back online within sixty seconds. If Ulysses received the symbol! at any time, something was wrong.

"Eyeball, Brushfire 1, commence video loop," said Ulysses over the tele-link.

"Brushfire, Eyeball, video loop in process," said a voice.

"Lancer, Brushfire 1, in position."

"Brushfire, Lancer, we are a go," said another voice.

"All teams, Brushfire is on the move," said Ulysses.

The Brushfire team consisted of Ulysses, Josh, and three other field agents. Just like Lancer, Brushfire was dressed as warehouse personnel and dockworkers. All teams had their tactical harnesses on underneath their civilian clothing. It was a thinner variation of an assault vest and made of Kevlar microfiber. Interwoven into the material was an array of circuitry that served multiple purposes, such as GPS tracking and positioning and communications. All signals emitting to and from the harness phased frequencies at random intervals, preventing hacking or interception from outside, while allowing the agents to remain synchronized to each other and connected to both Eyeball and Watchdog.

The parking lot for the warehouse and dockworkers was across the street from the service entrance to the plant. A group of workers arrived earlier than anticipated for their shift. Ulysses saw this as an opportunity to blend, so Brushfire picked up their backpacks and fell in line with the other workers headed toward the entrance. Each agent was dispersed throughout the herd. When they arrived at the guard gate, each agent produced their perfectly forged credentials and passed through.

"All teams, Brushfire is on-site," said Ulysses.

"Roger that, Brushfire. Proceed to dock 4 to retrieve the package. Lancer will rendezvous and ferry," said Eyeball.

"Acknowledged," said Ulysses.

He instructed Josh and two of the field agents to head directly to the tunnel entrance and wait, while he and the other field agent meet up with Lancer.

Part of Josh's plan to retrieve the medallion called for a piece of equipment that was too big to carry in as a worker without drawing attention. He came up with the idea to ship it to the plastics' plant in smaller sections, disguised as raw material. There was a tracking device embedded in the packing label, allowing them to pinpoint its exact location. Using what looked like a cell phone, Ulysses and

Lancer found the package within thirty seconds of entry to the dock.

"Eyeball, Brushfire 1, package located."

It was secured to a pallet that looked like any other freight, but was actually a hollowed-out container. Following the proper procedures, Ulysses updated the shipping manifest in the warehouse's computer while Lancer, using a forklift, took the pallet and headed toward the tunnel entrance.

With great precision, it was placed next to the wall on the west side of the tunnel entrance. Another Lancer agent backed an electric service van in front of the pallet and the entrance, obscuring the view.

"Brushfire, Lancer 3, cover in place, maintaining watch."

"Acknowledged," said Josh.

He and the remaining two Brushfire agents immediately opened the pallet to retrieve the items. In the mission prep, they practiced the assembly of the sled multiple times, trying to improve their movements and speed, each time shaving a few seconds off. Josh and one agent assembled the components of the sled, while another agent worked on the tow cable and automatic winch. Josh and his partner finished their set up within thirty seconds then went to help the third. They mounted the winch to the support struts and were attaching it to the concrete with an impact wrench when Ulysses and the other Brushfire agent rejoined them.

Ulysses acknowledged the other agents then checked the sled and the winch. He gave Josh a nod.

"Eyeball, Brushfire 2, package operational, awaiting signal," stated Josh.

"Acknowledged," said one of the intelligence agents inside the AGS van. Melina was standing back to make sure she was not in the way. She watched all the operatives with amazement. Each of them was working their stations with a calmness that surprised her, as she was completely tense. They were checking satellite coverage, perimeter movement, electromagnetic signals, all the while maintaining communications between all the teams. She looked over the shoulder of someone who was monitoring and tracking each of the field agents. She located Josh's signal labeled BF 2. It was clustered with a number of similarly labeled signals in one spot on the satellite image. She desperately wanted to speak with him, but knew that was an impossibility at the moment. She prayed for his safety harder than anything that she had prayed for before.

It seemed like time stood still. There was no chatter between any of the field operatives while they waited. All four of the Lancer agents did their job and maintained watch as they worked the warehouse loading docks. No one talked or acknowledged each other. Then someone broke the silence.

"Brushfire, Eyeball, incoming signal on mobile communications network."

Ulysses flipped open the burner phone and waited. He looked at his watch then back at the phone. At 4:36:50 pm, a text message came through.

It simply read'#.

"Eyeball, Brushfire, mission confirmed. We are a go," stated Ulysses.

One of the Brushfire agents pulled out an electronic device and attached it to the keypad for the outer door then pushed a sequence of buttons. The display lit up, and in three seconds, the indicator changed from red to green. The door locks clicked. At the same time, the other agents loaded the remaining contents of the pallet onto the sled. Brushfire was now just inside the outer door. Another agent was controlling the sled with the winch via remote control. The first agent used the same device to open the inner tunnel door.

"Eyeball, Brushfire, tunnel door has been breached. Brushfire going radio silent."

Melina held her breath as all of this happened. The operatives in the van watched their screens intently, each focused on their area of responsibility. The next eight to ten minutes was going to be very quiet for all teams.

"Brushfire, Eyeball, the clock has started."

Just as Herald had indicated in his Intel, behind the door was a singular hallway with a slight downward slope. Brushfire took off their civilian garments to reveal their field uniforms. They donned their individual packs, pulled out their night vision goggles, then started running toward the vault door. Brushfire 4 was responsible for the sled. He sat on it and opened the release on the winch to let gravity carry it down the tunnel.

Two minutes later, Brushfire and the sled arrived outside the vault door. Brushfire 3 began working on the locking system. He pulled out four separate electronic devices of various dimensions and switched them on. After punching in a few key codes, he handed one to each of the other agents. Josh placed his over the panel microphone; Ulysses, over the eyepiece. Brushfire 4 set the larger device on the raised floor pedestal in front of the other security access panels, and Brushfire 5 placed his beside the keypad.

With each agent holding their devices in place, Brushfire 3 stood back and synchronized all with a remote. "On my mark . . . three . . . two . . . one . . ."

All devices went from a red status to green simultaneously. The vault security locks clicked, followed by a hiss of compressed air. Brushfire 3 policed all the devices while the other four quickly entered.

"Time remaining?" asked Josh, speaking to no one in particular.

"Five minutes," said one of the agents.

"Let's move, people," said Ulysses.

Kelan was locking up his office at the Long Beach facility. He was making his way toward the exit when he saw Margaret coming out of her office.

"Hey," he said with a tired smile. "It's a bit late for you, isn't it?"

"I could say the same about you," she said.

"I was working on funding for the next mission. What's your excuse?"

"Crunching some telemetry numbers on a DRONE modification. We're trying to see if we can increase the response time at a higher orbital radius. I guess the time just got away from us."

"Time flies when you're having fun," he said.

"In this case, no, it didn't," she said.

As they had reached the elevator, she asked, "Are you up for a late-night dinner?"

"Actually—" he began to answer, as his cell phone rang. He looked at the number with raised eyebrows and answered.

"Sir, an alarm was triggered at one of our European facilities," said the voice.

Margaret's cell phone rang two seconds later.

"Which one?" asked Kelan.

"SV 8," said the voice.

Kelan's look turned serious when his eyes met Margaret's. He knew that she was receiving the same information. They both responded to their callers at the same time.

"I'm on my way."

Once inside the vault, each agent attached their tactical lighting system to the shoulder of their harnesses and removed their goggles. Brushfire 4 lowered the sled, leaving it ready for retraction, just inside the door. Ulysses and Josh walked the room to locate the medallion, while the rest of the team unpacked the extra equipment from the sled and begin assembling the X-9 VTOC microlaser. The main unit had four conduit cables that led to handheld units for output.

"Charging," said Brushfire 3 after connecting the last cable.

"Got it," said Josh as he found the medallion.

It was just as depicted in Herald's Intel. The medallion was, indeed, encased in a transparent aluminum shell affixed to a pedestal that was three and a half feet in height from the floor. Since there was no way to remove it from the enclosure within the window of the security system blackout, Josh's idea was simple. They were going to cut the pedestal from the floor and take it along with the medallion. Once it was free from its bindings, it would be loaded onto the sled and quickly pulled back up to the surface. Subsequently, it would be packed into the same false pallet that the sled and equipment came in then loaded for transport to exit the facility with Lancer. Josh and Ulysses walked around the pedestal to get a quick assessment as the rest of Brushfire made their way to the medallion's location.

"We've got a problem," said Josh.

"What?" asked Ulysses.

"The pedestal base has five impact bolts, not the four as anticipated," said Josh.

Ulysses turned to Brushfire 3 as he approached. "How long will it take to cut?"

Brushfire 3 knelt down to examine the base. "It depends on the tensile strength. These bolts are pretty sizable."

"We've got three minutes. There are four units and five bolts. Whoever finishes first will start on the fifth one. Let's get started," said Ulysses.

Kelan and Margaret entered the operation center and walked straight to the security duty station. There were three technicians clustered around one screen, talking back and forth. Everyone went silent when Kelan strolled up.

"Details," he said.

The technician who was assigned to the station and received the alarm began first. "Sir, each one of our security facilities has state-of-the-art surveillance systems. They are monitored twenty-four hours a day based on an automated program that relays video, audio, and status of access straight to this station." He pulled up all the secured global locations belonging to Alastar-McGlocklin and displayed them across the screen. "As you can see, all facilities are green across the board."

"I thought you said that there was an alarm?" said Margaret.

"That's the interesting part," said another technician. "The alarm was triggered by a failed status ping."

"What does that mean?" asked Kelan.

"As a matter of practice, we double up on all security measures. Even though all secured facilities are monitored consistently, we receive an intermittent ping that basically verifies that the facility is online and operational. If the facility fails to connect via a ping more than three times, an alarm is triggered," said the technician.

"SV 8 is not transmitting," stated the first tech.

"Okay . . . That doesn't make sense. According to the automated monitoring, SV 8 is online and in the green. One of these fail-safes seems to be faulty," said Kelan.

"That's what we thought," said another technician as he walked past the group to his station and began manipulating the keyboard, "so we began to run diagnostics to find the problem. First, we tapped into the video feed of the vault room." He pulled up a video snapshot. "This is a live feed directly from the vault. As you can see, everything is nominal, laser grids are active and pressurized O_2 is in the green. In this case, green means that there is no oxygen content within the vault itself." He punched in a few more keys. "This is a snapshot from the vault door up through the tunnel. Again, everything appears to be normal."

"Get to the bottom line quicker, please," stated Kelan.

"Y-Y-Yes, sir," stammered the technician working furiously with the keyboard. "I checked the audio units for both and listened. Once again, everything appeared normal, so I thought of one more thing. Just to make sure that the facility was safe, I tapped into external surveillance cameras owned by the plant . . . and this is what I found."

Kelan watched the tape for about ten seconds and began to get agitated. "What am I looking for?"

"Sir, please bear with me for a few more seconds and watch," said the technician.

"Wait . . . Right there!" said Margaret, pointing to the screen.

Kelan leaned in a bit and looked closely. Then he saw it too. One of the yard workers was at the corner of the camera screen; he carried a clipboard and appeared to be writing something. The image was a bit fuzzy, but it looked like he had dropped his pen and bent down to pick it up then moved on. A few seconds later, what looked like the same worker was in the identical position doing the same thing and dropped his pen. Kelan continued to watch for twenty more seconds and saw the same scene play out two more times.

"The video has been looped," stated Margaret.

Kelan looked at the technicians. "Did you check the other signal? the ping?"

"Multiple times, nothing is sending or receiving. Those signals are relayed by communication satellites. It's like trying to connect to an IP address through the Internet. SV 8 appears to be offline," said the technician.

Kelan looked at Margaret. "What assets do we have in place?"

"Let me make some phone calls," she said.

"We need eyes on the site to verify. Try to make it happen quickly," said Kelan. He turned away from the duty station to pull out his cell.

"Sir, excuse me for interrupting, but we were given explicit instructions should a situation like this occur," said the duty technician.

Kelan stopped in mid-dial and turned back around. "What? By whom?"

The technician looked at his other colleagues like he had just gotten in trouble by the teacher and was being sent to the principal's office. In this case, that was technically accurate; Kelan was the principal. He finally looked back with defeat in his eyes and tried to explain. "Mr. Pemberton. Some months ago, we were told that if there were a breach in any security facilities, specifically the vaults, from anything or anyone who was not authorized, we were to initiate a secondary protocol."

Margaret immediately asked the question that Kelan was thinking. "What secondary protocol?"

The technician hesitated. Again, he looked at his other colleagues, who knew full well the consequences of what was going to happen if they did not follow the instructions and Mr. Pemberton found out.

"Sanitize the facility." he finally said.

"What!?" said Margaret.

"Explain to me exactly what you were told," demanded Kelan.

The technician was visibly shaken now. His colleagues appeared to be upset as well. Something was going on, and Kelan wanted to know.

"Sir, it's what I told you . . . Mr. Pemberton told all of us that—" started the technician.

"Told all of who?" asked Kelan.

"Us. The guys running the duty stations."

"The three of you?" said Margaret.

The other technicians looked at the first one. They were all scared.

"All of us. Every shift personnel at this facility."

Kelan's eyes widened. He finally put two and two together. Pymm threatened his people. "What did he tell you to do?"

The technician felt defeated. "As I was saying, he instructed us to sanitize the facility in question without hesitation, should anything out of the ordinary deviate from standard procedures."

"Yet you called me . . . Why?" asked Kelan.

He looked at his other associates again. "We discussed it first and decided that you are our boss and needed to know. What he is asking us to do is without remorse or consideration for human life. We were hoping that you would have another alternative."

Kelan looked at Margaret for a half a second and then the other three. "What does he have on all of you that would make you initiate this secondary protocol?"

Another technician spoke up immediately. "He threatened to hurt our families, make them disappear . . . or something worse. If we don't do what he says, he will do it. The way that he said it, the look . . . he meant it."

Kelan nodded his head empathetically. He and Morgan shared this one thing in common; they both hated Pymm with an unbridled passion. "Okay, Margaret and I are going to see what assets we have in place at that facility and get them there as quickly as possible to verify if there is actually a situation or not. This could be something as simple as a power grid malfunction. We won't know until we get eyes on the site."

He looked at Margaret and nodded. She opened up her cell. Kelan was thoughtful for a second. He was intimately involved in the containment measures of each of the secured facilities as he designed them. The only lethal part of the countermeasures was the halon gas. Even if that could be initiated remotely from here, power has been cut off from the vault. There was no way to receive the signal.

He looked back at the first technician. "If there is a power failure, how would you trigger the halon release?"

The technician was puzzled. "Sir?"

"I designed the countermeasures of that vault. The only thing lethal enough to sanitize the area is the halon gas. If the power has been compromised and countermeasures cannot be activated by an intruder, how would you trigger the release?"

"Umm, per Mr. Pemberton's instructions, we installed redundant fail-safes. We have an uplink through all the global communication satellites to each of the facilities as a backup. Even in the event of a total power failure, the secondary receiver is connected to an individual power cell and would trigger the explosion, not the halon gas. It would be as simple as dialing a mobile phone number."

The blood drained from Kelan's face.

"What explosion?" said Margaret.

Kelan was already past that. "What's the yield?"

The technician looked down in shame.

"Answer me!"

"Total! It's a fuel-air bomb."

Kelan stared at him in horror.

Ulysses finished cutting his impact bolt first, so he started on the fifth. The total time for him to cut the initial was just under three minutes, which was cutting their timeline for the security blackout close. Brushfire maintained radio silence and worked together without talking. Outside of the hum of the laser and the occasional moan of the steel giving away under pressure, there was no other sound within the vault.

Kelan started typing commands into his mobile phone. "Don't do a thing until I've had a chance to verify a positive security breach, do you understand?"

"Yes, sir," said the first technician. He looked at his colleagues with a little relief. He, for one, did not want to be responsible for triggering a detonation resulting in ramifications that he would not be able to live with. Another technician shared his relief, but the third one looked pale.

"Russell? Are you feeling okay?"

Two other Brushfire agents finished cutting their impact bolts within thirty seconds after Ulysses.

Josh had just finished cutting his when Eyeball broke the silence. "Brushfire, Eyeball, incoming transmission on the mobile communications network."

He looked at the mission time on his watch. They still had two minutes left. He turned toward one of the other agents who had finished. "Take over so he can answer."

The agent assumed the position and activated his laser as Ulysses backed away to pull out his burner phone. He flipped it open as the message came through. Even in the darkness, Josh could see Ulysses's eyes grow wide.

Kelan and Margaret stepped away from the duty station to make their phone calls. The technicians were doing as they were instructed and waited. The third one started to pace nervously.

"Russell, what's going on?" asked the first technician.

"This is not good," he said.

"What's not good? We all decided to call Mr. Tindal once we had enough information. He's going to fix this. He is most likely right, this is a power malfunction of some sort."

"But that doesn't explain the looped video!" he said at almost a shout.

"Russell, calm down," started the second technician. "Just give Mr. Tindal a chance. He knows what to do."

Russell stared at them with a pained expression on his face. He looked from them to Kelan and then back and continued to pace.

"Eyeball! We are aborting the mission! Repeat . . . We are aborting the mission!"

The other Brushfire agent's eyes grew wide as they looked at Ulysses.

"What did the message say? Was it the abort code?" asked Josh.

"Brushfire is packing up now," stated Ulysses.

The agent who took Ulysses's place to finish the fifth impact bolt stopped and began disassembling the laser while the other agents started packing up the gear as quickly as possible.

Josh walked over and grabbed Ulysses's arm. "What did the message say?"

Ulysses took a deep breath. "Yes, it was the abort code."

The way that he looked at Josh told him that there was more. He would not let go of Ulysses's arm. "What else was there? What else was in the message?"

"There is a bomb. We have to get you out of here. Now!" stated Ulysses in a low tone.

Josh held his breath for a moment. For a split second, he thought that Melina was right, this was a dangerous mission and he was not prepared. Then, as if practically on cue, a calmness came over Josh that was completely unexpected. His next movements and actions were virtually instinctive.

"Do we know what kind of bomb?" he asked.

Without missing a beat, Ulysses said, "HIT."

The other Brushfire agents stopped in their tracks.

"What is an HIT?" asked Josh.

"High-Impulse Thermobaric. An aerosol ignition creates a blast wave. The vacuum pressure from the wave then ignites oxygen molecules between 5,000° and 6,000°. Anywhere there is air in this structure will burn, nothing will survive, the plant will collapse. Total destruction." gasped Brushfire 3.

Josh's eyes widened. *This cannot be happening. We are so close to getting this Artifact. All of the people above.* "Eyeball, this is Brushfire 2. Do you copy?"

"Brushfire 2, Eyeball, we copy."

"Belay that last transmission. We are continuing to retrieve the Artifact. Watchdog, Brushfire 2, have you detected any electromagnetic signatures transmitted to, or emitting from, this location? It would have to be something that could breach the depth of the vault."

"What's that going to tell us?" asked Brushfire 4.

"This facility does not currently have power, so the triggering mechanism would most likely be in the form of electromagnetic radiation waves, something along the lines of a cell phone with its own power supply. It stands to reason that if there is a bomb here, it would have to be triggered from outside using something like that and be powerful enough to transmit through the containment walls of the tunnel and the vault."

"Brushfire 2, Watchdog, negative readings on any electromagnetic signatures to or from your location. Can you tell us what's going on?"

"All teams, this is Brushfire 2. Herald has transmitted the abort code stating that there is an HIT explosive device on-site."

Everyone from Watchdog to Lancer tensed up. The situation was now very serious and extremely dangerous. Melina's hands went up to her mouth, and tears brimmed her eyes.

Looking around, Josh said, "Okay, I want the three of you to get back to the top entrance as quickly as you can. Ulysses and I are going to finish cutting out the pedestal."

"Now wait a second," started Ulysses.

Josh held up his hand while he continued to hand out instructions. "Lancer, Brushfire 2, have transport ready for the package and Brushfire ASAP. Brushfire will begin egress immediately."

"Brushfire 2, Lancer, copy that."

With a sense of urgency, Ulysses grabbed Josh. "Listen to me. You have to get out of here. We cannot afford to lose you!"

Josh saw the panic in his face. "Please, Ulysses . . . trust me. This is what you, Lucas, and Langston have been saying to me all along. Let me do my job. Get back on the laser for that fifth impact bolt. I will join you in a second."

Ulysses started to calm down and let go of Josh. He nodded once as if he understood and continued to cut.

The other Brushfire agents were trying to pack up the gear and place it on the sled. Josh looked over at them. "There's no time for that, leave it. Get onto the sled and ride it up as fast as you can. Send it back down once you reach the top. Help Lancer secure transport and prepare to receive Ulysses, the medallion, and myself when we are finished here."

They nodded and carried out their instructions.

"Watchdog, Brushfire 2, put me on speaker."

"You are on speaker," came the quick reply.

"Sentinel, online," said Josh.

"Sentinel is online."

"Sentinel, do you recognize my voice?"

"Yes."

"Can you hack into the facilities' emergency and evacuation systems above?"

"Yes."

"On my mark, I want you to trigger every alarm they have to evacuate the facility and the loading docks.

"Eyeball, work with Watchdog and figure out how to prevent and isolate an incoming signal that could trigger this bomb. If it is not within a standard proximity for something like this, then concentrate on a satellite uplink, cross-reference with all known points of origin of enemy locations. Brushfire 1 and I will continue to work on the medallion."

Margaret snapped her flip phone shut just as Kelan finished his call. "We've located an asset within the plant itself. We can have eyes on the door within twenty minutes," she said.

Kelan nodded. "I've just got—"

He stopped in midsentence and turned back to the duty station. Something was going on; one of the technicians was shouting.

"No!" yelled Russell. "You didn't see what I saw! When he told me that he was going to kill my family, his eyes! They were glowing!"

The second technician tried to reassure Russell by placing a hand on his shoulder. That just agitated him further. "Don't touch me! You weren't there, you didn't see it!" he screamed.

"Russell! Get a hold of yourself!" shouted the first technician. "He threatened all of our families, not just yours."

Russell stopped for a second; his eyes darted back and forth. It appeared that he was trying to process this information. Mr. Pemberton threatened their families too. That means that if any one of them failed to carry out his orders, all three of their families would be in danger, not only his. The other two were just sitting there, waiting for someone else to decide, to do something. The fate of his family was in someone else's hands. He started shaking his head erratically like a madman.

"No . . . No . . . This is not good," he repeated in almost a whisper. His eyes scanned the room looking through and around and at nothing at all.

He was losing it.

He saw Kelan and Margaret walking toward them.

"Eyeball, Lancer 4, Brushfire 3, 4, and 5 are at the tunnel entrance."

The Brushfire agents quickly disembarked the sled. Placing whatever they could find to give it weight, Brushfire 4 then released the switch on the automatic winch and sent the sled hurling back down the tunnel.

Kelan watched the scene unfold as he started walking toward the duty station. Two guys were obviously trying to calm down the third, who pushed the others aside and ran toward a computer terminal.

"Russell, no!" shouted one of the guys.

"I'm not going to sacrifice my family for anyone!" yelled Russell.

Slinging a chair aside, he began typing. The other two guys were about four steps behind him. Kelan started to sprint toward them with Margaret in pursuit. The two other technicians reached Russell, tackling him to the floor, but not before he pressed the Enter key.

Chapter 17

Leaders and Signals

Pierre Lautramont had just finished checking the previous shift's production list when he received the call. "Bonjour, c'est, Pierre."

His expression remained detached as he received his instructions relayed by the Americans.

"Compris. Je vais prendre soin d'elle." He hung up.

As the sled crashed against the vault door, the shouting over COMs began.

"Brushfire! Brushfire! Electromagnetic signature detected! Incoming signal! Point of origin, Long Island!" shouted Eyeball.

"Confirmed!" shouted someone from Watchdog.

Josh dropped his laser, braced himself between the wall and the pedestal, and started kicking it, hoping to loosen its hold as Ulysses continued to cut.

"Sentinel! Sound the alarm and evacuate the facility!" shouted Josh.

"Understood."

"Watchdog, can you shut down the link?" he said.

"Negative! The signal is being routed through multiple satellites! We can't isolate fast enough before it reaches the next one!"

"Shut down the satellites!" screamed Josh.

"Which one?" shouted someone from Eyeball.

"All of them!" he yelled.

"We can't! There's not enough time to fix the position or plot the signal's trajectory!" shouted Watchdog.

"Sentinel! Shut down all global communication satellites! . . . Now!" shouted Josh.

"Processing."

Within one second, the signal vanished off satellite relays.

"All global communications satellites are inactive. The signal has been terminated."

For the first time in modern technology's history, all forms of communication that use microwave radiation signatures ceased across the globe simultaneously. Although Sentinel's orders were not explicit, it ensured that the shutdown was specific only to the localized electromagnetic carrier waves that matched those of the inbound transmission. Since frequencies could possibly be phased, Sentinel further justified that all wave radiation across the spectrum should be stopped, preventing a signal jump to compensate. To the normal user, it would appear that cell phones could not get a signal or a call had been dropped. Mobile carriers across the world, on the other hand, would be working for weeks trying to figure out what happened.

All Artifact Acquisition Retrieval Team members' communications were not affected as they did not work on the same type of technology. No one really tested this; they all sat in their spots, stunned from the events of the last twenty seconds.

Ulysses burned through the last impact bolt as Josh pushed and kicked with all of his strength. With a loud snap, the pedestal finally moved free of its permanent bindings. Ulysses dropped his gear as he and Josh picked up the pedestal and moved toward the sled. Josh was the first to test their state-of-the-art communications after the shutdown. "Eyeball, Brushfire 2, pedestal is free. Loading onto the sled for egress," he said calmly, as if ordering a cup of coffee.

"C-Copy that," said Eyeball.

All types of Klaxons and alarms went off within the plastics' facility. Sirens and warnings ranging from a fire to a chemical airborne toxin radiated through the entire complex. All of this happened just after Pierre had hung up his phone. This might actually work in his favor. In the confusion of the evacuation, he could make his way over to check the tunnel entrance without arousing suspicion from the other workers or security. As employees were filing out, he grabbed his backpack, dropped in line, and walked with them to the nearest exit.

With the pedestal and the medallion strapped to the sled, both Ulysses and Josh climbed on either side and secured themselves.

"Brushfire 4, the package and remaining units are ready for extraction," said Ulysses.

Josh was glad that his friend was getting back into the objective. Josh did not know what had come over himself within the last few minutes. When Ulysses had mentioned a bomb, automatic motions and processes made him think and take charge without even questioning where this newfound commanding presence came from. It felt so natural and compelling, almost as if he had the answers for everything that came their way. It was as if he was being directed by force he did not recognize, but trusted completely. Josh made a mental note for him and Ulysses to have a long talk about what just happened.

"Brushfire 1, prepare for fast egress on my mark. In three, two, one, initiate," said Brushfire 4.

As Josh and Ulysses braced themselves, the sled took off like one of those air-compressed rides at an amusement park. The trip only took six seconds.

Hundreds of workers began pouring out of every available exit from all facilities, including the main building. Apparently, the alarms were generated across the entire complex and not just confined to the manufacturing plant itself. As one could imagine, there was a bit of chaos manifesting as people were confused and did not understand. Adding to all of that commotion was the fact that people were still coming and going for shift change. The ones that were leaving had turned around and come back to see what was going on, while the people who were in the middle of it were trying to leave as quickly as possible. It was quite evident that should they all survive whatever was happening, evacuation procedures and policies would most certainly be revamped and practiced.

Throughout the sea of people, Pierre tried to position himself at the side of the crowd to maneuver faster toward the exit. There were obstacles in the way as well as people pushing and bumping against him. He finally managed to get outside of the building then started to jog toward the south.

The sled decreased speed about twenty feet from the tunnel entrance, using the weight plus the gravity and slope of the incline, to slow the inertia. Once it came to a complete stop, the rest of the Brushfire team began to loosen the bindings for the medallion, Ulysses, and Josh. Lancer already positioned the transport near the electrical substation, twenty feet from the outer door, to the tunnel just on the other side of the electric van. Ulysses, Josh, and one other agent packed the medallion and the pedestal into the false pallet, while the other two Brushfire agents broke down the components of the sled and the winch. A tiny explosive charge was attached to each leg of the winch's tripod at the base. With all the activity resulting from the evacuation, no one heard the small shotgun blasts that freed the tripod from its mounting. It was then tossed on top of the sled and pushed through the inner vault door down into the tunnel. Both doors were secured by Ulysses as the rest of them made their way to the transport.

Pierre was a little overweight and definitely out of shape. He was sucking in large amounts of air by the time he reached the southwest corner of the main facility. He stopped and bent over with his hands on his knees as he tried to catch his breath. The closest exit of the manufacturing plant from his workstation was at the opposite end of the tunnel entrance. When he received the call, his plan was to walk through the plant to the southeast side. He did not count on having to exit the building and walk completely around it; he sure did not bank on having to run. He was still trying to catch his breath when he forced himself to continue.

As he approached the loading docks, Pierre looked around at all the workers trying to evacuate, while others were moving materials, as quickly as they could, away from the main structures. Most likely following protocols to remove combustibles to minimize any damage. At first, he thought the confusion from the alarms would aid in his reconnaissance, but it had turned into more of a hindrance than anything else. There was nothing standard to observe during this melee of unorganized activity.

Pierre was not the brightest man, but he was not unable to rationalize or think logically. Although the pattern of activity had changed due to the evacuation, there were things that he could spot if it did not seem normal for this type of situation. He slowly started scanning from the right to the left. He saw numerous people milling about, moving pallets and boxes from here to there. He looked toward the electrical substation and did not see anything out of the ordinary; there was a truck blocking the entrance. The tunnel door was really his objective anyway, so he moved in closer for a better look.

"Lancer 4, Watchdog, you have activity at your two o'clock. There is a Tango approaching from the south side of the complex, one thousand meters out."

"Watchdog, Lancer 4, copy that," he said as he looked in that direction and waited for the subject to come into view.

As Pierre approached, he saw that there was somebody just sitting in a cargo truck, not moving. That was not unusual if a driver was waiting for somebody to load pallets in the back for transport. He thought nothing of it as he moved around to get a better look of the tunnel entrance.

"Lancer 4 to all teams, currently tracking a Tango with eyes in this direction. Prepare for possible contact."

Continuing in his wide arc around the truck, Pierre reached the other side. He noticed there were a lot of people working on securing one pallet into the back. He thought it probably contained something heavy, and once again almost discounted it, but then something caught his eye. They were wearing protective gear, something like a Kevlar vest that the Groupes d'Intervention de la Police Nationale would wear in case of a riot. A red flag alarm went off inside of his head. He stopped cold in his tracks.

"Eyeball, Lancer 4, Tango has stopped and is still continuing visual. Looks like we may have been made!"

"Brushfire, Eyeball, status?"

"Package has been secured. Awaiting Brushfire 1, five seconds out," said Josh.

"Lancer 4, Brushfire 1, roll out! I will secure the Tango and rendezvous at the service entrance," said Ulysses.

"No! Negative. We are not leaving without all units!" said Josh.

"Lancer 4, safe flight!" said Ulysses.

"Copy that, safe flight acknowledged," replied Lancer 4 as he started the truck.

Ulysses prepared for a situation that may put, not the Artifact, but Josh's safety at risk. He established a code phrase that, when invoked, altered the parameters of the mission itself. Looking back to the events of the last ten minutes, he should have used the secondary protocol immediately once the danger had been discovered, but Josh had taken the initiative to work the situation, and Ulysses wanted to give him command latitude. He was not going to test his luck a second time.

Josh was now considered the precious cargo; the Artifact was secondary. He was the only member of the mission that was not aware of the ancillary agreement. The fact that both he and the Artifact were in the truck at this very moment was fortunate.

Pierre looked at the driver. Their eyes met, and he knew immediately that there was a problem. He was too far away to identify whatever was being loaded into the truck, but that did not matter. His instructions were to find out if the vault had been compromised, and it most certainly looked like it had. He reached into his pocket to retrieve his cell phone to report back. Upon flipping it open, he looked down at the display without moving his head.

There was no signal.

The request from the Americans for information on the vault could not be relayed. The nightmare of the situation became very real for him. A steady stream of sweat trickled down his face now, and it was not from the physical exertion. He had been given other instructions should the vault be disturbed without the proper authorizations. The memory of the meeting came back to him like a flood. He was told that if the facility was compromised for any reason, he should set off the security alarm that would call the Central Directorate of Interior Intelligence, or DCRI. The gentleman who issued this order was dressed in black. He was intimidating and scary beyond anything that Pierre had seen in his life. The man's eyes were red. Pierre was in indentured servitude and committed to a larger cause of which he did not understand or was even aware. He had no choice but to obey.

He was a Familiar.

"No! We are not leaving without Ulysses!" said Josh as he tried to exit the back of the truck.

The other Brushfire agents pulled him back and restrained him.

"Josh, please . . . we have our orders," one of them said.

Ulysses reached into one of the duffle bags that came inside the pallet with the sled. He pulled out a Milkor MGL with six 40-mm nonlethal shells already loaded. He chambered the first grenade as the truck pulled away, using it as a shield. When the vehicle was clear, Ulysses quickly had a bearing on the Tango and was ready to fire.

The truck was pulling away. Whatever the velours had stolen was most assuredly on it. That did not change his orders though. Pierre reached inside of his backpack and pulled out a small black control box. He fumbled a bit as he tried to punch in a code to unlock a triggering mechanism. Although he was not sure how the box would make contact, since he could not get any cell reception, it was not his place to worry about such things. He would do as instructed and initiate the signal.

When the truck had cleared the tunnel entrance, he saw a man standing there, pointing a gun at him.

Both Ulysses and Pierre stared at each other. Pierre's eyes grew wide, and his hands started to fan out in a reflexive response.

"Drop the detonator!"

An American, how typical. Pierre, being a true Frenchman, did not understand a word of English. "Déposez vos armes à feu, ou je vais appeler la police!" he responded, telling Ulysses to drop his gun or he would call the police. "Je peux les appeler avec cela!" he announced that he could call them with the black box.

He raised it as he made the statement, causing Ulysses to tighten up his grip and crouch into a firing stance.

"This is your last warning! Drop the detonator, or I will fire!"

As soon as Pierre saw Ulysses move into a firing position, his entire body started to shake. This crazy American was going to shoot him.

He needed both hands to turn the switch and depress the call signal. He estimated about fifteen meters between him and the crazy American and wondered how good a shot this person was. His eyes darted back and forth trying to decide what he was going to do next. He knew that if he failed to fulfill his obligation, the man in black with the strange red eyes would not be pleased. Would it be better to die an honorable death by filling his commitment, or should he surrender to the American and accept whatever the consequences might bring?

Pierre was more afraid of the man with the red eyes. In one swift movement, he brought his hands together, turning and depressing the switch.

Ulysses fired.

"Electromagnetic signal detected!" shouted someone from Eyeball.

"Where's it coming from?" said someone else.

"Can the signal be stopped?" said a Watcher.

"Where are Brushfire 2 and the package?"

Everyone was talking over each other trying to figure out what was going on, how a signal managed to get through.

Then the ground started shaking.

It felt like a rumbling coming up from the earth's belly. The people that were still in the process of trying to evacuate the complex slowed to a stop. They looked at each other and at the ground; then they turned toward the main building. A flash of brilliant light came out of the south side. The outer door from the tunnel blew with such force that it crashed into the electrical substation, causing power lines and transformers to crackle and hiss into a series of smaller explosions. The wave from the blast hit the electric van that was parked next to the substation, propelling it, and anything else that was in the force radius, outward. The foundation of the main building cracked from the pressure of the explosion, and one side began to drop. Illuminated plumes of flame shot out through the basement floors and radiated toward the top of the building. It was a pattern much like one would see from precisely calculated placements of shape charges like they used in structural demolitions. It seemed never-ending, all-consuming. The orchestration of the explosion was both a horrific and elegant at the same time. Of the survivors who would live to tell the tale, it would look as if the world was coming to an end.

As the building began imploding, the ground surrounding it started to roll and crack in various patterns indigenous to an earthquake. People were tossed about like rag dolls; vehicles, equipment, inventory, and pallets crashed onto their sides or into each other like marbles spilling out of a bag.

Lancer and Brushfire were at the fringe of the wave. The cargo truck shook as Lancer 4 powered forward to clear the service entrance. Josh and the rest of the team looked at the horror unfolding behind them. All communications were down at the moment of detonation, so they did not have any audio or visual of Ulysses and the Tango.

The impact of the repellent grenade hit Pierre square in the chest. Under good environmental conditions, it would have knocked the wind out of him, tossing him backward a few feet. The explosion happened so quickly that the blast, coupled with the grenade, carried him up and back twenty feet. He landed hard, shattering almost every bone on the right side of his body.

The moment that he fired, Ulysses turned to see the electric van heading straight for him.

And then there was blackness.

Chapter 18

Sorrows and History

The Hercules was two hours into its flight back to the United States. The mood was quite different on the way home. Feelings were very raw as team members were coping with the events of the last twenty-two hours. The actions of the mission garnered worldwide attention that no one anticipated. While the international news media was abuzz with the temporary global communications blackout, the top European story now was the massive explosion at a Paris manufacturing facility. It seemed as if every news outlet was running both stories conversely, with experts in the fields of telecommunications, satellite engineering, manufacturing, and seismology providing their two cents on what they thought had happened and why. When they ran out of anything they deemed substantial, they interviewed random people from all walks of life. They were asked how they coped without their cell phones. They talked with local sidewalk café patrons who either saw the brilliant light or heard what they thought sounded like a big boom. The media frenzy was worse than anything that prime-time reality TV could possibly offer, and the world was eating it up.

Melina sat in a window seat with her arms wrapped around her knees, slowly rocking back and forth. Tears were brimming her eyes as she watched Josh across the way. He was in so much pain, and once again, there was nothing she could do.

One of the Brushfire agents walked over. "Ms. Vargas, can I get you anything?"

"Thank you, Tim, but no." She looked up at him, trying to smile with quivering lips.

Her gaze returned to Josh; he followed her stare. Tim furrowed his brow a bit then looked down, thinking that he could have done more himself. As a professional, he tried to rationalize that he had followed his orders as instructed. That did little to console him or the rest of the team. Sometimes orders meant nothing in the aftermath. All they had now were scars of what could be considered a successful mission.

He sat down in the seat next to her. "This wasn't his fault."

"That doesn't matter, not to him. He doesn't see it that way," she said.

"He saved hundreds of lives with his actions."

"But he couldn't save them all . . . He couldn't save him."

They both looked over to see him just sitting there, staring.

Josh continued to look at the casket that held the body of his mentor and friend. Teammates, medical personnel, Melina, all had tried to comfort him through this incredible loss, but he was numb to everything surrounding him. He went through all the motions as the cleaner crew from Jonah Paris tried to ensure there was a separation between the mission and the incident. Medical personnel and emergency responders were all Associates, so they were sensitive to the secrecy of the operation and handled everything. They facilitated the movement of Ulysses' body, and the paperwork associated, to make certain that he could be transported back with the rest of the team.

Josh did not leave Ulysses's side once in the last nineteen hours. During that time, he ran through the many different ways that this outcome should have happened; things that he could have done to prevent this. If they had left when Ulysses called the abort, then he never would have encountered the Familiar. He would be sitting here, right now, angry that they did not retrieve the medallion. Josh looked past the casket to a smaller pallet that held the Artifact.

That stupid medallion.

Josh had half a mind to open the cargo hold and dump the thing out into the Atlantic. He looked back at the casket and, in his mind, could hear Ulysses telling him that would be a foolish thing to do, that he had better not consider something like that after everything they both had to go through to get it.

Josh felt all alone. How was he going to do this job without Ulysses? Did he even want to anymore? Why do so many people around him get hurt or die? He began to think about the past, but this time instead of pushing the memories back, he opened up his mind and began to relive.

It was the first day of school at McNamara Elementary. A very shy Joshua Arden held his mother's hand tightly as she walked him into Mrs. Blanchard's kindergarten class. The teacher greeted little Joshua with a smile and extended her hand. He reluctantly let go of his mother's and accepted hers, but still kept a wary eye on his mom. The teacher guided him toward some other kids, who were sitting in the play area, pushing trucks, and playing with dolls and blocks as they waited for the first bell.

As he sat down to reach for an unoccupied purple race car, a little boy pushed his tow truck up next to it. "You wanna play cars with me?" With the observing eyes of a five-year-old, Joshua looked at him then nodded. The two of them pushed their toys around making car noises. After a few minutes, other children joined in the fun.

Madeline Arden, Maddie to her friends, explained that they had just moved to the area. Without going into much detail, she said that Joshua might be going through a difficult time with the loss of his father. The teacher was very sympathetic, apologizing, and nodded her head in the understanding of the situation. Madeline knew the teacher had the wrong assumption, but she was not going to correct her. The less said, the better it would be for her and Joshua to move forward.

The truth of the matter was that Joshua's father had left them. He found himself, what he considered, a bigger and better deal and took off, stating that he did not want to settle for a family life. He was still young and had some living to do. He could not do any of the things that he wanted if he were tied down.

Loser.

Madeline wasted no time in packing up Joshua and what little belongings they had and got as far away from the irresponsible loser as fast as they could.

She had met the loser when they were in high school. It was a typical teenage sweetheart story, complete with aspiring dreams of what they wanted in their future. Neither of them counted on Joshua. When the baby came though, Madeline's entire outlook on life had changed. It was love at first sight. She started dreaming of a life as a family. That dream quickly turned into a nightmare. It was not for the lack of understanding, but it should have been her first clue when she wanted to get married, and the loser had said no. The drinking and the abuse started when Joshua was only eight months old. Although the loser never laid a hand on Joshua, Madeline feared that it was just a matter of time. She stayed with him suffering the abuse and protecting Joshua, because she had no other place to go. She was actually relieved when the loser said that he had enough. It forced her into a reality that it had always been just Joshua and her and that she did not need him in their lives. Since she and the loser were never officially married, she gave Joshua her maiden name of Arden. He might come back sometime down the line laying claim as the biological father, but Madeline would deal with that if, and when, it came.

Madeline and Joshua moved to a little town outside of Kenosha for a job. It was a Japanese plant that manufactured automotive belts and needed more line workers. Because of the unexpected gift from God, Madeline did not have the opportunity of a proper education after high school. She did not even get to graduate, getting her GED a year after the birth. Trying to fit in and give Joshua as much of a normal childhood as possible, she found this job to start all over.

Over time, Madeline and Joshua settled into the community. She managed to scrape enough money together to buy a small one-bedroom house fifteen minutes from the plant. Only wanting the best for her son, she gave him the bedroom, and she slept on the couch. She made every sacrifice a mother could for her child. She loved her son more than life itself. They did everything together, enjoying each other, and laughing almost all the time.

Through school functions and Joshua, she met and became best friends with Amanda Gibson. Her son, Harry, was in Joshua's class and also happened to be the little boy whom he met on his first day. It worked out wonderfully that their sons became best friends. Harry's father was no longer around either, so the similarities between the two boys and their mothers brought them all very close.

As years passed, Josh and Harry became inseparable. They had sleepovers at each other's house every weekend that they could. When the weather allowed it, they rode their bicycles home from school together every day. In the summertime, they built tree houses and always went fishing at the big lake behind the Benson's old farmhouse. Life really could not be much better from Josh's perspective.

Everything changed when he came home one day and saw his mom sitting in the living room, crying. She had just lost her job at the plant. At eleven years of age, Josh knew this was a big deal, but did not think about how different things would be for them going forward. They barely had enough money to get by as it was, and Madeline did not have a plan.

Amanda made the offer for her and Josh to come live with them. Madeline refused at first as she did not want to become anyone else's burden, but then acquiesced, as Amanda told her that it would be perfect for both her and the boys.

Madeline became sick a few months later.

Cancer is a horrible disease. It is a plague that does not reason, does not discriminate, and certainly does not show remorse for its victims. She was diagnosed with stage 4 lung cancer. It was caused by the chemical fumes of the compounds that made up the automotive belts. OSHA regulations were more of a guideline rather than a strict policy, so air filtration masks were not always worn by the workers on the mixture lines. Madeline never thought much about it. After years of exposure, it finally caught up with her.

Around the same time that Madeline and Josh came to live with them, Amanda was being pursued for a head nursing position within a lucrative medical practice in Kenosha. She had done very well at all the interviews and was considered the prime candidate. It would be a huge win for her, as the money would be almost double what she was currently making as an LPN at the local clinic. One afternoon upon returning from her shift, she received a call from the cushy Kenosha practice, stating that they appreciated her time and interest, but the opportunity was no longer available. She was not given any further details other than the medical practice was expanding due to a buyout, and they had more than enough staff to cover all needed areas. Unknown to her, or anyone else at that time, the purchaser was Alastar-McGlocklin.

Madeline was going to die. She knew this to be a fact, and so did Amanda. Although she knew it was going to be a tremendous inconvenience, Madeline begged Amanda to take care of Joshua. She had no money, no means of support or income, nothing of value that she could give Amanda in recompense for the support. Amanda did not care; she grew to love Joshua as much as she did Harry. The thought of him going somewhere else was not even considered.

One night, as he always did, Joshua came into his mother's bedroom to kiss her good night. She was in bed now all the time. He tried to remain positive when he was around her, and she did the same with him, but it was tough. He knew things were bad, and he was pretty sure that she was aware that he knew. She always managed to smile though. She helped him with his homework when she could, read passages out of the Bible, and tried to impart some of life's lessons that he could take with him as he grew up. She had nothing else to leave him, so she gave him the only thing that she could.

"Joshua . . . always remember how much I love you. No matter what happens, that will never change," she said weakly.

As he left her room, he turned around at the door. "I will. I love you too, Mom." He left with tears in his eyes.

She passed away in her sleep that night.

Things were hard for Josh going forward. He struggled in middle and high school from a social perspective because he was still dealing with the pain of his past. He would not let anyone get close to him for fear of being hurt, that they would ultimately leave just like his mom. Deep down, he knew that was irrational, as his mom did not have any choice, but his dad did. His mother probably thought he had forgotten, but Josh's memory was long around that one. Just the same, he did not want to shoulder the burden of maintaining an emotional attachment that involved love. He felt all alone in the world, even though he had Amanda and Harry. He thought he loved them both dearly, but it was different, something that he could not explain and did not feel the need to. He just accepted it for what it was.

Josh was a good-looking young man, but was viewed by his classmates as a social pariah due to his shyness. The stigma of this status reflected in his grades. Even though he was capable of achieving so much more, he did just enough to get by. His grades took an upturn when he and Harry had decided on colleges in which they wanted to apply. GPAs were important, so he had to get his at the right level by buckling down the last part of his junior year and his entire senior.

Neither Josh nor Harry was any different than other eager young college wannabes, so they sent out mass mailers and online applications to every college that they could think of who might be willing to look at two kids from a small Wisconsin town. They both decided early on that they wanted to go to the same college regardless of which. Their friendship was not going to end at high school graduation.

Every other week during his senior year, Josh would get some type of correspondence from college admissions. While some would start with the "Thank you for applying, but we regret to inform you . . ." spiel, those would come in the form of a single letter in an envelope; others would be thick, with tons of information and a congratulatory letter of acceptance. As excited as he was, he would always go to the financial section to see what tuition was going to run. There was no way that he could afford most of these colleges. He tried not to lose hope, but it was fading fast each time he opened up a fat envelope. Applying for the colleges was one thing, getting accepted and paying the bill was entirely something else.

One day he was pleasantly surprised by two thick packages: one addressed to Harry and the other to himself. Both were from Carnegie Mellon in Pittsburgh. They both had been accepted, and when they reviewed the monetary section, they found they both qualified for financial aid. In some situations, a full ride for a grant could be provided to capable applicants. Unknown to Josh, his grant was funded by a subsidiary of Jonah International. As they read the letters, their excitement grew. They began jumping around and giving each other high fives, much like at a sporting event. It looked like Josh had hope for his future. He wished his mom could have been there.

His head snapped forward as if coming out of a trance. His mind was back in his body, still sitting next to the casket holding his dead friend. He had a wild look in his eyes as he stood up and turned around in a slow circle, as if confused and trying to get the bearings of his location. Melina and Tim shot up out of their seats. It was the first sign of movement that they had seen in him since boarding the plane. Melina reached him as quickly as she could.

"Josh? It's okay. You're safe." She interpreted his startled state as a form of shock. Most likely, a latent reaction to Ulysses' death.

"What? No . . . Melina, I'm fine," he said calmly. "Well, as fine as I can be under the circumstances." He looked back at the casket.

"Then what is it?" she asked. Tim was standing right behind her.

"An epiphany," he simply said. "Do you remember what we were talking about on the plane ride over, the theory I had about Alastar-McGlocklin and their endgame?"

Melina was thoughtful for second. "Yes."

Tim stood there listening and looked confused.

"I'm convinced more now than ever that this is not just a coincidence. What happened here, on this mission, Ulysses's death . . . as significant as these events are, when you add that to the tally of all the other things that happened in connection with me, the likelihood of this being random decreases dramatically."

"I'm sorry to interrupt, but I don't understand any of this. Are you saying that this was not an accident? That it was planned as part of an unknown objective?" said Tim.

"I'm saying that his death was a possible outcome based on a choice or decision. It wasn't planned, but it happened because of the choices being made by me, and mostly by Alastar-McGlocklin."

Melina started to think. Based on everything that Josh had shared with her previously, it was all plausible and very real.

"I promise you, Tim, I will share everything with you and the rest of the team. I'm going to need all of you if I'm going to bring Alastar-McGlocklin down," said Josh.

"What?" said Tim.

He turned toward Melina. "As I sat here feeling sorry for myself, and about what happened to Ulysses, for the first time in a long while, I let myself sink into the blackness of all the bad things in my past. I remembered moments that I had desperately tried to block."

Josh walked over to his gear and pulled out the files. He spread them on a workstation table and started shuffling through them. He found the one that he needed.

"Here . . . ," he said, pointing. "The plant that my mother worked at was closed by Alastar-McGlocklin. That's why she lost her job. Years earlier after my father left us, she tried to find any work that she could to support us, there was nothing available, and believe me, knowing my mother, she looked everywhere. Miraculously, she found the job at the Japanese automotive belt plant. The only position available for her was on the mixture line, working the chemical vats." He looked at her intently for a second. "I will bet my paycheck that none of that was a coincidence, the job offer, the timing, the type of work . . . losing her job, and then somehow . . . the cancer."

Melina's eyes were wide with the speculation. "Josh, you're talking about a massive conspiracy that began when you were a child. How would you ever prove something like this?"

"The first step is to find out who the parent company was of the Japanese automotive plant. I will bet another paycheck that it was a subsidiary of Alastar-McGlocklin," he said.

"Josh, what are you going to do if you're right?" asked Melina.

"Embrace my destiny . . . and use all the resources of Jonah International to stop them."

He gathered up the files and put them back in the folder, turned, and handed it to Tim. "You are the first person outside of Melina that I've shared this with. Read through it, then I will answer any questions that you have." Tim took the file and nodded thoughtfully.

"What's your next step?" asked Melina.

"It's time for all those questions to be answered," he stated flatly.

"Who are you going to talk to first?" she asked.

"I'm going straight to the top," he said.

Kelan was a little in shock, but more angry than anything else. The news of the explosion in Paris was everywhere. His people at the Long Beach facility were more than a little stirred up at the thought that it was caused by one of them. He was still waiting on more intelligence to confirm, but his initial thoughts were that this was an act committed by the interference of one person, Pymm. He went behind Kelan's back to put in additional defensive measures at all the vaults. Measures that go against everything that Kelan believes in. He would never willingly sanction the death of anyone or destroy company property in the process. That person threatened and manipulated Kelan's own people, and that infuriated him beyond reason.

Russell had basically lost his mind at the realization of what he did. Kelan could have fired him for his act of internal treason, but in the end, he understood Russell's motives. The welfare of his family was at stake. He did what he thought was right at the time, but it did not excuse a life for a life. He suspended Russell from his duties and sent him home.

The death toll at the facility was hard to confirm for Parisian authorities. The devastation caused by the HIT left a crater in the earth where the complex once stood. There was nothing left, no bodies to find, no building, no vault—everything was utterly destroyed. The news reports stated that thirty-eight people that were known to work at the plant during that time were still unaccounted.

When Kelan had approached Blalock regarding what had happened, he expected more of a response than he received. Blalock was not necessarily unconcerned, but his focus was more about the exposure and the threat to Alastar-McGlocklin if this incident was tied back. It was things like this that made him hate Blalock more every day. Kelan's conviction for bringing him down had never been more intense than it was now. He already took the first steps in the overthrow. He needed to reach out to his contact and see about the next move.

PART THREE

THE TRUTH

Chapter 19

Answers and Glimpses

The memorial service for Ulysses Quaden was one of the grandest that Josh had ever seen. Jonah International spared no expense in honoring one of their fallen. As with everything else that Jonah touched, the service was very elegant, but not over-the-top, and planned to the tee. The event was very befitting; Ulysses would have liked it.

It was amazing to see how many people admired and respected this man. All the senior executives, not only from Jonah International but also from all the global offices, were in attendance. Josh, Melina, Langston and his family, and Lucas were among countless others paying their respects to a man who gave his life in service to a cause greater than himself. It was very unfortunate that the official explanation of death was listed as a commuter accident while attending a technical conference in another country, but the secrets must remain. It was highly suspected by the inner circle of truth that Sandra, Ulysses' wife, had knowledge of what his actual role was inside Jonah. He was a very devoted family man. He loved his wife and children with all his heart and would find it extremely difficult to keep something like this from Sandra, at the very least.

As the service continued, Josh watched her and their two children, Thomas and Adrianna. It broke Josh's heart that these kids were going to grow up without their father.

Money was obviously not going to be an issue; Sandra and the children would be well taking care of, to include college and all the amenities. It was just the thought of them growing up without Ulysses's presence in their lives. Josh envied what time the children had with him and wished he could have experienced the same. Although he had memories, albeit mostly bad, of his father, he wondered what it would have been like to have that type of relationship.

When the service was over, Josh and Melina paid their respects to the family. Upon exiting the church, Josh spotted Malcolm Holden. "I'll be right back."

She nodded and walked over to talk with Langston and his family.

As the global CEO, Holden had an entourage around him constantly; the ranges of roles were from other C-level executives to personal assistants. As with any corporation, a lot of professionals tended to gravitate toward the people with the most perceived power. Even though this day was a solemn occasion, they were still buzzing around him like gnats. As he saw Joshua approaching, he ended his current conversations rather quickly.

"Excuse me, Mr. Holden? Do you have a few minutes, sir?" asked Josh.

"Absolutely. What can I do for you, Joshua?" said Holden.

"First, my apologies for bringing something like this up on a day like today, but I wasn't sure if I would get another opportunity to speak with you. I know that you are a very busy man."

"Joshua, my door is always open to you any time."

He was startled by that statement. The global CEO of the largest corporation on the planet just told him that he was welcome to speak with him at any time. Josh wondered if he truly meant that or was only humoring him in front of his staff. As he looked Holden in the eyes, he could see that the invitation was genuine. Josh did not know how he knew, but that he just did. "Thank you, sir. I really appreciate that. I hope that this is not inappropriate and don't want to take up any more of your time than I already have, but I have some questions regarding certain activities that are related to my division, and I was hoping you could provide some answers or a point of reference for me to continue my research."

Even though the memorial service was not anywhere close to the moment of where Josh wanted to approach Holden, he was very aware of his surroundings and did not want to say too much or expose what he believed was the truth in front of too many people. He was cryptic on purpose and thought that Holden had a good understanding of why.

Looking over Josh's shoulder, Holden saw Lucas in the distance. He nodded as if secretly answering Holden's question.

It was time for Joshua to know the truth.

"I don't want to prevent you from continuing your research. I will be more than happy to answer any questions that you may have. Why don't we do this over dinner? Tomorrow night, my house, say around eight o'clock?" said Holden.

Josh was again a little startled at the openness. "That would be great, sir. Again, I really appreciate your time."

They shook hands then parted ways. As Josh approached Melina and Langston, she excused herself politely and stepped toward him. "Well?"

"He and I are having dinner tomorrow night . . . at his house," he said.

Melina's eyes were wide. "You're kidding? Just like that?"

"Just like that."

Malcolm Holden would consider his home to be modest for someone of his position, but for those that visited, it was nothing short of magnificent. He lived in the small town of Bedford Hills located in Westchester County, New York. His home was in the center of twenty acres of very well-manicured grounds with impressive iron fencing around the entire estate. Since he was expected, the security guard opened the gate immediately, and Josh's driver made his way up to the main doors. As the car pulled up, Josh marveled at the elegance. The CEO's home was beautiful, but not ostentatious. As Josh approached the front doors, they were opened by one of the house staff. Josh was taken to the library where Malcolm Holden was waiting.

"Joshua. Welcome," he said as he stood.

"Mr. Holden," said Josh, crossing the room to shake his hand. "Thank you so much for opening your home to me. It is very beautiful."

He shook Josh's hand. "It's my pleasure to have you here, but as far as the beauty goes, it was all done by my wife."

They exchanged a few minor pleasantries just before dinner was announced. It was discovered that Holden's wife had a prior engagement, so she would not be joining them. He was an older gentleman, so his children were grown and out of the home. It seemed that outside of the staff, it was just going to be him and Josh.

As they finished dessert, Holden folded his napkin and placed it to the side of the plate. "I believe that you have some questions. Why don't we talk in my office where it's a little more private."

As they walked down the hallway, Josh was more than a little anxious about what was coming. He had so many questions for so long, he tried to formulate where to start. He did not want to come off like an ambitious reporter looking for a Watergate. He also did not want to leave until he was satisfied. As they entered the office, Holden motioned to the comfortable chairs off to the side. Once they were both settled, Holden crossed his legs and just waited.

A few moments passed. "What can I answer for you, Joshua?" he finally asked.

"Sir, I don't mean to be presumptuous or disrespectful in any way, but I am hoping you know why I am here," he said cautiously.

"I do."

"I'm not even sure where to begin . . . ," he started.

Holden wanted to make the transition a little easier for him, so he began instead. "Joshua, listen . . . You need to be comfortable and accepting of the information that you are about to receive. Some of this may come as a shock, or disbelief, which is why we have been tentative in answering your questions. We have felt that when the time was right, and you were ready, we would provide those answers that you have been desperately seeking for so long."

"Why now?"

"Because the time has come for you to understand why you were chosen."

The confusion started, but Josh wanted to be patient, he was so very close. "Chosen for what?"

"To be the next champion in the fight to maintain balance between us and them."

"Mr. Holden, please . . . I can't do all of these cryptic riddles anymore. None of this makes any sense. I need straight answers," he said in frustration.

"Okay," said Holden, nodding in understanding. "Let's see if I can break this down to the very basics for you."

"I would really appreciate that, sir."

"I'll start by asking you a question. What do you think Jonah International does?" asked Holden.

"Well . . . it's one of the, if not the largest, multiconglomerate corporations in existence, specializing in a diverse array of ventures to range from antiquities, mergers and acquisitions, and relief efforts—"

"No. That's not at all what Jonah's true purpose is. What you just described is the company's mission statement as mankind sees it. You need to look at the bigger picture."

"As mankind sees it? What does that even mean?"

"Since the beginning of creation, we humans have been plagued with the consequences of our choices. God gave to man the power of free will and, with that, the right to make our own decisions. Good, bad, or indifferent, man has the power to choose.

"When you get up in the mornings, you decide whether or not to have breakfast in your home, grab something on the way to the office, or even pick something up in the cafeteria at work. That is a choice that you make. With each of those choices comes a reward or a consequence. If you decide to have breakfast in your home, a reward may be that you get to eat in the comfort of your home or maybe you save extra money by not spending out. On the other hand, a consequence of eating at home could be that the additional fifteen to twenty minutes that it takes can make you late for work because traffic may or may not be congested. Conversely, a reward may be an accident that was avoided," he paused for a second. "Do you understand?"

"I think so," Josh answered honestly. "Every cause has an effect."

"Exactly. There have been influences throughout time that sway those decisions. If you pick out something to wear, and Ms. Vargas said the colors did not match, there is a better than average chance that you will not wear that combination again. She has influenced you. Each choice that is made alters future events."

Holden paused for a moment thinking about how to phrase what he was going to say next. "As human beings, we are both blessed and burdened with the power of choice, but that power is limited based on what we are capable of comprehending. We think ourselves to be the center of the universe, that we are in control of our own destinies and know the difference between right and wrong. The truth is that we have never been in charge. There are powers beyond our understanding that have directed the course of humanity since the dawn of time."

He could see that Josh was thinking as he tried to put the pieces together. He wanted to give him time to process this.

"Extraterrestrial?" whispered Josh under his breath as his eyes searched for nothing, moving back and forth in thought.

Holden grinned slightly. "No, aliens do not exist. Think bigger."

Josh continued searching to put meaning behind the words that Holden had just said. We have the power to make choices. Results from those choices can either be good or bad. Sometimes our decisions are influenced, but not just by mankind. If it is not extraterrestrial in nature, what else could it be? Supernatural. The clarity of what was just said smacked him right in the face. Everything that Ulysses, Langston, and Lucas ever alluded to started to fall into place.

Holden could see that Josh was beginning to understand and leaned forward in order to give him the final piece of the puzzle. "Mankind cannot do this alone. The Chairman created Jonah International to maintain the balance between good and evil and provide hope to those where none exist."

"So you are telling me that angels and demons really do exist and that the Chairman is—"

"Why is that so hard to believe? Religious doctrines, pagan gods, ghosts, the occult, people have long sought to find meaning in those things for centuries. They've grown to place their faith in something that is not truth. After generations of following the wrong path, their beliefs are grounded in deception, leaving the truth buried. Today's society believes monsters exist in the form of vampires, werewolves, zombies, and other concoctions influenced by the enemy and made very realistic by Hollywood. This nation alone spends billions on a belief that life exists on other worlds. The purpose of all of that is to distract from the one true God. What better way to prevent man from making the right choice?" Holden said.

Josh's eyes started to dart back and forth again as he was trying to recall something that Ulysses had said to him. "Everyone has to make a choice."

Holden nodded. "Yes, there is no way around it. You are either on the side of truth, or you will be damned for all eternity."

Josh slumped back in his chair and put his hand to his head. It was swimming with so many different things, both current and from his past. The realization of all of this was like a rush of cold air swirling around him. His mind was opening up to the ideas of a world that was full not just of humans but of a supernatural presence. He had just been yanked out of the matrix and was trying to catch his breath.

"Please forgive me, I'm trying really hard to process this," he finally said.

"It's completely understandable, Joshua. To know that we are going through the motions here on earth as part of a much bigger plan . . . It took quite a while for me to come to terms with it when my eyes were finally opened."

"It's not that I don't believe you, please do not misunderstand, Mr. Holden. It's just that, this is so much to take in."

He looked Holden square in the eyes. "You said that I was the next champion in the fight. What do you mean?"

Holden was going to need some help with this question. "Lucas, will you please join us?"

In the blink of an eye, Lucas was standing next to Holden's seat. Josh was startled and jumped.

"Joshua, please don't be frightened," said Lucas.

"Oh man!" he said as he bent over in his seat holding his head as if he were going to get sick.

This is real. Everything that everyone had said to him was real. His mother, Sunday school, the crazy people on the street corners in Manhattan who did not really seem that unbalanced now.

He leaned back in his seat and tried to slow his breathing.

"Joshua, are you okay?" asked Holden.

"I'm good," he said, nodding his head, as if trying to convince himself that he actually *was* okay.

He looked at Lucas as if he were from outer space. This, in Josh's mind, was not too far from the truth. "Are you an angel?"

"Yes," he simply said. "I am called Lucaous. I am of the Guardian Host in the Majaliant Elodine. You are my charge."

"Like my guardian angel?" asked Josh.

"Similar, but slightly different with respect to your position."

"What is my position?"

Holden and Lucas shared a look.

"Joshua, the Chairman has selected you to be a leader within Jonah, to champion our cause for the balance of power," said Holden.

"Joshua . . . you possess a leadership quality unlike any other. Your heart is pure as well as your intentions. You have been given this gift to counterbalance the needs of mankind during this tumultuous time," said Lucas.

Josh started shaking his head. "I don't have any special gifts. I'm just trying to do my job."

Lucas stepped toward Josh and placed his hand on his shoulder. "You have been destined for this since before you were born. The events of your life have shaped the person that you are today, a kind man with an anger for injustice."

With Lucas's touch, Josh flashed back to the many events of his past. He remembered a tall man with blue eyes holding the door for him and his mother the first day of school. The picture in his mind shifted to the day of his mother's funeral. The same tall man with blue eyes came up to Josh and told him how very sorry he was for his loss. The picture shifted time and again as Josh remembered all the separate encounters on his interview day at Jonah all those years ago and countless other instances where he remembered Lucas's face.

He looked up. "You were there! In my past, as a child . . . college . . ."

"Joshua, I was there at your birth and have been ever since," said Lucas.

Josh's head cocked a little as he was still remembering. "You weren't the only one. There was someone else, someone in black . . ."

The look on Lucas's face turned to disdain. "His name is Pymm. He is the one that has been orchestrating all the negative elements that have affected your life."

Josh's demeanor turned serious. "My mother's death . . . Ulysses?"

"Aye. He has worked in tandem with Familiars to breed a series of happenings in hopes of preventing you from ascending to leadership. They have caused sorrow and pain at every turn. Through all . . . you still persevere."

A realization struck Josh. "Harry . . . Kate?"

"He was instrumental in dissolving your friendship. He used his influence and Familiars to set that course."

"I have gathered some pretty compelling evidence that ties Alastar-McGlocklin to my past. How far off base am I?" asked Josh.

"Not far, I'm afraid," said Holden. "They are the enemy's equivalent to Jonah."

"They have been around in some form for hundreds of years. I have had dealings with their agents in the past," added Lucas.

Josh looked at Holden then back at Lucas. "Why are they going to this much trouble for me?"

"Because you are the chosen one," said Holden. "You are the one that has been destined to turn the tide in favor of the Light."

Josh started shaking his head again. "I am just one man, I can't be that important."

"Joshua, look at all the good you have done since you have been affiliated with Jonah. By your actions, how many countless lives have you saved and given renewed hope? Max and his family, Tina from the cafeteria, Julie from the plant explosion, all the people from the Paris plant. I have watched you your entire life and seen the effect that you have with a simple act of kindness. Imagine a future with unlimited resources and the support of the Chairman," said Lucas.

"Joshua, your destiny can change others. The enemy knows this. They will do whatever they can to stop you and our cause in their ultimate quest," said Holden.

"The endgame?" asked Josh, hoping it was not the answer he knew it was going to be.

"Souls," said Lucas.

He looked at Holden like he had just seen a ghost. This seemed impossible for him to absorb and understand.

"Everyone has to pick a side. Whether they know it or not, it must be done," said Holden.

"As with your progression through Jonah, the decision to assume this responsibility is and must be yours, but know this . . . Your influence will reach further than anyone else on this planet during this time. The impact that you will have will shape policies, cultures, and the very way of life for most people.

"Fear not, the confidence in your abilities and gifts will present themselves as they are needed, just as they did in Paris. As with all decisions though, the outcome may not be to your liking . . . just as in Paris. You must be steadfast in all that you choose," said Lucas.

"No pressure," said Josh.

He paused while deep in thought. He longed for the days working the night shift at the library. Josh thought about the enormity of this information, of this new reality. He could not be the only person besides Holden that was aware. "How many others know about . . . the new world that I have just entered?"

"Besides the normal faith-based Christian population, most of the senior-level executives at headquarters, including the ones that interviewed you, key senior people at all the global Jonah offices, and very powerful people strategically placed in multiple positions across the globe." answered Holden.

"What about the rest of Jonah's personnel?"

"They are like every other corporate professional in the workplace. Everyone knows what they need to in order to perform their jobs and responsibilities. Most view Jonah as a great place to work, nothing more, nothing less," Holden said.

"What is the deal with Associates? How much do they know?"

"Associates know a little more about Jonah's global mission in maintaining the balance. They understand the ramifications of this ongoing war and are under the protection of the Chairman and Jonah. They have picked their side," said Holden.

"How many Associates are there?"

"They are just like Familiars, they are everywhere," said Lucas.

"How many of those people know about me, what I'm supposed to do?"

"Almost all," said Holden.

Well, that explained a lot of the odd attention that Josh had been seeing. "I don't want this type of responsibility," he whispered, looking down.

"Not everyone is destined for an ordinary life," said Holden.

Josh looked up at Lucas. "Are you going to stick around? I may need some guidance from time to time."

"I have been and always will be with you, my friend. That will never change," said Lucas.

Chapter 20

Mending and Warning

The days that followed became very educational for Josh. His new reality made him see things in a different light. He figured that in order to fulfill this destiny correctly, he needed to study up on the subject matter. He had some tutoring from Langston in theology as he wanted to make sure that he was armed with all the information relevant to the cause. He and Melina also began attending church on Sundays, it could not hurt.

The reporting structure was different now that Josh was in the fold. Holden had made it very clear that he reported directly to him and no one else. That pretty much gave Josh carte blanche within Jonah International. As part of his acclamation to this new way of thinking, he pulled in some trusted resources to help him with the day-to-day activities. Alice and Sally were now his assistants, and they were both more than happy to come work for him again.

Josh was in his new corner office on the upper levels. He sat on the couch with a book studying when Alice came in holding a cell phone.

"They found him," she said.

He stood up from behind the mountain of books on the table and took the phone. "Thank you, Alice."

He raised the phone to his ear. "This is Joshua Arden."

"Mr. Arden, this is Inspector Willis down at the one nine. We found your person of interest at a local eatery on Third. What would you like us to do?"

"Please bring him to the east entrance of the headquarters. I will have security meet your guys at the gate."

"I'll have the squad routed there immediately."

"Thank you, Inspector. I appreciate your assistance."

"I'm glad that we could help. If you need anything else, please let us know."

Josh flipped the phone shut and handed it back to Alice. "Once he gets here, have security escort him to my office."

Alice nodded and left.

Thirty minutes later, there was a knock on the double doors. They opened immediately, and in came Alice, with Harry trailing behind. He was flanked by two of Jonah's very sizable security officers. Harry's face drained of blood when he realized who was sitting on the couch. They all stood there for a moment while Josh assessed his old friend. He looked horrible. His very expensive suit look like it had not been cleaned in days and was wrinkled as if he had been walking in the rain. His hair was a little disheveled, and his eyes were sunken in to accentuate his pale complexion.

"Thank you, gentlemen," said Josh. They nodded, turned, and left.

"Alice, will you bring Mr. Gibson some juice. He looks like he's thirsty."

"Yes, sir."

As Alice left, Josh got up and motioned to two comfortable chairs in the corner of his office. Harry did not say anything as he took a seat. Josh continued to look at him, while Harry looked at everything but Josh. Alice came back in with a beverage and set it on the side table next to Harry's chair.

Josh looked at Alice with a smile. "Thank you."

"Harry, you look like crap," he said as the doors closed.

"I've had better days. I just took a ride in a police car. You know . . . you could have called me."

"It wouldn't have been as much fun."

Harry's eyes went wide. "This isn't funny!"

"It's not meant to be. What I need to talk to you about has to be done in person, and I'm pretty sure that you would not have taken my call."

Harry turned his attention to his surroundings. "It looks like you're doing pretty well for yourself."

"I get by," said Josh with a shrug.

"Why am I here?" he said, getting down to business.

"I believe that you're in danger at Alastar-McGlocklin."

Harry's demeanor changed from agitated to fear. Josh picked up on it.

"I think you're right," said Harry hoarsely, trying to clear his throat.

"What do you mean?" said Josh. He was concerned that something had already happened.

Harry began explaining the events over the last eight to ten months. He had put in excessive amounts of additional hours with no extra pay, in lieu of incentives and the promise of advancement when the timing was right. Because of the client's billing structure as a federal entity, he was told to charge his added hours to a separate accounting code that, in the end, turned out to be a violation of the statement of work contract and government regulations. His department head was furious over the matter and was considering pressing charges against Harry for fraudulent billing, even though he did as instructed regarding the charge code. A deal was presented to Harry in return for no prosecution. He was transferred to another department where they specialized in "creative accounting" to offset losses of bad investments by Alastar-McGlocklin. Every deal forward required Harry's ability to cook the books to avoid any legal hassles from a federal perspective regarding taxes. Harry's name was all over the illegal accounting procedures. He was now in a position of indentured servitude, with no way out.

Josh asked him what the special incentives were that prompted him to make the wrong choice to begin with, knowing full well what the answer was. True to form, it had to do with the material things that Harry had always longed for: a nice apartment on the upper east side, a new car, a clothing allowance, etc. It was all the same stuff that Kate thought was important and pushed Harry to achieve.

Josh leaned forward and shook his head. "Why didn't you call me?"

"And say what, Josh? I screwed up again, and I need your help? Please come bail me out . . . once again! Besides . . . We didn't exactly part on the best of terms."

"Regardless of what has happened in the past, you are still the closest thing that I have to family. I want to be here for you," said Josh, a little surprised at how easy that was to say. It looked as if he was finding forgiveness. Either that or it was a situation where it was okay if *he* picked on Harry, but nobody else could. None of that mattered now; he needed to ensure his friend's safety.

"Harry, listen to me . . . I think that Alastar-McGlocklin is coming down heavy on you because of me."

"Because of you? Can this for once not be about you?" he said frustrated.

Josh got up and walked to his desk to retrieve the folder of evidence. "This is going to sound crazy because you don't know everything, but if our friendship has ever meant anything to you, please listen," said Josh, sitting back down.

"I have very strong documentation proving that Alastar-McGlocklin has been systematically creating and altering events, stemming all the way back from my childhood, in an attempt to prevent me from becoming a threat to their future." Josh handed him the folder.

Harry had a look of confusion as he took the file. He started to thumb through some of the contents.

"You are another way for them to hurt me. This is why I had to find you."

"Josh, are you sure you're not just being paranoid? This seems a little far-fetched. How could they feel threatened by you?" said Harry. Realizing how he phrased it, he followed up with "No offense."

"Harry . . . I'm not being paranoid, nor am I offended. A lot has happened to me in the last ten months as well. There are things going on that I can't explain to you right now, but my hopes are that someday, I will be able to tell you everything. I'm asking you to trust my instincts."

Harry looked at him with skepticism.

"Have I ever lied to you?" asked Josh.

"No," replied Harry almost immediately. Of all that had ever happened throughout their friendship, that was the one thing that Harry knew to be true. He was ashamed that the same could not be said about him.

"Please, just look through the information," said Josh, pointing to the folder in Harry's hand.

"Okay, Josh."

For a brief, fleeting second, it felt like old times. They were best friends again, brothers in arms.

As Harry started pulling one document after another out while Josh explained, his expression turned from skepticism to concern, as he started to see what Josh was talking about. After about an hour of going over the information, he closed the file.

Harry just stared at the floor. Josh was not sure how to read him at the moment, but it could be one of two things. He was rethinking their entire childhood together and the events associated with the folder, or he was trying to figure out what to do now.

The next area was going to be a very touchy subject. "Harry, I need to talk to you about something else."

He looked at him waiting for the question. At this point, Josh was not going to pull any punches, but still wanted to be cognizant of Harry's feelings toward her and their relationship. "I need to know where things stand between you and Kate."

To Josh's surprise, Harry did not react overtly to the subject. His face remained stoic as he processed the topic. "Do you think she's involved in this?"

Pull no punches. "Yes, I do," said Josh.

This was going to be an emotional roller coaster of feelings. The possibility of Harry and Kate's relationship being a ruse just to get at Josh was going to be a tough pill to swallow.

Harry was processing every moment they had been together. Was any of it ever real? Did their relationship mean anything to her? Was she really that cold and calculated and just used Harry like he was nothing more than a means to an end? Or was all of this complete nonsense and they truly shared something special? That she really did love and care for him?

On the other hand, it confirmed what he had been thinking for quite some time. "So do I," said Harry, nodding his head slowly. He then looked back down to the floor.

Josh was quite surprised at his response. It was the last thing that he expected him to say. During the final few months of their friendship, he had always defended Kate against Josh no matter what the conflict. His loyalties were with her, what changed? Trying to be considerate of his feelings, Josh thought about what to say next. "Harry, I need to know why you think she may be involved. I need specifics, things that she has done or said that made you doubt her."

Harry was puzzled. "Why?"

"This is a conspiracy, a very elaborate and apparently long-running one. I need information on all the players if I'm going to stop it."

"If this is everything that you think it is, what makes you believe you can stop it?"

"I have a plan and many unlimited resources. This has to end before anyone else gets hurt or killed, the people that have perpetrated this must be brought to justice . . . one way or another."

Harry could see that Josh was serious. He meant every word he said, and Harry believed him.

He began recounting the events surrounding Kate immediately after their friendship imploded. After Josh had moved out, Kate moved in. His mother obviously did not know, because if she did, she would have mentioned it to Josh on one of their many phone calls. That indicated to him that Harry was ashamed, and rightfully so. Neither he nor Harry was brought up that way. He knew that his mother would not approve of the arrangement, and he would not be able to handle the disappointment from her. Amanda tried to keep an open mind when it came to Kate, but from everything she had heard, the little nuances in things Harry would tell her and the comments made by Josh, Kate was just another bad decision. The contact with his mother became less frequent, which Josh knew was also caused by Kate. After a couple of months, Kate began spending more time working and less time with Harry. Sometimes she would work late into the evenings to the point where he was already in bed when she came home. That was becoming less of an issue though as Harry's job demanded more of his time too.

As time passed, Harry became more suspicious of her activities. She would receive phone calls that were specific to work, in which she would talk freely in front of Harry. Then there were some where she saw who was calling and stepped out of the room. Harry did not think much of this at first, but then those types of calls came more regularly. After one such call, she put her phone back in her purse and went into the bedroom. Harry hurried over to check the call log on her phone, and the last one received had been erased. That was the first red flag.

One afternoon, Kate called Harry to tell him that she would be working late yet again. He decided this time, he was going to find out exactly what she did on those late evenings. He parked his fancy new car halfway down the block, outside of her office building, and waited. He came prepared to sit there most of the night, silently hoping he was overreacting. His hopes were crushed when she exited her building right around 7:15 pm and hailed a taxi. That was the second red flag. After a thirty-minute ride, the taxi stopped in front of a brownstone on the Upper West Side. She went in and did not resurface until three hours later. That was the third red flag.

He wanted to believe that none of what he was thinking was true, so he decided to give her the benefit of the doubt and asked how her night went when they saw each other the next morning. With a wave of her hand, she casually answered that there was nothing new and it was a typical late-night at the office. He stopped counting the flags after that.

Harry told Josh they were growing more distant as time passed, but still maintained a facade in front of people that Kate considered important. He did not make any waves with her, and she did not catch on that he was unhappy.

As he finished his story, Harry looked to the floor again, but this time, with defeat.

"Harry, why didn't you dump her?"

"Believe it or not, she is still the best thing that has happened to me in the last year. I didn't want to be alone. Pretty pathetic, huh?"

Josh looked at him and could see that there was no light left in his eyes. Harry still had low self-esteem. His job was hammering him hard, and Kate was taking advantage of him. He was getting it from all ends and definitely needed help.

"Let's clear some things up now. Between this massive conspiracy and what you have told me, I can see now that what happened between you and me was not your fault. I would be grateful if you accepted my apology for all of this," said Josh.

Harry looked stunned. Why would Josh accept the blame for all of Harry's mistakes? "Josh . . . why are you apologizing to me? I am the one who made a mess of things."

"I'm apologizing because I believe what has happened to you is specifically tied to events surrounding me. I would like a chance to fix this if you allow me."

"How? There doesn't seem to be a way out. Believe me, I've looked."

"As you have pointed out, I seem to be doing pretty well for myself. I intend to use my network to bring down Alastar-McGlocklin."

He leaned forward to emphasize the seriousness of his next statement. "Harry, I can get you out of this mess, get you away from Alastar-McGlocklin and away from Kate. Neither of them will ever bother you again, and you can have your life back. In order to do that, I need you to trust me and do everything that I ask. Can you do that?"

Harry's eyes started to get a bit of that light back. There was hope. He nodded his head slowly then quite vigorously. "Yes. I can do that. Does this mean that things are okay between you and me?" His question was very sincere and full of hope.

"Absolutely. I would like to be brothers again if that's okay?"

A smile broke out on Harry's face for the first time. They both stood and hugged each other. "I would like nothing more."

When they sat back down, Harry asked, "So what's the next move?"

Josh pulled out his cell phone. "Sally, I need a tactical package and tracker setup for Harry. Have Tim prepare a clone for his phone."

Three seconds later, she came in the office. "Harry, this is Sally. Please hand her your cell phone," said Josh.

Harry looked puzzled, but true to his promise to do as Josh asked, he handed over the phone. She smiled and left the room, and then Alice came in a few seconds later.

"Alice is going to take you to one of our tactical operations' technicians. He's going to check you and your phone for tracers. There is a better than average chance that you are being tracked by some people within your company. We're going to piggyback that signature so we can keep tabs on you as well."

"Are you serious? Josh, what do you do here?"

"A lot of things have changed in the last year, Harry. I promise you that as soon as this is over, I will tell you everything. For right now . . . I need you to trust me. I want you to continue doing your job and don't let on that you have suspicions. We need to keep you off their radar. If they don't think you're a threat, they will most likely leave you alone. Once I have everything else in place, I'll call you about the next move. Until that point, we will have people monitoring you to ensure your safety."

"What should I do about Kate?" asked Harry as he stood up.

"I need to figure out what her connection is before we make a move. Just like your job, don't let on that you know something's up."

Harry shook his hand. "Thank you, Josh . . . for everything."

"That's what brothers are for."

Just before Josh was to leave for the day, Alice knocked on his door then opened it. "Josh, there was a package delivered for you today." She was holding a box.

"Okay, thanks, Alice."

She placed the package on his desk. "Do you need anything else before I go?"

"Thanks. I'm good. Enjoy the rest of your evening."

He started to leave the office then stopped. He turned to look at the box. After a few seconds, his curiosity got the best of him. He took it over to his conference table, sat down, and began to unwrap it. It was in a plain brown wrapper with no sender or return address. It simply had his name in a formal script across the top. The package contained a simple wooden box. As he lifted the lid, he saw a handwritten note in the same formal script.

Beware those who would deceive you and stand against the Light, for their time in righteous justice is near.
Excubiarum will aid you in your long journey ahead.

An overwhelming feeling came across Josh. He was a little shaken at the thought of where this came from. He was almost afraid to lift out the note to see the contents. After a few deep breaths, he reached in very gently and removed the paper.

What was inside began to glow.

Josh's eyes grew wide.

Chapter 21

Turning and Burning

Kelan looked at his watch with impatience. Not only did it take two weeks for his contact to get back in touch with him, but now he had the audacity to make him wait even more. He was taking a big risk meeting in public. Kelan was not sure why he would pick such a place, a diner of all things. There were so many other preferable meeting locations and in much nicer parts of the city. If they were going to continue to do business, better arrangements must be made. This was completely subpar.

The diner had a couple of other tables occupied when a well-dressed young man walked in. He was flanked by what had to be two bodyguards. The muscle fanned out into separate directions, taking positions that allowed them the best visual observation of all doorways and the patrons, while their boss headed straight for Kelan.

He sat down across from him. "Hello, Mr. Tindal."

Somewhat mildly shocked and indignant, Kelan said, "Do I know you?" In fact, he actually did. He never forgot a face: the roommate.

"No, you don't."

"Well then, excuse me, I'm expecting someone else."

"You're expecting Ulysses Quaden. He will not be here."

"How do you know—"

"Mr. Tindal, my name is Joshua Arden. Ulysses will not be here because he is dead. I am the one who replied to your contact."

"What?" said Kelan, genuinely surprised.

Sentinel received the multiple contacts directed to Ulysses from Herald. That told Josh that he was not aware of Ulysses's death, and Kelan's reaction confirmed it.

"Yes. He was a casualty of the Paris fiasco. I suppose I should thank you for the early warning," said Josh.

Recovering from his shock, Kelan asked, "Were you able to retrieve the medallion?"

"Yes, but it was not worth the price."

"I sent the abort code. I had no idea that explosives were in the vault, and when I found out, I did my best to buy more time," he said defensively. "I didn't know the technician was going to trigger the explosion," he said in a softer tone.

"The signal is not what killed him."

"What do you mean?" asked Kelan.

"I stopped the signal from coming in on the satellite uplink."

Kelan was a bit confused. "Then how—"

"The HIT was triggered in close proximity. Someone was there and set off the explosive," Josh said angrily.

"Look, whether you believe me or not, I tried to keep this from happening. I never wanted anyone to get hurt, much less die. I've done some bad things, but never that."

Josh tilted his head a little, assessing Kelan's expression. "I believe you, Mr. Tindal," he finally said.

With a little curiosity, Kelan asked, "How exactly did you stop the signal?"

"I shut down all the global communications satellites."

"*You* did that?" Kelan was visibly astonished as he thought back to the magnitude of the event.

"Yes."

Kelan knew Jonah International had advanced technology that was not available commercially, but had no idea that something like this was in existence. With all the high-powered, state-of-the-art technology he controlled, Kelan seriously doubted he could have pulled off the same thing, much less in the span of time between trigger and event. Who was this man?

A few moments passed. "Why am I here?" asked Kelan.

"Why did you contact us?" returned Josh.

"Look, I don't have the time or the patience for games," said Kelan, getting angry.

"Answer my question first, then I will answer yours," said Josh calmly.

Kelan was trying not to lose his cool, but it was becoming hard. He wanted answers and was not accustomed to someone else running the conversation. When he talked, people always listened. This boy was obviously a player at Jonah, and since his only inside contact was no longer alive, it seemed, for the moment, this was his best option.

"All right . . . We'll play this your way—"

"This is your only play, Mr. Tindal. You need us more than we need you."

Kelan's eyes grew wide with rage at the blatant disrespect and started to say something, but then quickly realized that the boy was right. He needed Jonah's help in order to bring down Blalock. He could not believe this, but he was going to have to take some direction from this kid.

After a deep breath, Kelan began. "Per my arrangement with Mr. Quaden, I'm going to provide detailed information on the next two Artifact missions. My goal is to assist Jonah in acquiring these objects before my team does."

"Did you bring the information with you as requested?"

"Yes," said Kelan, looking around, "but I don't think this is an ideal place to review it."

"You can relax, Mr. Tindal, this diner is perfectly secure. The proprietor, as well as the patrons, is affiliated with Jonah. Satellite coverage is blacked out for three square blocks in all directions. Any trackers or tracers within these walls have been neutralized, to include localized microwave radiation signals."

Kelan's eyebrows furrowed as he reached inside his jacket pocket to retrieve his cell phone. He did not have any signal. They must be jamming it.

Josh remained neutral as he verified. "For all intent purposes, you are off the grid."

He shifted his gaze from his cell to Josh. "I could have been tailed."

"You were, by my people."

"Who *are* you? What position do you hold?" asked Kelan.

Joshua definitely had power. To what extent, he did not know. Bodyguards, affiliates loyal to Jonah, technological capabilities that rivaled or even surpassed his own—he most certainly was a major player.

"Let's just say that I have the full support of Jonah International," answered Josh carefully. "Now, if you are satisfied that we are safe, the information."

Kelan reached into his briefcase, retrieved his tablet, and placed it on the table in front of him. Josh looked at it with slight disappointment. "I was expecting something more portable, like a flash drive."

"We have measures in place that prevent the download of data without recording a thumbprint of the person, date, and time. I created those to ensure that classified data remained carefully controlled. Even I have to follow the same security precautions."

He was not necessarily lying about the measures, those did exist. He did, however, exaggerate the inability to retrieve data. Kelan had been collecting information on his tablet for months in his ongoing mission to bring Blalock down. Mission logs, satellite imagery, Artifact acquisition and retrieval plans, and other assorted Intel was also stored in there; but he was going to control what Jonah received. It looked like this was going to put him back in the driver's seat.

"No worries. I can remedy that," said Josh.

He reached into his pocket and extracted something the size of a phone and placed it on Kelan's tablet. It began to glow with rolling waves of blue light.

"Sentinel, please copy."

"Copy completed."

Kelan's eyes were fixed upon the device. "What did you just do? Who said that?"

"I copied everything on your tablet."

"What? You can't do that!"

The shout drew the attention of the two men who came in with Josh. He held up his hand to let them know it was all right.

"I can, and I did, Mr. Tindal," Josh said then leaned into the table. "What you fail to realize is that this is not a game for me. I'm not going to spar and deal with you over items or information that I need in order to prevent any more deaths. There is something much larger at stake than just the demise of Alastar-McGlocklin," he said, retrieving the device.

Kelan regained his composure. He needed to match this boy head to head to regain his Alpha slot at this meeting. He was not going to be bested by Joshua. "I am fully aware of the stakes and the powers behind them."

"Oh really?" challenged Josh. "Please, enlighten me."

"You may not be able to handle the truth," retorted Kelan.

"Do *you* even know the truth, Mr. Tindal?"

"Son, I know more about the reality of Alastar-McGlocklin than you do."

"Try me."

Kelan began recounting examples of the company's illicit corporate practices, scare tactics, illegal property seizures, embezzlement by Blalock, and the supernatural events that he had witnessed by the senior partners and their lapdog. He felt a little foolish talking about the latter. How on earth would Joshua take him seriously? After ten minutes of what Kelan quantified as proof, he stopped and waited for Josh's reaction.

"Mr. Tindal, I believe everything that you just said, especially the last part regarding the senior partners and their agent. I'm afraid, though, you still don't have the complete truth."

Kelan sat there, stunned. He could not believe that this boy agreed with everything he had just stated and still was not satisfied with the wealth of information that was presented.

After a moment, Josh asked, "Would you like to know the truth now?"

Kelan just shook his head and, with a smirk, said, "Sure."

"Please give us the room," said Josh to no one in particular. The bodyguards, the patrons, even the waitstaff left immediately, leaving only them in the diner.

Kelan eyed the process of obedience at the statement just uttered. There was no way that everyone across this diner heard Josh, and yet they followed his instruction without hesitation. He looked back at him with wonder and curiosity.

"Mr. Tindal, you will have to accept what I'm about to tell you, and show you, as the truth, even though you may not understand." He placed the glowing device on the table in front of him.

Kelan just stared at Josh waiting, not knowing what was coming next.

"Sentinel, genesis," he said.

Three-dimensional holograms exploded around Josh and Kelan and appeared to immerse them into another world. They were still sitting in the booth, but nothing resembled the diner around them. There were images depicting individuals whom Kelan did not know and places that he had never seen. All were shifting to match the tone and the words of Joshua.

"There is a war that has been raging since the beginning of time. Most people are unaware, purposely kept in the dark by the enemy."

Kelan stared in awe at the images around him. With his eyes wide and his mouth open, he looked back at Joshua as he spoke. "Mankind is just pawns in this war."

Josh continued on while the images shifted. He recounted a sequence of events surrounding his own life and how it was connected. Individuals came into view that Kelan recognized, such as Pymm and Blalock. As Josh talked about the explosion in Paris, Kelan jumped in his seat, as if affected by the fire itself. Through all of this, the images were starting to correlate in his mind. He was seeing patterns of events and accounts, connecting his own experiences. Everything that he had just witnessed was more than plausible in his findings. He was beginning to understand. The images abruptly pulled back into the small glowing device.

"This is much bigger than Alastar-McGlocklin or Jonah International. The stakes are more costly than anything you could possibly imagine," said Josh.

"I-I just can't believe this!" uttered Kelan.

"Nonbelief is for the ignorant or the foolish. Which one are you?"

Kelan's head snapped back and focused on Josh at that statement. His entire world had just changed.

Everything that he had ever known to be true was a lie. All of these years, Blalock was wrong. He was working for an enemy that he never knew existed.

"You asked me why you were here, Kelan," said Josh in a softer tone.

"Yes," he replied, starting to accept that Joshua was the Alpha in this meeting.

"I need someone whom I can trust on the inside to help cut this monster down and damage the enemy. I need more than just the Artifact data. You are in a very strategic position to work with us. In return, I can offer you a way out."

Kelan just came to the realization that his objective of taking over Blalock's position was now unattainable. It was not going to be possible for him to head a company that was going to ultimately be destroyed. He knew that Blalock and the senior partners would fight back, and he would most likely be collateral damage. It was going to be their power against Jonah's. From everything that he had just witnessed and heard, Jonah was clearly more powerful.

As if reading his thoughts, Josh said, "Kelan, you have to pick a side. You don't have any other choice."

"What's going to happen to me after all of this is said and done?"

"I've thought about that, and I would like you to work for me at Jonah International."

Kelan did not hide his surprise at this statement. It was completely unexpected and most decidedly not deserved. "Why would you want me to work with you, after all I have done to aid your enemy?"

"Because, Kelan, I believe that you were unaware of the true motives behind your actions. You have been used, much like many other people, for all the wrong reasons. Your expertise in covert operations is a skill that I can apply for the right ones. You as much stated that there is a line that you will not cross. Your heart is not black, there is still some good in there."

"I've done a lot of bad things that could be considered illegal," he said, looking down the table shamefully.

"All of those things can be forgiven. Jonah's influence is very wide, but you have to choose which side you are going to play for in order for that to happen."

He held out his hand and waited for Kelan. After a few moments, he grabbed it, and they shook.

"Okay . . . I choose your side. Where you go, I follow."

"Excellent!" said Josh with a smile.

At that very moment, it was as if the weight of the world had been lifted from Kelan's shoulders. He had not felt that good in years. He knew immediately that he had made the right choice and that there was hope. "What do you need from me?"

Everyone returned to the diner and assumed their previous activities. One of Josh's entourage walked toward him.

"We need your cell phone for a few minutes. We are going to fix it to where the bad guys cannot listen in on our conversations."

"My cell already has STU encryption capabilities," stated Kelan.

"We figured as much, but we are going to modify the encryption to isolate a specific frequency and signature," said the bodyguard as he reached the table.

"A secondary carrier wave—" started Kelan.

"Preventing anyone on your side from decrypting or even knowing that you're talking to us. We'll also need a passive neutralizer for the tracking," added Josh.

The bodyguard nodded as Kelan handed him his phone.

"I'm not being tracked," stated Kelan matter-of-factly.

"Actually, yes . . . you are," said Josh.

"Upon entering the diner, we detected an active tracking signature masked as a low-frequency pulse emitting from your phone," said the bodyguard, with a wave of the cell.

Kelan's look went from shock to anger in a split second. Someone in his department was tracking him. His cell phone was always with him. Who could have gotten close enough to—the answer smacked him in the face.

"It's a bit of a sting when you put trust in someone and they betray you," said Josh knowingly.

"We've also detected one of your DRONES in a low orbital radius," said the bodyguard.

"Did you authorize a mission to cover our meeting?" asked Josh.

The anger intensified on Kelan's face. "No," he replied in a low voice. That confirmed it. Only one person could have sanctioned the operation: Margaret.

"Chances are that was sent to keep tabs on you as well."

Josh nodded to the bodyguard, who then turned and left. "Kelan, I need you to be cool about this. The biggest thing that we have going for us inside of Alastar-McGlocklin is you. All activity needs to remain status quo. I don't want you burned before due time. Can you handle that?"

Kelan was a consummate professional in his field of expertise. Covert was what he did best. He cooled the anger down and straightened up. "Absolutely. This will not be a problem."

"Good. I want you to continue to operate on a normal basis, even if your objectives are in direct conflict with us. The enemy will notice anything out of the ordinary, so don't give them a reason to look. Continue with your personal research for evidence against Mr. Blalock. We will continue with activities on our end. When the time is right, we will pool our findings in preparation for the downfall. I promise that you will be there to witness Alastar-McGlocklin's death, which will include the takedown of Mr. Blalock."

"Outstanding," said Kelan, with a smile on his face.

This meeting was classified as a mission, so standard protocol had watchers and analysts on-site. One of Jonah's personnel from rHub came rushing through the diner doors and approached Josh quickly.

"Mr. Arden, I'm very sorry to interrupt you, but we have started the analysis on the data copied from Mr. Tindal's tablet. We came across an Artifact designation that we did not previously have cataloged. We have a problem, sir," she said.

"What is it?" asked Josh.

"A human target, Artifact 216."

"Oh no!" gasped Kelan. "I forgot . . ."

"It's Harry Gibson, sir. He's the target," she said quickly.

"What! What is this?" he said, turning to Kelan.

"We've been tracking him for four years now—" started Kelan.

"Why?" said Josh.

Kelan's eyes darted back and forth as he processed all the evidence. "Up to this point, none of it really made any sense. He was the first human target classified as an Artifact acquisition, but it was for surveillance only. All we did was track his activities . . ." he trailed off. A look of horror came across his face. "Find him. Now!" he said, looking at the young lady.

"What are you not telling me!" Josh said angrily.

"The project is being closed. We are shutting down surveillance," said Kelan.

"Why? What does that mean?" asked Josh.

One of the bodyguards said something into the cuff of his sleeve. Within seconds, three more men rushed into the diner toward Josh.

"Everything makes sense now! For one reason or another, we were specifically told not to track you, that our directive was Harry. They're using him to get to you. If he is no longer an asset . . . ," said Kelan.

"No!" gasped Josh as he understood. "Harry is in danger, activate his locator and find him . . . Now!"

Tim and the other bodyguards immediately started relaying orders to blanket the city using all resources.

As the scenario of what was happening played out in Josh's mind, he turned to Kelan to confirm a suspicion that he has had since he was awakened to this new world.

"Kate," he said flatly.

"She's one of mine," said Kelan.

A look of contempt came across Josh's face as he shot up out of the booth and headed toward the doors.

Weakness, by definition, is an inadequate or a defective quality. This can be applied to any number of things: a point in a defensive posture, a lacking element in a person's character, or even glass due to a thermal effect during casting. It's never been considered a positive attribute, no matter what the meaning.

As of late, this has been the one defining context to explain every aspect of his life.

Weakness.

A disappointing job due to the lack of conviction and forethought in thinking things through, a relationship built completely out of shallow desires and unfulfilled emotional needs, and lost time from the only person on this planet that has ever cared for him outside of his mother. All of these thoughts ran through his head like a roller coaster as he sat at a bar in the Village, drinking and trying to forget.

He had just ordered another one when she came up behind him and wrapped her arms around his waist. "Hey, lover."

He did not turn to acknowledge her, but instead shook his head in disbelief.

"Kate, what are you doing here?" he said as he took another swallow.

"I could ask you the same thing. You said that you were working late tonight."

"So did you," he said, taking another pull.

"Hey . . . what's with the attitude? Are you drunk?" she said, a bit snippy.

"Getting there," he replied, still not looking at her.

Dropping her hands, she slid in next to him, placing her purse on the bar rather loudly. "I don't appreciate being lied to."

"That's almost comical coming from you," he said, finally looking at her.

"What on earth are you talking about?" she said, genuinely surprised at the statement.

"Come on, Kate . . . don't you think it's time for a little honesty in our relationship?" said Harry.

With mild disgust in her voice, she replied, "Look, if you're having a bad day or something, that doesn't give you any right to take it out on me."

He turned his full body toward her. "You really don't get it, do you? I'm sick and tired of all the manipulation and lies, from you and my job. Did you really not think that this day would come?"

"What are you talking—"

"W Ninety-sixth Street."

Her mouth fell open from hearing the address of the brownstone on the Upper West Side.

"Yeah, I thought so," he said, turning back to the bar and draining his glass.

Trying to compose herself, she said, "Harry, I can explain . . ."

"Save it!" he said, holding up his hand to order another drink.

"If you just give me a chance—"

"To do what, Kate? Come up with a reason to justify why you have been lying to me all this time?"

For the first moment in their relationship, she did not know how to respond. That spoke volumes to Harry. The bartender delivered his drink. He took a swig then looked at her. "How did you know I was here?"

"What? . . ." she asked, pretending to be confused.

"I've never been here before, this is my first time. I told you I was working late tonight and didn't mention I was coming out for a drink." He paused for a few seconds before continuing. "How did you know I was at *this* bar, right here, right now?"

He could see that she was struggling and fumbled for words. He reached into a pocket, pulled out his cell phone, and gently placed it in front of her. Kate's eyes went wide upon seeing it. Josh was right as usual, they had been tracking him. He looked her directly in the eyes and waited for an answer he knew he would not get. He then turned back toward his glass and took another drink.

"Kate," he said very calmly, without looking at her, "I don't think this is going to work out between us."

As the bombardment of accusations and obvious contempt came one after another, she was unprepared to respond appropriately. She had been able to contain and control him better after she ended his friendship with Josh, but this rebellious attitude was something new. She had to think of her next move fast in order to salvage the connection and not blow her cover. He knew something, but she did not know what or how much. She needed some guidance, but remembered that she was given specific orders if something along these lines occurred.

"Look, Harry . . . I'm asking you for a chance to explain. I would like to think that after what we have meant to each other, you could at least give me that," she said in her manipulative way. "This is absolutely poor timing on my part, but I really need to go to the restroom. Please, promise me you will wait right here?"

"Whatever," he said, taking another drink.

As she started to move toward the restrooms, Harry said, "Make sure you take your cell. You wouldn't want to miss an important call."

She stopped in midstep at that statement without turning and knew that he was onto her. She then made her way through the crowd to the back.

Soon as she was out of sight, Harry picked up his phone, flipped some money onto the bar, and walked out.

Once Kate was in the hallway near the restroom, she quickly pulled out her phone and dialed Kelan. He did not answer. She was in a panic, then remembered her alternative and dialed a new number.

It picked up on the second ring. "Hello, my dear!" said the sickeningly sweet voice.

"Mr. Pemberton, I'm so sorry to bother you, but I've run into a bit of a problem with Harry. I tried to call Mr. Tindal, but he didn't pick up." she spat out hurriedly.

"My dear, it's no problem at all. I always enjoy hearing from you," he replied as if they were talking about China patterns.

She was kind of amazed at his nonchalance and indifference to the panic in her voice. "Sir, I believe that my cover is blown. He has all but figured out that he is under surveillance—"

"You needn't worry about Mr. Gibson anymore. His activities are no longer of interest to the corporation."

"I'm sorry, but I'm afraid I don't follow."

"The contract for surveillance of Object 216 has come to term. Your services on said contract are no longer required," he said politely.

"Oh . . . Okay?" she replied, not really understanding what that meant. "We're currently in a bar. He's waiting for me to come out of the restroom. What would you like me to do?"

"There's nothing for you *to* do, my dear. He has already left the establishment."

"What?"

"I will handle everything from here. Thank you so much for your services. We could not have done any of this without you," Pymm said happily then hung up.

Harry bumped into someone as he was walking out of the bar. He had a lot to drink in a short amount of time, so he should consider himself fortunate that he could walk at all. He did not drive with the possibility that something like this was going to happen, so he made his way down the street to look for a cab. He passed a couple holding hands, and doting on each other. His smile toward them was sincere, but inwardly he was asking himself why someone would want to put themselves through that. It all ends up being a sham for one reason or another. Of course, their girlfriends are probably not working for some bad guys as part of some massive conspiracy either.

As he continued down the block, he passed two men walking the opposite way. After a few seconds, the men stopped then turned to follow Harry. They trailed him for a block when he turned the corner. The new street was mostly deserted and lined with residential homes. Harry's cell phone began to ring as the two men caught up to him. One grabbed Harry and pulled him into a darkened alley while the other pulled out a knife.

Both men quickly left the alley after a few seconds. They could still hear the cell phone ringing as they rounded the corner. At the opposite end of the alley, on the other side of the street, stood Pymm with a smile on his face. He could hear the phone ringing too.

Chapter 22

Emptiness and Astonishment

As Josh finished his eulogy, he made his way back to his spot next to Amanda. She stood up with tears in her eyes and gave him a hug that seemed to last forever. Melina sat there with her heart breaking yet again for Josh. He and Harry had just begun to patch things up. The loss of his best friend would change him forever. As he took his seat, he stared at the floor beneath the casket. His mind was too weary to think or comprehend the events of the last week. He just wanted to get through the day.

Josh did not want her to endure the pain of the planning, so he made the funeral arrangements for Amanda. Wisconsin was their home, so that is where she wanted him buried.

He insisted that Melina travel with him; it was the only way that he could be absolutely sure she was safe. She and Amanda were all that he had left now, and he was not about to lose them too.

To ensure the safety of the service and the patrons, Jonah had a security detail that rivaled the president's. After Tim had read the evidence file on the trip back from Paris, he was in agreement with Josh's assessment; Alastar-McGlocklin, or a faction thereof, were out to hurt Josh by any means they deemed necessary. He was the senior operative from the tactical division, so he arranged and coordinated all activities and schedules surrounding security for Harry's memorial. Operatives were placed strategically throughout the service and the surrounding area. All routes to and from the service, as well as the hotel, were blocked off by the state police for the duration. There were field agents at the burial site; there were even operatives inside and around Amanda's house. Tim was not taking any chances with Josh or his family.

Prior to traveling to Wisconsin, Josh had asked Lucas if he could be present during their stay. Tim pretty much had everything handled from a human perspective, so Josh wanted to make sure that he had all the bases covered on the supernatural end too. Lucas had assured him that he would be in attendance, and there would be no interference from the enemy while he was on watch.

Everyone from Jonah's executive level, all the way down to Josh's friends, came for the service. Malcolm Holden and his wife were there, along with Langston and Debra. Jonathan Sinclair, Alice, and Sally also came. Sam and Janet Schulman pulled Max out of school to attend. Ulysses's widow, Sandra, even traveled out. When he saw her, he choked up; then when she gave him a hug, she whispered that if he could have, Ulysses would have been there too. Josh was in awe of how much he was blessed with his friendships, this company, and the honor of representing Jonah in their fight of balance and injustice.

The Associates and affiliates in the media industry ensured that there would be a blackout of coverage and activities from all markets to give the family the privacy they deserved. Josh was very appreciative and assured that should a time arise when they needed Jonah, he would be there.

To confirm that security coverage was complete, Jonah booked an entire hotel property of a major chain for the out-of-town guests. All staff working during the two-day event was vetted and cleared by Jonah's security personnel. Sentinel was on-site and online, running simulations and electronic security sweeps. Watchers and analysts were assisting the field agents with the standard mission protocols for surveillance. It could not have been more secure.

Everything was catching up to Josh, so he decided to go back to his room to rest for a bit. Two security agents were posted outside his doors as he and his two escorts arrived.

Once inside, he just sat upon the edge of the bed and stared out the window. Of everything that he felt, failure was the most overwhelming. Two people have died because of him. How many more will there be? How can he protect the ones that are left? Why is this happening? Questions and more questions kept filling his head and made it hurt even worse, but there was one that bothered him the most. Did Harry make the right choice? Josh needed to know.

"Lucas? Are you there?" he whispered.

"I am here, Joshua," came the answer from behind him.

He walked toward the bed and sat down beside Josh and waited.

"I'm not sure how this works," said Josh.

"You can just ask," Lucas said reassuringly.

"I need to know if Harry is safe now. Did he make the right choice?"

Lucas smiled affectionately at the question. There was always the possibility that Joshua would need reassurance in his actions or the decisions that have been made to date. This was anticipated well in advance.

"Joshua, Harry is at peace now. When your friendship was mended, he made some hard decisions after putting his trust in you and reevaluated his life choices. He is in a safe place now. He gave me a message to pass along to you."

Josh's eyes got big at that statement, and he looked at Lucas waiting anxiously.

"He said for you not to worry about him anymore, that he is better than he has been in a long time. He does not blame you for what happened, so do not blame yourself. He knows now that all you ever wanted for him was the best and sends his apologies for not seeing that."

Josh hung his head and sobbed as Lucas held him up. His emotions were finally cutting loose. He thought the expectation on him as a leader prevented him from showing what some would consider weakness. Lucas knew this not to be true. Joshua's emotions were the very thing that made him a great leader. His compassion for humanity, his anger for injustice, and his empathy toward those around him empowered him to lead with conviction and impartial bias, in the name of the truth.

"Can you please pass a message back to him for me?" he said, once his emotions had died down.

Lucas nodded.

"Please tell Harry that I am so sorry for the wasted time over the last year. Let him know that his sacrifice will not be in vain."

With that request, he straightened up, wiped his face, and said, "Now, we have work to do."

"Indeed," said Lucas.

Once everyone returned to New York, Josh called a staff meeting. Those who were intimately involved in the pursuit of taking out Alastar-McGlocklin was in a closed-door session in the rHub situation room.

As he entered, everyone settled down. "Sentinel, secure the room."

As the doors slid shut with a thump and a hiss of the seal, he took his place at the head of the table. "There is a lot to do before the end game, so I will be brief . . . To put it simple, I'm giving everyone the option to walk away."

People started mumbling and looking around. Josh held up his hand to get control. "What we are doing here is dangerous for everyone involved. You all have access to the conspiracy evidence. Just being near me or associated with me puts you at an incredible risk. Too many people have sacrificed their lives. My conscience would not be clear if more blood were shed because you are taking part. This is my fight, no one else's. If you stay, it has to be your choice."

Everyone was quiet. Josh gave each of them a look, letting them know that he was okay if they chose to leave. There would be no hard feelings, no fallout, and no repercussions.

Tim was the first person to speak up. "Sir, with all due respect, what's going on here is bigger than all of us. Our universal mission at Jonah is to help those who cannot help themselves. Since you have been with this company,

I've personally seen the impact that you have made. Some of us can actually say that we owe you our lives. You need our help his time. There's no other place that I would rather be, I'm in."

"So am I. I'm not going anywhere either," said Langston.

"I'm in as well," added Alice.

Each person either nodded their agreement or spoke up to say they were staying. Josh was humbled by their commitment. "Thank you all for your support."

He turned his attention back to the business at hand. "Okay . . . Like I said, I want to make this brief. Langston, how is the intelligence for the next Artifact mission?"

"Thanks to Herald, we now know that Alastar-McGlocklin is looking to acquire the Wallace sword. It's widely known to medieval aficionados to be on display in the National Wallace Monument in Stirling, Scotland, but that one is a replica. The actual sword somehow wound up in Toutle, Oregon."

"How in the world did it wind up in the middle-of-nowhere Oregon?" asked Sally.

"We don't know," said Langston.

"That doesn't matter, what does is that we get there first. According to Herald, this mission is off book, even for the RCT. They've hired mercenaries to retrieve this one. Tim, we need to be ready to respond to lethal measures. I'm not happy about that option, but I have no plans of losing anyone on this mission, okay?" said Josh.

"Understood," replied Tim.

Looking at Langston, Josh asked, "Did Herald give you a timeline for the mission?"

"At 0130 hours, two days from today."

Josh looked over at Tim who said, "Night ops, we'll be ready."

Josh nodded then looked toward Alice and Sally. "How's the market look today?"

"Their stock is at an all-time high. Investors are funneling a lot of money in," said Sally with a grin.

"The shell corporations are holding up nicely," added Alice.

"How long before we reach targeted levels?" asked Josh.

"At the current rate, we should hit the cap in five weeks," said Sally.

"Excellent."

Josh turned back to Langston. "Once you have completed the intelligence packet for the Wallace Artifact, I would like for you to begin working with Lucas on the Knight Blade mission."

"I can have Darius work on the operation's requirements as well," added Tim.

"That won't be necessary this time, Tim. The retrieval of this particular object is going to require a different skill set," Josh said, looking at Langston knowingly.

A bit confused, Tim asked, "How are you going to retrieve it without a tactical team?"

"With diplomacy . . . The Artifact is in the Vatican. Langston, Lucas, and I will be on point for this one."

"Well . . . at least let me provide security," said Tim.

"Fair enough," said Josh.

He turned back to the rest of the team. "Okay, they're going to try to retrieve the Wallace sword in two days. I would like to have it before then. Get the tactical packages, schedules, and transport secured by the end of business today. We leave for Oregon first thing in the morning."

"Excuse me . . . we?" said Tim as everyone started to leave.

"Yes, Tim, I'm going," stated Josh.

"Sir, given the circumstances of everything that is happening . . . you know, conspiracy and all, I don't think that is a good idea. You'll be too exposed."

"Duly noted . . . I'm still going."

"Yes, sir."

Since there was a three-hour time zone difference, Josh and the team arrived at Kingsley Field in Oregon around 9:00 am local time. The location of the Wallace sword was about 311 nautical miles north from the air force base. Josh was studying the geographical location and the topography on the trip in, and something bothered him. He kept thinking about what Sally had said regarding the "middle-of-nowhere Oregon." He was wrong to dismiss that notion. He had a hunch and wanted to discuss it with the team. Once everyone had lunch, he called a mission briefing.

"Sentinel, give me a real-time satellite image of the Artifact's location," he said.

The blue waves of Excubiarum began to pulsate. Immediately, a holographic satellite image of the Artifact's coordinates materialized on the table surrounded by the team. Josh looked at it for a few seconds and then started to spin the image by swiping his hand. "Create a digital reference highlighting the woodland areas."

The image changed from real-time to blue digital wire. Where there was forest, the color was highlighted in green. The Artifact location was highlighted in red.

To no one in particular, Josh asked, "What do you see?"

The tactical field agents were the first to notice what Josh had discovered.

"The target's location is sitting in the middle of an open field, surrounded by forest on all sides," said someone.

"The Artifact looks like it is in a small structure, a cabin," said someone else.

They all nodded their heads in agreement with those statements.

"Sentinel, show the proximity of the closest neighbors to the target," said Josh.

The digital wire frame expanded out to show a broader coverage of the area. Five yellow blips marked different spots around the Artifact. Each one showed the distance from the target, with the closest being 7.6 miles.

"Sally was on the mark. This truly is the middle-of-nowhere Oregon," said Tim.

"Why go to this much trouble to place an Artifact in a location such as this?" someone asked.

Tim was the second person outside of Josh to understand why. "It's a trap."

Josh nodded his head in confirmation. "Yes, it's a trap."

"Herald betrayed us," said Tim angrily.

"No, I don't think so," Josh countered quickly. "I believe he was betrayed as well."

"How do you know?" said someone.

"Call it a gut instinct. I've met the man, this is not something he would do understanding the implications of everything at stake," replied Josh.

"Then who do you think it is?" asked someone else.

"Not sure, but I think they're waiting in the cabin," replied Josh.

"What? Right now?" asked Tim.

"Yep. I also think that Herald's mercenaries are in position and waiting too," said Josh.

The field agents looked at each other with skepticism.

"How can you be sure?" asked someone.

"Sentinel, search for human objects closest to the Artifact's location using standard detection protocols," said Josh.

Within seconds, small purple digital symbols started to pop up along the perimeter of the forest surrounding the cabin. There were seven in total, and they were moving.

"Son of a—" started one of the agents.

"We need to abort," said Tim.

"No," said Josh calmly. "We came here to retrieve the Wallace sword, and that is what we will do."

"This will be suicide. They won't let us anywhere near that cabin. They'll pick us off one by one," said an agent.

"How do we even know that Artifact is real and not fake like the one in Scotland?" said another.

"This will not be suicide. We know that they are there now," said Josh.

"And we have the element of surprise," confirmed Tim, after thinking for a second.

"The Artifact is real. They knew I wouldn't make the trip if it weren't," said Josh.

"Wait, are you saying that," started Tim as he was thinking through the logic, "this is all about getting to you?"

"They already have the Artifact, Tim. Do you see any other possible reasons?" he said.

"If they are using that to get to you, then how do we expect to get the Artifact?" asked Tim.

"I am going to the cabin alone to get the sword while you and the other agents capture and detain the mercenaries."

"Sir, I strongly recommend that we abort. This goes beyond dangerous. Your safety must come first. We can find another way to get this Artifact," said Tim.

"We have to see this through. We don't have a lot of time left." He looked sympathetically at his team. "I'm not going to risk anyone else's life on something I would not be willing to do myself."

"You just said that the person orchestrating this is probably in the cabin, right now. If you are the only one going in, how are you going to be protected?" asked Tim.

"The biggest threats to me are those mercenaries. It will be fine. I have a theory and a plan."

There was a full moon that night. The mountain ranges glowed under the pale light as the forest creatures followed their nocturnal routines. An owl could be heard in the distance, while a deer wondered and searched for food. Under any other circumstances, one would find the peacefulness of the forest very serene and calming, compared to man-made environments. The only disruption that could be heard was a small unremarkable car turning into the clearing just beyond the forest edge.

Josh was trying desperately to have the confidence needed prior to entering the cabin. He drove slowly for two specific reasons. He wanted to make sure that all eyes were focused on the car and also give the cabin's resident clear warning that he was approaching. He came to a stop twenty yards from the structure. He stood next to his car for a few moments with the driver's door open, giving anyone watching enough time to ensure that he was the only visible occupant. He shut the door and approached the cabin. As he placed his foot on the front porch, the door opened automatically; he stopped. He could not see anyone in the doorway. Josh knew the next move was his; so with a slight hesitation, he entered. As he cleared the door, it shut just as it opened in a smooth motion. A fire came to life instantly underneath the aged hearth as lanterns and candlelight appeared to get brighter.

In the corner of the cabin sat the man dressed in black known as Pymm.

"Well, well . . . I must say that I did not think you would come!" he said, practically giddy.

"And why is that?" replied Josh very confidently.

"After all you have been through, my boy," he said, feigning sympathy, "you must be emotionally exhausted."

"I'm doing just fine. Thank you for your concern," he replied politely.

"Well done on your recent acquisition in Paris, by the way," he said, with a little distaste in his voice. "I'm sure that the medallion was well worth the cost." Pymm hoped to strike a chord with that statement.

Josh did not respond, but only stared.

They both eyed each other for a moment. For Josh, it was a matter of making his opponent aware that he was not afraid. Pymm, on the other hand, was just curious. It had been a very long time since a human had not cowered before him. The last one did not fare too well. Pymm politely motioned to a seat in the opposite corner of the room.

"So where is the sword?" asked Josh, breaking the silence as he took the seat.

"It is not here."

"Now, we both know that's not true, Pymm."

"You know my name. My reputation precedes me." His grin started to fade.

"I know a lot more than just your name."

"Then you also know that there is no possible way you can win."

"We both know that's not true as well."

The grin was gone. His eyes started glowing crimson. "It would be very unhealthy for you to challenge us."

"You and Alastar-McGlocklin are the ones that issued the challenge. I'm just responding in kind," said Josh, holding his ground. Inwardly, he was shaking, but was not about to give this thing the satisfaction.

Josh's cell phone rang. He reached into his pocket and pulled it out, his eyes never leaving Pymm's in the process. He listened to the person on the other end.

"Thank you," was the simple reply as he flipped the phone shut.

The grin started to return. "Trouble?" he said snidely.

"Not at all."

"I am almost impressed that you ventured out here all by yourself," said Pymm, focusing on the isolation. "I am equally impressed that you could receive a signal."

"Satellites. They have a little more reach than standard cell phone towers."

Pymm nodded his head slightly in agreement, looking casually around. When he returned his gaze back to Josh, he said, "You are still alone."

"What makes you think I'm alone?"

"Let's stop this charade, shall we?" he said, agitated.

"If you insist," replied Josh nonchalantly.

"Your team cannot help you. They are hopelessly outmatched and could not possibly reach you in time to make any semblance of a difference," he said, with glowing eyes.

Josh nodded in agreement. "You are correct, but their objective was never to help me. As far as being outmatched, they didn't seem to have a problem taking out the seven mercenaries positioned around this cabin," he said, with a wave of his cell phone.

Pymm's expression, as well as his features, began to change. His grin turned into a scowl with contortions that no longer looked like a human mouth. His hairline seemed to change, withering from long flowing black hair to scraggly strands of soiled and greasy threads. His fingers seemed to protrude into extended sharp claws with knotted joints. As he stood, he seemed to grow in size. He looked to be eight or nine feet tall.

Josh remained passive at the transformation in front of him. Inside he felt paralyzed and scared. He only saw stuff like this in movies. He continued to stay seated as Pymm began to speak in a hollowed and haunting voice.

"You have no idea of the power that I possess, boy! I can crush you with one hand!" he snarled.

"Actually, no . . . you can't," Josh said, surprised at the calmness of his response. "You're not allowed to touch me. That is one rule that cannot be broken. That's why you have been going after the people in my life."

Pymm turned toward the ceiling and howled like a wolf would at the moon. It was a screech unlike anything that Josh had ever heard before. That confirmed what Josh was made to understand; he was off-limits to the enemy.

"As for being alone . . ." He stood up and simply said, "Lucas."

With a brilliant flash of light, Lucas appeared to Josh's right. He was wearing flowing garments of silver, white, gold, and azure, which looked to be a cross between a pirate and a seventeenth-century Frenchman. He seemed to be just as big as Pymm and was shimmering with light.

Using his claws to shield from the light, Pymm then dropped his hands and growled. "Lucaous!"

"Joshua, it is time to leave," he said in an angelic voice.

"Not without the Wallace sword."

Black smoke swirled in midair and formed a spiked mace in Pymm's hand. With skilled precision, it struck the ceiling which then exploded outward. Tattered wings that resembled something like a dragon unfolded as he leapt into the nighttime sky and hovered. In the same instance, his clothing morphed into a crude armor that made him look like a gargoyle preparing for battle.

"Find the sword and leave. I will handle this," said Lucas without looking at Josh.

With that, his wings unfolded, and he floated up to meet Pymm in the sky. Josh pulled out Excubiarum and told Sentinel to locate the Artifact.

"You waste your time protecting these mewling creatures! They are insignificant nothings, troglodytes that were meant to be ruled!" spewed Pymm.

"That has never been for you and your kind to decide," said Lucas.

"We do not blindly follow orders from Someone who has lost sight of our place in this realm."

"You are as misguided as the rest of the fallen. You know not your place! Sometimes, you just need to do what you are told without question!" said Lucas with anger.

"A typical reply from someone with no will. You do not know the complete freedom of choice," retorted Pymm.

"My freedom is guaranteed, Demon. You are bound by the chains of your undoing. After all these millennia, you still cannot see that."

"What I can see is that you, too, are outmatched!"

Legions of demons appeared in the night sky. An evil, demonic smile spread across Pymm's face.

Lucas raised his arm. A flash of brilliant light streaked down, leaving a glorious sword in his hand. His garments transformed into a spectacular set of armor.

"I am far from outmatched," he replied.

Multitudes of angels, both of Guardian and Warrior class, streaked through the sky into a formation directly behind Lucas. Their sheer numbers appeared to surpass the demons two to one. Division commanders floated to Lucas's side to await his decree.

Pymm's anger consumed him at the sight. He raised his mace to signal the charge.

A faceplate materialized in place on Lucas's helmet as well as the division commanders. Their arms raised in a unified signal to prepare for battle. In unison, angels by the thousands assumed a defensive posture, much like the Spartans of ancient Greece. Storm clouds began to form throughout the night sky.

At Pymm's screeching cry, the demons moved forward.

In a voice that carried throughout the heavens, Lucas said, "Engage."

Thousands upon thousands of angels and demons clashed. As mallets met spears, axes met swords, brilliant sparks lit up the already-pale night sky. As the weapons connected, they sounded like thunderclaps and flashed like lightning, shaking the foundation of everything all around. The demons were sloppy and uncontrolled in their attacks, while the angelic forces held their ranks with uniformity and precision. Each time that a demon was vanquished, it disappeared in a dark swirling mist. When a angel met a blade, he shimmered and dissolved, leaving falling trails of light like the residual aftermath of fireworks.

Josh had located the Wallace sword then sprinted out of the cabin toward the car. As he tossed the sword in, he looked up to the battle before him. He recoiled at each strike and shielded his eyes from the volley of light. From everything that he could see, he watched in awe. How many other humans have ever seen such a sight? He only watched for a moment then realized his mission. He started his car and sped around to cross the clearing.

Pymm had just sent a Warrior back to the Host when he noticed Joshua fleeing. "Stop him!" he snarled as he headed toward the vehicle. A battalion of demons trailed him.

Lucas and a number of Warriors reached the vehicle before him and created a barrier surrounding the car as it moved. Josh drove as fast and as safely as he could, given the rough terrain of the clearing. As the demons fought the Warriors, they threw their weapons at the car, only to be deflected by the Guard. They howled and screeched as they were vanquished one by one. Pymm realized that he was outmatched and quickly fled back to the mass of demons. As Josh's vehicle entered the woods flanked by Lucas and the Warriors, Pymm let out a cry of outrage.

The vehicle sped through the forest, floating just above the surface of the ground, as it was carried by the Guard. The light of the Warriors faded as the car approached the rendezvous point with Tim and the other agents. They rushed up to greet the car with weapons ready in case Josh had been followed. The door was quickly opened by one of the agents, and Josh got out. He was breathing hard as if he had been running.

"Are you okay?" asked Tim as he eyed the surrounding area.

Josh quickly spun in a circle as he looked for any evidence of what he had just witnessed and drove through.

There was nothing, not even a trace.

"Did you see it?" he asked excitedly.

"See what?" asked Tim curiously, still in a protective posture.

Josh looked at him with puzzlement. How could Tim have not heard or seen the battle? He looked at the other agents, who were still surveilling the area to make sure that it was safe.

"Did you have eyes on the cabin during the entire time that I was there?" asked Josh.

"Absolutely. There was no way I was going to let you out of my sight," said Tim.

"From the time that I entered until now, what did you see?"

The field agents had just received the all clear from the watchers indicating that they were indeed alone and no danger was present. The agents began to relax; one retrieved the Wallace sword from the car.

Tim turned back toward Josh. "Once you had entered the cabin, we executed our mission and subdued each of the mercenaries. We have them locked in an RV, awaiting transport back to the local authorities. I made the call letting you know the operation was complete. After that we continued our surveillance on the cabin. Within seven minutes or so, I saw you exit the cabin in a hurry, you stopped for a moment and looked toward the sky, then got into the vehicle and sped away. I assumed that there was an unforeseen threat, so we readied our weapons in preparation to intercept, but you seem to reach us quicker than anticipated."

Josh slowly realized that he was the only one that had witnessed the supernatural event. If he expanded on this further, he would most likely sound like a babbling idiot.

They all succeeded in their missions. The Wallace sword was recovered, and no one had lost their lives.

Small victories.

Josh could live with that for now, but he had questions for Lucas later.

Chapter 23

Pieces and Purpose

A couple of days later, Josh met up with Langston. He smiled at the clutter as he entered his office. Historical documentation was not necessarily digitized in Langston's world of religious doctrine and anthropology, at least not the areas that mattered to Jonah, so there were books and paper everywhere.

"Have you learned anything significant about the Wallace sword?" asked Josh.

"No, not really anything other than what little data we received from Kelan. This Artifact was not even on our radar," he said, a little frustrated. "There's no references to the Wallace sword in any of the ancient text or definable connections with all the other Artifacts. I'm not really sure where to go from here."

Josh was thoughtful for a moment. "Why don't we get Kelan in here to work with you for a bit? He may know something that wasn't documented."

"Is that possible?" Langston said hopefully. "It would be nice to collaborate and figure out why this sword is such a big deal."

"I'll see what I can do."

The very next morning, Kelan and Langston were working in his office at Jonah. Josh managed to work out deception protocols, allowing Kelan to be free of any electronic tracking emitting from Alastar-McGlocklin or their affiliates. There was a team of Jonah personnel that worked an elaborate boondoggle to promote Kelan's physical presence throughout the city, in case there was ground surveillance. He was off the grid just like the diner.

Sometime after lunch, Langston and Kelan visited Josh in his office.

"How goes it, gentleman?" asked Josh.

"Well . . . we've managed to do a comparative analysis between all the known Artifacts and the ones that Kelan provided," said Langston.

"There's more than one that we didn't know about?" asked Josh curiously.

"Yes. The Wallace sword and one other Artifact that Morgan was tasked to recover. He apparently received the instructions to acquire both from Pymm. By Morgan's order, the sword was not sanctioned within my department, so he asked me to run the op off book, that's why there were mercenaries and not the RCT," said Kelan.

"Why would he not want to use the company resources to acquire?" asked Josh.

Kelan shook his head. "Not really sure. He never gave me a reason. Knowing him, he's got an agenda. I'm still trying to find out what that is."

"Anyway . . . we still haven't found anything remotely concrete regarding the importance of the sword as it relates to religious doctrine," said Langston.

"It's definitely important, Pymm was protecting it with everything that he had," said Josh.

"Wait a minute, Pymm was there?" asked Kelan.

"Yes. He was waiting for me in the cabin."

"And you managed to get the sword away from him," said Kelan, more as a statement of fact than a question.

"I wasn't there alone, I had help."

"Still, that is no small feat. He's a very powerful . . . person and doesn't strike me as the type to give in easily," he said.

"Make no mistake, there was nothing easy about it," said Josh, remembering the unbelievable events vividly.

"I would imagine not. His mere presence has all of my staffers scared senseless. If he had a payroll, I'm confident that all of my people would be on it. I'm not sure if there's anyone left that I can trust," said Kelan.

"You know, we've been looking at the Artifacts individually, trying to find a common meaning between them. What if the connection is not in the meaning, but the Artifacts themselves?" said Langston, getting back on track.

Josh's eyebrows rose at the thought. Kelan was intrigued by the idea as well. Josh pulled out the small glowing device and placed it on the conference table. "Sentinel, display all known Artifacts."

Eight Artifacts swirled into view. All three men stared at them, trying to make a visual connection.

"Based on the approximation of shape extrapolate which objects might interlock or connect," he said.

Sentinel began running variations of each object's dimensions and intersection points.

"No plausible connections found."

All three men looked discouraged. Josh sat down in a chair and studied the images. He watched each object swirl in place in an attempt to align the possibilities and angles himself. He looked at the latest acquisition of the Wallace sword. Nothing remarkable stood out, a metal blade with a hilt and a handle wrapped in tight leather.

Then it hit him, and he sat straight up. The sword had segments. Josh shot out of his seat. "Sentinel, where possible, separate Artifacts into their base components."

Pieces of the Knight Blade and the Wallace sword separated. The wool bindings from the Artifact known as the Loreto Challis separated from the silk. All the components floated in place after all possible separations had been completed.

"Based on new information, retain probable matches for connections, discard the rest," he said.

There were seven floating images remaining, each with an edge or slope that might fit together like a puzzle.

"Give me a digital wire frame, manipulable projection," he said.

The images instantly changed into a hard-light reference of distinctive colors. Josh began grabbing the pieces and aligning them in different ways.

After a few tries with various positions, he reached up and grabbed the blade from the Wallace sword. He positioned it over the hilt of the Knight Blade, and it slid into place.

Langston moved closer. With excitement in his eyes, he viewed the new assembly. "With the blade's position off center from the hilt, it leaves a circular pattern right here," he said, pointing.

"Yes, it does. Much like the circumference of the medallion," added Kelan.

Josh took the image of the medallion and slid it into the opened curved slot on the front. It went in halfway, but was stopped by the curvature of the ornate design of the hilt. He had an idea.

"Sentinel, based on the current position of the medallion, complete insertion and probable angle of the hilt while maintaining actual dimensions."

Josh released the wire frame as Sentinel completed the task. As the medallion slid into the final position, the hilt of the Knight Blade enclosed around it, meeting at the top. All three held their breath.

"Render the image," said Josh.

Before them was the swirling projection of a newly discovered Artifact.

"Is this something that you can work with?" Josh asked Langston.

"Yes!" he said, nodding his head. "Sentinel, please start a recognition program of the current object."

"Kelan and I are going back to my office to do more research based on this new information. If there are any pattern matches, we'll find it."

Hours later, Kelan and Langston returned to Josh's office. Excitement filled both their eyes while books filled their hands.

"You found something?" he said hopefully.

"It's called the Tor Embla. An ancient relic of worship culminating in the Byzantine era," said Langston.

"Once your computer identified the Artifact, Langston found a couple of obscure references in his books," said Kelan.

"He's being very kind . . . Sentinel identified the Artifact, Kelan's the one that located the ancient text in a Scandinavian script, dated around 1036 AD, as the earliest point of reference," said Langston.

"Is there a shorter version to the story?" asked Josh.

"Sorry, anyway . . . back in the early eleventh century, some Norwegians were said to worship pagan gods, a common practice of heathenism as a last-ditch effort to directly oppose the powerful wave of Christianity sweeping through the European territories at that time. As with all anti-Christian deities, direct worship of the false gods did not come without sacrifices, tributes, and," he paused for effect, "symbols of their power and virility.

"The most-worshiped pagan god, Blà Tàl, promised he would return and sweep away the Christian threat, leading a vast army of warriors and wielding the one true weapon of their destruction, the Tor Embla," said Langston.

"The worshipers of Blà Tàl have spent centuries in search of the Tor Embla, obviously, with no success. The cross-match of these three Artifacts is the closest thing based on the ancient scripts and drawings," added Kelan.

He presented Josh with a crude picture that was copied from one of the ancient textbooks, which matched the newly discovered Artifact.

"Humans have been looking for hundreds of years and never knew where to find it," said Langston.

Josh looked at the picture and asked Kelan, "Do your people have any information on this?"

He shook his head. "Not to my knowledge. Today is the first that I have ever seen it. That doesn't mean that Morgan or Pymm is unaware though."

Thoughtful for a moment, Josh said, "Mr. Blalock may not have knowledge of this relic, or its purpose, but I'll bet Pymm does."

He got up from his desk and paced around the office, thinking out loud. "It stands to reason that he has been using humans to do his work for centuries, acquiring Artifacts that he cannot find. What doesn't make sense is why he *couldn't* find or gather them himself? And, being the *person* that he is, wouldn't use what little power that he has to achieve this."

"Unless . . . ," started Langston, with the gears in his mind clicking.

After a moment, Josh said, "What?"

"When you and he were in the cabin, did he ever touch the Wallace sword?" asked Langston.

Josh shook his head. "Not that I saw, no."

"And he was nowhere near the SV 8 facility that housed the medallion. In fact, he had Kelan's people install additional security measures to destroy the facility rather than attempt to retrieve or move it himself," he said.

"I'm not sure I understand," said Kelan.

Langston started going through the books that they brought in. Thumbing through pages, he found the reference that would support his thought. "Here, the Médaillon des Âmes. Crafted in gold and *blessed* by a holy Roman Catholic Cardinal upon request of King Philip, for atonement of those who died." He handed the book to Josh then started thumbing for a reference in another.

"The Wallace sword. Upon William Wallace's defeat by Edward Longshanks, the king kept the sword and had it *blessed* by a Roman Catholic Cardinal as well, for the wrong that he did against God, country, and Wallace himself."

"Pymm can't touch these because they are holy objects," realized Josh.

"By themselves, I believe . . . yes," said Langston.

"But together," said Kelan.

"They take on a whole new meaning. I'm thinking that he still can't touch them, but needs someone, a human, who can. Someone to be the catalyst to strike up the notion that Blà Tàl is returning to fulfill his promise. We have the first two Artifacts," said Langston.

"He needs yours plus the third component to make the Tor Embla complete," said Kelan.

"We need to get the Knight Blade now," said Josh as he pulled out his cell phone.

Chapter 24

Catacombs and Banishment

Josh, Lucas, and Langston were aboard a corporate jet heading for Rome, Italy, within twenty-four hours. Jonah International had many private vehicles for various degrees of travel, but since this was a diplomatic mission, Malcolm Holden suggested that they take the converted Boeing 737-800. Under normal conditions, an airplane of this size carried 162 passengers, but this particular aircraft was anything but normal. It was fitted with the latest technology and best passenger comfort known to man. It even had crew quarters for long-term travel and destination stay, if needed.

As promised, Josh allowed Tim to assemble a security detail for his protection. The senior agent insisted on treating this as a full-blown mission, even if tactical retrieval was not needed. Watchers and analysts were on hand as well.

They arrived at Leonardo da Vinci International within eight hours of departure. The aircraft taxied to a secluded location where a caravan of vehicles, including security escorts, awaited. When they disembarked, Josh and company were met by a detachment of the Swiss Guard, the Vatican's personal security force. Josh, Langston, and Lucas were ushered to one of the suburban vehicles as preparations for departure were underway. Tim got into the vehicle at the last minute and took the seat directly across from Josh.

"Paladin is secure. Ready to roll," he said into his right sleeve.

Josh looked at him with a raised eyebrow. "Paladin?"

"Your call sign from this point on," Tim said matter-of-factly. Josh looked down a little sheepishly; Langston just smiled. "Gee, I wish I had a call sign."

Josh elbowed him.

"Do we have confirmation that the Artifact is still in Vatican City?" Josh asked Langston.

"Yes. My contact at the Italian Ministry of Cultural Assets and Activities says that it is stored in the Vatican Secret Archives."

"Do we have someone expecting us?"

"Monsignore Guinomenai, the prefect of the Archives, has agreed to meet with us personally. The Bishop has been an Associate of Jonah International for quite some time. This is a very important relationship for us."

"So don't screw it up, right?"

"I didn't mean it quite that way, but yes. We have privileges that a lot of other people do not."

"Have you been here before?"

Langston shook his head. "No, this is my first time."

Josh looked over to Lucas with raised eyebrows.

"A few," said Lucas, with a slight grin.

The route from the airport to Plaza di San Pietro was cordoned off by the Polizia locale; the motorcade made excellent time. Once they arrived, the Swiss Guard and security detachment assumed their protective positions as Josh and company were escorted into the side entrance of the Sistine Chapel.

The prefect was waiting for them. "Mr. Arden, it is a pleasure to have you here. Welcome to Vatican City," he said in broken English.

Taking the Bishop's extended hand, Josh said in near-perfect Italian, "Monsignore Guinomenai, thank you so much for allowing us to visit your beautiful city. We are humbled by your generous hospitality."

"Molto bene, Signor Arden!" replied the delighted prefect as he escorted them through the chapel. Langston and Lucas smiled as they followed.

As they walked through the Sistine Hall of the library, Josh marveled at the magnificently detailed artwork and craftsmanship. They came to the security entrance down to the Archives. The prefect entered his security card and code; and once the doors opened, Josh, Langston, and Lucas entered with the prefect. The Vatican had policies regarding armed security personnel; Tim and his people waited outside with the Swiss Guard.

The Bishop was well informed of why Josh was there, so he led them straight to where the Cavaliere Lama, the Knight Blade, was stored. It was in a nondescriptive steel case with an electronic keypad off to the side in an unassuming corner, with other boxes surrounding it. He punched in his code and opened the case.

The blade was gone.

"Impossibile!" said the astonished Bishop. He went on to say something in very quick Italian.

Josh looked over to Lucas, who translated that the Bishop had checked on the blade less than an hour ago and confirmed that it was in the case.

Without hesitation, Josh pulled out Excubiarum, the small object with glowing blue waves of light. "Sentinel, locate the blade."

Within milliseconds, Sentinel responded along with a visual representation, showing the objects movements.

"The Knight Blade is currently moving through the vatican catacombs."

Josh turned and started running back toward the Archive's entrance with everyone else in tow.

Upon exiting, he hurriedly explained to Tim the situation. With Excubiarum inside of his pocket, he told Sentinel to continue tracking the blade's movements and route coordinates to all security personnel for interception.

Once that was completed, Josh communicated to each through Sentinel. "Do not allow that blade to leave the city!"

Sentinel guided each of the security personnel from both Jonah and the Swiss Guard, in their own native language, from their current position to the moving blade. Each person had individual turn-by-turn verbal navigation, providing them the quickest route to interception.

The layout of the catacombs was like a maze. The main part was well lit with gates and ropes that funneled tourists as they oohed and aahed over famous Catholic tombs. There were some-not-so-nice areas that were viewable to the public, for a price. Then, there were the areas that were not well known except to the select few, chambers that were considered sacred by the Holy Roman Church. Most were forbidden to enter under any circumstances.

The person that handled the blade heard footsteps fast approaching. Panic began to set in. He ran, turning down a series of pathways and tunnels, which led into the forbidden part. The vatican catacombs were not as big as they appeared, but could be very confusing when twisting and turning without any bearings. It also did not help his situation to know he was being pursued. He emerged into an antechamber that opened up to a large circular hall with a high-domed ceiling. There were two stone tables parallel to each other on either side; the walls were lined with hundreds of skulls. He stopped just short of the archway on the other side and turned in a circle. He frantically looked around as if disoriented and did not know which way to go.

"Feeling a little lost?" came a voice.

He turned around quickly to see a figure walking through the archway.

"Hai paura di me!" replied the startled Bishop's aide.

"You have no need to be scared of me," came the silky sweet voice. "You have done well. Please, let me see the sword."

As the Bishop's aide started to comply, the approach of running footsteps became louder. One by one, Swiss Guard and Jonah security entered the hall, each with their weapons drawn and pointing at the two figures. The last to enter was the prefect and Josh.

Upon seeing that it was his personal aide that took the Knight Blade, the prefect shouted, "Don Emanuel! Come ti permetti!"

He continued to chastise his aide in rapid Italian while the guard and security remained motionless, covering their targets. Josh and Lucas moved to the front, their eyes never leaving the dark figure they knew as Pymm.

In near-perfect Italian, Josh told the Bishop's aide to lay the sword on the table. The aide was trembling, but did as he was instructed. As soon as he stepped away from the sword, he was subdued by the guard.

"Tim, please get the prefect to safety," asked Josh.

"Yes, sir," he replied with a slight nod. The Swiss Guard took point and ushered the Bishop and his aide out of the hall, while still maintaining a defensive stance against the remaining figure.

"I need everyone else to leave the hall too. Lucas and I will handle this," said Josh.

"Sir, are you sure about this? You'll be alone?" whispered Tim.

"I'll be okay."

As Tim and the security detail began to back out of the hall, Langston was the last to leave. He gave Josh a concerned look and a nod. Josh replied in kind as Langston finally stepped out.

"Well, well . . . here we are, reunited yet again," said the dark figure.

"I'm curious, Pymm," said Josh as he walked slowly in an arc around the hall. "How is it that you are in one of the holiest places on earth? I would imagine that this would be very difficult—you know, being a demon and all."

"Wouldn't you like to know?" he said snidely.

"He could only have entered a holy sanctum if he were invited," said Lucas.

Nodding, Josh said, "Like vampires . . . guess it would have to come from somewhere, that makes sense." He continued walking. "Familiars within Vatican City, quite the achievement in the supernatural world I would assume."

Pymm just glared at him.

"That is something that can be remedied over time," said Josh.

"Humans will always be loyal to us. They will never know any better," Pymm said with satisfaction.

"Not if I have anything to say about it. You know, for someone that is supposed to be smart and *superior*," he said, making finger gestures, "you're not very bright," said Josh. He was halfway around the arc.

Pymm bared his teeth and hissed at the insult. However, nothing supernatural happened to Josh's relief. His theory was proving to be true. Time to step up the tempo.

"How did you think you would get the Artifact out of here, the Bishop's aide? I know you can't touch the sword, and we have all the exits blocked. That plan didn't work out well for you at all.

"There's a better-than-average chance we have more Associates here than you do Familiars, and let's not forget the power emanating within the city. I bet there's not a single moment that a prayer somewhere is not being uttered. That's got to cause you a little discomfort, hmm?" stated Josh. He was not more than six feet from the Knight Blade.

This commentary and attitude were completely uncharacteristic for him. He felt compelled to force his position: to send the underworld a message. Pymm was physically agitated and getting angrier by the second. Josh stood there, silent for a moment, and looked at him. He almost felt pity for the creature. His side was chosen: the die cast. Pymm was bound by something that could, and would, never be broken.

Josh calmly walked to the table and picked up the sword. Pymm looked like he was in anguish, like he was being restrained by an invisible force that tightened around him the harder he struggled.

"Lucaous, this must be entertaining for you. Are you going to save your pet from me again?" said Pymm through the clenched teeth of someone in pain.

"It looks as if Joshua has the situation well in hand, therefore not requiring my assistance," he replied.

"Your powers are fragile here, aren't they? You can barely stand there with what little dignity you have left. Who is weak now?" asked Josh.

Pymm tried to raise his fisted hands, but could not get them any higher than his elbows. His eyebrows and forehead were expressing a great deal of pain. It was unclear to Josh whether this was out of physical distress or Pymm's inability to act upon his own will due to the rules that were in place.

Do demons even have a will?

He stepped a little closer to him, with the sword down to his side. He looked intently at him.

"This may not always have been the case . . . but for right here and right now, you are in way over your head," said Josh.

He walked back over toward Lucas with a purpose then turned around to face Pymm for the last time. The sarcasm and the taunting were now over.

"By the authority placed in me by the Chairman of Jonah International, I hereby banished you from these premises. By that same authority, I bind you from harming or influencing those to harm—my family, colleagues, or friends. You are now finished," stated Josh.

Pymm's skin started to crack; a glowing red-and-orange color emerged like embers of burning wood. Slowly, around his cheekbone at first but spreading more quickly like a fault line through the rest of his face. His arms and hands began to crack, his designer suit beginning to wither, changing from a smooth fabric to something rumpled and rough with scorched edges. He stood there motionless as his body was decaying, his face frozen in a silent scream.

"And, Pymm," said Josh.

The demon was turning to ash as his eyes met Josh's for the last time.

"Tell your boss to buckle up, the game is changing."

Pymm let out a final howl that faded as he dissolved into nothingness.

"Well done, Joshua. That said, it is not a good idea to provoke the enemy," said Lucas.

"They started it," he replied and turned to leave.

Kelan was in his office at the Long Beach facility reviewing the daily operations' logs when a knock came at his door.

"Hey, have you got a minute?" said Margaret upon opening it.

Kelan locked down both his computer and his tablet. "Sure, what's up?"

She closed the door behind her, walked over, and took a seat. She had a pensive look, obviously not knowing how to approach the subject. Kelan waited patiently.

"You've been a little distant lately," she finally said.

"Really? How so?"

"Well . . . you've been a hard man to track down."

Trying not to show surprise or animosity for the betrayal he felt, he waited for the rest. She could not have meant to be as bold as the statement came across.

"Still not following, Margaret."

"Sorry, what I meant to say was that I haven't seen a lot of you lately, both here and . . ." She indicated with a slightly sheepish head bob.

Suspicion was the last thing he wanted to encourage at this stage; they were too close to the endgame to blow it now. He feigned a look of exhaustion. "I've been working odd hours trying to close the 216 project. Resource assignments, reallocation of material assets, scrubbing the dossier for closure, all that stuff. As you know, we hired a lot of people to support this one operation. Some of the surveillance team specializing in the skill sets required for 216 is sought-after in the private sector for similar activities. I don't want to lose them to a competitor in case another need such as this presents itself. I have been working contracts to support as a third-party provider."

What he said had some bearing of truth to it. There were contracts in the works and a paper trail of all activities to back up everything he just stated, but he was not doing any of the actual work. It was all part of the services set up by Josh to cover his tracks while working with Jonah.

She nodded in agreement. "Farming out the resources, smart plan." She paused for a moment.

"Is there something else on your mind?" he asked, almost impatiently.

"I just miss you, that's all. We haven't seen much of each other in a very long time," she said, sounding sad.

Keeping up his cover, he said, "I know. It's just been very busy trying to manage the day-to-day operations while processing the 216 closure. I promise, things will change very soon." Of that, he was absolutely certain.

She smiled, nodded, and then stood up to leave.

"By the way, I noticed that there are a few log discrepancies in the DRONE rotation. It seems that a number of them have been sent out for test flights, but doesn't state why," he said.

"It's standard protocol when retrofitting and refurbishing maintenance parts, nothing really unusual about that," she said.

"Maybe so, but the flight plan for the tests was not logged for any of them."

"Really? That's not right. I'll check into the log times and the technician on duty to see what happened." The look on her face did not match the answer. She seemed like she was caught with her hand in the cookie jar.

"One time, I might understand, but this happened on four separate occasions. If it's the same technician, fire him. I want these logs personally reconciled by you. Keep me posted on the results," he said, waiting to see what she was going to say.

She looked a little pale and swallowed once. "I promise you that I will take care of this as quickly as I can. It will be my first priority."

With that, she quickly walked to the door and left. Kelan opened up his tablet and flagged the files to set up a trace for activity. He wanted to see what she would put in the logs. He pulled up a secondary screen on his PC with the satellite telemetry data from all four DRONE test flights. He already knew where they had been. Each flight coincided with his movements over the last two months. She was tracking him; the question was why and for whom. He had a good idea.

His mobile phone rang. He looked at the caller ID and answered.

"Did you get it?" he asked.

"Yes. We're on our way back to the States now. Do you have the information that I requested?" asked Josh.

"Yes, I'll transmit the file when you return."

"Where is she?"

"Monte Carlo."

Chapter 25

Hidden and Caught

It was an absolutely beautiful day. A light breeze was stirring down Avenue de la Madone, across the sloping hills toward the coastline. The peaceful waters of the Mediterranean were dotted with luxurious yachts belonging to Europe's upper-class elite, some of whom she claimed to know. Social standing was something that had always been important to her. In the six weeks of living in one of the most expensive suites in the Hotel Metropole, her only responsibility was to look the part of a wealthy socialite.

A late night of partying resulted in a midday wake-up call. Brunch was always the preferred meal, but not today. Instead, the option was for a midafternoon fare of a light salad and juice. No liquor until tonight, the residual of a headache still lingering.

Her plans were to spend the afternoon on the veranda off the main lobby, sipping expensive bottled water, while reading the latest fashion magazines. A routine that she had fallen into over the last week in order to be seen by anyone that might be important. The lobby was always buzzing with activity, whether for business or pleasure. It was one of the main reasons she chose to stay here.

Her second bottle of Christian Lacroix was delivered by her favorite waiter, Laurent, with a nice smile. After thanking him, she causally looked around to see if anyone was, indeed, watching before returning to her reading. As she thumbed through her magazine, she barely noticed a figure taking the seat directly across from her. After a few moments, she gazed up nonchalantly and froze.

"Hello, Kate," said Josh casually.

She slowly pulled down her Moss Lipow sunglasses; shock was ever-present.

"I like what you've done with your hair. Red is a good color for you."

"J-Josh! Um . . . how are you?" she said, looking around.

"That's not the first question that I thought you would ask," he said, his eyes never leaving her. He stared at her on purpose in an open attempt to make her uncomfortable. It was working as intended.

"I didn't see you at Harry's funeral. Did you have other plans for that day?"

"Josh, I can explain—"

"I'm not usually interested in anything that you have to say, but this time, I would really like to know. Please, continue."

She looked around nervously, trying to figure out what to do next. It was obvious to Josh that she did not have a lie prepared. Never in a million years did she think she would run into him again. She could see that he was enjoying this, and that made her angry.

"You know what? I don't owe you anything," she said, with an edge in her voice.

"Now, there's the Kate that I know. Nevertheless, you are wrong, you owe me more than you can ever imagine."

"It was Harry's decision to—"

"Oh, cut the crap! Have the guts to accept responsibility for your actions and not pin your excuses on my *dead* best friend!"

"I've missed our little talks." A satisfying grin spread across her face.

"You're going to be missing a lot more than that."

"Please, Joshua, don't make threats that you cannot back up."

"A lot has changed in the last year. You have no idea what I can back up."

"Is that so?" she said snidely and signaled to someone.

Josh sat in his chair with his legs crossed. "The local muscle that you hired is currently being detained," he said, gesturing toward the main doors of the hotel. There were two guys flanked by three of Josh's security detail. Her expression changed somewhat when she saw them.

"They won't be able to help you today."

He then began to recount her actions over the last year. He told her he knew the true nature of her relationship with Harry, that she had been secretly working for Alastar-McGlocklin, about her contract with Kelan Tindal, and that her high-powered job as a pharmaceutical rep was a sham and cover. He went on to say that she probably never even knew why she was hired, that she most likely did not question the life she was about to destroy, because of the promises of money, wealth, and status were all that mattered.

The indignant, in-control look was now gone. She kept staring at Josh. "I know everything, Kate."

"Okay, you can't blame me, for—"

"For what? Caring about no one else besides you?" He held out his hand as someone walked over and handed him a manila folder.

She shifted in her seat uncomfortably and watched a person she did not know walk away then turned to Josh as he pulled out the contents and placed them on his lap.

"You've had a pretty normal and boring life, Kate . . . or should I call you Rachel?"

To his satisfaction, the response was immediate and could not be hidden. Her eyes widened, and the glass in her hand slipped, shattering on the floor.

"Rachel McReavy. Born and raised in Bethlehem, Pennsylvania." He thumbed through the pages of the file. "Nice picture." He held up a photocopy of her driver's license as a teenager.

"Nothing looks out of the ordinary: straight-A student, except for that B in biochemistry in your junior year. Your dad, Stanley, was a master electrician, your mother, Martha"—he flipped a few pages—"was an accountant. You were offered a full ride to three different colleges and turned them all down. Your entire life is in this package."

He put the pages back in the folder and tossed it on the table between them.

"What could possibly have happened to turn you into such a horrible person?" The question was sincere; he really wanted to know.

She stared at the folder with tears brimming her eyes. "You don't know anything about me!"

"I know that you left everything and everyone behind thirty-eight months ago when you were approached by Alastar-McGlocklin. They agreed to change your life, your name, your very existence . . . and all you had to do was get close to a person of interest, guide him in certain directions, lie, deceive, destroy, and report back on everything that he did.

"I know that you were given specialized training in the art of deception, to pull off the deep cover assignment, and most importantly . . . I know that you were reporting to more than just Kelan."

Her eyes told him that he was correct. "I wonder if Mr. Blalock even knew that you were double-crossing him as well."

She was like a statue. How could he have possibly known this? She was so careful in everything that she did. She planned it all out meticulously. "How do you know all of this?"

"Like I said, a lot has changed."

He leaned toward her and said in a very serious voice, "It would be in your best interest to listen to what I have to say."

Kate and Josh stared at each other for what seemed like an eternity. She could see that he was angry about what had happened; he could see that she was starting to understand the seriousness of her situation.

"We need some privacy," he said.

She was confused by the statement. Then, she noticed that it was very quiet. She looked around, and everyone was gone; the lobby was empty. No customers or hotel staff could be seen. She slowly and nervously rose from her seat. She walked around the outside onto the veranda; it was deserted. She walked slowly back into the lobby, turning in circles, as she moved toward the front of the hotel. Peering outside, the street was completely vacant of people. She did not see a soul, except for Josh, who just sat there, waiting for her to return to her seat. By the time she sat back down, she was shaking.

"What did you do? Where did everyone go?" she asked softly.

"You think what you have is power. You have no idea what true power really is," he said softly, barely in a whisper. "It is not something that can be acquired, but given from something much greater than yourself . . . and only to those who will use it justly and selflessly."

"What are you going to do to me?"

"Not what you deserve, that's for sure. You played a direct part in the death of Harrison Gibson, my best friend, my brother, and for that, you should face American justice, that is your first option."

She was really scared now. Tears started to stream down her face. That was the first time that Josh noticed the poor soul known as Rachel, and not the manipulative harpy he knew as Kate.

"What is the second option?" she asked, fearful of what he would say.

"I leave you to your own fate of what awaits you in the world and the people that you've wronged," he said. "Either way, I have frozen all of your assets. Your accounts will be closed, and all of your personal items repossessed. Your passport has been revoked and driver's license suspended indefinitely. Your cell phone doesn't even work."

She picked up her phone from the table; it did not have any signal. She looked at him in disbelief.

"You will be checking out of the hotel today. I've taken care the remainder of the balance. You will be allowed to take your clothes with you, and the money you have left in your pockets, but that's it.

"So you have a decision to make: option one or two. If you go with the first, I will take you back to the States, you will be protected until you stand trial. If you choose the second, I cannot help you. You'll be at the mercy of anyone or anything that comes for you."

"What do you mean *anything*? I don't understand. You make it sound like going to jail is better than just starting over," she said.

"The second choice is by no means starting over. It's leaving you to your own fate, which in your case is the worst-scenario possible. Without someone to look out for you, the evil in this world will find you, it always does."

"What in the world are you talking about?"

"The option to make the right decision. Things aren't as they seem, you have no idea what's out there. You have to make a choice, Rachel. I'm giving you the chance you never gave Harry. You will have to trust me if you want absolution for your actions. As I said, you're not getting what you deserve, which is no choice at all. You need to decide. There is a time limit on this offer."

Two hours later, Rachel/Kate stood in front of the hotel with four designer suitcases at her feet. As soon as Josh was finished, everyone returned and continued on with their day as if nothing happened. She turned down his offer and chose the second option, stating that she would be better off on her own. Josh was truly sorry to hear that and genuinely wished her the best of luck.

She approached a few people that she knew from her stay and asked for help. They politely smiled and walked away. Even the hotel staff, who had pampered and catered to her every need, barely, if at all, acknowledged her presence. Her favorite waiter, Laurent, breezed by her without as much as a look.

It was like she did not exist.

On the curb, suitcases by her side, she stood there and wept. Everything that she had worked for over the last three years was now gone, all lost in the span of three hours. Taken away in an act of revenge over someone whom she, admittedly, had treated badly.

She was not directly involved in Harry's murder. She did not even know that was the endgame. How could she? If she had, she would have surely done something to prevent it—wouldn't she? She had no say in the decisions or the outcome—it was all Mr. Pemberton's doing. Rachel/Kate was just as much a victim in this mess as Harry. How could Josh leave her like this? She had nothing but her clothes and a few hundred dollars to her name now. Practically destitute with no means of getting back to the States to start over. Where would she go now? What would she do? She needed time to figure this out. However, once she was back on her feet, she would find a way to get back at Josh for everything that he had done, had taken from her.

All of these thoughts and emotions swirled through her head in an instant. So clouded by the fact that she was wronged in this situation and unjustly accused, she never allowed the possibility of what Josh offered to be a way out. A recompense for her actions and salvation for her soul.

Greed has a way of condemning the ignorant, and they are the perfect marks for the enemy.

A taxicab pulled up to the front of the hotel; the driver got out and approached Rachel.

"Miss, are you in need of assistance?" he asked.

She wiped tears from her face, stunned that someone actually seemed to care. "Yes, but I have no money to pay you with," she lied.

"That is quite all right, miss," he said as he began loading her suitcases into the trunk. "Mr. Pemberton has sent me."

As he finished loading the suitcases, he opened the back door for her.

"Oh, thank you!" she said, getting in.

The driver quickly walked around and got into the cab. As he shifted into drive and started to pull away, he caught the eye of a gentleman observing from across the street. The man was impeccably dressed in all black. A smile creased his face, and the driver nodded to him.

"Wait a minute. How did he know that I needed help?" said Rachel.

The doors locked automatically as the car turned the corner.

Chapter 26

Accusations and Confrontations

Kelan walked down the corridor toward Blalock's office. His boss had called him in at the last minute, but did not state the nature of the meeting. He wanted to be prepared just in case Blalock wanted updates regarding mission statuses, but without an agenda, he would be walking into this cold.

He smiled as he approached her desk. "Hey, Betty. How are you this morning?"

"I'm doing just fine, Mr. Tindal. How are you today?" she said with a smile.

"Great! Things actually couldn't be better."

"That's wonderful to hear, sir! I'm glad that things are getting better for you! I've been really worried about you lately. You've seemed so stressed and run-down. It looks like you have managed to turn things around."

"You have no idea. The big man is expecting me," he said as he continued to walk toward the double doors. "Betty, I hope you have a wonderful day!"

"You too, Mr. Tindal!" she responded as he entered the office.

When he closed the doors behind him and turned, he noticed that Margaret was sitting in a chair at the front of Blalock's desk.

"Hello, Morgan," said Kelan as he approached. "I was not aware that Margaret would be in our meeting today."

His hands were folded neatly on his desk. He then gestured to the opposite seat. "Please sit down, Tindal."

Kelan took his seat as requested. "I get the feeling that we are not here to just talk about the operational finances."

"Tindal, I'll get right to the point. It has come to my attention that you have committed acts of treason against Alastar-McGlocklin."

Interesting and a bit shocking, but not completely unexpected. "What acts might those be and how did they happen to come to your attention?" he said, answering Blalock but staring at Margaret.

"I have substantial proof that you have been less than honest in your reports, both from a financial perspective and around Artifact mission protocols," said Blalock.

The timing was about right. Kelan suspected that Morgan's exit strategy would have to include a scapegoat; it made sense that it would be him.

"Morgan, I'm not sure what this is about, but I can assure you every report that I have filed has been to the letter of the responsibilities that you have given me," he said.

Kelan looked back and forth between Blalock and Margaret. He had a smirk upon his face, and she looked nervous. Margaret being here confirmed what Kelan had already known, she had gathered her evidence and was now coming forward to present her findings.

"So what you're saying is you have never fabricated any mission data or manipulated operational cash reserves to promote any type of personal or hidden agenda, is that correct?" said Blalock.

"Not necessarily. Mission data has never been altered without express written consent by you, nor have we transferred or moved any operational funding unless it was sanctioned by you as well. That would also include the off-book missions," said Kelan.

Blalock gave him a stern look for that last comment. Truthfully, his manipulative looks did not bother Kelan anymore.

Huh . . . how about that?

Where at one time Kelan had feared him, he now pitied the man and his attempts at subterfuge. Josh and

Langston had told him that Blalock was close to pulling out and most likely would leave him holding the bag; he was the logical choice for the corporate witch hunt that would likely follow. So far, their assessment, and his gut feeling, had been spot-on.

"I'm assuming that you have proof of this accusation?" asked Kelan.

"Margaret," Blalock said roughly.

Startled by the sharp voice, she jumped slightly in her seat, losing a couple of papers out of the file that was on her lap. As she bent down to quickly pick them up, Kelan saw that one of them had some financial values on it. If he were a betting man, it most likely had to do with the missing money that was used to fund the Wallace sword mission. She quickly replaced the pages and handed the file to Blalock.

He took his time thumbing through some of the pages, as if he had never seen them before. Kelan saw him perform this technique in the past; he used it as part of his mind games when negotiating deals. He would frown at whatever he was looking at, turn some pages as if comparing one against another, then make a muffled sound like he was either disappointed in his findings or saw something that could be used to his advantage. No matter how he used this technique, its intended purpose was to make the opposition feel uncomfortable and let them know who was in charge. It had an even bigger impact when he was sitting behind his judicial bench of a desk.

"Hmm," said Blalock, studying a page.

Right on cue. Kelan almost wanted to laugh.

"Tindal, it looks like there is an unaccounted discrepancy of about $2.3 million within the last eighteen months. Can you explain this?"

"Yes," he responded casually, "the $2.3 million was the total amount of reallocated funding across five separate Artifact mission accounts. An amount of $1.7 million was moved by me to fund the unsanctioned Wallace sword expedition, which only came from three of the five active accounts."

"What Wallace sword mission?" asked Margaret, confused.

"It was the mission that I was asked to plan and execute without direct utilization of my department and the RCT."

Blalock was clearly upset about this disclosure. Kelan did not really care. "Sir, I believe you were aware of how we were funding this mission. I brought this to your attention some months ago and requested your approval to contract the mercenaries to execute it."

"Mercenaries!?" said Margaret.

"Yes," he said casually as he continued to address Blalock. "At the same time I discussed this with you, I also brought to your attention that additional money had been shifted from two other mission accounts totaling $600,000, which was unaccounted for by my planning."

He could see that Blalock knew very well what he was talking about. He was not sure what agitated him more, the fact that they were discussing this in front of Margaret or that he knew whatever leverage he had against Kelan over this topic was diminishing slowly.

He decided to turn the screw just a bit more. "I believe your directive was to adjust the accounts accordingly. You said, and I quote, 'The $600,000 will go away as if it never existed.' I followed your instructions to the letter and basically cooked the books . . . so to speak."

Blalock's eyes were wide with internal rage. While Kelan's face was unemotional, inside, he was laughing like a child in a candy store. Kelan turned and looked at Margaret as if to ask, "What else you got?" She just sat there, afraid to say anything or look at either of them.

"Morgan, again, I'm not sure what this is about, I have done everything that you have ever asked me to do. I don't appreciate being falsely accused of something in which I had no direct influence over the outcome."

Blalock looked at Margaret, who continued to avoid eye contact. "Sir, there is the matter of the modified reports surrounding surveillance data transmitted from the DRONE," she said, pointing to other papers.

He shuffled them around until he came to the ones that she mentioned. He read the first couple then looked at Kelan. "Tindal, what is this about?"

"I believe Margaret is referring to the onboard system failure of the 216 DRONE when we lost the signal and subsequently the Object."

Blalock looked through the papers and did not see anything out of the ordinary. He then looked at Margaret. "You say these reports were modified?"

"Yes, sir. The initial diagnostics of the systems didn't produce anything of significant value to indicate why the DRONE malfunctioned. We were still in the process of reacquiring 216. Mr. Tindal had created false readings for the report and asked me to post those to the central server once his review was completed."

He had a look of disappointment. "Is this correct, Tindal?"

"Yes, sir, it is."

Both Blalock and Margaret were surprised by his truthfulness.

"Would you care to explain?" the boss asked.

"Absolutely. I had Margaret post the falsified reports to basically satisfy your need for an immediate status," he said.

"Excuse me!?" Blalock blurted out.

"Look, Morgan, we didn't have enough information back then to understand why our electronic surveillance failed. After we completed the level 4 diagnostics, it was determined that the equipment was not faulty, it just simply didn't work. We both know why. You demanded answers before we had enough time to get them. I made the call that was necessary to focus our time and resources to the objective: reacquiring 216. It was a judgment call and my responsibility. Taking more time to run further analysis would have made little difference."

Margaret sat there, waiting for the hammer to fall, but Morgan just looked at him. They did not break eye contact as he evaluated Kelan's response. "Right then. I suppose if I had been in your shoes, I might have done the same thing."

This response surprised all three of them. Margaret was out of her league in the company of both, with regards to the volley of power. Morgan was disappointed that she had not provided any favorable evidence that could be used to mask his true motives. The extra money that he had paid her was an investment, which he now regretted.

She could see that she was striking out. There were a few more things that she found in Kelan's personal file that could be of use though. Margaret was holding those as a last resort, mostly because she did not understand and wanted more time to investigate, but now, she was going to have to say something to ensure her own survival. Maybe Kelan could fill in the missing pieces of some of her findings, such as the encryption anomalies on his cell phone.

"Sir, if you look at the last part of the file, there is something else I can—"

"That will be quite enough, Ms. Havilland. I believe that we have taken up enough of Mr. Tindal's time." He placed the papers back inside the file. "Kelan, when Ms. Havilland approached me about suspicious activities in your division, she assured me that she had proof that everything led back to you."

Her eyes got wide. "That's a lie! You paid me to find dirt on Kelan. I did everything that—"

"Enough!" said Blalock.

And there it was, glimpses of the truth revealed by a woman freshly scorned. Margaret had no idea what she had just done, but did understand the implications of what she just blurted out.

"Ms. Havilland, your services are no longer required," said Blalock in a professional tone.

"You can't do that!"

"Regardless, Margaret . . . you're fired," said Kelan, backing Morgan up.

He flipped open his cell phone. "Jones, we have an A186 in progress, Margaret Havilland. Mr. Blalock's office."

Her eyes were spinning; her head reeling from the events of the last fifteen minutes. Within seconds, two security people knocked at the door then entered. Blalock waved them forward with one swift gesture. As they approached, Margaret stood slowly, her legs shaking.

"Why are you doing this? After everything that we've been through?" she asked Kelan.

"You should have come to me first if you felt there was a problem. Questioning my loyalty to this company, in front of my boss, was a mistake. I expect better from my subordinates."

"I'm sorry," she whispered.

Kelan responded unemotionally, "Apology accepted." He nodded to the security people. They gently guided her to the door and left.

"Morgan, my sincerest apologies for wasting your time over this matter. I have no idea why Margaret would go to such lengths to question my actions. I hope you know that my only objective is to do the right thing by this company. You have given me a lot of freedom to do my job. I don't want to misuse that trust."

"Nonsense, my boy, I should have never doubted you to begin with. These were outrageous accusations, and I should have questioned them more carefully before calling them to your attention."

"It's quite all right. I am the one to apologize. Margaret was one of mine. I just don't understand what would have caused her to turn against me," said Kelan, feigning concern. He knew full well why she turned and who was behind it.

"Well . . . I don't suppose we will ever know," said Blalock.

They discussed operational finances and the plans for the next Artifact mission before politely closing the meeting. They parted with a handshake, which was uncharacteristic for any of their meetings. Kelan was not sure if this was a sign to the events yet to come or a gesture signifying the end of their working relationship. Both explanations were plausible in any case.

As he was leaving, he made a mental note to contact Josh to thank him. His team supplied the results from the trace information on the surveillance that Margaret had been running. Jonah's supercomputer was, indeed, amazing. When Josh had copied the information from his tablet at the diner, a subroutine was embedded by Sentinel in return. This routine allowed Sentinel to maintain a passive link, establishing a one-way synchronization from Kelan's computer. It needed to network to Alastar-McGlocklin's mainframe just once in order for the routine to find its way into the core of their central server. Once embedded, it pushed all information regarding the DRONE status and surveillance schedules on Kelan directly to Sentinel. His suspicions were then confirmed.

Sentinel was capable of this and more without the subroutine, but Kelan was not yet ready to embrace the complete truth.

As Blalock watched him leave, he fumed at the outcome and the incompetence. This was a minor setback, but there was still time to find something that he could pin on Kelan, to divert attention when the moment came. He needed to come up with more quantitative evidence to explain the loss of assets and focus the board and, more importantly, the senior partners on a target other than himself. He figuratively patted himself on the back for his ingenuity thus far. By the time anyone was the wiser, he would be sitting in a villa in Austria, earning 20 percent. As for Margaret, he would deal with her decisively.

Chapter 27

Endgame and Aftermath

It was like any other day. His routine did not deviate in the slightest. He finished breakfast at 6:25 am; then his car dropped him off at the private entrance of Alastar-McGlocklin's corporate office at 7:55 am. Per his usual route, it was a solitary stroll, encountering no one except the guard at the entrance. He was reading an investment article in this month's *Forbes* magazine as the elevator doors opened on his floor. Without looking up, he started down the corridor.

"Betty, call Leland Hamilton and reschedule the 8:30 am for this afternoon. Tell him something else came up," he said as he came to his office.

There was no immediate response, so he looked up. She was not there. In fact, her desk light and computer were off. It did not appear that she was in yet. This was odd; she was always in the office before him. He looked at his wristwatch to make sure he was not, in fact, early. This was very peculiar, indeed. For a brief second, he was worried something had happened to her. He thought better of it after a few moments. She was late, and this was unacceptable. He sighed, realizing that he was going to have to get his own coffee as well. He continued reading his article as he opened the doors. Walking across the expanse of his office, he practically jumped when he noticed Kelan leaning against the desk, with his arms folded.

"Tindal. You gave me a start. I don't recall having you on my calendar for today," he said as he tossed his coat on a chair. He walked behind the desk.

"I'm not, Morgan."

Blalock went about emptying the contents of his case and arranging files. He waited for Kelan to continue, but he said nothing as he stood there.

Frustrated at the intrusion, Blalock said, "Then why are you here?"

"I am here to bear witness to a historic event." He moved away from the desk.

"Tindal, I have no time nor am I in the mood for any of these games," he replied gruffly.

Kelan simply smiled and walked toward the couch. Blalock's gaze followed him, shocked by the total lack of respect. He had enough of this and was about to inform Kelan that he was treading into a very dangerous territory when he noticed there was someone else sitting on the couch.

"What is this?" he said, looking back and forth between the two.

"Mr. Blalock, my name is Joshua Arden."

His expression changed to one of caution mixed with realization. His name was not unfamiliar, although Blalock would not understand the significance that it carried until it was too late.

"Why are you in my office? How did you get in here?" he demanded.

"I am here to collect on a very long-standing debt. How I got in is irrelevant."

"I'm not sure what game you are playing, but—"

"I can assure you, sir, this is not a game," said Josh.

Blalock looked at him with an icy stare. He did not know this boy, but there was no show of respect as an individual or as the head of the world's largest mergers and acquisitions corporation. He picked up his phone and began dialing.

"If you're calling for security, they won't answer," said Kelan.

Blalock continued; the phone just rang. He tried other numbers; no one picked up.

"The building is empty. There are no employees here," said Kelan.

Blalock replaced the receiver harshly. "What is the meaning of this?"

Josh gestured to a chair opposite the couch. "Mr. Blalock, please have a seat."

"I will not stand for this!" He gathered his things and headed for the doors. As he opened them, there were two gentlemen standing just on the other side. They appeared to be some sort of security. As Blalock tried to push by, they maneuvered to block his path. Frustrated, he turned around to look at Kelan.

"Tindal, you are fired!"

There was no acknowledgment of the statement. "You need to listen to what this man has to say."

"I have to do no such thing! *I* run this company, I give the orders!"

Josh glanced at his watch. "Mr. Blalock, at 9:00 am EST, Alastar-McGlocklin and its subsidiaries will no longer exist." Still seated, he stared at Blalock. "In forty-five minutes, you will be the head of nothing."

With a slight nod from Josh, the two security people escorted Blalock to the chair across from him. A little stunned at the statement, he sat down.

"I'll come right to the point. Alastar-McGlocklin's stock has done very well over the last three months. Your corporate earnings have been the largest recorded in decades. Investor's confidence in the company's mission and growth potential is ranked highest among the leading Global 100. This company, and your position, is the best that it has ever been in twenty years as the acting CEO," said Josh.

"Anyone who is anybody of significance in the financial market knows this," he replied snidely.

Kelan handed Blalock a professionally bound investment portfolio. "As of the close of the market yesterday, what you have in your hand is the financial position of Alastar-McGlocklin Inc. and their investor standings. The group of investors highlighted currently own 54 percent of the shares in your company."

Blalock's eyebrows furrowed as he started looking through the portfolio.

"Jonah International is in the process of financing a leveraged buyout for the remaining 46 percent," said Josh.

"Do you understand what is happening here, Morgan?" asked Kelan.

"It looks like Jonah International is trying to make a play for this company, but it will fail. They don't have the controlling interest." He tossed the portfolio onto the table between them.

"Your current investors are actually shell corporations owned solely by Jonah International. We already own the 54 percent, therefore, the controlling interest," said Josh.

Blalock's eyes grew wide. "The senior partners and the board of directors will not allow this to happen! You cannot do this legally!"

"There's nothing that the board can do. As we speak, federal agencies are investigating each of them for tax evasion and fraudulent acts to commit insider trading. More than likely, most will be indicted. The board will dissolve during the buyout. You know as well as I do that they have been lining their pockets for years," said Kelan.

"I have the legal precedence in this matter according to the Department of Justice. As for the senior partners, they will not be interfering," said Josh.

"You are a very foolish man if you believe that," said Blalock.

"Ignorance to the obvious is foolish. I'm very aware of who your senior partners are and the influence they hold. Believe me when I say, my network is more powerful," he said.

Blalock stared at the defiance. Even he was not that bold to make a declaration like that in the open. "They have an agent—"

"Yes, I know, Pymm. I've already taken care of him."

Blalock was surprised at the tenacity of this man. While trying not to show it, he was beginning to question Josh's associations. "Who exactly are you to boast of these connections or this type of power? I've never heard of you before, and I know everyone with influence on this planet."

Kelan smiled knowingly as he remembered wondering the same thing. It did not take him long to become a believer in what Josh could accomplish though.

Josh leaned forward. "Morgan, if you knew half as much as you thought and applied it to a cause greater than yourself, you would be in a very different position now."

"And what position is that?" he asked.

"Alastar-McGlocklin's assets, holdings, and properties will begin a voluntary liquidation within the week. All surpluses, as a result, will be set up into a trust to support, and make restitution, to the countless lives that have been destroyed under your leadership," said Josh.

Blalock shot up out of his seat. "You do not have the power or the authority to—"

"Sit down!" said Josh. The two security personnel had hands on either side of Blalock to guide him back into his seat.

"Understand this. There are no more employees. They received their notifications yesterday evening with a sizable severance to get them through to their next opportunity. This isn't just happening here at headquarters but across the globe. The market bell will ring in twenty-five minutes. At that time, the announcement of the sale of Alastar-McGlocklin will be broadcasted internationally. All global properties of interest will be seized and sealed by the end of the day."

Astonishment crossed Blalock's face. "This maneuver is insane. You will lose billions over this deal!"

"Something like that would only matter if it were about the money," said Josh.

Blalock looked as if he was just slapped across the face. "What else would it be about?"

"Justice. Fairness. Improbable absolution for the atrocities committed by greedy men who care about nothing," he said in anger.

Josh leaned back on the couch and took a deep breath. Blalock just sat there with a stone expression. He still had a card or two up his sleeve, or so he foolishly believed. "My lawyers are going to have a field day with you."

Kelan shook his head. "You just don't get it, do you?"

Blalock slowly turned to look at him. "You're in this just as much as I am."

"Kelan no longer has any legal ties to Alastar-McGlocklin. He works for me now," said Josh.

"I have proof that he performed illegal activities while working for this company," said Blalock.

"All of which can be tied back to directives issued by you, performed under the duress of job security and threats," said Josh.

"We'll see what my lawyers have—"

"You have no lawyers, Morgan. You have nothing anymore," said Kelan.

He gritted his teeth at that statement. Kelan looked toward Josh for the delivery of the final blow.

"Mr. Blalock, for your crimes against humanity, illegal corporate activities, your private quest for power and money at the expense of others, and the indifference to the human condition, Jonah International has seized all of your personal worldly belongings to be distributed, or liquidated as necessary, in reparation to those that you have hurt the most."

"You have no right and no proof!" screamed Blalock as he was restrained by security.

"All of your activities have been thoroughly documented and delivered to the federal authorities. Evidence of all transactions for all accounts has been secured from the central servers. This also includes the ghost servers that you thought were hidden," said Kelan.

"As far as the right," said Josh, "it is very unfortunate that you do not have direct knowledge of the damage you have done in my life. Your punishment on this earth might have more meaning to you if it did.

"Because of your actions, I grew up without a mother. I lost my best friend, who worked for your company. People close to me have lost their jobs, their homes, and their very dignity because of your blatant disregard for anything other than yourself, and that is only the people directly connected to me. You have inflicted your brand of cancer on countless others. For all of those who could never fight back, this is their reckoning. My influence at the Justice Department will make this your new reality!" he finished.

"Why are you doing this?" asked Blalock in a shallow voice. He was now becoming aware of his situation.

"I don't like bullies," said Josh, without breaking eye contact. "I don't like you."

Josh nodded to Tim, who in turn, spoke into his sleeve. Within seconds, federal agents burst through the doors. Tim and the other security agent helped Blalock out of the seat and turned him around as the government agents pulled out handcuffs.

"Morgan Blalock, you are under arrest for the crimes of . . ." one agent started as they cuffed him then escorted him through his office doors for the last time.

Some weeks later, Josh was settling into a mundane routine of day-to-day activities. It was honestly a welcome relief to the varied degrees of excitement experienced over the last few years. So much happened; so much was lost.

Alastar-McGlocklin's global dismantling was progressing as anticipated. Scores of affiliates from consulting firms specializing in corporate restructures to human resourcing and placement agencies would be employed for quite some time before the dust settled.

Morgan Blalock was being indicted on several counts of espionage, insurance fraud, murder, and numerous other charges that would most likely have the federal judicial system tied up for years. The damage under his reign would take months to compile and catalog to accurately document the full extent. Whether or not he would make it to trial was a subject that came up from time to time behind closed doors. Of all the uncertainties of everything that happened, ruling out the senior partners exacting their brand of justice was not one of them.

Josh had the opportunity to speak with Lucas regarding what he had seen in Oregon that night. He told Josh that he had been given the ability to see a world that most humans would not or could not handle, much less understand. His eyes would no longer be clouded in the mist that separates the realms. Accepting this reality was something in which he would need to come to terms. He would need his new senses to aid him as a champion for mankind.

Melina knocked on his office doorway. He looked up and smiled. With the immediate threat to her and Amanda's safety over, both could now resume their lives free of protective custody and seclusion. The hardest part was not being able to talk with Amanda or see Melina. Josh could not risk their safety until this final mission was complete.

"Are you ready?" she said, crossing over and giving him a kiss.

"Still waiting for the others."

Just as he said that, Langston walked in.

"Hey, guys . . . where's Kelan?" he said, looking at his watch.

"Right here," he said, trailing in just behind him.

Josh smiled, looking at the frazzled expression on Kelan's face. "Are you settling in okay?"

"Getting there," responded the new Director of Technical Operations.

He turned and looked out the window; his smile faded. Although some could say that Joshua's campaign against the evils of a corporation was a success, he could not help but feel sadness over the situation. Whenever an enemy is defeated, the measure of victory cannot be about the winning of the battle but more about the degree of losses that it took. He had come to terms with everything that had happened in his life over the years. His sadness now was about those whose lives would never be the same. This was just one battle; the war would rage on.

"Hey, you okay?" said Melina.

He looked at her; his smile returned. "Yeah, I'm fine."

He picked up his jacket as everybody walked toward the door. Right now, the only thing that mattered was where they were going for lunch.

Epilogue

The hallway was long and lifeless, drab walls with a polished tile floor. Lighting was sporadic, with hanging fixtures of fluorescent tubes like something in an old high school. Rooms lined either side of the hallway every nine meters. Nondescript and unassuming—a perfect place.

The only sound was the clicking heels of black patent pumps beating out a steady rhythm. Upon rounding the corner, she opened the door to a darkened room on the left. Four sets of eyes sitting at a table with a single hanging light immediately turned toward her. In silence, she closed the door and took her place.

"Do you have the information?" one of them asked.

"As much as I could obtain." She pulled out a file with documents inside and laid them on the table. "As far as we are able to tell, they are now located within the borders of the United States."

"All of them?" asked another.

"No, one of them is still unaccounted," she said.

"Do we know its current location?" asked a third.

"Unfortunately, no . . . they were not able to retrieve it in time before the company collapsed," she said.

"That is unfortunate indeed," said the remaining person at the opposite end of the table.

"The loss of their resources is going to be felt."

"Our cause will still move forward. Granted, with this setback, it will take a little longer, but will move nonetheless," she said.

"The boy is a problem now."

"Agreed."

"He should be dealt with decisively."

"There are rules against that," came a voice from the other side of the room.

"For you, yes . . . ," she said.

"What are you suggesting?" said the voice.

"A hard-line approach. Failure to prevent the ascension is not something my superiors, nor yours, are prepared to discard lightly. Those directly involved will be handled appropriately. However, all hope is not lost. Contingencies were developed in the unlikely event he would come to power," she said.

"And what are these . . . plans?" someone asked.

"Soon," she said.

All the occupants of the table looked at one another with a mix of satisfaction and trepidation. The consortium was heavily invested in the promise of a New World order. Waiting idly for the change was difficult, at best, but not intolerable.

She stood in preparation to leave. "Ministry has activated a hellfire gambit."

A wide grin crossed the face of the voice on the other side of the room. Crimson eyes began to glow.

"You may begin preparation for the coming chaos."